LUCID

LUCID

ADRIENNE STOLTZ
RON BASS

razOr
bill

An Imprint of Penguin Group (USA) Inc.

razOr
bill

A division of Penguin Young Readers Group
Published by the Penguin Group
Penguin Group (USA) Inc., 345 Hudson Street
New York, New York 10014, U.S.A.

USA / Canada / UK / Ireland / Australia / New Zealand / India / South Africa / China
Penguin Books Ltd, Registered Offices: 80 Strand, London WC2R 0RL, England
For more information about the Penguin Group visit penguin.com

Published simultaneously in Canada

Library of Congress Cataloging-in-Publication Data
Stoltz, Adrienne.
  Lucid / Adrienne Stoltz, Ron Bass.
    p. cm.
  Summary: "What if you could dream your way into a different life? What if you could choose
to live that life forever? Sloane and Maggie have never met. Sloane is a straight-A student
with a big and loving family. Maggie lives a glamorously independent life as an up-and-coming
actress in New York. The two girls couldn't be more different—except for one thing. They
share a secret that they can't tell a soul. At night, they dream that they're each other. The
deeper they're pulled into the promise of their own lives, the more their worlds begin to blur
dangerously together. Before long, Sloane and Maggie can no longer tell which life is real and
which is just a dream. They realize that eventually they will have to choose one life to wake up
to, or risk spiraling into insanity. But that means giving up one world, one love, and one self,
forever."—Provided by publisher.
  ISBN 978-1-59514-636-6 (paperback)
  [1. Dreams—Fiction. 2. Love—Fiction. 3. Friendship—Fiction. 4. Actors and actresses—
Fiction. 5. High schools—Fiction. 6. Schools—Fiction.] I. Bass, Ronald. II. Title.
  PZ7.S8758355Luc 2012
  [Fic] —dc23

                                         2012014448

ISBN: 978-1-59514-636-6

Printed in the United States of America

1 3 5 7 9 10 8 6 4 2

To my dear wife Christine, who creates the happiness and peace within which all other creation is possible. And to my precious daughters Jennifer and Sasha, for teaching me the most essential truth in human experience: that unconditional love exists.

—Ron

For Flutter and B.
—Adrienne

CHAPTER ONE

MAGGIE

Right now I'm Maggie. Actually Sloane Margaret Jameson, but I've been Maggie since that afternoon when my kindergarten teacher called my mom, Nicole, to tell her that Sloane punched Devin Cruikshank in the mouth. When confronted, I readily confirmed that Sloane had indeed done that, despite the fact that I had warned her not to and was completely disapproving of her antisocial behavior. Although if anyone ever deserved a punch in the mouth, Devin Cruikshank makes my lifetime top ten. Nicole said she didn't know there were two Sloanes in my class. I informed her that Sloane was my usually invisible best friend who often mischievously appeared to get me in trouble. My name, as of that day and forever after, was exclusively Maggie. And for all my reservations about Nicole's parenting skills, she totally went along with this like a little lamb.

Among these reservations is the fact that Nicole is rarely around to do any parenting at all. This was less of a problem when my dad was living with us. Despite his dedication to the short stories he wrote and the students he taught at Columbia, he never once failed to show up for whatever my sister, Jade, or I needed. Nicole tries her best, but as a mid-level editor at *Elle* with a spectacular bitch as a boss and no control over her schedule, it gets hard.

My schedule, meanwhile, is unpredictable. I don't go to school so that I can be free to go to auditions. Which explains why at 11:34 on a Tuesday morning, I'm lying on the floor of our West Village apartment, alone of course, listening to the absolute silence. Nicole had these windows installed that I swear are constructed of magic glass, which makes all life in the outside world mute. In the quiet, I can imagine what everyone else alive is actually doing: my friends from my old high school going to class, people hailing cabs on Houston, chefs prepping starters at trendy downtown restaurants for the lunch crowd, women going into labor, brokers trading commodity futures at Goldman Sachs, shoppers sliding credit cards at Barneys, hot dog guys slopping onions on dogs at a Sabrett's wagon, dog walkers walking dogs on Hudson River Greenery, truck drivers double-parking to deliver tulips.

And instead of being out in the action, I'm the one lying on the floor, counting all the things I'm not doing—instead of what I *should* be doing, like studying the scene for my audition tomorrow or the GED materials stacked up beside me. I love the chance to be alone with myself, even if Emma says I'm really a lonely girl and just don't want to face it. Being alone allows me to procrastinate with my rambling thoughts for as long as I want.

Until my phone rings.

It's Mrs. Manoti, the nurse at Jade's Montessori school, anxiously explaining that Nicole is at a photo shoot somewhere with no cell service and her assistant gave the nurse my cell number. Once she gets over the seemingly incomprehensible fact that I don't go to school and am therefore available to answer my cell in the middle of the day, she tells me that my seven-year-old sister "passed out" in class.

Most girls my age are sort of addicted to drama, but I'm blessed to have inherited both my father's eyelashes and his ability to be calm in a crisis. The nurse, however, is clearly terrified that any serious illness might conceivably take place on her watch. I feel her throwing my sister like a hot potato into my arms through the receiver, thrusting responsibility on me. What else is new?

I dig my shoes out from under the GED workbooks scattered on the floor around me and bolt out the door. Once I'm on the street, the world comes to life as I'm hit with the noise outside my windows: a jackhammer, the subway beneath me, cars ignoring the anti-honking laws. The day is bright and crisp. Still, as I focus on getting to my little sister, I don't feel like I'm a part of any of it.

The stocky nurse whispers to me that Jade is asleep in the next room. But I hear curious scurrying sounds from behind the door. I open it slowly and catch a glimpse of my sister quickly reclining on the vinyl table, the sanitary paper crinkling loudly beneath her. She pretends she's asleep. I sit next to her and put my hand on her forehead. No fever. She doesn't stir. She's actually giving a great performance. I give her a wet willy.

That gets her to peek one eye open.

"Oh. I thought you were Nurse Manatee," she says, and sits up. Mrs. Manoti does resemble a manatee now that I think of it.

"Would she give you a wet willy?"

"You never know with that lady," she says.

Jade looks chipper. Her freckled cheeks are rosy; her skinny arms hug my neck as tight and fierce as always. She tosses her thick russet-colored hair, rolls her eyes, and whispers, "I fell asleep for like maybe ten seconds. I don't get why everyone is freaking out."

She pulls a fistful of tongue dispensers out of her jacket pocket and starts fiddling with them.

"Are you stealing those?"

She nods matter-of-factly. I wait patiently for the why.

She jumps from the table and grabs her backpack. "I want to make popsicles. And maybe a log cabin. Let's blow this fruit stand." And heads out the door.

An hour later, I'm in the pediatrician's waiting room, visions of brain tumors dancing through my head, heart pounding like someone who is not actually so calm in a real crisis, when the doc and the kid emerge smiling. Dr. Edelstein was my pediatrician as well and I have puked on him many times.

"It's only a blood sugar thing," he informs me. "It can happen when kids go through growth spurts." He hands me a prescription. On it is scrawled something I can't for the life of me read, but I think underneath, it says *Fun Size*.

He nods, confirming the diagnosis. "Yep. Doctor's orders, Jade is to carry an emergency Snickers with her at all times."

Amazingly, she agrees.

I don't take Jade back to school after the doctor. All afternoon, we lie on the grass by the river and make dandelion chains while Jade's minuscule Yorkie, Boris, terrorizes the larger dogs. Jade fills every single second of this perfect afternoon with her delightfully boring chatter. This includes her irrational fear of snails, behavior and hygiene secrets of assorted classmates, reaction to last night's *The Daily Show*, which she somehow seems to sort of understand and which clearly explains why she fell asleep in class, speculation about my love life (colorful and unfounded), and an enthusiastic and completely public rendition of her latest original booty dance. She turns and looks at her skinny butt bouncing.

"It's got a mind of its own. You can't teach this stuff, Maggie. I was just born this way!"

At around seven, the sky turns a rose gold over the river. On my way to acting class, I drop Jade at Nicole's office for dinner so that they can go eat Indian. Meaning tandoori, not cannibalism. *Elle* is on the forty-third floor of the Time-Life building. The office is less glamorous than a girl would dream: dreary, fluorescent-lit halls lined with the ghostly photos of cover girls past.

"Hello, sunshine," Jerome greets me ironically, air-kissing both cheeks. He mimics my concerned face with a scowl before he sweeps Jade up into a salsa dance. I can't help but smile.

Jerome is my mom's prematurely balding, insanely beautiful assistant. The man has no pores, and the shape of his lips looks like some mountain range I don't know the name of. He has the slight body of a dancer and escaped the small-town small-mindedness of Podunk, Oklahoma, to Chelsea, where he's gotten more boyfriends strutting the aisles at Whole Foods than I have in my whole life. We have a complicated relationship because I worship him, but when push comes to shove, his loyalties lie with my mom (a boy's gotta pay for those Prada shoes), ever the guard dog of her annoying schedule. My mom once suggested she and I do a couples session with Emma. I brought Jerome because I talk to him more often.

While Jade tries on shoes twelve sizes too big, Nicole and I debrief on our separate conversations with the doctor. She, of course, pretends to be completely reassured and already sent Jerome to buy the Duane Reade out of Snickers. I'm relieved to see that she has been silently scared to death and in her unspoken way is grateful to me for having stepped in to play Mom again.

It's funny all that lies between the lines. As an actress, I wonder if an audience would understand what's actually being said between my mom and me without dialogue. The way she takes off her glasses when we come in, how she lifts her shoulders and sighs when she greets me, the extra beat in the hug she wraps around Jade. I take note of the small crinkle lines on her eyes and the pinch of her eyebrows, her thin voice. I know from all this the complexity of how she feels. And I guess in my ability to get inside her, as her true understudy, I find some compassion and lose my irritation. For the moment.

Jerome is teaching Jade how to trot like a model in five-inch Louboutins. As I watch her spindly spider legs pump and the red soles clomp, I resist the urge to scoop her up and huggle her. (*Huggle*: verb. A brilliant word Jade made up when she was two that exists somewhere between "to snuggle" and "to hug"; e.g., "Hey Maggie, want to huggle me?") Usually I'd be worried about her breaking an ankle in those shoes, but after the day we've had, that feels like peanuts.

Nicole comes up behind me and kisses the top of my head, which I hate.

"She's fine, Maggie," she says, trying to convince herself and me. I open my mouth to argue and decide better. Nicole is right:

Jade is fine. What I'd really be arguing about is the fact that I think a mother should be concerned, should be the one to show up to the nurse's office and hold her daughter's hand at the doctor's even if her daughter is fine. But having that argument is like going to an empty well looking for water. So I just walk away.

Class that night is frustrating because we're doing group work and I had been hoping for some individual focus before tomorrow's big audition. Particularly since the afternoon adventure with Jade gobbled up all my prep time. I'm more nervous than usual, and doing my best to pretend I'm not.

After class, I turn down an urgent invitation from Andrea and Jason to hit Rose Bar. They're both over twenty-one, and I never mention that I'm not. Knowing someone's real age always seems to add to the already competitive nature of friendships with fellow thespians. Not that getting into Rose Bar would be a problem for me. I don't know if my face is showing premature signs of aging or if walking in like you own the place really works, but I rarely get carded.

Instead, I wander down to Union Square Café, which is my go-to spot for dinner when Nicole is working late. Nicole is almost never home for dinner, so they know me there by now. The place is packed as always, but Jimmy gives me an inconspicuous table, and I order my usual chicken Caesar, dressing on the side, no croutons or anchovies, a pot of green tea, and don't have to mention no bread on the table because I know I'll have no problem resisting it. Jimmy likes to leave it on the other place mat when he collects the silverware from the empty spot. As though Bread were my dinner partner.

I settle back to watch the crowd. It's funny; I always have my Kindle with me just in case, but I never touch it. Ever since I can remember, my favorite game when I'm alone is to imagine the lives of strangers. When I was younger, the noodle shop was filled with deposed royalty, secret agents, circus stars in the off-season. Now I'm less creative.

For example, that couple on their second bottle of wine just met this afternoon. She's a ventriloquist and lip reader. He's been mute since birth. The prospect of a future together is mutually irresistible. However, she's mourning the loss of her beloved dummy Chester, who recently leapt from a truck and was crushed by an Escalade, driven by a past-his-prime power forward for the Knicks. She has his finger in her pocket. Chester's, not the forward's. Unfortunately, the mute is allergic to the eau de toilette of the aging blonde nearby who has never learned how to properly eat her spaghetti. She thinks the scent is attracting the retired detective she met on eHarmony, who is sitting across from her, wolfing down his pasta and trying to remember if he saw her face on the *America's Most Wanted* list. Meanwhile their waiter is so preoccupied with his mother's Alzheimer's . . . well, you get the idea.

I notice very few other diners are solo, but the ones that are have something to read propped up on the table. A paperback, a magazine, a newspaper. Something to help them forget that they're eating alone. I just think that's sad.

Sometimes, someone comes over and says, *Aren't you the girl who was in such and such?* Tonight it's a cute guy, maybe ten years too old for me.

"Hi. I'm totally not hitting on you . . ."

Totally. That's why you are standing inappropriately too close and your hand is still on my shoulder.

"But I swear I saw you in an off-Broadway Ibsen I caught last fall. You were heart-stirring. Will you sign this? I know it will be worth a lot one of these days."

Once a guy said something similar and then having learned my name, Facebook-stalked me, which was creepy. Even though I'm no longer even on Facebook, when this guy hands me his napkin, I sign *Julia Roberts*.

"Your girlfriend will be more impressed when you show that to her and tell her you met an actress. She's lucky to have such a handsome, polite guy."

He laughs and opens his mouth, maybe to tell me I'm lucky because he doesn't have a girlfriend. I cut him off. "Enjoy your dinner." He folds up the napkin and goes away.

Emma is convinced I'm secretly a lonely person. She will not let go of that idea. It seems like it's all we talk about. Walking home in the night air, I wonder how anybody could ever feel alone in New York. It's like when you're walking with someone, you're stuck with just that one person. When you're walking in New York alone, you're with everyone. It's possible Emma is lonely and she's putting it on me. She sure is obsessed with it. She's grasping for an easy answer. One theory fits all. That'll be $300, please.

But the truth is, I think she doesn't have a clue how the dreams began.

One of my favorite games while I'm walking, especially at night, is to wonder what different people would think if they knew my secret. Emma is the only person on the planet who does, and I have enough faith in our doctor-patient privilege to know she hasn't spilled my beans. Nicole, for example, wouldn't know what to do. So she'd try to be my friend instead of my mother, which is what she's comfortable doing, which is part of my ongoing list of parenting grievances. But she'd be scared. She has, for such an intelligent person, an amazingly small reality box in which to live. She needs life to be no bigger or harder to solve than the stuff she edits for the magazine. What would happen if a real crisis occurred, someone got cancer or a brain tumor or something? I think she'd handle it by reducing it to editorial size, denying its real scope and consequences, and telling herself that she's being practical by not getting overwhelmed. But the truth is, the most important things about life are overwhelming. That may be terrifying, or tragic, but that doesn't make it necessarily bad. And certainly, not something to run away from.

Jade, on the other hand, would be initially thrilled to learn that fairy tales are true and she'd demand to be part of it. She'd get jealous and want to be a part of the magic too—but she'd never deny it was real. And that is high on my list of reasons why I love her.

My dad. My dad would tell me not to be afraid. That I should treat it as a gift, as something precious that was mine alone. And if I ever felt lonely with it, he'd be there.

I used to tell my dad about my dreams. Sometimes the real ones, and sometimes I'd lie and tell him about dreams I didn't have. I somehow expected that he would know the difference. But he never did. Either I'm a good liar or a good actress. Or he did know the difference, and he's the good liar. I wish I could ask him.

I turn down Horatio, and the streetlights are illuminating the cherry blossoms like pink snow. This is our first spring on this street. We've moved a lot, though we keep to the West Village so Jade doesn't have to change schools. Nicole has great luck flipping apartments.

My friends think it must be unsettling, but the nomadic thing has its virtues. I get to redecorate my room more than anyone else I know, and Jade and I have become partners in creating our personal new neighborhood from the bodegas, boutiques, and restaurants that we choose together. But more important, when you have to keep changing your environment, you are constantly aware of how wide the world is and how many choices really lie out there for you.

I quietly let myself into our darkened apartment, assuming that both Nicole and Jade are sleeping. Once in my room, I stand for a long moment, staring out the window at the Hudson. Suddenly, I feel someone standing behind me. I know who it is and what I'm going to say. Putting on my game face, I whirl around and stab my finger out as I shout:

"Who the fuck are you looking at?!"

Nicole stares back at me. The look on her face is intolerable.

"Shut up!" I keep going. "You have nothing to say to me!"

"Um, actually I do. If you don't lower your voice, you're going to have a seven-year-old out of bed, watching you act like a raving bitch."

I turn from my image in the full-length mirror to see Nicole's amused smile.

"So I'm a convincing raving bitch, huh? Wow. I wasn't sure I had it in me."

"Honey, believe me, you do. You're going to nail that audition."

She comes in and flops down on my bed. "Want me to read the other side of the scene?"

Nicole is always slightly disappointed that I need to rehearse alone. It isn't that I don't want her criticism and comments, which I certainly don't; it's more that I have to get my head in a space where it's my own world, completely uncontaminated by any other reality. Changing the subject is always our most comfortable way for me to refuse this.

"How's Jade?"

"Great. Ever notice that kid talks a lot?"

"Never happens to me. Must be something you're doing wrong."

"Again."

A companionable mood now established, she feels free to go on and pretend that she isn't expressing concern that my look would not be strong enough for the audition.

"So, how have you been sleeping?"

That's a loaded question.

"Are you implying the circles under my eyes are too dark? Anything else that's not pretty enough to win the part tomorrow?"

"Wow. So glad you're not defensive. Kudos to Emma."

Now I have a choice. Nicole is just being Nicole, trying to relate to me the only way I sometimes think she knows how. I could let it go or push it. True to form, I make the wrong choice . . .

"Sorry," I say. "You don't get to be passive-aggressive about my looks and then blame it on me. If you're going to do something like that, you're going to have to own it."

Nicole sits up, holds out her arms for me to crawl into a hug. Which of course I do. This is our thing. We fight, then make up. We're friends, and then she wants to be my mom.

"Baby girl, it's not only okay for a rising actress to be insecure about her appearance, but I would think you were from another planet if you *weren't*. The only thing is, you've chosen a career where you'll be picked apart daily, and you have to own that."

She slides from the bed, pulls me toward the mirror, steps behind me, and puts her arms around my waist. Her elegant face perches on my shoulder, looking at our reflection.

"Now tell me what you see."

I see an ordinary girl, who could, I guess, be pretty in the right light, with the right attitude. Pretty enough that my looks won't hold me back, but they sure as hell won't make up for any lack of talent. I study the image. A ballerina's body, slightly too thin, certainly not appropriate for any voluptuous role. Thick black hair that can look sort of glamorous in a head shot after a good stylist has tamed it. But it is an enormous pain in my ass to manage and makes me feel like I'm walking around with an Eskimo hoodie in the summer heat. I hate to walk around in the sun anyway, hence my pale skin, which may be lacking vitamin D but at least is clear and creamy. My face has good angles for catching light, and my eyes do a nice job of popping on-camera. They are icy blue pools contained by a navy perimeter. My lips are too thin for some casting directors. Two have referred me to plastic surgeons, but there's no chance I'm going down the collagen trail. My favorite part of me is a part that the make-up department on every set or show I've done considers a flaw. There is a gap in the lashes on my right eyelid, from where a tiny chicken pox, the itchiest itch you can imagine, left its scar.

All of this runs through my mind in a tenth of a second. What I actually answer is . . .

"Angelina Jolie with bigger boobs and much nicer lips."

Nicole rolls her eyes at the irony. Angelina out-sizes me considerably in both departments.

"When did you see Angelina's boobs?"

"Mom, you gotta get out more. *Us Weekly*."

Of course, since I look absolutely nothing like Angelina Jolie in any way, Nicole has to tell me how much prettier, more natural, and wholesome (every girl's favorite word) I am. After enduring fifteen minutes of Nicole praising every inch of me, I shoo her out the door, throw one last menacing glare at my image in the mirror, and get ready for bed.

Once the lights are out, my brain turns on. I hate when that happens.

In the dark, at night, before I fall asleep, my mantra is "fine." I tell myself too many times that Jade of course is *fine* and that Snickers are the miracle cure for narcolepsy. I tell myself the callback will go *fine*. It's an okay role in an intriguing indie film, but working with the director would be a dream come true—and the same goes for the hot young star already cast as the lead. As is often the case, my character is twenty-two (my look adapts easily—in life and work—to seem older, which is probably why I never get carded), and the casting director commented at my initial reading that my being underage could be a "slight problem in one scene, but not to worry." So I lie in bed for half an hour and worry, telling myself it will be *fine*. Nicole would say, *Don't be a prude, don't be afraid of your body, but draw your own boundaries.* My dad would say, *Don't ask me a question you don't want the answer to.* Which would indeed be giving me the answer I didn't want to hear.

As usual, Sloane flickers through my thoughts as I drift off. I close my eyes.

CHAPTER TWO

SLOANE

In the next instant, I open them to see the same tree outside the same window I've been waking up to my entire life. She's an elm, my tree. Her mood frequently reflects the weather, as if she has seasonal affect disorder. But today, despite the spring sunshine filtering through her early leaves, her branches seem weary. As if she feels like me. Even though I slept, I didn't rest. I dreamed, as I do every night, through Maggie's entire day in Manhattan. My bones feel tired and heavy.

My name is Sloane Margaret Jameson. I've never punched anybody named Devin Cruikshank in the mouth because I've never met anyone named Devin Cruikshank. Plus I'm not a puncher. I'm more of a head butter.

I roll over and stare at the dull stars on my ceiling. They are the kind that glow in the dark, so when it's not dark, they just look like jaundiced stickers. I bought them and a package of astronaut ice cream on a field trip to the Boston Museum of Science. How did they ever think to dehydrate ice cream, those brilliant rocket scientists?! When I got home from the field trip, I carefully studied the constellations and did my best to re-create Orion. I then decided it was more fun to make my own. There's Stella the Horse, who talks like Mr. Ed. She has a sharp tongue and can't be trusted. There's El Delicioso, the grand Nutella crepe in the sky. I ran out of stars halfway through making an elephant, so he kind of looks like a teacup. But I call him Rooibus (which is my favorite African tea) and imagine the stars in his trunk went supernova a zillion years ago and disappeared.

The noise of my family downstairs annoys me in the way a mosquito can be more distracting than a jackhammer. Lately, I'm always the last one out of bed in the mornings. It's been a long time since there was something that I was eager to get out of bed for. Actually, it's been a year.

I'm not depressed. At least not clinically according to my Internet research. I clearly have a few issues. Having a huge secret like I do makes life a little lonely. Lonelier still being surrounded by people, wonderful people, so close each day and not being able to tell them. I imagine that being a double agent, or a cheating wife, or in the closet must be similarly lonely and tiring.

I'm not an actress like Maggie is in my dream, but I think I do a pretty good job of convincing everyone I'm okay. And really, I am okay. Really. Not every day feels this heavy and hard.

The anniversary of my best friend Bill's death is coming up. And it conveniently coincides with my seventeenth birthday. I hate attention anyway. I'm so uncomfortable being the focus of anyone's attention. I squirm when I'm in the spotlight. I like to be behind the camera.

Luckily, the annoying buzz of my family downstairs is preventing me from wallowing in my pity puddle. Soon enough my feet hit the hardwood and I'm in the bathroom waiting for the water to get warm.

Downstairs smells like coffee and pancakes and eggs and my mother's freshly washed hair. I guess she got to the hot water before I could. And then I catch the scent of decaying sea animals. My seven-year-old brother, Max, has covered the entire table with his haphazard and negligently constructed "science project." It is apparently a diorama of our local coastline (giving Max the benefit of the doubt), including real dead mussels, eelgrass, part of a bird's nest, the indescribably gross shell of a mangled horseshoe crab, all not quite held together with Elmer's wood glue, which now disfigures our entire kitchen.

I love Max. He is scrappy and puckish and capricious. He has a brilliant imagination and used to let me play his weird games with him. He would walk into a room, intertwine his little fingers through mine, and pull me into hours of running around. Once worn out, he would snuggle his fuzzy head into my cheek so that I could feel his warm body breathing against mine, and we'd read books.

Then, about a year ago, he and his cronies reached the decision that girls have cooties. So now I'm no longer his sister, but a *girl*.

My mother is cooking for too many people, which is fewer than usual. She really overdoes all the homemaking stuff. There is ridiculously meticulous attention to cleanliness, for example. Not that cleanliness is a bad thing, unless you turn it into one by hiding behind it. For example, she'll spend half the morning cleaning up Max's crap, none of which would have been necessary if she actually disciplined him for once and told him not to make a mess in the first place. I bet if the consequences had to do with video games or snacks, he'd listen. I wonder from time to time if she lets him make a mess to give herself one more thing to do. She's got the fullest schedule of anyone in southeastern Connecticut or probably the Free World. I think she does it to make herself feel better for "temporarily" abandoning a promising career in marine science to give birth to my older brother, Tyler. On staff at Woods Hole, she used to study the dynamics governing the transport of fine-grained sediments in coastal and estuarine waters. I've listened to my dad tell me how much she loved that work. But she never went back to it. After Tyler, she was pregnant with me before she knew it. Once you're out of the game, there aren't a ton of employment opportunities in the area. I suppose our family just grew roots. Deep roots stuck in the Mystic soil.

My mom and I used to be a lot closer. She didn't suddenly get cooties, but this last year things have been really bad between us. I know it really hurts her. I just don't know what to do about it.

Without turning from the stove, she says in her sunniest, most innocent voice, "Morning, sweetie. You know I was thinking?"

Uh-oh. "Thinking" is a euphemism for "I'm about to throw something out there that I know is probably going to piss you off." The fact that she isn't even using a normal tone of voice makes me resent that she clearly feels like she has to walk on eggshells around me.

"This Saturday might just be the perfect time for us to zip up to Providence to start looking for your prom dress. What do you think?"

I think you're deliberately trying to provoke me.

"Since I have no intention of ever going to something called a *prom*," I snap before I have time to think this through, "I wonder whatever would we do with a dress?"

"Sounds like someone's brushing up on her irony."

My dad has entered the kitchen and butted in, in his customary good-natured and completely fair way. I'll have none of that this morning.

"Dad, Mom knows how I feel about going to this prom. And instead of engaging me in a direct conversation about it, she throws in a passive-aggressive attempt to manipulate the situation, with complete deniability. This is what we call the 'I'm just saying' syndrome, where we don't take responsibility for saying things we shouldn't."

"Fascinating." My dad takes a maddeningly calm sip of his coffee. "A straight-A English student with no understanding of the term *passive-aggressive*. Which actually applies to your statement rather than your mother's."

Other than the fact that he is completely right, he is way out of line.

"Sloane," my mother says through pursed lips. "Will you step outside with me for a minute?" She doesn't sound exactly angry. Or hurt. She sounds determined and purposeful. At least we might have a real conversation for a change.

"Sloane," she says. "You're absolutely right, I was afraid to bring the prom up with you because I thought you might react this way.

But let's cut straight to the chase. You and I both know there's a lot more involved in this than the junior prom."

I'm kind of speechless. This is a combination of firmness and genuine concern that I thought I'd been longing for. But now that we're actually talking, I realize the things I want us to talk about are of course impossible.

"When you were fifteen, you hounded me to let you begin dating. And I insisted that you wait until your sixteenth birthday. You were so patient, but now an entire year has gone by and I don't think you've had one proper date in all this time. What happened?"

I look down at my feet. Hating myself for feeling awkward and inadequate to come up with a smoothly convincing lie.

"Nothing happened. There still isn't a particular guy I want to date. I guess I just didn't understand your stupid rule and wanted to see if I could get you to change your mind." My eyes burn as I say the words so I focus on the grass. I feel her watching me and just want to be out of her spotlight. I look up and surprisingly have the grace to say, "And I'm really sorry for being such a snide little brat."

"Again," she says, bending down to pull out a weed from the bed of daffodils.

Who knew she had a sense of humor.

I'm about to head for the bus stop when Gordy texts me, offering to pick me up. This is an unusual treat since my house is not on the way to school for him. I then get a second text with a request for some of my mom's breakfast leftovers and figure he must just be hungry and broke. Gordy is my best friend since birth. Our parents are good friends and used to force us to play together as kids, but our forced friendship turned into a real bond.

With a tinfoil-wrapped Jameson McMuffin in hand, I wait on the corner for my ride. We live in an old house on Gravel Street, dating back to 1834. Some guy named Daniel R. Williams built it and sold seine fishing nets from the basement. The basement is ten feet deep and was a station on the Underground Railroad, which I love. And Matilda Appleman Williams, old Danny's wife, used to hold weekly séances in the front parlor. I've dabbled with a Ouija board in her honor.

The house sits sideways to the street, and I'm sure when it was built, there weren't any other houses around blocking the view of the Mystic River. Now we have a partial view from the front of the house. We can see the Dyer Dhows and their colored sails spinning around in front of the seaport. Sunsets swirl pastel along the moving water. The egrets, night herons, laughing gulls, and sweet little plovers all go about their business and we get to watch.

Gordy's truck pulls up, and before I even climb in the cab, I can tell the ride to school is going to cost more than breakfast. Something's up. He doesn't wait for me to ask.

"Sloane." He has his serious voice on. "Coach Manard told me last night that the school is organizing a memorial for Bill. A big service, down on the football field so everyone can be there. He asked me for your number because he wants you to say something. I knew you'd think it's lame and you'd probably just hang up on him or say something snide. So I told him I'd ask you myself." He turns to me. "Will you please do it?"

I want to throw up.

"You mean stand up on the football field in front of the whole school—not to mention Bill's family? What would I say? That Bill was an extraordinary human even though lots of you didn't know him at all and virtually none of you really knew him well?" Gordy is used to my rants, but this must be hard for him too.

"You won't be alone up there," he says, taking a hand off the steering wheel and putting it gently on my back. "I'll say something, and your brother is coming home from school for it too."

"*Tyler's* coming home for this?" How could Gordy think that would make me feel any better? Tyler drives me bananas. He always has. Nothing he could say about Bill's death would make me feel better. He is six-four, sort of good-looking if you like really conventionally boringly "handsome" types. A lot of my friends think he's cute. He never worries. He has no problems. His life has always been good and easy, at least when it comes to the conventionally boring expectations that he seems maddeningly satisfied with. B+ average? No problem. He bragged about it like he was valedictorian at MIT. First-string quarterback on the third-worst team in our league? Loved it. Was beating off cheerleaders with a stick. No kidding.

"Tyler wants to be there. He and Bill were tight, Sloane. Not like you and me and Bill, of course." He slides a look in my direction. "You weren't his only friend." He says this last bit softly. And it feels like a piano crashing on my heart.

Bill and Gordy and I were a tight threesome. But I guess, sometimes, I feel territorial about our shared grief. And it's not fair of me. In the past year Gordy and I have wobbled like a tricycle missing a wheel. We haven't figured out a way to become our own bike.

I take a deep breath and stare at the bright green trees blurring by. Maybe somebody does need to stand up and tell everyone that an irreplaceable human life is gone, and the empty expressions of "so sorry for your loss" make me want to start pounding those phonies to jelly. The worst ones pretend it was their loss. As if sitting next to Bill for one class and never talking to him except to borrow an eraser makes them authorities on what kind of guy Bill was. I mean, I actually heard Mia Wallace brag about how "close" she'd been to him because he'd kissed her once at a keg party two years ago. She was sobbing, telling the story of that kiss like it was a soap on Telemundo, while her girlfriends flocked around comforting her, eating it up like vultures. Bill told me she'd basically jumped him and shoved her tongue down his throat. Of course, he added that she was a nice girl, because Bill was incapable of trashing anybody.

But Gordy isn't one of the phonies. And it isn't fair of me to take it out on him. I tell him I'll think about it, thank him for the ride, and fib that I have a test first period and need to get into class.

At lunch with Lila and Kelly, I decide not to even mention the memorial. No matter how much I love my girls, I can't really talk to them about Bill. I've just never been able to.

Lila can't stop indirectly asking me to set her up with Gordy, which she knows is an absolute nonstarter, even though I love her to death and Gordy would be so much better served dating sweet Lila than the cheerleader sloppy seconds that my stupid brother Tyler left behind.

Gordy is an athlete too, wide receiver and quarter miler, and thereby unfortunately friendly with Tyler. He is sort of gorgeous, and if I am to be honest, also in a conventionally boring way, but on him, I don't mind it because he has a good soul. He sits with the Abercrombie-and-Fitch-looking crew at the bottom of the hill. Sometimes I sit with them. Sometimes I sit with Lila and Kelly or with the nerd herd from most of my classes. Most often I just sit up on the hill and see who sits with me. I'm kind of a social floater. I don't really belong to any one clique but can navigate most of them (except for maybe the hard-core metal heads).

Kelly is on a relentless mission to get me to double with her and Chuck to the prom, which is coming up sooner than I want to think about. Today she reveals Chuck has several candidates prescreened to be the lucky man who wins my hand in promitude. It is true that Chuck isn't an athlete (boy, isn't he); however, he is a burner, a slacker, and completely unworthy of brilliant Kelly, except that he is cute and a really fun guy. His friends are just stoners. They usually stumble into lunch a little late reeking like they just rolled out of Scooby-Doo's van. Kelly spends twenty minutes waxing poetic about their depth of character, and I pretend that I'm not in danger of losing my lunch at the thought of a good-night kiss from Brad "The Weed" Wilcox.

Throughout the day, a couple of people ask me about the memorial, or tell me how sorry they are for my loss. Right. I try to keep it together until the final bell rings—and then I hightail it to the darkroom.

As always, the darkroom is my one refuge. I love the quiet darkness of developing film. And the fact that you shut the door and turn on a light and no one can come in for fear of overexposure. My own, and the negatives', I suppose.

I pour developer into the tank and start the timer. I like the rhythm and repetition of the process, inverting the tank four times, tapping for air bubbles. Repeating at the start of each minute. Pour out the developer and pour in the stop bath, reclose the lid, and invert back and forth. The pattern is like a prayer or a mantra and helps my busy brain to slow down.

I have been serious about photography since my dad gave me one of those Lomo toy cameras that take those cool seventies-style square shots. He used to take me out for hikes on Bluff Point or excursions in our boat around Fishers Island or walks along Napatree to let me develop my sense of light and composition. We haven't done this together in a long time, but I kept it up.

I don't want to be a photographer for a living or anything. I just like observing. I think that helps with my writing, which is what I really want to do. And maybe teach college-level literature like Maggie's father, Benjamin, used to do. Although I wouldn't stick to American lit. Too many drunk white men. I want to live in New York, that's for sure. I will go to Columbia, which I always state with certainty, despite my terror of a slim envelope arriving in the mail next spring. Getting into Columbia is the hatch door in my escape plan.

Just before six, Gordy knocks on the darkroom door. Even though I didn't tell him that's where I'd be, he knows where to find me. He takes me down to the Green Marble, my favorite hang-out spot, for a coffee.

All our lives, Gordy has been my true brother and I have been his true confidante. I have seen him through every mismatched girlfriend, his torn medial collateral ligament, which threatened his high school football career (the horror!), every foray his mind would take into literature or philosophy or anything that approached the meaning of life. He is sweet to the bone, and I would spare him any pain and unhappiness and failure that it would be in my power to spare him.

But do I tell him my heart? No. Why not? Because, right or wrong, I fear he wouldn't completely understand. And that would break both our hearts in pieces.

When we were eight or nine, there was this one night we camped out in my backyard and sort of swore or promised or at least speculated that if we weren't married by the time we were old (which I think meant by high school graduation at the time), it probably meant we were destined to be together "in that way." For several years thereafter, Gordy would frequently begin sentences with "When we're married." This usually preceded some joke, like how he'll give up farting indoors. Real mature. I perceived this as Gordy's excuse to kind of keep the door open between us. Like if we wanted to be together, the option was always there. And I would sometimes do the same so that he wouldn't feel rejected. He sometimes still lapses into that, and I have to admit that I sort of like it. I will actually marry some great, misunderstood genius—a modern equivalent of Salvador Dalí, Franz Liszt, maybe Genghis Khan.

Still, I'm comforted by the belief that someone solid and decent is there to fall back on.

Over coffee, Gordy stares at me in that way he has when he's intending to be meaningful. "Don't make me do this tribute alone," he says. "Please, Sloane. I know you think this is dumb, but we're not doing it for them. We're doing it for Bill. And he deserves that. You can be as agnostic as you want, but you don't know that he isn't somewhere listening."

"I'm an atheist, Gordy," I say. "There's a difference." And then I feel bad for making a joke out of it, and I tell him I'll do it and that I love him.

Which, of course, he already knows.

In bed with the lights out, my mind races. I wish Maggie was real so she could drive up to Mystic and "say something" for Bill. She would nail it cold.

Then the cold panic creeps in about whether these dreams of mine are insane, and where it will take me, and the incredible irony that it's Maggie who has a psychiatrist. My big fear is that one day I'll be normal, and fall asleep, and Maggie won't be there. I'll just have normal dreams, a good night's sleep. And she'll be gone.

But my biggest fear of all is the one I have to always tell myself could never happen. That one night Maggie will go to sleep and I'll be the one who's gone.

CHAPTER THREE

MAGGIE

My eyes open to a gray and rainy West Village morning. There's a sinking hole in my stomach, which is always there on the morning of a callback. Perform and be judged. It's worse than just an audition because they've liked me enough to want to see me again, which gives me hope, but their assessment will be more focused this time around, meaning all my flaws and limitations will be unmissable.

I can handle being turned down, obviously, because it happens more often than not and I'm still walking around. But coming home and dealing with Nicole's inane comforting when I lose the role requires me to audition for her, to make my disappointment okay for her. In Nicole's eyes failure and victory are indistinguishable; all that matters is not feeling bad so that you haven't been parented poorly. Even with very nice parents, there's an aspect of everything that's all about them. I won't do that when I'm a parent. I'll make different mistakes, of course.

I watch my reflection in the subway windows as the train heads uptown and realize Sloane is better suited to play Jolene, the character I'm trying to land. Sloane has actual boobs. And all that silky, buttery blond hair. And green eyes. Actually green. No matter how well I nail the lines, I still just look like me.

I climb the subway stairs at Columbus Circle into a full-on downpour, not quite getting my umbrella open soon enough, which is not great for my hair. Nicole would say that means good luck, but I'm not feeling very lucky today. I shouldn't think about Nicole this morning but should concentrate on Jolene and what she would feel, think, and say about the rain, about hair, and about being stuck blabbing with your shrink two hours before you need to become a completely different person. Which, come to think of it, is a specialty of the house.

I go upstairs to Emma's office. The teensy waiting room has an inappropriately super-feminine décor and I wonder if Emma actually took the time to pick out those cheesy fake flowers or if they just came with the office space. It almost turned me off her when I first came to talk about my parents. But somehow, once in her office, the walls felt like steel, strong enough to hold my biggest secret, so I let it spill out of me in the first five minutes. Maybe I was avoiding talking about my parents, or maybe I wanted to be relieved of it, but either way that threshold decision has tied me to her. She's the only one in my life who knows that every night I dream I'm someone else.

I flick on the appointment light and wait, knowing that even though she doesn't have a patient before me, it will take her just under three minutes to collect me. In two minutes and forty-two seconds by the watch my father gave me, Emma opens the door with that phony heartiness and energy that always makes me wonder why I have to be completely straight with her while she's always playing a role for me.

She always begins with small talk, like it's putting me at ease.

"It's raining out," she sagely notes.

"Sure is." I go with it because it eats up minutes where I won't have to talk about Sloane. Luckily, I get to discuss my big panic over Jade's conking out in class, the brain tumor fears, the bonding afternoon in the park to the point of reenacting Jade's booty dance in the middle of her office. I just keep running with it until Emma asks me why I'm so reluctant to discuss Sloane this morning.

"Because it's like every other morning," I answer, sitting back down on the couch.

And here we go. Am I mad at Sloane this morning? How can I be mad at a fantasy? Easy—there are no consequences, and all you're really doing is being mad at yourself in a disguised and therefore safer way.

Emma pleads her well-worn case that Sloane is my fantasy because I want a family and good friends and stability and a normal home life with my loving dad around, in which there are no auditions, rejections, dieting, constant focus on my appearance, my technique, and on and on with everything that is not ideal in my world. So-called actor friends who are insincere, competitive, actually adversaries. Men who either don't realize or care about my youth, who want things from me that of course I will not give but make me worry I'll be punished for not giving. A life so solitary that I need to fabricate friends by making up stories about every stranger I encounter.

Meals alone. Walks alone. Movies alone (at least the R-rated ones). No boyfriend. And finally, finally, after example after example, the dreaded word *loneliness*. She goes on and on about how I'm deluding myself by pretending that I'm comfortable or even happy.

It just pisses me off, so I try to flip it on her and bust holes in her snotty little theory. Why aren't I Sloane's fantasy? I'm an actress; doesn't every high school girl want to dream of something like this? I live in Manhattan instead of Mystic, Connecticut. Which is the fantasy? My sister is adorable and my best friend and has her own set of cooties. My mom is never breathing down my neck, never trying to control me in any way. Most importantly, the whole world is truly open to me. I can choose to live in London or Paris or Rio or China, and I don't need an escape plan to make it happen. I am the perfect fantasy for a girl who desperately wants to believe she has options but who has been rooted in one small town, one cozy home, one common life.

"So tell me this," I say. "Everything in Sloane's life is a mess and is making her unhappy. You tell me why you think I'd want to invent that."

"You love to talk about the freedoms in your life," she answered, "but those freedoms are all external. Emotionally, you have to suppress so much. You perform for your employers, you keep your sister's spirits up, you can't really confide in your mom, and you have no truly close friends. Sloane lets you be selfish, angry, even unfair, but all in the package of a basically decent person with a comforting support group. I don't know why you're so resistant to seeing this."

And then she smiles.

"Of course I do," she says. "You don't want to give her up."

"Any more than she wants to give me up."

"You have to say that immediately out of your fear that if the balance were to slip for a moment, you might lose her. In a way, Sloane is a healthy fiction. It's you as your own most intimate friend. Even more than identical twins, you know every secret of each other's heart. While Sloane is in your life, you feel you will never truly be alone."

"That'll be $300, please," I say. And she laughs.

"Maggie, the problem is that this is a detachment from reality. One you do everything possible to defend. But things like this, and I must I admit I've never seen one quite like this, can't remain stable forever. Something will change. It may just go away, which could happen fast or slow. Or it could morph into a different kind of detachment from reality as you desperately fight to cling to it. I am talking about schizophrenia, multiple personality disorder. Maggie, there's no cure for those types of mental illnesses. Once they take hold, there's no way back."

She has never said this before. I'm so frightened I don't even think of some smart-ass comeback. She really means this. She is really scared of it. She is really scared for me. Which means one thing more that I hadn't really thought about. She actually cares what happens to me.

"Maggie, if I could wave a magic wand and let you stay in this fantasy forever, it would be very, very, very bad for you. Can you imagine why?"

I can't. And in spite of my customary skepticism, I really want to hear.

"Trying to live two lives keeps you from truly committing to any life at all. Imagine you and Sloane each getting married, each having babies, and imagine someday having to explain this surreal kind of bigamy that you're living in. Where you have these other children who are imaginary—"

"Stop!"

It takes a second for me to realize that I'm crying. Emma stands and comes to me and puts her arm around my shoulders and actually dries my face with her fingertips. And I actually let her.

Great, now I'm crying right before a big audition. When our session is over, I lock myself in Emma's bathroom for a good ten minutes. I smooth my hair and fix my makeup. Ready for my close-up, Mr. DeMille.

My callback is in the office of June Weitzmann, a really wonderful casting director. Making a good impression on her is actually far more important than landing this role. I always tell myself this kind of stuff when I'm playing the lower-your-expectations game. As soon as I walk in the office, I'm being judged. Even the receptionist sizes me up and can't resist a critical comment.

"Hi, I'm Maggie Jameson. I'm a little early."

"Excuse me?" she says, her brows furrowing together.

"I'm a little early. I'm not scheduled until three. I can just wait here, or . . ."

"Oh!" She forces a laugh. "I thought you said you were a little surly. Make sure you enunciate for Tucker."

Great. Thanks for the tip.

She eventually escorts me into a large loft space, empty but for two chairs, a long table strewn with script pages, and a bunch of storyboards leaning against the wall. Astonishingly, the director himself is there. Tucker Martin's last film took first at the Tribeca Festival. He is the real deal. As I stand before them, my heart is in my throat. And the more kindly June and Tucker speak to me, the more I realize that my panic is showing and the more frightened I become. I mean, seriously, I want to run.

Tucker chooses a different scene than the one I'd rehearsed and allows me to read from the sides (which is what they call printed pages of a scene). To my credit, I've already memorized all of Jolene's lines, so I'm able to keep eye contact pretty consistently. I rise above my fear and manage to be actually pretty terrific. I guess because I want it so bad. Last night, I told myself it was no big deal. But staring into Tucker Martin's eyes, things feel different. Maybe I am just as competitive as every other actor.

When I finish, there is a beat. June glances over to read Tucker. He is still staring at me, his face indecipherable. June tells me it was lovely and thanks me for coming down and says she'll call. My heart sinks.

Tucker turns to her and asks if he can speak to me alone. I've been on hundreds of auditions, callbacks, readings. This has never happened before. June squeezes my shoulder warmly as she leaves the room.

"I'm not going to cast you," he says in the kindest way he can by choosing a matter-of-fact voice to treat me as a professional rather than a brokenhearted girl, which is what I am. "How old are you?"

I lie by ten days.

"If you want a career in this profession, and if you'll work hard enough, you're going to make it. I'm not saying you have a chance; I'm saying you will make it. And my guess is sooner rather than later.

There's an elegance and a refinement to you that is at odds with the core of this character. The day will come when you have the technique to overcome something like that."

I want to jump up and down and squeal, in an elegant and refined way, of course.

"We'll work together someday, Maggie. And it will be my pleasure."

I walk around town in the rain for about two hours imagining the, oh, thirty or forty films that Tucker and I will make together during our mentor-protégé collaboration. My favorites are a startlingly reimagined version of *Lear*, with me as Cordelia (somehow I envisioned Tucker actually playing Lear and carrying me out of frame in the finale), and an original conception of my own in which my character is alcoholic, blind, with either one or no legs (depending on how my technique has developed), and oh yeah, also in love with a ballerina. But it's tragically unrequited.

Eventually, I fall by *Elle* to borrow some clothes from the magical room of never-ending high-fashion wardrobe items. Some of the upside of having your mother indentured to a fashion magazine includes free cosmetics and facial products of all kinds, introduction to some well-known cover models (who are frequently as misunderstood by history as, say, Genghis Khan), entrée to endless parties, a few of which are actually cool, seats at fashion week, and a free pass to borrow goodies you could never afford. I'm in need of a few goodies to outfit me for a photo exhibit tonight.

Jerome, whose taste is somewhere between stellar and impeccable, helps me choose an Hervé Léger bandage dress and some killer McQueen heels, and when I look at myself in the mirror, I suddenly forget the audition.

As I'm dressing, Nicole asks as casually as she can manage (which is not very) if I'm disappointed not to get the role. Uh, no, I think, not disappointed at all. Didn't even want it. Just spent all those hours preparing for the hell of it.

I tell her that my technique isn't there yet but that some mildly encouraging things were said, and I'm fine. If I tell her I am actually swooning with ecstasy, I'll never get out of here. Gallery openings never have an adequate amount of hors d'oeuvres, but they are always the highest quality of deliciousness. I feel like I haven't eaten in days because of my nerves, and my stomach is like that Venus flytrap from *Little Shop of Horrors*. Feed me, Seymour.

I walk into Flowers Gallery, and my name is on the list. In my *Elle*-borrowed outfit, I feel good. Most of the glitterati haven't arrived, which works into my evil plan of collecting all the crab toast I can nab. The opening is in honor of Mona Kuhn's new collection, shot in the South of France. The guy who owns the off-off-Broadway theater where I did the *Glass Menagerie* when I was fourteen is tight with the guy who represents Mona, who is my most favorite photographer, so I begged him to invite me. Of course, I can only imagine how insanely jealous Sloane will be tomorrow morning. Hey, it's a $60 train ride; she can get her butt down here.

Actually, that could never happen. I've tried to look up Sloane in information in Mystic, Connecticut. She doesn't exist. My dad took us up there for a month one summer, and I used to bike by what I thought was her house. A nice family lived there. Not hers. I'm absolutely positive that Sloane has done the same for me.

Five crab toasts and two braised lamb shanks later, I'm stuffed, which is not a good look in a bandage dress. I'm drinking red wine from a glass that seems never to empty because the waiters are so good at their job of filling it up. I turn down several cocktails from assorted males who like to look at the part of your bandage dress where there's no dress. Do these guys think we don't see where they're looking? This always amazes me. Nicole says, sure they know, but they don't care. Nah. Guys think they're bulletproof. And, irony of ironies, just as I'm hating on the men in the place, in walks . . . well . . .

He is tall, which I'm ashamed to admit is sort of a requirement (sorry, short guys). He has incredible hair, which is kind of golden and amber and stays gorgeously long and in place with no product. Magic hair guy. His eyes are nearly black, but I'm so in the spell of charisma that I don't realize this means the hair might be dyed. So what? I stand my ground. Stare straight at him. And just wait to see what happens.

It starts with a slow smile. I don't smile back, but I don't blink. Here he comes. And to my surprise, the first thing he says is . . .

"Aren't you Maggie Jameson?"

I'm stuck for a comeback. Here's what I come up with . . .

"As a matter of fact, I actually am."

This has to be the dumbest single way any human ever acknowledged their own identity.

"I've been looking for you. Actually, that's a slight exaggeration. I've been looking for a woman to play a role that you could crush. I have a short list. Nine names. I'll be honest enough to say you were seventh. But looking at you tonight, I hope I can persuade you to hear me out."

This is the life of a wannabe ingénue. Should I be more upset that the guy ("Thomas Randazzo, born Tomaso, of course," he tells me) is not hitting on me, or more thrilled that he wants to cast me, or more skeptical that he's pretending to want to cast me in order to hit on me? I decide that with that hair, he doesn't need any excuses to hit on anybody. And since I'm way too young (a lot more than one year and ten days) to live out this fantasy, I'm gonna hope he's casting me.

"I work for Rosalie Woods. We're casting a primetime series for ABC."

Rosalie is the primo casting director on planet Earth and surrounding galaxies. ABC is an Earth-bound television network. I am literally pinching my arm to see if this is somehow a dream within a dream.

"It's based on the Innuendo books. I'm sure you're familiar with them."

For those who have recently revived from a prolonged coma, the Innuendo books (presently five of them) have made vampires obsolete in terms of youthful romance. I devoured the whole series in one weekend. They are well written, deep, and really hot. The bidding war for the film rights was extensively over-reported.

"And you simply have to find the perfect Lara."

"I sure do. It's not you. You were born to play Robin."

Robin is maybe the fourth lead, the edgy, unconventional, free-spirited, well, babe. Lisbeth Salander but elegant and refined.

Thomas hands me his card. Now some guys could go to the length of printing a card like that just to get lucky. Once again, not with that hair.

"We haven't gone out to anyone yet. We're waiting for Macauley Evans to wrap his feature in South Africa. He's going to be directing the pilot, and obviously he'll be key in the casting."

I recover my senses.

"Thomas, I'm almost speechless. The chance to read for Robin would be an opportunity that I could scarcely imagine."

"Don't be so modest, especially in that dress."

Red flag. Maybe it isn't about the role and is more about the bandage. Or he could just be pointing out that I'm not exactly telegraphing shrinking violet tonight. He isn't ogling my goodies. In fact, I'm probably the one ogling. As if he can hear my internal debate, he brings it back to work . . .

"I saw you in *The Mamet* on HBO."

One scene. Fifteen lines. If you sneezed hard, you'd have missed me.

"You blew Andy Garcia off the screen. And I thought, this is what Emmy Rossum was supposed to be in *Phantom*. Then I remembered I'd seen you do Holly Golightly in summer stock in the Berkshires and you were incandescent. Audrey Hepburn at sixteen."

Fifteen. Barely.

"I just have this instinct, I mean, you know, that's how we work in my business. You feel that spark, and you just know. I'm sure I'm sounding like, I don't know, a casting agent. Sorry about that."

A smile as nice as his hair. He stares at me, comfortably, pleasantly.

"There are a few things you'd be right for. At some point, we should get together and talk about that."

At some point. What point is that?

"But by all means, let's play out the Robin thing first. Funny bumping into you tonight; I wasn't going to come. In fact, I have to give Mona a hug and run off to this thing at the Standard."

I like the Standard. I'd like to go to the Standard. Invite me to the Standard. He holds out his hand. His hand! Gentlemanly and businesslike.

"Real pleasure to meet you, Maggie. We'll be in touch."

I shake his hand. He lingers for just a second longer than he should. Then he gives a little wave. And he's off.

Either this guy has so much game he just Jedi-mind-tricked me into thinking he wasn't hitting on me and making me wish he would, or I have a little crush on a man who could be the key to some big opportunities.

The bandage business has no pockets. So I'll have to hold on to his card for the rest of the night. Like I'll ever call him.

CHAPTER FOUR

SLOANE

A sparrow is trapped in homeroom. I walk in right before the bell and kids are freaking out because the poor little thing is slamming itself against the glass of a partially open window desperately trying to escape. No one knows what to do. Some swat books at it, many yell and disorient it further.

"Stop," a calm voice says from behind me.

I can only see his profile, backlit from the open door. And then he walks into the room. It is a face of such strikingly unique beauty that it actually stops my breath. A beauty so compelling that I admire it for its own sake without even fantasizing being close to it in a personal way. I gasp softly, but no one notices. That's how completely he's captured everyone's attention.

He steps to the window with a commanding presence, and the rest of the class falls back. At this point the sparrow is fluttering its wings hysterically against the glass. The boy reaches out with his bare hands and gently cups them around the terrified creature. It seems somehow to calm at his touch. He simply reaches through the open part of the window and releases the sparrow, who flies madly off without so much as a thank you. The boy stands for a moment, his back still to me, oblivious of the rest of the class, simply watching the bird fly away.

He goes to a seat in the back of the room. At this point every eye is on him, the new kid in homeroom who just performed the Miracle of the Sparrow. He picks up a well-thumbed paperback of Kafka's *The Trial*, a particular favorite of mine. But his choice of leisure reading isn't what has me hypnotized. It is something more mysterious, and even perhaps darker, than the book itself.

This guy is reading his book as if he is alone in the world. He seems to have no awareness, let alone interest, in any of us. There is nothing in the absolute stillness of his beautiful face to suggest arrogance or conceit, and this gives him an aura of limitless inner power. But the most striking part is that there is a darkness to it. A danger. Although I'm not sure what could be at risk.

Unlike Maggie, I have no acting experience except for one summer at Stage Door Manor in the Catskills. I went there because I knew that the study of acting would help me in writing characters. I have written short stories since the age of six (okay, those were really short). And when I was eight, I finally had the courage to write one about my greatest fear. It was not a nightmare; it was a waking fear that would often keep me from sleep. There was a sorcerer floating beyond my second-story window. He was invisible, and yet I knew exactly what he looked like. Because he wanted me to.

He looked like this boy now sitting in my homeroom, reading

Kafka. Or at least that's what I realize in this moment, as goose bumps cover my flesh. I knew that if I ever let my guard down, the sorcerer would be able to come through my window, into my bed, and take control of me. I had rituals at night to keep him at bay. I wrote stories about these rituals, which always worked. There are eleven of them. I often wondered if I would ever have the courage to write the story of them not working.

I don't know him, and yet somehow I do. Enough to not like him. I know I will never like him. It isn't personal. It isn't a judgment. It is a fact as true and unchangeable as gravity.

Mr. Sanchez introduces the gorgeous new boy as James Waters. Then he begins reading every banal announcement ever invented by homeroom teachers. There are fire drills in our future, bake sales (the horror!), the posting of rules for our dumb mathalon (a marathon of mathematics), tutoring sign-up for tutors and tutorees, we will no longer be served polenta in the cafeteria because it was too hard to scrape off the walls after last Thursday's "incident." And through all of this, every cell of my being is focused on the beautiful boy six rows behind me. It feels as if his pale gray eyes are boring into the back of my neck despite my absolute certainty that he hasn't noticed I'm alive. And then, dear Mr. Sanchez wipes James Waters from my mind.

"I know that all of you are, I suppose the phrase is, 'looking forward to' the opportunity to honor the memory of William Rainey on the athletic field next Friday afternoon. I never had the pleasure of personally knowing Bill, but I have heard from so many students and faculty members of his gentle intelligence, his kindness, his sweetness of spirit, and of course, his athletic prowess.

Now I suppose all of you know that your classmate in this very homeroom, Sloane Jameson, will be one of the principal speakers at this event . . ."

Everyone turns to look at me. Some actually slide their chairs around to have a better view. It would be a relief if the floor beneath my desk could open wide so I'd plummet to hell.

"Now I haven't actually spoken to Sloane about this . . ."

Let's keep it that way.

". . . but I'm going to take the liberty . . ."

Uh-oh. This is never a favorable sign.

". . . of suggesting that any of you who has a personal memory or story to tell about our Bill—perhaps humorous, perhaps poignant, but certainly revealing—"

Is there any possible way that by simply wanting to die in this moment, I could will myself to make it happen? An aneurysm perhaps?

". . . might email or text or Tweet or, to date myself, even dare to telephone Sloane with your story, in case she'd like to include it. This memorial is for all of you. And not to put poor Sloane on the spot . . ."

Just in time.

". . . I know that none of you will think the less of her if your stories are not used. Sloane, have you already prepared your remarks?"

"Can we just go back to that polenta thing again?"

One voice laughs from the back of the room. And even though the laugh isn't overtly cruel, I know that it is mocking my poor attempt at humor, and I am humiliated beyond belief. I didn't know it was possible for a human blush to last thirteen minutes. Regular color and body temperature don't return to my skin until long after the bell, when I dash from the room to the girls' room to splash my face with cold water.

It is embarrassing how easily embarrassed I am. But this incident was intolerable, especially given the subject matter. James Waters was the only one who laughed out loud, but it felt like the whole room had me tarred and feathered and was chuckling at my discomfort.

As I enter each of my morning classes, I say a heartfelt atheist's prayer that James won't be there. He isn't in French, calculus, AP European History, or physics. I keep my head low in the halls all day, trying to be invisible. As I head off to lunch, I realize that since my fifth period is free study, my only remaining risk is sixth-period AP Lit. The one wild card is lunch. I just have to avoid seeing him or letting him see me.

Lila and Kelly are up on the hill. I join them and plop down on the grass as if reaching home base in a game of tag I'm playing all by myself. It's not like I have a bull's-eye on the back of my shirt. It's not like he or anyone else even remembers homeroom at this point. Get over yourself, Sloane. I just need to push him from my mind.

No. Such. Luck.

"Have you seen him?" Lila is practically foaming at the mouth.

"Who?"

"The love child of Johnny Depp and the most beautiful woman who ever lived, whoever she is. Or was."

"Well, don't keep me in suspense."

Kelly taps me on the shoulder. She points. He is no more than twenty yards away. He's not sitting isolated and alone on some demonic throne as I'd imagine but is at a picnic table with a group of kids, apparently engaged in friendly conversation.

"Oh, the new kid in my homeroom. What about him?"

Kelly isn't buying my casual tone. "Enough with this 'too cool for school' shit that you pull incessantly. If you're not going to admit that this dude is an objet d'art, that can only mean that you have a crush on him so disabling that you've lost your will to lie persuasively."

I pretend to take a long, professionally discerning examination of the art object in question.

"Well, compared to The Weed . . ."

"That was a cheap shot; he's a very nice kid and quite attractive."

"Mmm, don't have him stand next to the new guy in any group photo if you want to convince anyone else of that."

"So you admit he is hot," Lila prods.

"Well. He's more . . . unusual . . . than actually hot. Sort of an off-kilter James Franco kind of thing. Maybe James Dean. But prettier. Maybe a little too pretty for his own good. He has the kind of looks that probably change with the angle and the light, so he might be interesting to photograph."

"Preferably naked," Lila adds. "And even more preferably, I'm the one holding the camera."

"Or holding whatever," Kelly suggests.

Kelly is the only one of us who has had actual sex. As opposed to, I suppose, virtual sex. Lila is very pretty and very religious, which adds up to total horndog. She would be president of the Everything But Club if one existed. She actually thinks she's saving herself for marriage. An interesting definition of "herself," since there's only one thing she's saved.

As for me, I'm a virgin for a reason that is personal.

Kelly tucks a strand of Lila's hair behind her ear and tells her, "Sorry to be the buzz kill. He belongs to, drumroll, please, Amanda Porcella."

"That can't be true," Lila says. "Because as a Catholic, I know that there is a God in heaven."

"They went on Outward Bound together summer before freshman year. Their dads work together at Pfizer. His folks are divorced, he's lived with his mom in San Francisco all these years, but now that she's remarrying, it's dad's turn."

"So I've never been on Outward Bound," Lila offers, "but I'm guessing it takes more than building a lean-to together to 'belong' to each other."

"Depends on what you do in the lean-to after it's built."

"Okay, now I know you're full of shit because Amanda has been in CCD with me since we were six and she'd never ever go all the way before marriage for any reason."

Kelly turns toward the boy, with a sweep of her hand: "Gentlemen of the jury, I present to you exhibit A."

I stare at James. And for no reason in particular say, "I don't see him with Amanda Porcella. She's homecoming queen. She's popular and friendly and cheery. I just don't think he'd find her interesting."

"Sloane, let me introduce you to a species called 'male.' She's interesting."

"Not to him." And then, without thinking, I say, "This isn't me being cool, and it isn't sour grapes; there's something about that boy that . . ."

Kelly looks interested. She watches me stare. "Are you writing a story about him as we speak?"

"Of course not."

Kelly laughs. "Bullshit. Okay, if you were writing a story about him, who would he be?"

I think for a moment as I watch him talking with the group, eating his sandwich, unaware that Amanda has angled herself toward him hoping for attention. "He's not a boy who will ever give himself to anyone. And he's not going to bring anyone any happiness."

"Wow." Lila speaks for the two of them, and I feel embarrassed to have said something so pretentious and judgmental and, well, mean. "Well, the good news is I don't have to compete with you, and as far as I'm concerned, I could love me a little unhappiness. In the right flavor."

Kelly turns to me. "You may just be making up one of your stories, but I think you're right."

And at this moment, the boy who couldn't possibly have heard anything we were saying slowly turns. And looks directly into my eyes. For exactly two seconds. And then he walks away.

Those are the eyes of a sniper, or even an assassin. But then we just read *An Occurrence at Owl Creek Bridge*. And anyway, what does it mean to have the eyes of a sniper? Is he analytical? Is he cool under pressure? Is he cold-blooded? Is he coldhearted? I think that gray eyes don't absorb any light, don't give back any color or life. They are self-contained. They care nothing for you. And are therefore fascinating, in the sense that aren't we all compelled to read the unreadable?

Sixth period. The seat to my left is unaccountably empty. I find myself performing one of my eleven rituals. I move my thumbs to the other fingers of its hand in a complicated pattern I memorized.

Index, ring, pinky, middle, pinky, pinky, ring, and on and on. The sound of that bell is a relief. I stop and reach down to pull out my book.

. And then he walks in the door. And sits next to me.

"This afternoon, we welcome James Waters, a new transfer student from California," Ms. Lambert announces. "James, we are just finishing our postmortems on the relevance of *The Great Gatsby* to modern male-female dynamics in terms of romanticism, class and social status, power relationships, and the tools each gender uses. So for the weekend, if you can read *Sound and the Fury*, the Benjy section, we begin that discussion on Monday." James nods like he's read it before, and I immediately bristle. "So, guys, what do we think about Daisy? Does she exist today?"

She looks around the room. Absolutely no hands. Which is usual. They're waiting for me. Today they're out of luck.

"Sloane? Are you comatose? I don't think any of us will know what to do if someone else has to speak first. Does Daisy exist today?"

I used to like Ms. Lambert. Until this moment, actually. No way will I ever speak again in this class. And from the seat to my left . . .

"She certainly does. I've dated her." Wild laughter. Including our apparently smitten teacher. Damn her. And without realizing that my brain has disconnected from my mouth . . .

"As long as guys would rather be with a girl they think of as their intellectual inferior, Daisy will live on."

"Goodness, we have ourselves a debate. And in the affirmative?"

James turns to me, but I keep my gaze fixed on Ms. Lambert.

"Ms., uh . . ."

Diabolical. He clearly doesn't remember me from homeroom, or at least my name. I'm now forced to look at him to answer. The sorcerer draws first blood. I turn to the gray eyes, trying to be completely natural and unconcerned, which aren't really things you can "try" to do.

"Jameson. Not sure the relevance to the question you haven't started to answer." Zing.

"I wasn't being asked a question, actually. I was asked to take the affirmative in defense of a complex female character. And I just wonder why you feel Daisy is intellectually inferior to any other character in that book. Ms. Jameson."

"Have you actually read the book?"

"Not only have I read it, but I've made the distinction between someone who is stupid and someone who is foolish."

There is actual applause. I never realized that I was actually hated by this class. This is the worst of all possible moments to find it out.

"Well?" Ms. Lambert is loving this.

"If you say so. As long as guys would rather be with a foolish girl, Daisy will live on."

"An interesting debating tactic. It's like you're hoping everyone will agree that the quality you most dislike in the character is the one that attracts men to her. I'd love to hear the list of qualities that attract men to you."

This is followed by a cacophony of zoo noises so gross and prolonged that Ms. Lambert, the traitor, has to call for order. My anger emboldens me to say:

"Well, I suppose . . . green eyes. Blond hair. Silky skin. Standard body parts wrapped in a tight package." The zoo noises return, but now they are on my side. "Everything that means nothing."

"And what is it about you that means something?"

"Interesting tactic, switching the subject of the debate to your opponent. Sadly I haven't been the object of Fitzgerald's fascination."

"Okay, fair point. My assessment of Daisy is that she cares about her own agenda and doesn't apologize for it. She may have many characteristics that Fitzgerald dislikes. She's careless, reckless, flirtatiously manipulative, superficial, and chooses material things over romantic love. But she's in control. Maybe her foolishness is a brilliant act to get what she wants."

The class waits for my response. Unfortunately, I know he's right. I've reduced it too simply.

"I've never looked at it quite that way before. But when you don't care about anything but yourself, you may be more powerful, you may even be more interesting, but you are less worthy company." I watch him think about what I said.

"I guess. But why is it an admirable quality to be worthy company? Because it's important that other people want to be with you? I think that's a dangerous road. I don't judge people's worth by how popular they are."

"Daisy's selfishness makes it impossible for her to truly connect with anyone. If you're defending her, admiring her, dating her, whatever, does that mean you don't place much value on human connection?"

I feel the crowd turning on me again, as if I distorted an interesting discussion into a personal attack. As if. Okay, I sort of did. But he did it first, I think. And even if he didn't, what, I'm supposed to just get bitch-slapped in AP Lit?

"That's probably what we are really debating. The basic reason that romantic connection is so difficult is that men objectify women. For Tom, Gatsby, and Nick, and probably the male species in general, it's all about them. The woman fills a place in his life, and that's her only value. Basically, she's just part of his relationship with himself."

"So all the fault lies with you and your brothers."

"Except that we couldn't be the pigs we are if women didn't buy into it. Women have enabled this situation from the beginning of time. Daisy is actually the man in the book. She's using Tom to have money, position, and safety. She's using Jay to feel loved. She's using Nick to feel worshipped and valued."

And that's Amanda Porcella?

"So what'd she use you for?" I can't resist.

"Sloane . . ." Ms. Lambert starts to interrupt, but James just looks at me like the rest of class isn't there and answers.

"I guess we used each other. Read Rilke's poem about two individuals living side by side, who can grow, if they can love the distance between them, which makes it possible for each to see the other whole against the sky."

"I read it. In fourth grade."

Lots of good-natured laughter. Maddeningly, some of it from him.

"Then you know it's saying that blurring the lines of individuality in a desperate attempt to stay connected is, ironically, the greatest enemy of true connection."

Every eye on me.

"I have to say I agree."

He turns to Ms. Lambert. "Do we keep score in this class?"

She laughs. "Starting today."

She goes to the board, writes *J* and *S*, and puts a hash mark under *J*. There is enthusiastic applause. And I should be feeling like a big loser. But weirdly, I'm excited because I feel somehow connected to him, even though moments ago that was the last thing I wanted.

For all of his air of superiority, and the fact that he just schooled me, he engaged me as an equal. Maybe we will strike up a prickly but mutually respectful relationship. As Ms. Lambert spends the rest of the class calling on other kids, I spend the rest of the class planning several alternative conversations to chat him up with as soon as class is over. How convenient that this is sixth period. Maybe we will wind up at the Marble, sipping vanilla lattes dissecting the brilliance of *The Trial*. Actually, he probably drinks espresso. Or just black coffee. Nothing sweet and foamy.

The bell rings.

He stands up without ever looking at me. Stops at Ms. Lambert's desk. Says something that makes her laugh and her eyes involuntarily dart to me.

And then he just walks out. Of the room. Of my good graces. Of our prickly, mutually respectful future together. Of any universe I may ever inhabit.

CHAPTER FIVE

MAGGIE

The phone is ringing when I return home from a cattle call audition for a nationwide TV commercial. While it's not high art, scoring the role of Woman with Headache or Girl Drinking Coke pays great money. And I'm a working actress. And smart enough to know that having some savings in case I ever want to go to college is a good idea.

When I quit school so that I'd be able to audition and work, my father devoted himself to my homeschooling. He created a library of lesson plans for me, bringing me through my "graduation." They are personal and fun and tailored specifically for me by someone who really gets how my brain works. I whizzed through them all, binders and binders of every subject, by the time I turned sixteen. I've been dragging my feet for the past year on taking the GED and just being done with it. For the second time, I have an actual test date, so I try to force myself to peck away at the preparation material each day. It's easy to find distractions from sitting down and doing the actual work. Like this damn ringing phone.

"No, she's not home. This is her daughter."

The voice on the other end of the phone asks incredulously, "Jade?"

"I'm Maggie, Jade's older sister. What's wrong?"

"We have to reschedule your sister's MRI . . ."

My sister's what??

". . . because Dr. Strong has a surgery in the afternoon and so needs to see her in the morning."

I silently choke down my terror, my fury at that idiot Nicole, while composing my thoughts.

"Um, my mother hasn't mentioned this; can you tell me what the MRI is for?"

"I'm sorry, I wish I could. Is there another number where I can reach your mother?"

When I arrive at *Elle* to have it out with her, Nicole is at her desk obsessing over an article titled "Electric Facials, Botox's New Best Friend," because facials and Botox are much more important than being available for your children. The open layout of the office lends a great stage for our smackdown. Jerome actually makes a bag of popcorn in the kitchenette and puts his feet up to watch.

Nicole takes and holds the position that she kept this a secret from me so that I "wouldn't be worried." Or respond in an inappropriately dramatic way, as, she points out, I am now. I ask how that's working out for her. I also ask if she will advance me enough money for a bus ticket so that I can take Jade somewhere far away from her and neither of us will ever see her again. I hear a chuckle from the beauty editor sitting ten feet away.

I suppose a good part of my outrage is fueled by the fact that I am basically Jade's functioning mother more than half the time. I have enormous responsibility and now am being left out of crucial information and decisions affecting Jade's very life.

Nicole informs me in that patronizing tone she calls "patient" that this is completely routine. The medical protocol requires a scan to rule out "anything structural" before committing completely to the Snickers regime.

The clincher is that when I ask Nicole how we should tell Jade about it, she informs me she told Jade about the appointment a few days ago and said, "Don't tell your sister. You know how she worries."

I lose it. Whereupon Nicole has the gall to remind me that she is my mother (considering the way she behaves, I suppose a reminder is in order), as well as being Jade's mother (right), and that she doesn't appreciate my choice of language or tone of voice.

Thus unappreciated, I take my words and my voice and Jerome's popcorn and storm out the door. Unwilling to be under the same roof with that woman, I call a few friends from class and wind up crashing at Jason's because he sleeps at his boyfriend's most nights and needs someone to feed his kitten anyway. Dorothy (named after Bea Arthur's character on *The Golden Girls*, Jason's favorite TV show, which he only started watching when the reruns became cool) listens intently as I explain the situation. She responds with purring and cuddling. I could easily start coming to talk to Dorothy instead of Emma.

I ignore my mother's calls. Dorothy and I do, however, listen to her voicemails. My favorite, the one I actually saved instead of angrily deleting in case I ever need to petition for full custody, wonders if I could bring Jade to the hospital at the appointed time so that she can meet us there and not miss a staff meeting. This from the woman who wasn't going to tell me about it at all. For anyone seeking an example of cognitive dissonance, I'd like to present my mother.

She can miss her damn meeting.

Suddenly, I glance at Jason's bedside table and notice the second book of the Innuendo series sitting there, like a sign from heaven. With a nudge from my fuzzy new friend, drunk with the anger I feel toward Nicole, I dial Thomas. Relieved when he doesn't answer, I leave a message telling him I'd love to get together to discuss the opportunities he was mentioning. I fumble the end of the message, saying, "This is Maggie Jameson, we met at the Mona Kuhn opening," realizing too late that's what I said as my opener. I press 3, expecting the AT&T lady to interrupt and ask me if I want to delete and rerecord my message, but he apparently uses a different carrier. So now he has a bunch of beeps and a soft "shit" from me to wrap up the voicemail. Won't hold my breath to hear from Hair Guy.

I show up at the hospital an hour before they are supposed to arrive. When they do, I scoop up Jade and take her off for a chat without acknowledging Nicole's existence. She tells me she's frightened of being stuck in the tunnel but hasn't mentioned this to Nicole because you know how she worries. This is what happens when parents ask seven-year-olds to keep secrets from adults. I tell her that we will solve it by my going in with her and holding on to her foot while she is in the tube so that we can be secretly talking to each other between her toes and my fingers. She likes this idea, though preferring I could actually be in the tunnel with her.

She does great. Her sweet toes and my fingers have a Morse code conversation and listen to the pounding of the machine, just barely louder than the pounding of my worried heart.

Jade is, of course, fine. The test was just protocol but gives me peace of mind to know that there isn't any reason for concern. We put the MRI image of her brain on the refrigerator and I scrawl on it with a Sharpie: *Nothing going on in here*. Jade thinks it's funny. I forgive Nicole. Snickers become my sister's fifth food group. And everything returns to normal. Except that I now think about the mortality of all of us a lot more than I ever did.

"What do you mean by that?" Emma asks at our next session.

"Well, it isn't just a question of whether Sloane or I will disappear one day. Jade is at risk too."

"If you give Sloane up, let her go, then you won't have to worry about Jade anymore." She sits back in her chair and tells me, "This is a pricey fantasy you're indulging in. You're starting to learn the true costs, and there will be more to come."

Which just sounds cryptic and foreboding. But what if she's right?

I take my petulance and depression to the Washington Square dog park with Jade's Yorkie, Boris. She is sleeping over at her best friend Tomiko's, so I am Boris's bitch for the duration. I don't like Boris. And I probably never will. He's only a little dog, and never did anything bad to me at all. I don't like his attitude, which is big enough to barely squeeze into an airplane hangar, but I also think he's ugly, which is exacerbated by the fact that every young female I meet (and guys who have so little game they address their pickup lines to a girl's dog) is constantly adoring how adorable Boris is. He's not.

I like big dogs. Big, shaggy ones who love you to pound them with your fists because they can barely feel it. And they slobber all over you and are completely disgusting and are completely comfortable letting assholes like Boris pretend to push them around. Because they have the thing I admire most in dogs and men. Confidence.

So when I see some perfectly pleasant-looking guy being pushed around by some strutting, entitled bitch, I want to look the other way. I'm not sure why I don't. There's a couple across the grassy run, with no discernible dog, setting up some kind of home video something. They have claimed a prime bench under one of the leafy oaks. He is setting up lights and screens to replace the natural sunlight with the specific lighting angles he wants. And she is bitching at him nonstop, like she knows what the hell she's talking about. I've been on enough sets to know that he does and she doesn't. However, she's totally gorgeous, which makes me tense up. Whenever I see an actress with a stronger look than mine, I try to resist the urge to go all alpha dog, but I never succeed. Thus assured that she could have no talent, I wander over, hoping to lose Boris in the process, figuring this is none of my business. I'm sure the guy is getting something out of it for the aggravation.

I sit on a bench, absurdly close. Obviously within earshot. Her complaints are all about the lighting. She has very specific ideas about what his setup should do to her bone structure. The guy pays no attention to her whatsoever. So now I like him. She is, however, incredibly hot.

Through masterful eavesdropping, I'm able to figure out that Andrew is in film school at NYU, which is pretty prestigious. Carmen, astonishingly enough, is his classmate. He's making a student film and is confident in his abilities, obviously having made several before, and I realize that they must not be a couple at all. I hate to admit that it actually makes me feel a little satisfied. He's too good for her.

Once he starts directing her scene, their dynamic changes completely. He is in total command. She eagerly follows his every suggestion, all of which are made respectfully, in low tones. She even lets him give her line readings, which always drives me crazy. She is actually good. Not just good for a film student, but good for an actress. When the scene is over, they do a second take, and he says it's a wrap. She looks at him like a puppy waiting to be praised. He says, "Nice." And she jumps into his arms like a trained chimp, jams her tongue down his throat, and I realize they must be a couple after all. I'm not even trying to pretend I'm not watching at this point.

Then she says she was channeling Audrey Hepburn from *Philadelphia Story*. I can see in his eyes that he knows. If he says the word *Katharine*, he's in the doghouse.

"Katharine," he says softly.

"Katharine who?"

"Katharine Hepburn was in *Philadelphia Story*. You're thinking of channeling Audrey Hepburn in *The Nun's Story*."

"Excuse me?"

"Well, I'm thinking the purity, the spirituality, the grace . . ."

"So this is you being an asshole, yes?" She puts a hand on her hip.

He grins. "This is me making a little fun of you for being pretentious."

"Except you're the one being pretentious," I say out loud. They both turn to me.

"Thanks," says the actress.

"Fair enough," says the director, and they proceed to politely ignore me as he shapes her performance for their next scene. So Boris and I sit and watch. We don't discuss our reactions, but I sense that despite our differences, he agrees with my approval of their individual techniques. For some reason I can't quite put my finger on, I begin to really like them as a couple. Even when they argue. It makes me wish I could find a guy to argue with. It's not as easy as you'd think.

When they finish, he begins to strike the set, and she walks straight over to me and sits beside me on the bench.

"I have a dog at home in Barcelona. But he's a big dog. I prefer bigger dogs."

"This is Boris. You hate him, admit it."

"Well, *hate* is such a strong word. Let's just say that he repels me on every level. At heart, he's probably a loving and gentle creature, but I somehow doubt it."

"Wow, you're a shrewd judge of dogs."

"Men too," she says, glancing at Andrew.

It's clear that he was listening to everything we were saying because he turns and nods his appreciation for the compliment. Boris merely yaps. The actress holds out her hand, tells me her name is Carmen (which I already knew from my eavesdropping) and that her boyfriend (which is exactly how she introduces him) is Andrew, don't call him Andy.

"What will happen if I do?" I ask, just to see how she'll respond.

"Tell her, Andy," she commands without a hint of a smile.

Without missing a beat, he says, "I'll feel marginalized, diminished, and be reminded of my inferiority in every way to Andy Bachman, who was my nemesis in first grade."

Carmen studies me. "You're an actress."

"Why would you say that?"

"Because I told her I thought you were an actress," Andrew pipes in without looking up.

Carmen nods. "You were mouthing my lines, after the first take. Would you like to try the scene?"

I laugh. Actors are such a competitive species.

"This is his short film for workshop; I'm just helping him out while I'm working a shoot on the Upper East Side. Believe me, you'd be doing me a favor if he cast you instead."

He reminds Carmen that her call is in an hour, offers her cab money, and to my surprise she grabs my shoulders and kisses my cheek as she leaves.

Meanwhile, her boyfriend has packed up and is ready to go. He glances at me.

"You weren't only mouthing the lines, your face was in character."

He looks at me so directly. His eyes are deep brown with nice lashes I hadn't noticed before. Then a smile, which is somehow shy and lopsided. I instantly want to be his friend.

"I was trying to pretend I wasn't watching you," he says, "but I was. You were really good. I mean, in that moment when she says, 'It's been a while,' your eyes went straight to anger, which I think was the best choice."

"Then why did you wait a take to suggest it?"

"I wanted to see if she'd find it for herself."

For a second he looks as if he's afraid he was being disrespectful, and he quickly adds, "She's very experienced. She did eight films in Spain, including two with Almodóvar." I nod, impressed. He keeps looking at me as if he has something more to say. But instead says, "Nice meeting you."

"I'm Maggie," I say.

He smiles. "Nice meeting you, Maggie."

And heads off toward his day.

Boris is now humping a labradoodle of indeterminate gender, who doesn't even seem to notice. I pull out my phone to snap some doggie porn for Jade and notice a text from, oh my God, Thomas. It says:

Drinks at 6?

Now. There's an art to this. Which unfortunately I have yet to master. Boris will be no help. Andrew probably wouldn't have either. Where is Carmen when you need her? If I write *Yes*, does that seem too perfunctory or, on the other hand, too eager? How about *Why not?* Nope, too obviously straining for casualtude. Okay, let's go with *Sure*. It's incredibly boring but avoids any negative I can think of at the moment. Wait a minute. What if I try *Love to I just have to move something around*? Less available, but dishonest. And I'm saying it's so important that I'd cancel something else. Is that bad? I mean, I do want him to know that I'm desperate for the role. Maybe *Can't make six, let's do six thirty*. Only if he has a seven o'clock, he'll just cancel and who knows if I'll get another chance.

And then, a whole other debate crashes down on me. What kind of drinks are these? Professional—or personal? Is this a *date*?

If I keep this going until six, I won't have to worry about it.

I text *I think I can make that work. Looking forward.* A little bit of everything. *Push send. Push send.*

"Boris?" I say. "What do you think?"

Thomas chooses a place that is notoriously impossible to get into. Not that the doorways are small, but they are guarded by snippy hostesses whose only pleasure in life is to pretend that they are better than you because they won't let you into a restaurant that nobody would let them into either.

I've actually made it past the sphinx guards of this joint before. A celebutante named Crystal in my acting class likes to take me and Andrea places. I would say that Crystal, like Genghis Khan, has been sadly misjudged by history, but she has been sadly correctly judged by Page Six. I like her, though. And I love the truffled mac and cheese at this place.

I find Thomas at a quality table in the garden. He's dressed impeccably but casual, and I can't help but wonder how I'd look in his cashmere sweater. His hair sits soft and perfect, his face relaxed and handsome. The garden is lit with a glow, and I feel like I'm walking into a romantic movie where Thomas is the hunky lead.

Seeing me, he pockets his BlackBerry, stands, kisses one cheek, and holds my chair. He smells good. He asks what I'm drinking. I ask him what this meeting is going to be about so that I can properly select. He likes that. He says, "Chapter one of you taking over the world. Or at least New York."

I order champagne and immediately feel the stab of fear in my belly that I might get carded. Then I remember he already knows my age. The waitress doesn't ask and leaves us to the business at hand.

In these situations, an actress has to consider, or act by reflex or instinct, with respect to certain bodily movements. Does one touch one's hair? Does one cross one's legs so as to carelessly reveal only the knee or a hint of thigh? Does one lean forward while touching (though certainly not unbuttoning) the top button of her shirt? What is expected? What will be interpreted in what way? Body language while being interviewed by a male casting director can be a type of nonsexual foreplay. Having said all this, at my age I think all of the foregoing is risky. Consequently, I have to be careful not to do it. Which is not as easy as you might think. Particularly when confronted with someone as foxy as Thomas.

"I'm a little nervous," he says, which makes me feel better.

"Don't worry," I respond with my best smile. "I promise I'll take the part."

He does seem nervous. He keeps unfolding and refolding the napkin in his lap.

"I'd like to see you have a real shot at this role. The truth is Rosalie or either of the two other actresses could knock you straight off the list. There are high stakes on this show, and networks tend to go for safer choices, which means faces they know. Although with the fourth lead they might well take a chance, particularly if we can lock in the star we want for Lara. I want to be completely honest, I don't yet know if you're best for the part or not."

"Look, I appreciate the lack of bullshit. And I appreciate the shot."

"I want to be honest about something else," he says, and my heart jumps. "I want to get to know you better. There are nine years between us, and if that doesn't scare you, it sure scares me. But I hate the game of pretending I'm not really interested. Like you say, all the bullshit we all live through every day." At this point, *I* must have been the one to look nervous because he adds, "I swear to God that nothing about any of this will affect your chances in the slightest."

The first bullshit. Even if he doesn't mean it to be. He just rang a bell that can't be unrung, and my response will not only affect my chances, it well might determine them completely. I've been here before, though never with stakes like these. Still, I made my rule on this long ago and promised myself I would never reevaluate it on the spot or on impulse. The rule is to only respond with complete honesty about the personal side of it, with no business considerations whatsoever.

"Okay, I'll be honest too," I say. "You're obviously very attractive. I'd like to get to know *you*. But I'm not at all interested in casual dating. I only want to be with someone I care about right now. And that takes time." I know that what I'm saying is totally dorky, but I barrel on. "Truthfully, with me, considerable time. If all that is something you're really comfortable with, I'd like to know you better."

He stares in my eyes, and I try hard not to blush. I feel really nervous and a little excited.

"Are you free for dinner Saturday night?" he asks.

"It's my birthday," I say, instead of answering.

"Thank God, fourteen at last!" And I laugh. He says he has a business thing and can't pick me up until eight thirty, but if that was okay, he would be "so honored" to have dinner with me on my birthday.

For the next hour we talk about business. He makes several strategic suggestions, including a way for us to encounter Rosalie socially, that he might never have made without my having agreed to a dinner date. He also talks about a pilot and two films that he is involved in casting and how I might be considered for roles. I have an idealistic heart, but it's latched to a practical mind. As I listen to Thomas, I have to put aside my illusions about the ideal platonic relationship between casting agent/mentor and little me. If he doesn't want what he wants already (and he does), he's going to eventually. And I'd better start thinking about how I'm going to feel about that.

The problem is that I don't know.

The other problem is, I've been thinking about this for so long that I've lost track of what he's talking about, and since I've been doing that actress audition thing of looking deeply into his eyes and leaning slightly forward, I'm in trouble.

"So what do you think?" he asks. How convenient.

"Actually, I'm torn." Please fill in the blanks. Please. Please.

"Well, it's more a basic career choice."

"That's exactly what I was thinking. Two roads diverge in a yellow wood and all that. But which path to take?"

"My advice is, follow your instincts."

"Thank you. My instinct is to take your advice."

Boy, he loves that. He changes the subject (to something else I'm not following) and I never do find out what I was covering my butt about. Before I can decide whether he's a letch in sheep's clothing or the future father of my future children, he stands up. So I do too.

He kisses me on both cheeks, asks if he can drop me, and when I tell him I'm good, he actually says, "A lot better than good." Ugh. Okay, nobody's perfect.

When he offers to put me in a cab, I suppress the instinct to say that it's only a couple of blocks and I can walk, for fear that he would walk me home and try to kiss me or something. Or something. So I get in the cab, go around the block, overtip out of guilt. And go to bed thinking about him.

Unfortunately, I know I won't be able to dream about him.

CHAPTER SIX

SLOANE

I was so distracted this morning I forgot my lunch, so I'm destined to try to digest this slimy-looking cafeteria pizza. In line to pay, I scan the tables for the one face I hope to see. No sign of him. I take my sorry-looking lunch outside. In the past week, I haven't actually spoken to the guy. More to the point, he not only hasn't spoken to me, I don't believe he has ever once looked at me or acknowledged my existence. Admittedly, it seems completely unintentional on his part, as if I'm just any other kid in a world of kids to which he is simply indifferent. It's a weakness of mine that I take this kind of thing personally. In other words, I would have preferred that he avoided me instead of forgetting that I exist. After all, hadn't we had this titanic battle of wits? Hadn't we proved to be two genuine literary intellects at a mediocre school?

I suppose thoughts like that are more about my insecurities and need to bolster my own self-esteem than about the worth of our school and its student body. I'm so panicky about Columbia, worried that my straight-A credentials from our tiny pond will be laughed out of the running in comparison to my competition, which will be from the very best schools in the very biggest cities. The facts are only 9 percent of applicants get in, and 97 percent of the applicants are in the top 10 percent of their classes. Factor in that 57 percent of those admitted are Asian, African American, Latino, or Native American. And that only 7 percent are from New England. So 7 percent of 9 percent means that my chances of getting in are 0.63 percent, which is 1 out of 160. My mind can go on like this for hours. Days, really.

Just to beat this poor dead horse so that it can never come back to life, I'm not an athlete, I don't debate, play chess, cheerlead, sing a cappella, or really do anything except volunteer at the vet's. I just study hard and take photographs for yearbook. In short, I'm irresistible. I have literally cried myself to sleep over how vanilla and translucent I am and how achingly devoid of accomplishments that could let me stand out from the crowd.

Which is, I guess, why I feel so down about being ignored by Sparrow Boy. He did something more memorable in that offhand moment than I will do in my entire life. And I suppose that if he recognized a special connection between us, that would give me a little fairy dust. So, I'm not really upset about wanting attention from him; it's just a crushing confirmation of my own averageness. It's certainly not that I like anything about him. Without even trying, the guy is completely obnoxious. For example, having arguably (slightly) won our first skirmish, he retired victorious. He suddenly is quiet in class and answers only when called upon, at which point he delivers a brilliantly polished one-liner and then steps back to leave the field to lesser beings. Unfortunately, now that includes me.

Worse, he sits in the back of the class, never anywhere near me, let alone next to me. So I can't see what he's up to.

Picking up my Faulkner paper from Ms. Lambert's desk, I notice (as in, shuffle through the papers to find) his A+. Next to which, my naked A looks like a C–. So I casually stop by after school to ask Ms. Lambert what is missing in my paper to make it less than an A+ effort. Annoyingly, she tells me not to be so hard on myself, she's only given one A+ in her life. I decide not to warn her she has spinach stuck in her tooth and ask casually, "Anyone I know?"

She gives me a look confirming that she knows that I know who the hell I'm talking about. She then volunteers that she asked James to dial it back in class. Having me speak all the time was a great thing for the class, sort of a backboard for the other students to bounce their ideas off. With James, she fears it would be a tennis match between the two of us, which would inevitably freeze the others out.

"I get the theory just fine. I only wonder why you didn't ask me to dial it back. Or is that a request one only makes to the A+ caste?" I ask with a smile I hope doesn't look too snide.

She looks at me for a long moment and decides to tell me the truth. After leading with, "This isn't a criticism," which is always English for, "Hope you can take it," she tells me James isn't a student who *needs* to put himself forward all the time.

I will stop talking in class. I'll show her.

After two days, he has taken over my role. Answering every question with a fresh and insightful observation on everything from the question to some thought of his own that seemed completely random until he draws it all together in this synthesis that I honestly feel only I can fully appreciate. And Ms. Lambert, a little. It is just as well; I wouldn't be able to enter into the discussion anyway, because all I can think about is him.

Maybe he is the sorcerer outside my window. And his earth-bound ability to render me helpless in English class is hiding some deeper, more terrifying, and worse intoxicating power that I don't even want to think about, even though I can't stop thinking about it for fifteen seconds.

At lunch, he sometimes reads under the oak, and I always try to position myself with Lila and Kelly so that I can clearly see his spot without looking directly at it. But today he's not there either when I plop down with my slice of pizza. So I now can't wait for lunch to be over, not to mention fifth period. AP Lit is the only time during the day when I'm sure to see him. He seems to have no set schedule, so it's impossible to bump into him as we move between classes. The whole not-knowing-when-I'll-see-him-and-never-actually-seeing-him thing has me on edge.

I'm probably just searching for any distraction from worrying about my speech for Bill's memorial. Honestly, I would rather pull every tooth out of my mouth with rusty pliers than do this. And I haven't even started writing it, which is completely unlike me.

Kelly actually brings it up at lunch, wondering how I'm doing. I appreciate her asking, but there's just not much to say. And in a rare moment of poignancy, Lila says, "I miss Bill. He had the best smile."

He did. It was kind of uneven, tilting up more on the left, like he had a secret. But by nature Bill was forthright, direct, and open. He made everyone comfortable. He'd probably find some way to make me relax about the memorial and come up with something simple and true to say.

Just as I'm enjoying the fact that thinking about the speech has driven whatshisname from my mind, he returns to my thoughts in the person of the most beautiful girl who has ever attended this school. Amanda Porcella simply steps into our circle and sits down with her lunch as if she does it every day.

"Hey guys, mind if I join you?" She starts unwrapping her sandwich without waiting for an answer.

I like Amanda. She is the kind of girl that guys want to be around and girls love to backbite, but I've always thought she was really nice and funny. She is probably the most beautiful female ever to live in our town, bright, hardworking, and clearly a decent person. But her beauty unavoidably became her defining trait. She is never conceited, never holds herself above anyone else, but naturally sits at the top of the heap. She's head cheerleader as a junior (an unheard-of feat), vice president of the student body (guaranteed to be president next year), and half the girls in the school treat her like the self-centered bitch we all expect that kind of girl to be.

I can't pretend to know her really well, but we see each other out and kid around and enjoy each other when we do. Not that she needs my pity, but I feel bad how unfairly judged she is by females and how she's sought after by males for lesser reasons than she deserves.

Still, it's not like she's ever sat with us at lunch before.

For all my positive thoughts about her, it still kind of surprises me that this particular guy would be interested enough to make her his Daisy. Then again, I don't really know shit about him.

"Look," she says hesitantly, "I feel a little weird doing this, but I promised him, so anyway . . ."

Him? Oh my God. Does she mean "him"?

"What do you think of Matt Fields?"

Oh.

"I think he's super-hot," Lila offers.

"He's a little quiet," Kelly adds.

"He's a nice guy," I say.

"He likes you. He asked me to suss you out."

Matt is super-hot, and a nice guy, and a really good friend of Gordy's. If I were in the market for a guy, I'm not sure where he'd fit on my list. But more importantly, I've known Matt since third grade, and neither of us has ever shown any romantic interest in the other. We've never even flirted at parties or anything. This doesn't add up.

"Matt Fields?" I ask, trying not to sound as dumbfounded as I feel. "Really? I didn't think he thought of me that way."

"Maybe he never thought he had a chance with you. If you want, we could double or something."

"Double?" I ask innocently, knowing full well where this is going.

"James and I are gonna get a burger at the Seahorse tomorrow night. I can ask Matt and you can come, and just see what happens."

Think fast.

"I'd love to hang with you, but I think I'd rather bring Gordy. Matt's a nice guy, but I don't think of him that way and wouldn't want to give him the wrong idea."

I watch her thinking over my bait and switch.

"Cool. That'd be fun. So . . . seven o'clock? I'll bring the Twizzlers."

I laugh. We all saw *Twilight* in a big group when it came out, and I taught her how to use licorice as a straw for her Mountain Dew. Sophisticated stuff.

"I'm excited to hang. It's been too long." She stands to go, but not fast enough for Lila.

"So how long have you and James been together?"

"We started dating two summers ago at Outward Bound." And then she smiles at me. "Not that it's necessarily flattering to be compared to Daisy Buchanan."

I smile back. "The way he put it in class was extremely flattering."

She already knows that. In the silence I can't resist asking the thing I know I will hate myself for asking. "So he told you all about that, huh?"

"Yeah." It's hard to tell from her tone how she feels about that. "He said you were super-smart." She waves to the girls and heads down the hill.

"Wow. I didn't know this kind of stuff happened in real life." Lila's eyes are wide.

"Burgers and Twizzlers?"

"No. The queen bee of our school pulling every move in the book to keep your hands off her man."

As ridiculous as it sounds, and almost certainly is, my heart jumps with a little excitement at even the false accusation that my hands would ever get so lucky.

"My hands."

"Of course. First, she tries to find you another boy to take you out of circulation by picking the finest unattached guy around. I'll bet you anything that she told Matt that you're hot for him. Ask Gordy. I bet he can find out."

"Okay. Any particular reason why she thinks I'd be competition? I mean, my entire interaction with this guy was one embarrassing argument in AP Lit."

Kelly intervenes. "I think Lila could be on to something. What if he also mentioned how cute you are?"

"Like raved about your rack!" Lila is president of my rack's fan club.

"Lila," Kelly says. "Focus."

"Okay," I say. "First of all, how many guys tell their girlfriend that they think another girl is cute? Especially when their girlfriend is Amanda Porcella. Second of all, there were no moves being pulled from any book. She just invited me out with them."

"Not exactly," Kelly reminds me. "She invited you on a double date with another guy."

"Stop it, you guys. Amanda is a good person. I hate it when you rip on her. I guess the thing about being enviable is that people envy you."

"Ouch." Kelly grabs her guts as if harpooned.

"Burn!" Lila adds. "Look, I envy *you*. So if you aren't into Matt, step aside."

"Matt's got nothing on The Weed," Kelly halfheartedly tries.

I stay on point. "Amanda is the most desirable girl in this town, so it makes sense that he'd want to be with her. I just hope he'll treat her right."

At which point the girls mime their famous world's-smallest

violin concert in honor of my deep concern for poor Amanda Porcella.

"Do me one favor." Lila suddenly seems serious. "Tomorrow night? Keep an open mind. If James Waters has any interest in you, I want your radar fully operational. Don't shut yourself off the way you do sometimes with guys." She grins. "And I want immediate details."

That afternoon I ride my bike to the Noank-Mystic Veterinary Hospital, where I have worked after school since eighth grade. Probably deserving of another violin concert, my connection to poor sick, abandoned, or mistreated animals is emotional to the point where it can interfere with my eating, sleeping, and thoughts. I had lots of pets growing up, two cats named Schmulie and Sharona, a golden retriever named Riggins, a bunch of chicks who followed me around the house like I was their mother even after they grew into disgusting chickens, ten tropical fish, numerous hamster/guinea pig/gerbil guys, a tree frog that lived in my bathroom, and a ferret named Fedora.

Then Tyler developed allergies almost as offensive as his personality, and all living pets were banished to my uncle's farm (where I still visit them as often as I can), to be replaced by a hypoallergenic Coton de Tulear named Mishka. A lovely, rather foolish, extraordinarily empathetic creature who died just after my sixteenth birthday. Mom, to her credit, has hounded me (no pun intended) to replace Mishka. But so far I haven't the heart.

The town vet is Dr. French, who is pushing eighty, still supergorgeous and distinguished, and always treats me like a lady, as opposed to a granddaughter, which I appreciate. He is a perfect person inside and out, and I am blessed to know him and work for him. I started out cleaning cages, feeding and watering, grooming, and shooting off my mouth at people who obviously didn't respect their animals the way they should. I still do all of the above, but now I sit in on surgeries and even assist, I answer the phone and do billing, and have recently been given the responsibility to recommend adoptions. I love helping the strayed and abandoned find good homes. It sort of renews my faith in the world.

As I'm cleaning out cages, I realize perhaps I'm only fascinated with James because he is an exotic. As if a puma were to be in one of these cages alongside the mutts and mixed breed kitties. He rolls into town, dripping with mystery and braininess that he got from traveling and relating to other exotics. And the juxtaposition is so stark against the L.L. Bean drabness of our town. Not to mention his face. I mean I've never seen in real life a guy with a face that you absolutely couldn't take your eyes off no matter how much you needed to.

"Hey. Hi."

That voice. It belongs to exactly that face. I freeze. My gloved hands won't release the mess I'm sweeping from a schnauzer's temporary home. I'm tingling, inexplicably warm, my stomach has dropped to my knees, and the whole world seems to be slightly shaking.

I regain control of my motor skills and drop the poop, pull off my gloves, and turn around.

It's really him. I have to sit down. I make it to the seat behind the desk and try to pretend I wasn't just cleaning up shit.

He's followed me here. How did he know? Why has he come?

And what the hell am I gonna do about it? And I thought he didn't even know I existed.

"Do you work here?" he asks.

Okay, so he didn't follow me here. So he doesn't know I exist. So his eyes are just so hypnotically pale and gray with flecks of violet (which I hadn't noticed before) that I'm humiliating myself by not even being able to blink. He's going to say, "Sloane. You're staring." If only he knew my name. Which thank God he apparently doesn't. Oh my God. He asked a question, didn't he? Come on, brain.

"No. I'm just sitting behind this desk because the person who actually works here likes her seat kept warm while she's away."

Why did I say that? I sound so bitchy.

"Awfully nice of you. Maybe sometime you'll do the same for me."

Why did he say that? What does that even mean? From another guy that could definitely be a come-on. My mind flashes with images of keeping his seat warm for him.

"I'm hoping to adopt."

Why can't we try for natural childbirth first?

"What are you looking for?"

"A dog and a cat. I left mine with my kid sister in San Francisco. And I really, really miss them."

Incroyable. He loves animals. He's nothing like I thought he was. He's a dear, sweet, caring, gentle, perfect, perfect, perfect . . . person.

"Well, it's not San Francisco, we have a limited selection, but let's take a look-see."

Look-see? I said "look-see"?? I'm a forty-seven-year-old cat lady whom no devastatingly desirable young man would ever fantasize brushing up against on the way back to the animal cages. Which is, of course, a lucky thing, seeing as he belongs to my friend. Actually, more of an acquaintance. Which is exactly the wrong way to be thinking. Girls don't poach other girls' boyfriends. Right, like I even could.

"So what kind of dog did you have?"

"He was kind of a goofy mixture, some Mexican cross of I-don't-know-what. I was surfing down in Baja and rescued the poor guy, threw him in my truck, and snuck him across the border, without realizing what an idiot I was for trying to get away with that. He really hit it off with Beckett, my shepherd. I think when Beck died, Churro missed him even more than I did."

While he was surfing in Baja? He rescued some mutt? And smuggled it across the border? And loved it so much that he can't wait to adopt another rescue? Wow.

"So what about the cat?" I ask as I reach my hand in to pet an old beagle named Baily.

He pauses for a moment. I glance up, thinking he's found a pet to adopt. He's not looking into a cage but straight at me, studying me.

"It's a little personal, but what the hell. We're FOS."

"FO what?"

"Friends of Scott. Fitzgerald, right? Anyway, the cat originally belonged to a girlfriend. And Peaches would, well, sleep with us. Which eventually became sleeping on top of me. When we broke up, me and the gir—not me and the cat—I was awarded custody because apparently Peaches spent the first week of my absence looking for me and pissing on her pillow. Like it was her fault. Which it actually was."

Sleeping with a girlfriend while he was in high school or, God forbid, even younger. My mind fills with these possibilities: her parents were very understanding. Even in San Francisco, unlikely. They were camp counselors together. Sure, like what camp would put up with that? Only one possibility remained. An older woman with her own place. Yikes.

"I was actually going to bring him . . ."

"Peaches? Him?"

"Yeah, he and I are very secure in our masculinity. But when he saw my bags being packed, he started sleeping with my sister, and she sort of got attached."

"So Peaches is basically a slut."

"Well, stud."

Is this guy going to one-up me for the rest of our lives? Sure, like we have a rest of our lives for topping.

He chooses a ginger kitten from the litter that our library cat dropped. True to his perfection, he picks the runt that is least likely to be adopted by someone else. For the dog, he chooses the ugliest mutt we have and, yes, this dog who has never paid a moment's attention to me licks half his face off.

"He's got your eyes," he observes.

"How kind of you to choose the butt-ugliest animal in the state of Connecticut for that remark."

He stares at me for a moment. I know I'm blushing, but there's nowhere to hide in here.

"First of all, I was commenting on the color. Your eyes are green, and you hardly ever see that in a dog; he must be part Australian shepherd. Second, he's not ugly in the least. He just doesn't look like anybody else because he's a mutt. So he doesn't meet some conventional standard of what a pretty dog is supposed to look like. And last, because you seem to take it personally, be assured that you meet conventional standards of what a pretty girl is supposed to be." I feel my face burning, but I can't tell if it's because I'm flattered— or pissed off.

"Wow," I say. "You really know how to compliment a girl. You can be assured that you exceed every standard of how to insult someone."

He laughs, and for a minute I wonder if he's laughing *at* me. "Come on. The last thing you need to be defensive about is your appearance. You're really pretty by any standards."

I know I should be flattered, I know I should be swooning, but I'm too annoyed. "So what's the first thing I need to be defensive about?"

"Oh, I'd say the first thirty-seven of the top ten are all your attitude."

"I should be defensive about my attitude?"

He laughs again. The jerk. "Be defensive. Be very defensive." And then . . .

"Look, I'm sorry we got off on the wrong foot. Again. Seeing as how we're going to be working together." The cat purrs as James massages her ginger fur and buries his face in her neck.

"Excuse me? We're going to be what-ing together?" I grab the cat from him and try to put on a collar.

"Didn't Dr. French tell you that I signed up as a volunteer?"

"What?" The cat squirms, looking for more petting from James.

"Hey, you're paid staff; you'll get to boss me around."

"I'm not sure that's a good idea." I finally manage to wrangle the cat by scratching her belly with one hand and slipping the collar on with the other.

He smiles a genuinely charming smile and manages without a bit of meanness to say, "You don't have to be sure. You just have to get used to it."

He picks up the leash of his unnamed Australian shepherd mutt, scoops up his scrawny ginger cat, and on his way out the door . . .

"See you Friday night."

I should be relieved. All my stupid remarks and defensiveness haven't alienated him. He clearly feels completely comfortable with me, friendly even. So why has my heart collapsed into a black hole?

I want to be special to him.

CHAPTER SEVEN

MAGGIE

Jade clearly has something on her mind as Boris and I escort her to school. We are sharing a blueberry muffin and I'm getting surprisingly full. Usually she scarfs the entire crumble top before I can get my fingers in the bag, but I look down and realize she's barely taken a bite. I ask her what's up.

"You wouldn't really get it." She sighs. "It's about a boy."

The sincerity catches me so off guard that I cough on a bite of muffin.

She shoots me a sideways glance and grabs the bag from my hand. The conversation seems to kick-start her appetite for breakfast, which makes me happy. The girl's ankles are the size of my wrists. As she plucks the blueberries from the muffin to eat separately, she not-so-delicately reminds me that I have never had a real, actual boyfriend. Nor do I seem to have many friends who are boys who don't like other boys. I convince her I may still be able to provide some worthy advice for her dilemma.

Apparently Josh Hinkle, a freckle-faced friend of hers I have met on several occasions, is now "vibe-ing her." She actually uses those words. She isn't mutually interested in shifting their status from Just Friends to Boyfriend/Girlfriend (not even sure what that means in second grade, but I know it's harmless and involves lots of heart stationery and sparkly stickers). She doesn't want to lose him as a friend or let things get weird.

I tell her just to be honest. To have a direct conversation with him and let him know how she feels.

"Maaagggie!" She giggles, rolling her eyes. "You so don't get it."

"What did Nicole say?" I ask.

Jade gets quiet for about half a block and I let her. She doesn't answer my question. Instead she asks me a different one.

"Why do you think Mom hasn't found anyone since Daddy?"

"Tough shoes to fill," is all I can think to say.

By the time we get to school, she has decided she is going to get Josh to see that Tomiko is the girl for him. Problem solved. How very Jane Austen of her. She hugs me tight and ditches me with her mangy mutt.

I head to the dog park near Washington Square so Boris can take care of business. Okay, I may have an ulterior motive. I choose this particular dog park not because it's convenient, but it was there—and right around this time of day—that I saw Andrew and Carmen. Not that I'm trying to bump into them again or anything, but I still can't shake the feeling that Andrew and I could be great friends.

Wondering how Jade's morning at school is going, I must admit that Emma may be right. I don't have much of a social life. Especially in comparison to my seven-year-old sought-after sister. But I am certainly never lonely. I don't know where Emma gets that from.

It's usually only in bad movies that this happens. I walk through the chain-link fence and see Andrew sitting on a bench, by himself. The moment feels like what I imagine Jade experiences when we play Go Fish and she picks a card from the pile and screams, "I got my wish!"

He's reading *Catch-22*, one of my dad's favorites and thereby part of my home-school curriculum. No canine or Carmen or camera in sight. He just seems to be hanging out in the dog park. I walk toward him and he looks up.

"I've been waiting for you," he says with a pleasant smile, with that endearing lopsided thing. It makes him seem honest and nice but also conveys a scent that we are already conspirators. This happens to me in some roles. Where you meet someone and there's an instant mutual feeling that the two of you will have a shorthand and a common view of life. I can always use another friend. This guy would be a good one.

"I was counting on your waiting for me. That's why I came," I say. "It sure as hell wasn't because this is Boris's favorite place to take a crap."

"Of course not. From the look of him, Boris's first choice would always be something you'd have to wash or, better, replace. Perhaps some precious keepsake like the tattered blankie your grandma crocheted for you and FedExed from her shtetl in southeastern Armenia, which has comforted you in your bed ever since, being soaked with the tears from the heartbreak of your second husband's untimely demise at the hands of a charging water buffalo in Cape Town. Not that they have hands; it's simply a figure of speech. If not on your blankie, Boris might prefer to crap in an expensive shoe."

Boris barks on cue. In that nasty, misanthropic way he has.

"I do that too."

"Interesting. Why would you pick the expensive ones? Speaking personally, I'd just crap in a sneaker."

"Food for thought. Actually I mean that I make up stories about everything. Kind of compulsively." I elbow him. "But they're better than yours."

He pretends to frown. "And that was my best one ever. It's going to be really hard to impress you."

"Which will make it all the more worthwhile."

"Do you like me enough yet to do me a favor?"

It turns out that when he showed his short film to the eminent and volatile Professor Duncan, the prof told him that his star's Spanish accent was too strong to be believable as an Inuit. Andrew made the mistake of responding, "So what?" which prompted Duncan to make the issue grade dependent. The answer was supposedly simple, in a school filled with aspiring actresses: just get one to spend half an hour on a dubbing stage redialoguing every one of Carmen's lines.

The problem with the answer is that since Andrew is dating Carmen and wants to continue to do so, recruiting any of her classmates could result in her discovering that her boyfriend rolled over and trashed her work. The other problem is that instinct told him Professor Duncan doesn't give a shit about the first problem.

"Do you have an Inuit accent?" he asks hopefully.

"Depends on whether I get Inuit." It gets a genuine laugh from him.

The Post Production Center at NYU's Kanbar Institute of Film and Television provides all of the state-of-the-art hardware, software applications, and operational/technical support necessary for the editing needs of an artistic filmmaking community that produces about eight thousand student projects a year. It isn't like being on a real campus—NYU is just a bunch of buildings around Washington Square—but being in such an amazing facility, surrounded by young creative types going about their work, rekindles the oft-visited dilemma of whether I'd enjoy four years of college.

The half an hour is closer to three. The entire film is Carmen talking to the camera. Every syllable has to be synched perfectly. An accent as extreme as Penelope Cruz's not only sounds different, it makes your mouth move differently over different lengths of time. Also, Andrew has a lot of potential as a director, not so much as a sound technician. He apologizes a lot for screwing up in about every way possible. Boris is only to blame for one retake.

I do a super job. Partly from professional pride, and partly because I really want to impress the hell out of him. Not that I'm hoping to star in his class projects or anything.

"You know what?" he says. "This actually plays."

"Right, Director Boy. You now have a C– ceiling on this project."

He insists on buying me lunch, which I feel weird about because he's a student and I'm a working girl who can almost certainly afford it more than he can. And as much as I really like the guy without knowing him, the fact is I don't usually accept favors from people I don't know. Or from people I do know. Which I tell him, and he points out that I'd just done a favor for him, so don't give me no freaking guilt trip, woman.

He winds up taking me to a nice place by his apartment in SoHo for moules frites (mussels and fries in this yummy buttery sauce). It is Boris friendly and we sit outside watching busy shoppers bustle along the street. Boris yaps at some heels and Andrew and I trade approximately 400,000 imaginary stories about everyone eating, serving, walking by our table or through our imaginations. He shows potential.

He remarks that an old woman in a fedora dragging a purple roller bag behind her not only sells hallucinogenic mushrooms out of cookie tins but is Aaron Jerome's grandmother and goes to all his shows. I have no idea who Aaron Jerome is. Andrew's eyes get wide in mock disbelief. Aaron Jerome is SBTRKT, he tells me. Still not computing. He explains that Aaron, or SBwhatever, is some great DJ from London. Andrew reveals he has a show on WNYU (from midnight to 3 a.m. on Tuesdays, not primetime broadcast, but nonetheless . . .) and is a music junkie. Which in some cases can translate to too hip to be actually cool. But on Andrew it works because he's a total dork about it, so it's like reverse cool.

However, no one's perfect, particularly in the cool department. Just as my frites disappear and I'm reaching onto his plate, in walks Carmen. Turns out she's been desperately looking for him in his favorite lunch spots because she lost her key to his place and needs to retrieve her sides to rehearse. Apparently, his iPhone died a surprising and secret death this morning. I shoot him a look, but he pretends not to notice.

At first, she doesn't acknowledge me at all. Then, without looking at me, "Thanks for babysitting my boyfriend. I like that top." She turns to me. And with the most comfortable smile, "Did you wear it just for him?"

"Actually, just for you." The words fly out of my mouth before I have a chance to think twice. "Imagine my heartbreak when you weren't around."

She scrutinizes me. "Being a fellow actress, I can imagine even more than that."

"Should I be scared of you? Because if you're going to cut me, please not the face." At which point she laughs long and hard and phony. Andrew clocks it all, and his face is oddly neutral. Which is interesting.

As she pockets his keys, "So what's up with you guys?"

"Up?" Andrew says in only a slightly squeaky voice. "We bumped into each other at the park and . . ."

"I'm buying him lunch to pay him back for a favor."

"I hope he was worth it," Carmen says straight back.

"I'll find out tonight, right, Andy?" Yes, it is a test. I'm hoping he has the guts to tease her a little.

"Looking forward to it," he says brightly. I breathe an inward sigh of relief that he came through. I really don't want to be disappointed in this guy. Now the actress is worried. So I say, "Tonight's the audition he's been helping me rehearse for."

Her relief is pathetically transparent. No, this skinny kid isn't stealing her boyfriend. Like she really should've been worried. The thing you learn rather young is that a spicy bombshell always holds a trump card where men are concerned.

She gives Andrew the forty-five-minute kiss I expect her to. I've seen shorter weddings. Classier, too. When she is sure she's staked her claim, she shocks me by grabbing my face and kissing me goodbye. On the mouth. I'm still blinking by the time she disappears through the door.

He is smiling, we are getting along, so why am I getting this unpleasant feeling in my stomach?

"She's quite a character"—he grins—"more than a handful."

And then . . .

"Why do we love who we love? It's just so inexplicable, huh?"

"My very thought."

And with that I know what the feeling is in my stomach. I want Andrew to want to be with me. I don't know what I'd do if he did, but I sure don't like hearing about how much he loves Carmen. I'm a girl. And I want the guy across the table to want me with every beat of his heart.

The Apple store is just down the street, so I tag along as we wait this obscene length of time for a Genius to tell us the phone is broken. Once we officially establish the obvious, we have to wait for an iPhone Specialist to set up his new one. So we get on computers, watch a selection of cats farting on YouTube, one of whom can actually hiccup at the same time. He (or she, I didn't get a good look) is my favorite.

Andrew touches me to get my attention, to punctuate a sentence or a joke, or to express his delight, like when I stop him from clicking on "Why I became a call girl" (I explain that this is the shortest clip on the Internet—just a skank saying the word *Duh*). Once, he actually slips his arm around my waist, and I honestly don't think he even realizes he's doing it. It's sort of like the way Gordy treats Sloane, and as a girl who never really had a close guy friend, I find it all really comfortable and even a little exciting.

Out of the blue, Jerome calls breathlessly telling me that Nicole has been "actually pulled into a meeting" (poor dear thing) and can no longer pick up my kid sister ten minutes ago, which is how long Jade has already been sitting on the curb feeling like the loser kid who was forgotten. Which she's absolutely not, although she absolutely has been.

It's four thirty, right when the cabs are switching shifts and Wall Street is getting out, so there are none to be found. Amazingly, Andrew says he can drop me because he happens to have one of those nerdy, adorable GEM cars (which are like the Jetsons' cars, but they don't fly—imagine a fancy golf cart for six), and his place is only four blocks away.

I'm super-curious to see his place but don't want Jade parked on the curb for longer than necessary. His GEM is on the street (parked nose in like a Smart car) and we unplug it and we're off. It might move faster if we were running on the ground like a Flintstone-mobile.

Andrew makes up for the lack of horsepower by weaving his way through horrific traffic like a Formula One champ. This is the most masculine thing I've seen from him so far, which is saying something considering he is driving a toy.

Jade is on the curb, knock-kneed with her cute little backpack, and flashes the smile of instant all right at seeing us. To further cheer her up, he lets her drive. It is only for a block, but she is ready for an arranged marriage.

We hit our place and he just comes up with us like he lives there. His invitation is assumed. I am completely and charmingly ignored. They start with her vintage Guitar Hero, at which he ruthlessly kicks her ass.

"You know," she points out, "a proper boyfriend may not let

me win, but he probably doesn't snort like a donkey as he does his stupid victory dance."

"That was my best Braylon Edwards," he tells her, busting out his Dougie again in case we missed it the first time.

"Your best what?" I ask, thoroughly lost.

"Wide receiver. The 49ers. Deliverer of enthusiastic end zone recitals." He offers these clues as if something will click for me. It doesn't.

"He was more like this," Jade says, standing up, rocking her hips as she alternates wiping the sides of her head with her left and right hands. Girl's got rhythm. But more importantly, how the heck does she know who Braylon Edwards is?

Andrew claps respectfully and tries to mimic Jade's moves. They look ridiculous and adorable as they stare at each other with huge smiles, popping their hips and raising their shoulders just alike.

Andrew restarts the game and Jade winks at me. I realize she has no idea who Braylon Edwards is and probably no idea what an end zone recital could mean. She was just pretending to impress him. Go, Jade!

Jade offers to give him a tour. I'm not invited. I'm unsure how the tour of a three-bedroom apartment can take an hour and fifteen minutes, which feels like seventy-two hours when you are trying to busy yourself waiting for it to be over. I could have written a master's thesis on annoying siblings, complete with copious revisions. At last, after polishing twenty nails and reading *Vogue* cover to cover, I sneak down to her bedroom door and eavesdrop. I hear my obnoxious sibling asking, "So you like her, right? Like, you *like* her like her?"

"I have a girlfriend."

"But she's cuter, right?"

"You're cuter."

"I'm too young for you."

"Would you move to Arkansas?" I think he's joking.

"Would that help?"

"No, it was just a dumb joke. And your sister has more wonderful things about her than I can count, the best of which is that she is completely crazy about you."

"Okay, but do you *like* her like her?"

I barge into her bedroom like a house detective only to discover them playing cards in the fort that they built from stuff that Nicole has forbidden be used for such purpose. Far from apologizing, Andrew deals me in, then kicks my ass at Hearts.

Eventually, Jade asks (well, actually orders) me to make them some dinner. The angel hair arrabiata, and don't screw up on the al dente. Andrew says he's insulted, meaning he is offended that Jade hasn't realized he can cook rings around me. Which he proceeds to do.

Just as he is plating our scrumptious feast, including a hand-grated mountain of asiago, his new iPhone goes off. The ringtone sounds suspiciously like "Wind beneath My Wings." Before I can subtract a masculinity point, he assures me this is Carmen's special ring. So I subtract twelve points.

I watch his face as he listens to a just-audible rant on the other end of the phone, about as carefully as I've ever watched anything. Is he in love with her? Is that what love looks like? For some reason, it doesn't look like the kind of love I'd want to be in, but what do I know.

My stomach jolts uncomfortably when I hear him offer to be "home" in twenty minutes.

"I thought she was working, but she came home to cook a surprise dinner. Sorry to, well, *not* eat and run, I guess." He doesn't look nearly sorry enough for me. He looks like he can't wait to get "home."

He kisses Jade and hugs her hard. He thanks her for the hospitality. I walk him down to the street and watch him get into the GEM.

"What are you doing tomorrow?" I ask suddenly, leaning into the window.

"Whatever you want." He's smiling at me, like he's wondering what took so long for me to ask.

And it's just that simple. I have a new friend.

"Meet me at the corner of Fifth and Fifty-seventh at eight thirty," I say. "Don't eat breakfast first."

He leans out the window and impulsively kisses my cheek. Then he peels out in his oversized roller skate.

Later, when I'm getting into bed, I think of my dad. How he used to tuck me in the night before my birthday and tell me all the places he was going to take me the next day. He always left out the best one as a surprise.

And I cry myself to sleep.

CHAPTER EIGHT
SLOANE

I wake up in a cold sweat. I'm not ready for this day. I wish I could sleep right through it. Today is the memorial, but it feels just like the day after Bill died. I would've preferred to just keep dreaming of Maggie than face a world where something like Bill's accident could happen.

I'm sure she feels that way about her dad being gone too.

The sky is just beginning to light ahead of the sunrise. I jump out of bed and race downstairs in my pajamas, hoping to catch my dad before he goes for his run. He's on the front porch in his Cornell sweatshirt, tying his Saucony running shoes.

I sit down next to him and lean my head on his shoulder. He smiles, grateful for the affection, but immediately aware that something is up. One of the things I really love about him is that he'll let me say things like this in my own time. So he just kisses me on the head, and looks patiently into my eyes, and waits for me to say . . .

"I had a horrible dream. I've had it before. We live in Manhattan. But you're dead. I mean you don't die in the dream. You'd been dead for years. And last night in the dream I was lying in bed the night before my birthday, and remembering you and all the things we'd done together and missing you so much. And it just felt so real. And when I woke up, I was still missing you."

He stares in my eyes, and I can tell that he's trying hard to look calm and unconcerned. But if my daughter were to ever tell me she has a recurring dream in which I'm dead, I guess I'd be a little worried too.

"I'm sorry, Bug," he says as he hugs me tight. "How often do you have this dream?"

I don't say anything, just keep hugging him, draped over his shoulder. I pick at a small hole in the sleeve of his sweatshirt.

"Lots of times?" he asks.

"Why? Would that be a bad thing? I mean they're not always sad."

"So what are they like?"

I hug him tight and then let go. "I can't talk about it this morning, I have to go write my thing about Bill. You're coming, aren't you?"

"You know I am. And tomorrow is your birthday, and I'll still be here. I'm not going anywhere."

But of course, one day he would. As Bill did. As everyone we love does, unless we go first. The one thing that I'm carrying around that nobody else does is Maggie. What's it going to feel like the day I stop dreaming about her and her sister and that grouchy dog? And then, the thought that is always the caboose on this train: it is entirely possible that one day, Maggie will go to sleep and I'll simply be gone, and everything around me will be gone with me, and she'll have normal dreams, and her own normal life. This is the craziest possible thought that any human has ever had.

And the only comfort is, I know Maggie has it too.

I go back upstairs and shut my door. There is a mountain of crumpled pages strewn around my desk. I glance at a framed photo of me and Bill and Gordy at the beach two summers ago. It isn't a posed shot. Kelly just happened to snap it when we were going for a swim. Gordy's strong back is diving under this big wave like he's a dolphin. And Bill is right in front of me, his back to the wave, breaking its force so it doesn't pummel me over. You see my profile, my head tilted up toward the sun, and my smile is so big it seems to take up my whole face.

I pull out Bill's iPod (Gordy and I pass it back and forth when we miss him) and listen to the very last mix that Bill made for me. It's on my iPod too, of course, but today I want to hear it on his. It's called Jabberwocky, after the dragon constellation on my ceiling. It was Bill's favorite.

I sit down and stare at my laptop, and this wave of self-loathing swamps me. I'm a wretched person. I have this one opportunity to stand up in front of the world and give them some glimpse of what Bill, and loss, and grief, and the loneliness that life can drown you in mean to me. And I find myself procrastinating with thoughts of this dumb "double-date" at the Seahorse tonight. Do I really not have anything to say about the only person who knew all my constellations? Or maybe there's just too much to say.

How can I possibly even scratch the surface of honoring Bill at an event like this? The adult world that runs our school considers this a teachable moment (a new phrase for our era) where children will learn to process loss and grief and loneliness by sitting in the football bleachers and being presented with the truth of mortality. There's nothing to be taught. Only something to be felt. And I swear to God no one needs to sit in football bleachers to feel it.

Just to make my morning complete, I'm two-thirds out the front door when I hear, "Hey, Slime!" Tyler has never called me anything else. He apparently made the drive home from University of Vermont last night.

I don't think I have it in me this morning to navigate this encounter. I pretend I haven't heard him and just keep walking. One of the things about being six-four is that your legs are very long and you catch up to diminutive feminine types in about three strides.

"Good to see you too!" he booms with what he considers irony. "No hug?"

I look at him and realize that of course I don't actually hate my brother. He is decent and good and this is all my problem because I'm jealous of his easy path through life.

So I hug him. And I mean it. And he feels that. And he hugs back.

"Glad I caught you. I really want to talk to you about Bill's thing today."

From his pocket, he pulls out a wad of folded-up paper, like four or five pages. He looks at it nervously, shaking his head.

"I wrote up this thing, you know, about sort of being Billy's mentor and all, you know, at quarterback and just generally about guy stuff."

"I'm sure it's eloquent."

He stares at me for a beat. Smiles a small smile. "Don't ever change, kid. I wouldn't recognize you."

"I'm sorry. I'm really sorry. It's just a tough day."

"Well, that's why we're talking. I thought maybe it might be better if I didn't say anything and just left it to you and Gordy."

He seems awkward making this extremely generous and considerate offer. I can't remember ever seeing him awkward before.

"Thanks, Ty. It's really sweet of you. But Bill was your friend, and you deserve to say your piece to honor him."

"Yeah, he was my friend. And we were real close. But not like you two were."

I almost choke. I can't tell how he means that.

"Billy was special to you. I mean, very special. I'm your brother, and I'm not super-bright, but I know that much."

"Thank you," I say. And somehow I'm blushing that he knew or had even noticed that Bill and I were special to each other. Which of course we were.

There's a silence.

"So, uh, how you doing?" He clearly has forgotten our Mafia bit, one of our few inside jokes. So I answer . . .

"No, how *you* doin'?" in this Jersey mobster voice.

"No, how *you* doin'?" Now he's smiling, relieved of the burden of his kindness and free to joke around. It takes about ten more "how you doin's" before the loser cracks a smile and the winner who keeps his (or in this case her) face straight gets to punch the loser on the arm.

A horn sounds. It's Gordy, picking me up in his old Land Rover, which is unexpected and extremely welcome. Tyler and I walk out together. He and Gordy do their dumb guy fist bump, do their dumb guy joke, do their dumb guy sports talk stuff, and just before my brain melts into a slushy, I'm alone with Gordy cruising down the street.

"Thanks for picking me up."

"How are you doing?" This is a serious question. I shrug because he knows I'm not doing well at all. He nods in agreement. Gordy has these beautiful, clear eyes, and today they remind me of when we were six years old for some reason. He looks directly into mine and then turns back to watch the road.

"I know I said you wouldn't be alone up there, but would you mind being the only one to talk today? I wrote my speech out, and I've rehearsed it a bunch of times, and I cry every time. I just can't get through it."

I wind my fingers through his free hand and squeeze hard.

"We can do this any way you want. But I think since you're feeling like that, we should try to prep you to give the speech. Maybe we'll change a line or two."

"I tried that."

"Have you tried swallowing real hard, just before you get to the place before you cry? It always works."

"It won't. It won't." He starts tearing up.

I haven't seen him cry since the night he drove to my house to tell me that Bill had been killed in the crash. The patrolman had called Bill's folks, and his dad called Gordy crying and asked if he would tell Bill's friends. Gordy immediately jumped in his car, tears on his face, and drove about ninety miles an hour to my house so I wouldn't hear it from anybody else. That's the kind of guy Gordy is. And gorgeous, too. Just ask anybody.

"Pull over," I say softly. "Let's see the speech." He pulls over and shows it to me. It's folded up about twenty-five times and since it's in pencil is almost indecipherable. I scan it. Really sweet, really from the heart. I'm proud that he would even think of saying something this emotional in front of the guys.

"I love this, Gordy. You have to give it. And you and I are going to sit here and rehearse and rehearse until you're happy with your performance. And it doesn't matter how many classes we miss."

It takes about eight readings until he isn't crying anymore. He thanks me for the tip about swallowing, which seems to be helping him. I wouldn't make too large a bet on whether or not he'd cry, but at least he'll read it. As many times as I've seen him cry (which might be five or six), he always swears that no one else has ever seen him crying, even his mom. Guys are weird.

We get to school in time for first period, only missing homeroom. By lunch my heart is jumping on the way to the hill. I am so ashamed to even be thinking about you-know-who when Bill should be the only thing on my mind. But the truth is I can't think about much else. Not only is he not in his usual spot under the tree, but Kelly says casually, "Don't bother looking for Mr. or Mrs. Porcella. They were both missing from my second period today." She raises her eyebrows in an attempt at lewd inference.

"Think they're having a hot lunch?" Lila is more direct.

"Hope so for her sake," Kelly adds. "She looks like she could use it."

So I bawl them out for joking about my friend and spend the

rest of lunch praying that the girls can't hear my heart pounding through my chest. Of course he and Amanda are together. Why shouldn't they be?

I fight to think of Bill and how he deserves my full attention and loyalty today. Which makes me feel worse because I can't seem to do that. Every cell in my body is aflame with jealousy over a guy I don't know who doesn't even like me. That's how I roll.

By the time almost a thousand people are filling the stands, I still haven't tamed my mind. I feel completely numb. I keep looking for James everywhere. The cheerleading squad files in wearing their uniforms, with Amanda in the lead. No James. No James anywhere. Then, just as Gordy gets up to speak, squeezing my knee on the way—

—I see him. He enters at the far end of the bleachers carrying Pablo, the mutt he adopted on Wednesday. He simply climbs the steps and finds a seat. He keeps hugging that little mutt and kissing its head as if they were alone in the world.

Lost in the dangerous alleys of my obsessed mind, I suddenly realize that Gordy has been talking, is in the middle of his speech, and is looking right at me while I have been fixated on Pablo and his owner. I can't believe that I'd let Gordy down this way. I finally snap out of it and focus on what he's saying about our dead friend.

"I can't help but think about the life he had yet to live, all of the things we may get to do that he won't: enjoy summer again, graduate from high school, go to college, fall in love for real . . ."

The eye contact between us seems to jolt him and he starts to cry. Everyone around me is deeply moved and touched, and the more Gordy has to swallow and start over, the more everyone connects to him. In this moment I want to believe that we are all connecting a little more to Bill's memory. Maybe a group remembrance isn't as horrible an idea as I'd thought it'd be.

Then suddenly, he's finished. The crowd applauds in support of Gordy and in appreciation of Bill. I stand and meet him halfway. I give him the biggest hug out there in front of everyone, he hugs me back, and it's like we are all alone, even though every eye is on us.

He goes to his seat. And it's me alone at a microphone.

"I didn't write this out beforehand," I say. "Like many of us, I loved Bill so much, I love Bill so much that there are no words. Let me share just one story."

I scan the crowd and see my family in their section. My dad with his calm and supportive look. My mom with tears in her eyes, which I appreciate so much that it almost makes me cry on the spot. Tyler is there, and even his standard maddening smile seems on my side for once. He is holding Max's hand, and I remember how much Max loved Bill and wonder if my case of the cooties could have anything to do with him being gone. Bill always played with him, brought him treats, and most importantly talked to him like an equal. Max looks devastated and lost holding Tyler's big hand. And then my baby brother stares straight into my eyes and I'm filled with love.

"There was something that I wanted more than anything I'd wanted in my life before. Or even since. And there was a very good reason why I couldn't have the thing I wanted. And I was inconsolable. I cried. I thought I was the unluckiest, unhappiest person on this planet and that things could never ever be right again. I tried to hide it from my family, from my girlfriends, from Gordy. But I couldn't hide it from Bill.

"So Bill hugged me. Actually, held me. And we were totally silent for what seemed like a day and a half. And when he thought I could hear him, he told me that it was important to just let myself feel bad as long as I wanted. And it was also important to remember at the same time how lucky I was for everything in my life that brought me happiness. And to know that I would feel that happiness again someday.

"So I tried. And the thing that I kept clinging to was how blessed I was to have Bill in my life. Then he died. And I thought of that day that he held me, and I realized that I still have Bill to cling to and always will."

Feeling empty, because I should have done better, I put my head down and start back toward the bleachers in absolute silence. Suddenly, there is this really strong applause, and for some reason I look up directly at James. He has that ugly dog in his lap, and he smiles at me.

Somehow that comforts me. All the time my mom is hugging me and Tyler is telling me I "crushed it," and Max is staring at me with admiring eyes, and my dad is waiting his turn for our special hug . . .

I can't stop thinking of James.

When Gordy and I arrive at the Seahorse, James and Amanda are already there. The Pony, as we all fondly call this place, is basically in the parking lot of a marina. It has the best burgers in town, and when I was little, I loved their grasshopper pie and the Miss Pac-Man machine. Tonight Amanda and James are sitting in a booth by the fish tank, clearly into each other.

Amanda says something that makes him laugh, and I roll my eyes. What a guy won't do to get laid. In all the years I've known her, she has never said anything that could make a human laugh.

Not that being funny is as important as being a good person, or really smart, or really beautiful (okay, maybe that one). But funny is important to me, so I project. And basically, all the hopes I had for some kind of personal connection that was promised by that smile completely disappear. Maybe he's just a typical guy.

We sit down. Amanda jumps up and gives me a kiss, which at first I judge as being phony and solely for James's benefit and then realize it's because we haven't spoken since Bill's memorial. She is a nice person, Amanda Porcello. Without looking, I can hear Gordy exchanging amiable guy grunts with him. I pull myself together and look up, only to find James staring straight in my eyes.

"I loved what you said today. Both of you."

He says both of us, but he is looking just at me.

"It speaks really well of Bill that he could have friends who loved him so much. Sorry, in your words, love him so much."

"Thanks," is all I can come up with. Clearly, I'm on top of my game.

Immediately, Gordy launches into the Celtics and the playoffs, a sacred ritual that Gordy believes all males observe. He is about to get his head handed to him by a guy who is far too interesting to waste hours of his life on such things. In fact, James would probably rather discuss the Celtic beheading game in *Sir Gawain and the Green Knight* than give two shits about basketball playoffs.

Amazingly, James knows more than Gordy, like all the really boring stuff about where players went to school and how many rebounds and how many "dimes" (which turns out to mean assists) each player has racked up. He is an enigma, this one.

Like he says, "KG has to make himself big down low so Rondo

can get him the ball on the block." And Gordy nods like that's English.

In the middle of *SportsCenter*, Amanda winds her arm through James's and puts her head on his shoulder. Normally, I would find such a display of public affection either sweet or nauseating depending on the couple. But here, it's clear this is a simple act of possession. It reminds me instantly of the way Carmen kissed Andrew at lunch.

Why is Amanda even bothering? Of course, it probably just feels good. Or maybe my attraction to him is showing, and I am making a fool of myself by drooling over her boyfriend, and Amanda is just instinctively doing what girls do when that happens.

How could I ever have thought this would be a good idea? And when will it end? I glance toward the door. When I look back, he is looking right at me. Again.

"What are you reading these days?" he asks. It seems like he's actually curious, not forcing conversation.

"*Decoded*. It's Jay-Z's autobiography."

He nods. "I've read that. I wish that he spent more time actually explaining his hustler years rather than defending why he still raps about the game," he says.

"He and Beyoncé are such a cute couple. Baby Blue is like a hip-hop princess," Amanda contributes.

"I'm bummed," I tell him, "that so far he's barely said anything personal about Biggie at all, just that he still wears his platinum Jesus chain every time he records."

"I think that's because he can confess his love for Biggie without having to feed juicy details to curious bystanders just to sell books."

Then he smiles a very nice smile. "Sort of like you today. You didn't have to tell us what that thing was that you wanted so badly. It was enough to know that you loved him and he comforted you. I thought that was really cool."

I think my heart will burst. I don't think any compliment has ever meant more to me. He heard what I said about Bill in the way I was hoping it would be heard. It makes me feel understood.

By this time our companions, terminally bored with the world of hip-hop, are deep in their own conversation about a locker room fight in the girls' gym.

We spend the next two hours essentially lost in conversation with each other. We have many shared interests. He knows more about politics. I know more about history. He plays flamenco guitar. I would love to sleep with a guy who plays flamenco guitar. He loves animals. Turns out he skipped school today because he wanted Pablo to feel comfortable in his new home. We are both movie nuts. Through living in San Francisco, he could see in a theater all the indies I have to beg Derek at Mystic Video to stock for me. He loves big action stuff and special effects, which I can't stand, and we both adore silly comedies.

The big topic turns out to be travel. Because he's done it and I haven't. Yet. I force him to explain every detail of his time in France, China, Scotland, even East Africa.

I don't feel self-conscious or nervous talking to him at all. I thought I wouldn't be able to eat when we sat down. But before I know it, I've plowed through my hamburger and Gordy is sweetly wiping ketchup off my cheek as I quiz James about the safari he went on with his dad. Normally something like ketchup on my face would send me into hysterical embarrassment. I'm having too much fun to care.

When we've all finished our grasshopper pies and paid the check, my heart sinks. I feel like Cinderella after the ball. I can have his attention for a dinner's worth of conversation, but a girl like Amanda holds his heart. We say our goodbyes and he and Amanda walk together toward his car in the parking lot and I want to cry.

On the ride home, Gordy can tell I'm sad. Of course, he thinks it's about Bill. He does his best to cheer me up, which essentially means making fun of me until I can laugh at myself. He tells me I look like his Labrador Tiller the time Tiller swallowed a tennis ball. I check my reflection in the visor mirror and he is sort of right.

Gordy promises we'll celebrate my birthday and Bill tomorrow. And he promises it won't suck. I'm so lucky to have Gordy.

In bed that night I toss and turn, inventing scenarios where I can somehow see James again like that. Eventually, I realize this is just self-torture. Because even if I could have dinner with him like that every night, each moment would hold the heartbreak of knowing I want something more.

And of course, the ultimate curse. Only Maggie can dream about him.

CHAPTER NINE

MAGGIE

I study the girl in the window. Hair piled on top of her head, huge black sunglasses, enjoying a coffee and Danish among a sheik's ransom in diamonds and emeralds. She's having breakfast at Tiffany's. Once a year, on my birthday, Holly Golightly is me. At least for breakfast.

His image steps beside mine, and without turning to him I say: "Eu acredito que você está na liga com o carniceiro."

Not missing a beat, he translates, "I believe you are in league with the butcher." Film student or not, the fact that he knows my favorite film well enough to recall that line means one thing. This is going to be a good day.

I point down at the pavement. There is his breakfast, a neatly wrapped almond croissant and a large coffee. I noted at lunch that he liked heavy cream no sugar. He just stands beside me and starts to eat, and we are silent like that for quite a while.

"Do you think if I bought you a Cracker Jack ring, they would engrave it for us?" This happens in the film and is extremely romantic.

"No. See, that was a movie. This is Tiffany's. That actor doesn't really work here, or sadly anywhere anymore." I turn and look at him. "Thank you for knowing that film and liking it."

"My pleasure."

"I'm taking you on a tour of New York today. All visits will be to film locations, or reasonable reproductions thereof."

"Awesome. Any particular reason?"

"Yes. Shall we go?" I say.

"As soon as you've told me what's your favorite scene and why."

"You first."

"I love the very end where they're standing in the rain in an alley and they've just found her runaway cat and they're in this three-way hug and cry, although some cynics have suggested that it was rain on Cat's face rather than tears."

"You left out the why."

"Because I saw the film when I was sixteen, and that scene completely defined romance for me. One day, I will find a woman who will let me chase down her runaway cat and hug me in the soaking rain."

He is so unguarded and genuine. I'm ashamed of the calculation in my silence.

"Your turn," he urges.

"The truth is, I'm deciding which scene to choose on the basis of what I want you to know about me."

"Perfect."

ADRIENNE STOLTZ AND RON BASS

"I like the scene where she gets the telegram that the Brazilian rich guy is dumping her, and she trashes her apartment in hysterical rage but then concludes that she's going to use her perfectly good free ticket to fly to Rio anyway." I watch him think. "What does that say about me?"

"It says you had your heart broken once, and it's on your mind."

"Actually, I've never had my heart broken. But watching her performance made me think, *so that's what it's like*. And how I'll deal when it happens to me."

"So. How will you deal with it?"

"I'll run away to Rio."

"No you won't. You're not the type to run away from your problems."

"You have so much to learn about me, this could take a while."

I put my arm through his and lead him off to be my companion through the one day each year that I can't bear to face alone.

We pop into FAO Schwarz and I tap dance on that brilliant piano keyboard thing. Thanks to my extensive dance training, I'm able to approximate a little ditty known as "Chopsticks." It's not as easy as Tom Hanks makes it look in *Big*.

Standing outside the Plaza, he sings "Memories" to me from *The Way We Were*. You know, "Memories / Light the corners of my mind / Misty watercolor memories / Of the way we were." He has a surprisingly sweet voice and sings to me as if I'm Robert Redford and this is our last chance to find true love together. We attract quite a crowd. Somewhere about thirty seconds from the end, I get scared that he is going to play to the moment and try to kiss me. Being an

112

actress who has kissed dozens of guys (in character, not in skanki-
ness), I'm not sure why that should be a frightening thought. He
doesn't, and some twelve-year-old girl in the crowd says, "Kiss her,"
as if it really matters to her. Sweet.

We cross Fifty-ninth into Central Park, so of course I take off my
shoes to suggest another Redford film, *Barefoot in the Park*.

"They should have cast you," he says. "Jane Fonda is such a
ballbuster."

"Did you get a look at her body in those days?"

"Hard to miss, it was so awesome. All that Jazzercise and span-
dex and leg warmers. But a hot bod isn't so important."

"Carmen has a rockin' package."

"She sure does. That's not why we're together, though. You've
got so much to learn about me, this could take a while."

We lie on the grass in Sheep Meadow and ignore the tourists
sunbathing. I want to talk about Carmen, but he doesn't. He's
drumming his rib cage, humming some song he's currently obsessed
with. It's totally dorky and kind of annoying since I can't grasp his
passion for seventies easy-listening.

I mention that I'm up for the fourth lead in the *Innuendo* pilot,
hoping he might have some good advice. My agent, Cindy, doesn't
know about it yet, and she is always so enthusiastic about everything
anyway that we don't have a genuine connection. Talking to Nicole
would requiring me enduring Nicole's unhelpful suggestions for
wardrobe and hair makeover to help me land the role. My friends all
have personal agendas relating to their own careers and jealousies.

And besides, I trust Andrew to tell me the truth. Unfortunately,
he does.

"I hope you don't get it."

"Excuse me?"

"I'll miss you."

I haven't stopped to think that it's 90 percent likely the show will shoot in Los Angeles. I'd have to relocate. Nicole couldn't come with me, and therefore Jade couldn't either.

Sloane can't wait to get to Columbia, escape the nest, and be on her own. I've been on my own. But not on my own the way I'd be in Los Angeles. I've never been there. I sort of picture it as a place with shallow, grasping, competitive people, at least in my profession. I feel smaller and more vulnerable than I've felt in a long time.

"So you better give your mom my cell, for the next time Jade needs to get picked up on a curb somewhere." Andrew looks sorry the moment he says it. I just stare at him. "What?" he asks.

"I'm just sitting here being scared. Like some little kid who's thinking about running away to join the circus."

"Okay, let's break it down, Mama. What are your chances of actually getting this role?"

I exhale. Smart place to start. "Less than zero."

"How old are you?"

"I just turned seventeen," I tell him.

He smiles sweetly. "It's okay to be a little scared. Two years ago I was a little freaked out to come to New York for college, and it's not even like you'd have the structure of school out there. But if this happens for you, you would be absolutely clinically insane to turn it down. Do whatever you have to do to give yourself the best chance at this."

"Whatever?" I ask.

"What are you talking about? Couch-casting?"

I say nothing.

"Here's one piece of advice that I know is true. No casting couch for you. Ever."

We walk south, and passing through Times Square, Andrew steps in front of a taxi that hasn't quite come to a full stop and pounds on its hood. I know exactly where he's heading even before he does his best Ratso Rizzo with, "I'm walkin' here! I'm walkin' here!" Dustin Hoffman should have won the Oscar for *Midnight Cowboy*. In fact, he should've won for half the things he did.

At the top of the Empire State Building, where Cary Grant waited in vain for his true love in *An Affair to Remember*, we stare out over the city. He looks through those high-power binoculars. When I was small, I was obsessed with them. I imagined you could zoom anywhere in the city, into windows, into people's lives, and watch a moment in time.

"My dad and I used to do this every year. Spend the day together visiting film locations. And since he died, I haven't done it alone." Without looking at him, "So, thanks."

"I'm so sorry." I feel him watching me.

"He was the most brilliant, intuitive, and loving person." I turn to him. "He got off an airplane in Chicago and had a massive coronary walking through the terminal. He died before he hit the ground. It was good for him that he didn't suffer. And that he had no fear. No regrets."

I must look terribly sad because Andrew says, "But there was no chance to say goodbye."

I shake my head, no. And start to cry. He puts his arms around me and I let him.

"He took me to my first movie, my first everything. And when Nicole pushed back against the idea that I could be an actress, he really ripped her. He said it wasn't just rude and discouraging, it was ignorant. He completely believed that I could succeed."

"I'm just thinking what would happen if my dad ever called my mom ignorant."

"Well, what would happen?"

"She'd kick his ass."

"He started that game of making up stories about strangers. He wrote stories for a living, and he always said the stories seemed like a way to hide ourselves while revealing others, but really we were only revealing ourselves. And so, we would look back on the stories we made up and figure out what they meant about us."

"Now there's two people who make up better stories than me."

"At least." Andrew gets me to smile, which was, of course, his evil plan ever since I cried.

"Thanks for telling me about your dad. I wish I'd met him."

"I never talk about him. I think you're the first person I've done that with except for my shrink."

He shakes his head. "You need a shrink less than anyone I ever met."

"Well, like I said, you have a lot to learn about me. In the interest of not being coy or unfriendly, let me just say that I started seeing her when my dad died. Now we basically just talk about my dreams."

In little more than an hour, we stand on the deck of the Staten Island Ferry. The sun has just disappeared and the water is purple. He's stumped. I tell him *Working Girl*. He nods, as if vaguely remembering. I try to help . . .

"Alec Baldwin says, 'Tess, will you marry me?' and Melanie Griffith replies, 'Maybe.' He says, 'Ya call that an answer?' And she says, 'You want another answer, ask another girl.' "

"Wow. Great line. Gotta use that."

"You have my permission. So the day shouldn't be a total loss."

"The day's just begun."

I like the conspiratorial promise of fun in his suggestion. But I am really excited to see Thomas. "Not for me, not tonight. I have an appointment."

He looks me right in the eyes. "Break it. And I'll break mine."

"It's about the series. It's with the casting director."

There's a flicker across his eyes. This time, his smile is against the grain.

"Just so long as there's no couch."

I think about that. Being on a couch with Thomas and what he might want to do on that couch. And what I might want to do on that couch. And how all of that couch business might or might not affect my chances at *Innuendo*.

"Well." I certainly have his attention. "The casting director is this older guy. Maybe twenty-five, even. And he wants to date me. He said so. Just put it out on the table. And he says that this has nothing to do with my chance to read for the role. And he says that he has other opportunities I'd be right for. And, of course, that also has nothing to do with whether I see him."

"Are you attracted to him?"

"Very." I try to see if he looks disappointed, but in the fading light his face is hard to read.

"I'm sorry to tell you that you already know what you're asking me. If you hook up with this guy, and I don't just mean kiss him good night and lead him along, but if you sleep with him, he'll give you a shot at this role. So you'll keep sleeping with him. And that doesn't make him evil. And it doesn't make you opportunistic. And I don't want you to do it."

"The bummer part is, if he'd just been a lawyer or something, I might want to date him. He hasn't been funny yet, and that's sort of the last hurdle. But being who he is, I don't know if I'd wonder that I was dating him for the wrong reasons. Do you know what I mean?"

"Yeah. I know what you mean. But I think you should absolutely trust yourself. If this is the guy for you, don't let his job stand in your way. In fact, don't let anything stand in your way."

And then he said, "Finding the right person. The person you belong to. Is the most important thing there is."

I tell him, "Today's my birthday. My seventeenth birthday."

"Get out of here! Your actual birthday?"

"All day." I'm quite the phrase maker.

"Cancel your stupid casting thing and let me take you to Katz's for pie à la mode and a fake orgasm."

I laugh. That's everyone's favorite scene from *When Harry Met Sally*. I wonder how many fake orgasms those poor waitresses have to live through every night. I wonder what it would be like to have a fake orgasm with him.

Later, staring into my closet, I realize that I have no idea where Thomas is taking me for dinner. Major problem. I text and call. Nada. Well, I could dress down the middle, but what the heck does that even mean? What's more embarrassing? Underdressed or overdressed? The obvious answer is overdressed because underdressed indicates too cool for school, what do we care what anybody thinks. Overdressed means desperate to impress. But my spider sense tells me to dress to the nines. This guy likes me, he knows it's my birthday, he's not taking me to the sushi place around the corner. We start with a little black dress. How little? Maybe not so little. Tight and short makes a girl look young; that's not what I'm going for. Tight and longer is more sophisticated, which can be its own trap because you don't want to look like a young girl trying to look older. But I go with that dress because it fits me best. Four-inch heels, no way to hide these, just have to take the shot we're not going bowling. I raid Nicole's jewelry box for some chunky cool pieces. I sweep up my hair and let one strand fall over my bare shoulder.

I feel confident, which makes me think I'm not so interested in this guy. Why would that be? I thought I was interested. I told Andrew I was interested. He even encouraged me to be interested. That's why I do not want one attractive male telling me to go for another. What I really want is every attractive male to want me for himself. Okay, that's simple. There's nothing wrong. I'm just self-centered.

When he appears at my door, I resist the urge to tell him that I'm going to run and change. There'd be no point unless I ran all the way to the magic closet at *Elle*. I'm wearing my very best and it isn't nearly good enough. He is actually in black tie. And looks as fine as any model in a Tom Ford ad. He apologizes, explaining that after supper, we have to attend a private screening of a client's film at Donna Karan's co-op on Central Park West, after which we are "obligated to fall by the after party." It turns out that the same film was having a preview downtown, which was too hoi polloi for us insiders, but all the little people would expect us to make an appearance at the party.

Subsequent remarks make it clear that he does not want to be labeled as someone who is impressed by wealth and fame and power. I sure am. I have serious stars in my eyes. It's true that probably lots of those people are jerks. Probably lots of them are far nicer and more interesting than those of us down in the hoi polloi give them credit for being. I'm looking forward to finding out who is which. Believe me, if I had glass slippers, I'd be slipping them on.

He bundles me into a Town Car, nothing extraordinary, but it was a royal carriage for me. All the way to dinner, he keeps telling me how incredible I look. It's repetitive but doesn't get tiresome. He sounds like he means it and that I've sort of exceeded his expectations. I have no mixed feelings about any of that. I like it.

Dinner is only at Jean-Georges, which is walking distance to Donna's place and one of the half-dozen best restaurants in Manhattan. Thomas apparently eats here a lot; everyone knows him. I like that too. I like wondering whether the day would come when everybody there knew me. Sitting there with him, I felt like there wasn't much I wouldn't do to have this be my actual life. Not meaning on the couch, but how hard I'm willing to work to make premieres and elegant dinners part of my existence.

Tonight, he orders champagne. As if he can read my mind, he smiles and says that if they card me, it would be the first time in a place like this that the staff want their other customers to know how young the most beautiful woman in the place actually is. No card is requested.

Throughout the meal, he has impeccable manners, never seems in a rush to make our screening, gives me all his attention. In fact, he makes me feel as if he would be happy just sitting here and talking to me and looking at me for the rest of his life.

There is never an awkward silence and he never brings up business. The entire conversation is about me. My background, my preferences, my ambitions. He still hasn't been funny. But he really thinks I am. Which makes me wonder what it would be like spending my life with a guy I could always make laugh but who could never make me laugh. I do love an audience.

At a quarter to ten, they bring a hunk of baked Alaska with a sparkling candle. When I blow it out, my silent wish is that Sloane will have a date with James as perfect as this one.

We walk the six blocks to the building that I recognize as the place from *Ghostbusters*. I smile to myself, thinking that it's totally in keeping with my birthday theme. I'll have to bring Andrew here sometime. Thomas is taller than I remember as he walks beside me. That's a good thing. His hair is still spectacular, but the rest of him has sort of caught up to it. An even better thing.

The apartment is breathtaking. I've never been in a more sophisticated home. Light-filled areas flow into one another in a loungey, sexy way. Everything is decorated in a classic black-and-white palette with sumptuous fabrics and smooth surfaces. The glass external walls open up to terraces overlooking the park. Gorgeous people mill and mingle.

I'm introduced to two dozen persons of power; several are names I know, and above all, Rosalie Woods, who is super-nice and treats me as if I belong here. In fact, there is a moment when we are alone, and she tells me that Thomas has been telling her how great I'd be as Robin and she can now see why. She says she can't wait to see me read for the role. And then we are ushered to sit down.

My heart is in my throat through the entire screening. I'm barely aware of the film we are watching. I can only think, Is this the moment? Is this my chance?

Thomas sits between me and Rosalie. He never holds my hand or does anything overt. Our thighs brush occasionally, and I feel a charge from the warmth.

When it's over, everyone looks me in the eye during the good-byes, one producer gives me his card, a talent agent from ICM suggests lunch, Rosalie squeezes my hand and says, "See you soon."

It is thrilling and feels like a dream I'd have—if I dreamed about my own life.

Before we head out, I excuse myself to use the bathroom. On my way I bump into one of the actresses from the film. She is gorgeous and groomed and glares at me as I begin to compliment her performance.

She interrupts me with, "So how long have you known Thomas?" There is an edge to her voice that really sets me back.

I mumble something clumsy about scarcely knowing him at all and that he is interested in me for something they are casting.

"Sure he is," she says, brushing by me. "Nice shoes."

Of course I'm now incredibly insecure about my shoes. I curl my feet under my dress in the Town Car as we head to the after

party. I decide to tell Thomas about my encounter with the unfriendly starlet.

There's a moment of silence. And then he tells me just a little
too casually that they used to see each other. "It was no big deal, it
ended a while ago, but actresses are competitive by nature, no of-
fense. It's all just stupid industry stuff," he says.

None of that lands well with me. And I suddenly worry that the
guy I've been painting as a prince all night is really a wolf in a nice
suit.

Then he turns to me. "Are you seeing anyone?"

"Nope. Are you?"

"No. I told you that I wanted to date you. Why would I say that
if I was already seeing someone?"

That was pretty direct. My faith in him restored, I relax. But the
best I can respond with is, "So since I'm out with you tonight, why
would you have to ask me that question?"

"Because you haven't said you want to date me. Because sometimes women spend time with me because I have something to
offer, like the girl you just met. And you haven't said anything that
would be misleading or unfair if that were the only reason we were
together tonight."

"That's a mouthful. What does it mean?"

"It means I want to kiss you."

In the next nanosecond, my thoughts flash from first, do I want
to kiss him? Definitely yes and no, which is not uncommon for me.
Second, what's the consequence of not kissing him? He'll be hurt;
he really stuck his neck out. Maybe I'll never get a second chance.
Although that might not be a bad thing. Draw the line now. He

sure can't say I led him on; in fact, he just acknowledged I hadn't. I might lose the role. Or he might take rejection as a challenge, making him even more interested. My last flash of thought was what would Andrew say?

Then I lean and kiss him. I try to keep it tender, sweet, and sincere. His lips are soft; up close his skin smells like something I can't name but really like. But I feel this kiss is letting us both down. Because as it's happening, I can't stop wondering why I'm kissing him. I know that I want this life, the life that this one night promises, more than I know I want him. If that is terrible, it is at least honest. Luckily, he's not a mind reader and seems to very much enjoy our kiss.

The party is in some fancy club, a blur of people he wants me to meet, and I feel so conflicted about the kiss that I'm not paying much attention to anything but my disappointment in myself. So of course, the party lasts about ten years.

Then at my front door, he suddenly grabs me and kisses me hard, and I feel the jolt that I want to feel in a moment like that. So I kiss him back and feel happy. He can see that and it makes him happy too. He says he'll call me. I say he'd better.

The apartment is dark. I have a text from Nicole that she's working late. Jade left me a note reminding me she and Boris are sleeping at Tomiko's. The postscript wishes me a happy birthday. She's drawn a picture of her and Boris holding a big cake with stars as flames on the candles. It's not baked Alaska, but it looks pretty delicious.

As I put on my pajamas, I think of that kiss at the door. And I go to bed smiling.

Best birthday in a long, long time.

CHAPTER TEN

SLOANE

I open my eyes to blinding sunlight. The sunniest, brightest morning I can remember. My elm looks like she's dancing. And I want to cry. It's my birthday.

The weight of Bill is all I can feel. Maggie just had this amazing day, even though she was sad about her dad. Maggie chooses the healthy perspective every chance she gets. And I have trouble not focusing on the darkness. Sometimes I wish I really were Maggie. Only Maggie.

Maybe I am.

There's one sharp knock on my door and then it flies open and Kelly flashes through it and pounces on my bed and me.

"Happy birthday, Kitten Breath. Wow, you look awful."

"Do I know you?"

She pulls a small leather pouch from her pocket.

"Gordy told me he's kidnapping you for the whole day, so I

wanted to get in while I could. Here, open it. And don't forget to look excited."

Kelly is an incredible artist. She made me a necklace from two exquisite pieces of malachite. It is unique and so lovely. She can tell how much I appreciate them and her. She gives me a kiss.

"So how was the big double date? I mean Lila is jonesing for details."

"Well, it was nothing special. The minute our eyes met, we knew we belonged to each other, and ignoring our dates, we climbed on the table, tore each other's clothes off, and fulfilled Lila's every fantasy."

She stares at me with a funny look. "You sure it's only Lila's fantasy?"

"What's that supposed to mean?"

"You're not doing as good a job as you think you are of hiding how you feel about him," she says, snuggling next to me. "And I think you're only obsessing on him because you can't have him."

Then she wrinkles her nose and says, "I think you're forgetting that not having him is the good news. You were right when you said he's not going to bring anyone any happiness. He's like a heart pulverizer. Dating him would be a constant angsty stomachache. You've been gloomy enough this year."

I smile, a little uncomfortable with both the transparency of my crush and the confirmation that it's delusional. I'm also worried she's probing into why I've walled myself off. So I squirm. "What are you even saying?"

"I'm saying that you'd rather moon after some unobtainable fantasy than risk having a real relationship with the guy who's right in front of your nose."

I blink. "You mean Gordy??"

Kelly rolls her eyes. "Thanks for proving my point. Yeah, how stupid of me to think that the best-looking guy in our town, who also happens to be the sweetest and nicest guy ever, and completely perfect for you in every way since preschool, is a guy you should be interested in. What a crazy idea!"

I laugh. "Kel, Gordy is like . . ."

"Don't say it. Don't say he's like your brother. That's your choice. That's been your choice. That's how you keep yourself safe from going for it. And I think it's crazy."

She climbs off my bed. Takes my hands in hers. "Sloanie girl, you are seventeen; this means you are officially, legally, only one year underage. You are allowed to be kissed with a moderate amount of tongue. Make me proud and give Gordy the first shot." She kisses me, without any tongue, and disappears.

As I'm getting dressed, I decide to wear my good jeans and a cotton flowy top that shows off my shoulders. I wear my new necklace. And take the time to do my hair. I mean, it's just breakfast with my folks. And then hanging with Gordy. But it's my birthday, so maybe I should make a little effort.

I can smell my dad's special pancakes being slightly burned, I can hear Max's excited yelp and mom's soothing voice, and I recognize how lucky I am. Maggie's family doesn't make much of her birthday. Jade gave her a card and a hug. Nicole sent her an e-card and a gift certificate to Net-a-Porter (both sent from Jerome's email address as if a reminder had popped up on his calendar that morning).

A little chill runs through me. Why would I want to fantasize that I'm a lonely girl with an inattentive mother and a tragically dead father and no real friends to speak of besides my little sister? Doesn't it make more sense that I'm Maggie, dreaming of a life where she's about to scarf pancakes burned with love? That's craziness, I know. But maybe I need to think of my life as the dream life. Maybe that will help me appreciate and enjoy it more.

Downstairs, the birthday brigade has decorated with balloons and a big cheesy banner and they are all wearing those shiny cone hats and Daddy has piled like eight pancakes with a huge candle that is already lit. They applaud as I enter the room. I curtsy, like the royalty I am this morning. The first hug comes from Tyler; Max is lined up next and actually nuzzles in. He doesn't even de-slime himself after. My mom holds me tight and rocks me in her arms.

"I'm not entirely sure that I'm willing to give you up to Gordy for your whole birthday. He really is too possessive."

The last hug comes from the only dad that Maggie and I have left, and in that sense it is the most special of all. He murmurs in my ear, "Sleep well?"

"Very. With lovely dreams." I can feel his relief. At least for the moment. And I'm relieved. Protecting my secret is sometimes exhausting. There have been moments like yesterday morning, where I test the water, consider telling the truth. But the fear of the dam crumbling and the tsunami of my insanity drowning us all is far greater than the burden of secrecy.

They gather in a circle, waiting for me to blow out my pancake candle. My silent wish is that they could always be safe and be together. Even if someday I disappear. If it ever happened, I couldn't bear the thought of dragging them down with me.

I stuff myself with about half the pancakes. Tyler takes pity on me by stealing several from my plate, and I pretend to be angry.

Gordy arrives. He seamlessly fits into the picture of breakfast in our kitchen. He helps himself to pancakes and admires Max's present to me. It is a frame he made himself out of clay. The photograph inside is of me and Max and Bill from just over a year ago. We are all climbing the elm. Bill's strong arms are supporting Max on a low branch in a way that made Max feel like he was doing it himself. I'm upside down like a monkey.

Max shows me that the frame has a secret compartment on the back where he has hidden a folded note with a birthday message. When I read it, tears stream down my face. Everyone wants to see what it says, but Max insists it's private. Not that I would share it with anyone anyway.

Last year my birthday breakfast looked very similar, except Bill was there. He gave me the coolest present I've ever received. It's an old Viewfinder, one of those red binocular-shaped toys that you put slides in. He had created a wheel of personal slides. Images of all the places in the world we always talked about wanting to see. And on each one, he had superimposed pictures of us. So there was me and Bill in a market in Morocco, on a bridge in Paris, with Sherpas on a misty trail in the Himalayas. I catch Max in my room looking at it a lot.

Gordy hasn't given me a heads-up as to what he has in store for today, other than "it won't suck." Once he's scarfed the rest of the pancakes, he tells me to get stuff to go out on his boat. As I'm packing up a little bag, I get a text. It's from Amanda. Happy Bday! Luvd hanging w/ u. We're in NYC this wknd but c u Mon.

129

We.

So much for living the dream. My day, my life is ruined. I can tell myself all day that "we" is simply her family. But a picture of Amanda and James dressed as Daisy and Gatsby kissing in a rowboat in Central Park flashes into my mind. I'm happy for them. Really. The world is the way it's supposed to be. And I will adjust to it. I'll have to.

Gordy keeps his boat at Maxwell's Shipyard. It's a twenty-two-foot Seacraft with huge twin engines on the back. I love going fast in this boat. Gordy is a masterful driver and always makes me feel safe. We cruise across the sound over to Fishers Island, which is the most indescribably beautiful and serene place I know. After docking at the abandoned Coast Guard station, we hike across the not-yet-open golf course, and brilliantly colored pheasants streak across the ground in front of us.

Gordy takes my hand and silently points out three baby deer with their wobbly just-born legs. And while I stand there holding his hand, Kelly's absurd little theory comes back into my mind. And I look over at Gordy's profile, trying to see him with fresh eyes. And I see exactly the guy Kelly described. Rugged and beautiful at once. Kind and strong. We are connected to each other in a way nothing else could duplicate.

We get to Isabella Beach, which is my favorite beach, not just because of the dunes and the soft sand but because when you look out, all you see is an unimpeded view of the Atlantic and the horizon and the sky above.

He has packed a lunch with all of my favorite stuff. He made deviled eggs with plenty of hot Chinese mustard, Vietnamese spring rolls stuffed with crab meat (which he drove to New London to get from this little restaurant), followed by my de rigueur pièce de résistance, a gooey, dripping, cheesy meatball grinder from Universal Package Store. Dessert is homemade brownies and Joe Froggers (ginger cookies that whalers used to take to sea because they were not only protection against nausea, but they're made with no dairy so they don't spoil). He scored a six-pack of Stella Artois (which I appreciate as beyond the normal range of our Natty Light budget).

We sit on the tapestry he brought, eat our feast, and then play a few rounds of our competition Lightning Crossword. This consists of purchasing two ninety-nine-cent crossword puzzle books from the checkout line at the A&P, choosing one at random, and madly seeing who can finish first. I have never beat him at this. He knows more words than I do; he just doesn't feel the compulsion to use them. He is, after all, a jock. He also scored higher (slightly) on his verbal PSAT. However, I crushed him in the math. Which he still resents.

As I race against him, I point out that it would be polite to let me win because it's my birthday. "And," he says, "because you're just a girl."

He kicks my ass.

After this, we lie down beside each other and take a nap in the sunny breeze. I always feel comfortable and safe with him. I wonder what he's dreaming about. I wonder if he's dreaming of me. As always, any daytime naps that Maggie or I take don't seem to count. We never dream then.

When I wake up from my dreamless nap, Gordy is looking out at the white house on the cliff down the beach.

"Should we live in that one when we get married?" he asks.

"Oh, absolutely. We'll have to do a lot of work, of course. Tear down walls and make it a lot bigger so the kids will have room to run around."

He looks at me. I can't tell what he is thinking.

"Kids need room," is all he says.

On the way back in, we stop in the lee of Mouse Island so Gordy can pull up one of his lobster traps and pick out a couple of two pounders for dinner. The sun is setting beyond the tiny island, casting gold flecks in the water. I take the wheel and hold the boat into the wind as he hoists the trap onto the boat. His arms are so strong and he's not at all afraid as he pulls the lobsters from the trap and snaps rubber bands over their pinchers.

Back at his place, we are alone. His folks are visiting his mom's dad in Maine. Grandpa Tuck has been fighting cancer for a while and lives alone. I've met him lots of times, even spent a week up in Maine one summer with Gordy when we were nine. His grandpa taught us to whittle, and I made a seal out of driftwood that had washed up on the rocky shore of the little island he lives on. A jellyfish stung my leg, and I made Gordy pee on me because that's the only way to neutralize the pain. He made me close my eyes. But I peeked.

So now I watch Gordy fling living creatures into boiling water that will scald them alive. He doesn't find this any more cruel than eating a hamburger and feels that I'm irrational in being upset to witness the execution. I don't know if cows scream when you slaughter them, but I guess they must. I know I would. So I listen to the lobsters' screech (which is actually only water bubbles moving through their shells since they have no vocal cords; apologies to the

Little Mermaid), and I wonder if I could spend the rest of my life with a man who is unaffected by that sound.

Kelly's theory has become an internal debate. Could I spend the rest of my life with Gordy? Sure. Could I sleep with Gordy? Wow. I don't know. But I certainly don't go "ick," so what does that mean? Probably nothing.

While we eat, I realize that this would be incredibly romantic or scary with any other guy. Maggie is unflappable. She just rolls into the fanciest restaurant on the arm of this older guy and doesn't feel nervous at all. I'm rarely that self-assured. With Gordy in his kitchen, I feel confident and comfortable. Like just being myself is enough.

Gordy stares at me as I pick apart a piece of lobster. I can tell he wants to talk about this cheerleader Melissa who he dates whenever he needs a date. Her distinguishing trait is that she sucks. She is the classic bitch that boys always go for because they figure she must be too good for them. She is not too good for The Weed, let alone Gordy. Every time she treats him like shit, he laughs it off, telling me that it's just because he won't really make her his girlfriend.

But tonight, he asks if maybe he should give her a shot to be a real girlfriend, him having to find a prom date and all.

"You aren't serious. This is a skank from skanksville. She is not worth the fifteen seconds we're wasting on her right now."

He smiles. "You always say that. Nobody's good enough for me. That's why you're always stuck hanging out with me. Seems like you'd wise up and palm me off on somebody sometime."

I study him, looking to see if he's wondering what I'm wondering. No way to tell, so I take the first step.

"You ever think what it would have been like if we'd ever dated?"

"Nope. I don't like rejection enough to fantasize about it." And he laughs.

"Seriously. 'Cause I think about it sometimes."

"It would depend on the reason we started. If it was casual, I might be lucky enough that it would be sort of like now. Only with sex." And he wiggles his eyebrows to make a joke of that word so I won't think it has ever been on his mind for real. Which of course I now do. Not that there is anything wrong with that.

"What if it wasn't casual?" I ask. "What if we wanted to see if we were actually right for each other?"

"The truth is"—Gordy takes a deep breath—"I think you'd have realized that there isn't enough of me to keep you interested in that way. And maybe it would have broken us up, or made things weird between us."

I stare in his eyes. I feel so terrible.

"This is a silly conversation, and I'm going to end it in one second and get back to my birthday with you. But before I do, you need to hear that there is more than enough of you to be of interest forever to any girl in this world."

There is a silence.

"I actually baked a birthday cake," he says. "From a box, but still. I'm really scared to try it."

"We'll drown it in Häagen-Dazs and hot fudge. Do we have hot fudge?"

He smiles. "And salted caramels. After all, it's your birthday."

We talk and eat and watch my favorite movie, which is *Breakfast at Tiffany's*. He doesn't get me home until one thirty.

Sitting on my bed is a small neatly wrapped package, obviously a paperback book. Nice ribbon, though. But there's no card. I open it to find . . .

A copy of *Siddhartha*, which of course I read when I was twelve. The book was dog-eared and well used. Inside the title page is neatly printed: *This is the first copy I ever read, and the notes are a little embarrassing, but first impressions often are. It struck me that there are thoughts in here I'd like to talk to you about someday. Happy birthday.* —J.

CHAPTER ELEVEN

MAGGIE

Emma hands me a book titled *Exploring the World of Lucid Dreaming*.

"I hope you'll read it. There are some thoughts in there I'd like to discuss with you," she says as I begin to read the summary on the back of the book.

Of course I've done enough research into my, let's call it my condition, to know that lucid dreaming is when you are aware you are dreaming. Tibetan yogis are really good at it. It's not really a quick answer for our particular situation because I know I'm dreaming when Sloane is awake, just as she knows she's dreaming right now.

"I think you have constructed an extremely intricate, recurring, controlled lucid dreamscape. And I think you did this out of necessity to try to comprehend your life and yourself in a world where your father no longer exists." She says this very slowly, looking right at me. I'm critical of her delivery because it feels so rehearsed. But also because it doesn't make sense. I wish it did.

"Thank you for taking the time to come up with that. But there are two problems with your theory. First, I've been dreaming of Sloane for as long as I can remember, before my father died," I start. "I know all about her life, when she was a kid." Emma interrupts with the answer she has prepared, knowing I would say this.

"You believe that now. But it could've begun when your father died and your unconscious created the belief and the memory that you have always dreamt of Sloane. Your mind filled in the details of her past."

"Okay. Well, I don't control Sloane."

"You may not feel like you are controlling what Sloane does in your dream, but you are using her nonetheless. There are parts of you that you're not willing to look at, so you keep them in the dark by living them out through Sloane. If we can get you to understand that, then you can consciously use your dream of Sloane to gain clarity about your own life, and you won't need her anymore. And it's time we begin to do that. Now."

Her voice lowers, gets almost ominous. "At the moment, you at least still have control of your world, the real world. If we let this go much longer, I'm afraid that could change."

I start to imagine what that would be like and it terrifies me so much I actually close my eyes.

"Thanks for the book," is all I say.

That afternoon, I am suddenly motivated to read my GED material. I leave the book on lucid dreams next to my bed. Maybe by osmosis I'll pick something up.

I get so engrossed in the Congress of Vienna, basically because the characters read like a dynamite stage play (Metternich, Talleyrand, those guys), that by the time I look up, it's four o'clock, and like any good mom, I realize an hour late that Jade isn't around.

I know she had no playdate today because I'm scheduled to take her to ballet, which Miss Twinkle Toes never misses. Maybe she just forgot about me and headed to Ms. Jeffries's studio with one of her friends. But when I call the class, they are concerned because she isn't there.

I call Nicole, basically because I love wasting my time under stress, and it is, after all, my best opportunity to talk to Jerome and hear yet one more excuse about how my mother is the world's most unavailable person. No, she didn't take Jade to ballet, didn't say anything about it, and has been in budget meetings for the last four hours.

I dial the school. No one answers because anyone who would answer a phone is gone for the day. Nice job.

I come to my senses and call the kid's Hello Kitty cell phone. No answer, which is alarming because she never switches it off. So as a rational and mature person, I'm positive it's a brain tumor. She's lying on a street somewhere, being stepped around by compassionate New Yorkers.

I call Jerome back.

"Jade is missing, at risk, and just a little more important than your getting yelled at for bringing a note to Nicole during some bullshit meeting. If you don't go in there, whatever happens is your responsibility." And then I hang up fast. And don't pick up the phone when he calls right back. It's his ball. He's stuck with it.

I grab my jacket, head down to the street to trace the three different routes that Jade takes on her walk home. Sure enough, eight minutes of panic later, Nicole calls. She actually laughs and takes credit for not being angry with me for interrupting her stupid meeting. What a paranoid I am to be worried when Jade is simply taking an ice-skating lesson at Chelsea Piers.

Gulping back my rage, I ask when she signed Jade up for skating lessons, and why she didn't bother to tell Ms. Jeffries at ballet? I'm told that Jade was supposed to call Ms. Jeffries. Kids today, what are you going to do? Blind with matricidal impulses (can you call it that if the person isn't really a functioning mother?), I listen to the cherry on top of this whole horror sundae . . .

Jade didn't sign up for skating lessons. She is being taught this afternoon by her new friend Andrew. Who drove her there in his GEM. And who never even bothered to mention any of this to me yesterday. Amazing. And I actually was beginning to like this guy.

I run up the West Side Highway, covering the mile in record time. Low and behold, here they are in the Sky Rink, a young man teaching a little girl to ice-skate. Why am I so angry?

Jade sees me and waves like crazy, and for some reason I don't wave back. Andrew smiles at me, as if he's done absolutely nothing wrong, and when I very definitely don't smile back, he simply goes back to work with Jade and ignores me for twenty minutes. He is, maddeningly but predictably, fabulous with her. She's laughing, flirting, and sort of learning to ice-skate.

I sit down on the hard bench and wonder what my deal is. Never mind wanting to control Sloane's world. I'm irritated beyond belief that no one in my own life is doing things the way they should be doing them. Why wouldn't anyone think to let me know this after-school date was taking place so that I wouldn't worry? After a bit, Andrew leaves her to practice on her own and skates up to sit beside me.

"Okay, what happened? Did you lose the role or your boy-friend?"

"Neither. More like my faith in humanity."

"How come you're looking at me when you say that?"

I blink. "Oh, I don't know. Maybe because we spent an entire day together and you never mentioned this."

"Why would I?"

There is nothing worse than a question like that. Because any honest answer would reveal that I'm angry because I feel left out and insanely jealous of my seven-year-old sister's friendship with some guy who I'm completely platonic with anyway. Like it would matter. It is so unfair to have those humiliating feelings exposed as the result of a question so unassuming and innocent that I can't credibly blame the guy for asking it.

"Well, for one thing, I've told you that Nicole is brain-dead and negligent, so you should have assumed that she wouldn't tell me about this, and I'd be a little concerned when my sister went missing."

"I did think of that. Which is why I told Jade to make sure you knew. And if she didn't, I'm very disappointed in her. As to your mom, she is forgetful. However, she is also incredibly hot."

"How would you know that?"

"Jade showed me a picture on her phone."

"Why are we talking about this?"

"We're trying to distract you so you'll stop being angry with me. And start cheering for Jade so she has enough confidence in her skating to go to Ashley's party. She asked me to come up with a lie for her to use to get out of the party because she's embarrassed she doesn't ice-skate. So I offered my services, which is the least I can do for a friend who invited me on a sleepover with three of her girlfriends. Don't worry, I declined for obvious reasons. Much as I might have enjoyed the event."

So I start cheering for Jade. And I stop being angry at him.

Maybe I am so pissed because I feel like Jade and I have become his kid sisters, who are fun passing time with until he can go home to his smoking-hot girlfriend.

I ask if he wants to grab dinner. He asks Jade what she's in the mood for, and I remind her that she has a sushi date with Nicole. It'd be easy to get Jade out of it, but even if I'm no longer feeling angry about it, I certainly don't want to be grouped in the little sister category. And besides, I tell him, I need his advice on a certain matter. "Sadly, however, I don't have two friends who would include you in our sleepover."

He laughs and says, "If there's no pillow fight in it for me, I'm not sure I can render my services. We'll work out payment over dinner."

Jade and I go to the locker room so she can get changed to meet Nicole at Nobu. She confides the following things to me. Andrew really, really likes her. And she knows this because he bought the pale blue sparkly skates she was wearing so that she wouldn't be the loser kid with the ugly rental skates at the party. And she could keep them forever and ever. And then she asks how old Andrew will be when she turns sixteen. I tell her that he will be twenty-eight and will seem really old and boring to her at that point. But will still be her friend.

I take him to a place with super-comfort food, especially the home-baked pie, especially the blueberry. I tell him that dinner is on me, and he tries to order two pounds of caviar.

I keep to small talk during the matzo ball soup and hush puppies. Before the meat loaf, I hesitantly bring up my main conversational course. I want to talk to Andrew about Thomas mainly because I don't have anyone else to talk to, but also, as a man, he will be able to think like Thomas thinks (girls think we can do that, but we are kidding ourselves). As a friend, he will tell me the truth.

"How did you feel about the kiss? Not the one in the car, the one at the door."

I'm taken aback a little. But it's a fair question.

"I was pretty excited. And I guess I was relieved to be honestly excited."

"Because you were afraid you might be using him?"

"Yes."

He sighs. And looks at me in a very tender and wonderful way that paradoxically makes me afraid of what he's about to say.

"Don't be. You can't use somebody who's using you."

"Is that what you really think, or are you just . . ."

I stop myself. I was about to use the word *jealous*. And I realize in this one instant that this was, of course, exactly why I asked him to dinner, exactly why I'm telling him all of this. I want him to be jealous. The truth of that shocks me so that it takes me a beat before I can come up with a lie to cover . . .

"Or are you just a guy who thinks that all guys are the same and all girls need to be protected from them."

He stares at me evenly. No smile at all.

"No, I'm not that guy. I'm the guy who knows that this particular guy is a flunky to an important casting director, and yes, I checked him out and he is a flunky, is not looking to cast you in anything. Because he doesn't have the power to do so."

"Fine. I'd like it better if he just really liked me."

He says nothing. Takes a bite of meat loaf and annoyingly starts to hum a tune I sort of recognize. As if our conversation is over.

"What makes you so sure," I say, "that he doesn't?"

"That's not it at all. I think he wants you and likes you. A lot. He's going to a lot of trouble, sticking his neck out even at the risk of rejection, which I'd bet this guy doesn't do all that often."

So now I'm really confused.

"So now I'm really confused," I say. "If I want him to like me, and he really likes me, are you telling me not to date him just because he's a flunky?"

He looks at me as if I were rather slow.

"Nobody told you not to date this guy. Actually, my advice, for what it's worth, is that this sounds like exactly the kind of situation you should pursue."

Why does this feel like the last thing I want to hear?

"You said the guy is trying to use me."

"Bad choice of words on my part. The guy is dangling career stuff, thinking that's what it takes to get you interested. But actually, you're relieved that this isn't about a role, and you guys can date simply because you're hot for each other. As long as you're clear on who he is and what he can or can't do for your career, you're smart and careful and you'll do what's best for you."

"But you don't like the guy. I mean, you don't like him for me."

"I've never even seen the guy, and this is only about what *you* like. Look. It's hard to tell the difference between how we want someone to feel about us and how we actually feel about them. If the person is attractive, we always want them to want us, and sometimes we get so busy trying to make that happen, we forget to keep track of whether we actually want them or not. Plus, we always want what we're afraid we can't get . . ."

"But you're telling me I can get him."

"Sure. But the important thing is what you're telling me: that you actually want to get him."

This throws me into a tornado of mixed emotions. On the one hand, do I really want Thomas or just want him to want me? On the other hand, it does explain my confusion over Andrew because, as he so wisely says, we want every reasonable candidate to want us. The truth is that I meet very few guys who I could ever even see myself wanting to be with, and this one comes complete with the world's sexiest and most possessive girlfriend, so of course I want him standing in line for me, somewhere just behind Thomas.

"How did you know you really wanted Carmen, instead of just wanting her to want you?"

"I still don't know. She fascinates me; I know that much."

Of course, I'm overwhelmed by a desire to learn absolutely everything about their relationship.

"Well, I won't comment," I comment, "because you haven't really asked me for advice on that."

"Thank you."

This kind of cools me off on the whole Andrew thing. We finish our dinner pleasantly enough. More talk about French and Italian movies. Make up a few of our funny stories about the waiters, the other diners, and particularly the stunningly put-together hostess.

Out on the street, I offer, "I'll just grab a cab; you probably have to get home."

"I've got time to drop you." Meaning, he indeed does have to get home.

At which point, a cab pulls over, dropping off a woman who proves that you can at least be too thin, if not too rich. I give him a friendly wave and just jump in the cab and take off without really saying anything.

On the way home, I feel kind of bad. Almost as if I've broken up with a boyfriend or something. This shows how limited my experience is with actual boyfriends. I'll call Andrew tomorrow and be all friendly and everything.

I enter the apartment to encounter a beaming Nicole. I don't think I've ever seen her so darn happy. She is positively bursting to ask . . .

"Who. Is. Thomas?"

Oh boy.

"Thomas who?"

"Thomas who sent you no fewer than fifty yellow roses. With an incredibly romantic note."

As I draw a breath to kill her with the poison boiling in my tongue . . .

"Which of course I haven't opened or read. I'm just getting back at you because you've been holding out on me."

The flowers are beautiful beyond belief and come in a crystal vase that shames our whole apartment. The note says, *Thinking of you.* And then it says, *Instead of working, sleeping, or doing anything else.*

Should I call him? No. Of course I should. It would be smarter not to. But also rude not to. Was he staring out his apartment window at the city, wondering which twinkling light was mine? I've never had a boy do anything like this for me before. Andrew is right: Thomas really does like me. And thinking about it, Thomas is pretty close to perfect. Lying there in bed, I can't come up with any real imperfection. And he may be a flunky now, but we all have to start somewhere. He certainly has entrée to a world full of exciting introductions and premieres and dinner reservations. What's wrong with falling for a guy who also might be able to help me reach my dreams?

I grab my phone. And before I can talk myself out of it, I'm dialing his number. He picks it up on the first ring.

"Hi." And his voice is silk and everything soft and warm and excited to hear from me. All in that one simple word. And before I can say anything, he says . . .

"You're going to need your beauty rest." And before I can ask why, he says, "Because you're reading tomorrow for Robin."

My heart pounds and stops all at once. Andrew was wrong. Thomas is anything but a flunky. My man delivered for me.

"Rosalie is going to be there. And hang on to your flannel jammies, so will our director. He's back from Africa. I'd sent him your reel. I don't want to oversell this, but he's absolutely open to you. It's a shot, a real one."

"God bless you."

"Believe me, I'm happier than you are."

Not possible. I do Jade's booty dance alone in my room because I can't contain my excitement. We talk for twenty more minutes while I get ready for bed. He listens to me brush my teeth. And then, when I turn out the light and crawl under the covers, he says . . .

"Good night, beautiful. I hope I'm in your dreams."

And I'm reckless enough to say, "In a funny way, you already are."

CHAPTER TWELVE

SLOANE

I wake up with James's copy of *Siddhartha* between me and my pillow. I spent all day yesterday reading *Siddhartha* through two and half times, apparently falling asleep in the process. I love his underlinings and notes in the margins. And I love the way his lower lip is like a shelf someone carved out of something I'd like to touch.

In the bathroom, I decide to put on some makeup, trying to do it so that none of the girls will notice and James won't notice but will just find me attractive and not know why. I'm obsessing over some mascara, making sure there are no telltale clumps, when Max stumbles into the bathroom without knocking.

"Sorry!" he says, and closes his eyes quickly. But he doesn't shut the door. He just stands there with his eyes closed.

"I'm dressed, Max. You can open your eyes," I assure him. He opens one slightly. Thus reassured, he comes in and elbows me away from the sink so he can brush his teeth. In the mirror, he studies my reflection as I try to perfect my "natural" look.

I want to say something to him about his birthday note but don't want to make him feel awkward or even more repulsed by my feminine presence. And then as if he's reading my mind, which I really wouldn't be surprised if Max has the ability to do, he says . . .

"I borrowed Bill's words for your card. He said them. That day we climbed the tree." He stares at me directly in the mirror. I'm afraid I'll cry if I look at him, so I keep working on my eyelashes.

"It is a beautiful card. They are beautiful words, Max."

He nods. He knows. That's why he used them.

He spits and begins to rinse. I look down at his head and want to burrow my face in it for comfort but am afraid of ruining the moment. As he slurps water straight from the faucet, which is a new "guy" habit of his, he confesses, "I found Bill in the sky. In the stars. Like on your ceiling."

He turns off the water and looks at me directly. His face so open and clear and innocent.

"I'll show you one night," he says. And walks out of the bathroom.

And as I'm savoring this shared moment, he reminds me not to get used to it. He calls from down the hall, "You look a lot prettier without all that gunk on your face, Sloane."

I stare at myself in the mirror. There is still a slight crease on my face from where I fell asleep on James's book. I think of the line I was reading, the one James had underlined and put an asterisk next to: "Siddhartha stood alone like a star in the heavens . . . That was the last shudder of his awakening . . . Immediately he moved on

again and began to walk quickly and impatiently, no longer home-
wards, no longer looking backwards."

I steel myself to get on with my day. A deep breath and I float
down the stairs. My two seconds of serenity are immediately broken
when met with my mother's inquisition.

"You look happy," she says. It's not a statement but a question.
Why?

"Thanks. So do you." I try to focus on the scrambled eggs and
toast she slides under my nose.

"Could it have anything to do with the book you were reading
all day yesterday?"

I don't look up. "Maybe. It's the kind of book that makes you
feel good about the world. I'll let you read it."

"Hello!" she says so I have to look up. "I'm asking about the
freakishly gorgeous young man, I can't even use the word *boy*, who
dropped said book off."

"That would be James. He's new."

She sits down directly across from me.

"He obviously likes you. You obviously are happy that he does.
Why won't you talk about it?"

"Oh, don't worry, I talk about it with lots of people. But I think
what you mean is, why won't I talk about it to *you*?"

She flinches a little, as if my words pinched her.

"And the answer?" she asks calmly.

"The answer is that I'd rather not."

There's a really long silence while she tries to control her tem-
per. At last, she simply stands and walks out of the kitchen. She
doesn't even turn off the burner under dad's bacon.

I'm so mad at her for being that way I can hardly see straight. I don't want her knowing anything about James. She's clearly trying to be all chummy with me about it only so that she can suss out what sort of regulations she needs to implement. My mom rules under martial law when it comes to dating. Under penalty of grounding or worse, I wasn't even allowed to date until my sixteenth birthday. It embarrassed and frustrated me beyond belief, not that I was batting away dates. It sort of equated boys and punishment in my mind. And it certainly didn't leave communication lines open where I want to sit down and have a chick chat with dear old Mom. I obeyed her stupid rule, and now that I'm old enough and some guy drops off a book, she has to be all up in my business. I'm so sick of being under her microscope. I leave my eggs and go back upstairs to redo my makeup.

I turn my dad down twice on his unusual offer to drive me to school. On the third offer, I just say thanks and wonder if he has some dad thing on his mind. Please let it be anything other than my dreams. He only asked that once how I slept, so hopefully he's simply forgotten.

When my dad gets angry with me, his voice gets low and really slow, and it just scares me to death.

"What's going on with you about your mom?"

So the dad thing is actually a mom thing and not at all about my dreams.

"I'm sorry I snapped at her at breakfast. I'm just tired, which is no excuse. I promise I'll apologize soon as I see her."

"Not nearly good enough. You've been angry with her for a year. It started abruptly, right around your sixteenth birthday, and it's actually getting worse."

"Daddy . . ."

"Be quiet. Your mother and I discuss it all the time. It is breaking her heart and mine. It is completely unfair, and I want to know right this minute what it's all about."

"I don't know, Daddy. I feel it too. I keep hoping it will go away. I know it's not anything she's doing wrong. I'm hoping it's just like a teenage daughter separation thing, where I have to push her away so I can leave or something."

"That's the worst excuse I've ever heard. Teenagers can pout and have tantrums, but this has been going on for a year. If it doesn't change and change soon, the next step is talking to a professional."

I wish I could take the train into New York and start seeing Emma. I wish Emma actually existed. If she did, I could ask her why this is happening to me. I could ask her about Maggie.

"I mean it, Sloane. This has to stop. We're a family. The world doesn't revolve around you. Do you understand me?" He glances from the road, sees the tears filling my eyes. "Do you?"

"I do," I say. And then the truth just slips from me. "I don't know what's wrong with me."

But of course I do. I just don't know why.

He drops me at school. There is no thought of a kiss goodbye, or even saying anything. I try to close the car door without slamming it, but maybe it sounds too loud anyway.

Ashamed, I go straight to the bathroom and look in the mirror. Sure enough, the stupid mascara has blackened under my eyes so I look like Gordy when he suits up for a game. I carefully wipe it away, feeling like an absolute monster to be treating my mom so meanly. I remember her hurt face in flashes of clips from the past year where she attempted to talk the way we always had before and I just slammed the door.

Besides, there's nothing to talk about. I'm indulging in a tweener fantasy that the most beautiful boy who ever lived could possibly like me. How would I say that to her and what would I say to her endless questions at every breakfast as to how the big non-romance is going? Talking about my fantasy and longing is humiliating and for some reason would be exponentially more humiliating with her.

I walk into homeroom and there he is, in the back as usual, with an empty seat next to him. The second he sees me, he waves me over. I forget I have a mother. I forget everything. Except, try not to run. At least not too fast.

I slide into the seat beside him. He stares at me pleasantly but very intently.

"Good morning," I say.

"Hi. I'm sorry for staring; I was just noticing something, that's all."

There follows an extremely long two seconds of silence.

"I'm waiting," I say.

"Your lashes are so long."

It may be hard to understand, but that sentence sets my heart to racing more than if he had proposed marriage or something. He thinks I'm a little attractive at least. Right?

"Thanks. And thanks for the book. I'd read it long ago, of course . . ."

"Of course," and he smiles at how pretentious that was. But it is a really kind and friendly smile. As if he knows I'm trying to impress him, and that's okay because he complimented my eyelashes. I wonder how he'd like them without the residual mascara. A worry for another day. I think you can have them dyed permanently. Mental note to check that out. I mean, who knew he was an eyelash guy.

"What happened there? Were you in a duel?" He points to the tiny gap in my fabulously long lashes caused by a chicken pox scar from when I was a kid.

"You should see the other guy," I say, and he laughs.

"I've got to skip sixth period," he says, "because I promised to drive somebody somewhere. But Pablo and I are coming to help out at the vet's later; I'll stuff envelopes and he'll lick. So I'll see you there. Maybe we can grab a bite or something."

I'm paralyzed. Frozen. So of course I say something surpassingly stupid. "So we can talk about *Siddhartha*."

He leans across his desk toward me. "So we can talk about anything we want."

The bell rings. He reaches down and grabs his bag, looking up at me with those eyes. And I will myself to move. As I pack up, it sinks in. That was a date. He asked me on a date. Not even with the cover of an excuse. He wants me to know that he wants my company. He wants to be with me. Alone.

I just sit there as the room empties, and just as I'm about to dissolve into a blissful wisp of smoke, two little words break through my ecstasy: *Amanda Porcella*. The someone he is driving somewhere during sixth period. The someone he is probably having sex with on a daily basis.

Wow. I'm an idiot. He's way too decent, and certainly way too smart, to think he could two-time his girlfriend in a class of eighty kids, all of whom watch and gossip about them constantly. Obviously, this isn't a date at all. He would think of it as grabbing a burger with a friend from school. Same as if I were Gordy or The Weed. It is only a date in my mind because that is my fondest wish in all the world.

I'm not ashamed for wanting Amanda's boyfriend for myself. Every girl at this school wants him. Nothing bad just happened. James simply asked if I wanted to hang out, and if I can keep from mooning over him and be fairly intelligent and entertaining, we can become people who hang out together. And I would like that. It won't be horrible because I want more; this will be second best and I will make that good enough.

I find Gordy and sit with him at lunch. I apologize for not calling him yesterday, explaining that I was into some heavy reading all day. I want him to know how wonderful my birthday was, thanks to him. Gordy thinks it took second place to my roller-skating party in fourth grade when he broke his wrist trying to "shoot the duck" (a challenging skating move). He asks if we can grab dinner together tonight. I can tell something is up, and he faux casually mentions that he took my advice and shit-canned the odious Melissa. Good freakin' riddance.

He seems a little sad about it, even though he's trying to play it off lightly.

"Want to grab dinner at Pizzetta? I could use a breakup pepperoni pie." His big shoulders shrug and he takes a sip from the tiny straw sticking out of a juice box.

"Of course," I tell him. There's no way he's eating breakup pizza alone. Even though I never would have accepted James's offer of dinner anyway (for fear that Amanda or others would misconstrue), I feel some regret at having given away the possibility. But he's Gordy, and he'd do it for me.

James never shows at the vet anyway. Not a very reliable volunteer. I probably won't mention it to Dr. French, though. Obviously, driving someone somewhere wound up being much more exciting than hanging out with me and the animals. Not my problem. Not my business. I'm off to cheer up my best friend on the occasion of his slut-ectomy.

I kiss all the creatures good night and lock up. The envelopes with Dr. French's monthly newsletter can wait another day. I unlock my bike and wheel it out to the curb just as—

An old red Porsche Targa whips around the corner and skids to a stop right in my face. He leans out of the window with a goofy smile. I would never in a million years guess he owns a goofy smile, and it makes him more devastating than ever.

"I'm so glad I caught you. I got held up."

"You don't have to explain anything to me." It sounds a little too snippy the moment I say it. Hopefully he won't take it that way.

"Anyway, if you're still free to grab dinner . . ."

I walk my bike to his window. In my nicest, softest voice I say, "I never said I was free for dinner. You just assumed I was, probably because you don't get a lot of people turning you down."

"I think that's a compliment, right?"

"A little bit of both."

He laughs. "So. Are you? Free for dinner, I mean."

156

"No, sorry."

"Me neither. How about tomorrow?"

This is more than heart-pounding. This is not enough air to expand my lungs. This is tingling in all weird places. I look down at my feet and try to create a look that is ironic, gently disapproving but still friendly. I'm not sure Meryl Streep could invent a look like that.

"What?" he asks pleasantly. I decide not to look up.

"I'm just wondering what Amanda would think of what you just said."

The silence is so long I'm not sure he's actually still there.

"Look at me," he says in an especially sweet way. So I do. "Everyone thinks Amanda and I are together, so I shouldn't be surprised that you think it too."

Does that mean he's not dating her?

"We're not. I'm not dating her or anyone. I actually never dated Amanda. We hung out for two weeks during Outward Bound and stayed friends after."

"So she was never your girlfriend?"

James turns a little red. "I mean, we hooked up. And it was pretty clear that she was hoping things might continue. But then I met someone. Someone I'm not with anymore. Amanda knows all of this. And everything is fine between us. You can ask her and she'll tell you that."

I hold my breath. Unfortunately, he seems to have no more to say.

"And you're telling me this because . . . ?"

"Um, you asked."

"Oh yeah." And we both laugh. Here we are, in the vet's parking lot. Laughing at me. I have no idea what to do. So I just keep laughing. I must look like an idiot. At last he says something.

"Sloane, I asked you out on a date. And to be honest, it's the first time I've asked anybody on a date in a long time. And I really hope you say yes."

What on earth could someone like him ever see in me?

"Yes. I'd like that very much."

We just look at each other. He's still in his car. I'm standing at his window with one hand resting on the door. He reaches out and strokes my pinky finger. It feels like I've stuck it in an electrical socket. But in a good way.

"So, can I drop you somewhere?" he asks.

"Um, I've got this bike, see."

"Right. But I could pick you up tomorrow morning and drop you back at the bike, in time for school."

This isn't real. Maggie is dreaming this. By osmosis she picked up something from that book Emma gave her and she is making this happen. I'll never find a way to thank her enough for the opportunity. Too bad I have to turn him down.

"If I leave this bike out tonight, I'll be in even more trouble with my mom and dad than I already am, which is considerable." I feel like a little girl saying this to a guy driving his own Porsche.

"I met your mom on Saturday. I think she likes me. I could put a word in."

"Rain check." I force myself to mount my bike, give him a casual wave, as if this is all in a day's work for a girl who was frequently asked out for burgers by the hottest guy to ever blow into our sleepy town. The sophistication is somewhat undercut when I strap on my monumentally dorky bike helmet.

He's just sitting there watching as I pedal away. Too giddy to steer straight.

CHAPTER THIRTEEN

MAGGIE

I decide not to mention my audition for *Innuendo* to Nicole or even to Jade. It's not that I'm afraid I'll jinx myself, or even that I want to avoid Nicole's comforting when I lose the role. It just feels like too big an opportunity to casually chat about. I have Thomas to talk to, and he's on the inside, so I'm leaning on him quite a bit. I actually consult him about what socks to wear and whether it's best to eat oatmeal or eggs for breakfast. He humors me by considering the choices as heavily as I am. I wind up going for one of Jade's neon pink Pop-Tarts because that's probably what the character would choose.

Two hours before the most important audition thus far of my life, I'm scheduled to meet with Emma. I debate canceling since Thomas is much more fun to talk to and can give me actually helpful advice at the moment. Despite my dropout sensibilities and artistic bent, I am not a flake. So I show up on time for the appointment.

I start off by telling her I haven't read the book she gave me and that Sloane is off-limits as a topic for the next hour. Instead we could make good use of this time by preparing me for the audition. I envision meditating to some relaxing music, maybe sneaking in a nap while she guides me to my "happy place."

Emma has other plans and says that she can help me "focus" by reaching back into life experience to channel the wild, tempestuous, promiscuous, and downright crazy Robin.

My entire experience with sexual intercourse was once, at the ridiculous age of fourteen. Of course, I've been forced to talk about this forgettable moment in about 80 percent of my sessions with Emma, who just considers this a treasure trove of Freudiana. In reality, the penis involved belonged to Robert Parkens, who was nearly seventeen and the big brother of my friend's friend who was hosting a party where (shocker) booze reared its ugly head. In fairness, I had been mooning over Robert, who was attractive in a tubercular artist kind of way (he'd actually written forty pages of what was never to become his novel), and that made him some kind of bohemian dreamboat. My luck, he thought I was hot, which I promise I was anything but.

So, cautionary tale, he got me up in his bedroom, and I got really drunk (which I thoroughly enjoyed until about three o'clock in the morning, waking up in bed in my own puke). We started making out, which I also thoroughly enjoyed, at least as much as he did. This (along with the little white lie that I was sixteen) encouraged him to believe that this was the magic moment. It wasn't horrible, it was slightly painful, and what it was not was magical or thrilling or anything like it was supposed to be. The making out had seemed spontaneous and exciting. The last part got kind of technical, and fumbly, and was over in about fifteen seconds.

Emma takes the position that this is some deep wound and maybe, somehow, could have created virginal Sloane. Boy. I explained one hundred times that I was not raped, and although I hadn't really thought about the deflowering aspect until I was too drunk to think about much of anything, I was basically down with it and the only negative consequence was that I didn't want to go through exactly that experience again and have been sort of afraid that maybe that's how it will always be for me, a non-event. On the positive side, I try to look on it as simply a matter of the wrong guy and that the next time will be with someone, well, I'm truly in love with.

For the record, Robert is a perfectly nice guy. He wanted to see more of me (no pun intended) even after he found out that I was fourteen and didn't want to sleep with him or anybody for the indefinite future. The truth is I just felt too young for it and didn't have a mom like Sloane's to tell me so—or that it was okay. Sometimes I wonder if I always will be too young to date.

So, of course, Emma awkwardly tries to connect this to the whole Thomas thing, and it just makes me want to slap her silly. For all of my confusion about how I feel toward Thomas, Robert Parkens is not in the mix. Emma feels conflicted about Thomas too. And so we spend the hour discussing her conflicts instead of mine, which is a relief.

It seems that while the last thing she wants is for me to jump into a "sexual relationship" or become "sexually active" with anyone before my psychosis is resolved, she also wonders whether falling in love and having a genuine attachment would obviate the need for Sloane entirely. Then there's the inappropriateness of Thomas's age (like he was fifty or something), the complications of potential workplace conflicts, and my own ambivalence about how I want to feel toward someone I do that with.

The part I don't tell her is that for all my bravado, I'm more than a little bit scared to be in a genuine relationship, where God forbid the guy I might fall in love with would learn that there's no *there* there in me and I would have my worst fears confirmed, that I am not deserving of the right guy's love.

With five minutes to go, Emma brings out the hammer, ignoring my request to keep Sloane out of this. Why haven't I brought up the relevance of Sloane to the whole Thomas question? Maybe because there isn't any? Wrong. To truly be in a relationship, I need to be ready to share my whole self, my true self, and I'm not. In fact, my secret is about the most disabling one she's ever seen in this context.

She goes on to remind me of the potential danger of simply going permanently and irrevocably bananas (a technical term), which terrifies me, particularly when she explains that the panic I might feel hiding Sloane from the hypothetical man I will love could be the very thing that pushes me over the edge.

Three hundred dollars, please.

Thus prepared for my audition, I wander around Central Park in a complete daze, actually contemplating calling in sick and begging for a do-over. Right. That would certainly happen. So instead, I decide to get in character. I buy a chili dog and flirt with the Sabrett's guy in Robin's New Orleans accent (conveniently borrowed from my *Glass Menagerie* triumph). He actually asks me out. Maybe I'll tell him about Sloane and see how it goes.

By the time I get to Rosalie's offices, I have expertly gone through my scene thirty times and am feeling pretty cocky. Thomas greets me very professionally and reintroduces me to Rosalie, who is super-supportive (which means treating me both as an actress she respects and someone she personally likes). I'm introduced to Macauley Evans, the director. He has the most intense eyes. They are laser-focused on me. I don't think he blinks for the entire five minutes we chitchat. Game on.

Of course, Macauley wants a different scene. In fact, five different scenes. I tell him about the scene I'd been asked to prepare, and he says that's great and we'll do it last. As in, I don't really care about that scene, but I'm throwing you a bone to see if you can impress me. All eyes on me, I feel totally confident going through the scenes. And I wind up killing. Meaning, I'm very, very good. I know it, they know it. It feels almost like a dream.

People ask me if the best performances are when you lose yourself in the character and actually are channeling Robin. Absolutely not. You need to do both things at once. You are always in control, always know what you are doing, but are so completely fluent in what your character would do that you are confident you can't make a false step. I guess it sounds a little bit like lucid dreaming, like what Emma wants me to do with Sloane.

In the goodbyes, no one is falsely encouraging, which is completely expected and at the same time devastating. I'm sure there will be more experienced, more marketable, and more talented actresses reading for this, and one of them will get the role. Today is a total triumph, great for my future, I tell myself. Sure. That's why I feel so deflated as I head out the door.

Thomas walks me down to the street. He tells me I did wonderfully, knowing that's not what I want to hear. When he says that I have a terrific chance, I can tell he's lying through his perfect teeth. What I don't know is whether I should be angry or grateful for the lie. Andrew would tsk-tsk me and ask me to forget what I should be feeling and dig around to find out what I was actually feeling. This is why Andrew is a pain in the ass, and Carmen is welcome to him.

Thomas surprises me with a goodbye kiss on the street. It makes my stomach do a tiny flip. He gently pushes me against the wall of the building and plays with my hair.

"Please have dinner with me tonight. I'll cook for you. I'm a good cook," he assures me with a smile.

I feel nervous and confused and can't think fast enough. So I lie.

"I have a family thing. But I'll call you in the morning so we can pick a date for you to impress me with your Iron Chefness."

He seems happy enough, repeats his lie about my chances, and goes back to work.

I walk down the street toward the subway. My stomach is growling from only eating a chili dog all day. My heart hurts from having clearly lost my big chance to play Robin. My head aches from wondering what to do about Thomas. I pull out my phone and text Andrew to see if he'll meet me at Union Square Café.

I get there before him and take a seat at a table by the window. Jimmy starts to clear the silverware and I tell him I'm expecting someone. You would've thought I told him I poop gold bricks.

"Good for you," he says with a big encouraging smile and takes time to polish Andrew's fork with his uniform. Jimmy thinks I'm lonely.

Andrew arrives thirty minutes after me. He looks different. It's not a haircut. It's something in his attitude. I'm not sure I like it.

"How'd it go?"

"I crushed it. They loved me. And I'm still probably twelfth on a list of ten."

He can see how disappointed I am. And that's why I texted him.

"I'm sorry. You're probably right. Don't tell yourself you shouldn't feel sad about it. Because wanting it so bad is part of what you need to go where you're going. What you were able to do today shows you're going there. And I'll bet very soon. It just takes one role. And maybe this wasn't the one."

What a lovely way to put it. He is back on my good-guy list.

Jimmy comes over and shakes Andrew's hand like he's meeting the fireman who rescued his cat from a tree. I'm not lonely or in need of rescuing! Jeesh, Jimmy.

I order my chicken Caesar without the chicken, dressing on the side, and wedges of lemon. Andrew adds something called a Maker's sour. He then orders two burgers and another Maker's sour for himself. I don't complain because I really enjoy the look that Jimmy gives me, which is: You're going to drink and expect me not to card you? I just smile, waiting for the inevitable carding. Which doesn't come. Probably because he's afraid he'll scare away my one and only dinner companion.

Once he is gone, I ask Andrew, "What is that drink you ordered and why in hell do you think I'm going to drink it?"

"It's my favorite drink, really strong, and we need to toast me with it and you need to take at least one tiny sip. Because we're celebrating."

"Anything in particular?"

"I broke up with Carmen."

Whoa. He's got that lopsided grin going on and he's drumming his hands on the table. I can't tell if he's genuinely that happy or pretending.

"Give me the details."

"I just had to do it. She was really shocked. I thought she was going to be angry and tell me all about how much better she can do, which she absolutely has and can. Instead, she got kind of teary and asked me for another chance."

"Why wouldn't you give her one?"

"Because I had a sudden burst of sanity. I only want to be with someone I actually love. Love has never happened to me. I guess I'm afraid it never will. But all of a sudden, I have this rock-solid conviction that I don't want to settle for less."

"Wow. Good for you. What made that happen?"

"You."

My stomach does a real flip on that, one I've never felt before. Is he maybe telling me something that would ruin the one and only true friendship I have? Channeling my top acting skills . . .

"How did I do that?" I smooth the napkin in my lap nervously.

"Because you are my favorite person. In the sense that I really like and admire you. And my advice to you will always be exactly that. Don't settle for less than love; you don't have to. And even if I don't like myself as much as I like you, I should. So I should follow my own advice."

That was a close one.

"That's the way of the universe," he says. "One door closes and another door opens."

Oops.

"Any particular doors?"

"Thomas, duh. How's that going?"

I tell him about Thomas offering to cook for me at his place and how I lied to get out of it. I ask him what's up with me? And he's flattered that I think he might know. I tell him that he's cheaper than Emma and that I will feel less constrained to kick his ass if I don't like the advice.

At this point, Jimmy arrives with the drinks.

"I hope you made mine a double," I tease with a straight face. Jimmy tells me that if he loses his job for this, my future acting career will be burdened with financially supporting him and his partner. "Fair enough," I say.

I lift my glass: "To finding the woman you belong to." He clicks my glass. I take a manly swallow and don't gag. It's actually pretty tasty.

"So what do you think, could Thomas be the man I belong to?"

He says nothing, just looks at me.

"Less suspense, more advice, please."

"Maybe you're asking me this question for a second time because you're hoping for a different answer."

"What's the answer I'm hoping for?"

"You want me to say no so you won't have to go through the scary part of finding out for yourself. Don't be. Whatever happens, you can handle it."

"Thanks," I say ironically.

"Stop that. Here's the one thing you can't handle, a compliment."

As I get into bed, I use Emma's book as a coaster for my glass of water. So Andrew thinks I should only date someone I'm in love with. And Emma thinks that falling in love will make me insane. But that kind of contradicts her other little theory that Sloane is the twin sister best friend I've never had and I'm such a lonely sad sack I had to create her. If I fell in love, I wouldn't be lonely. Not that I am. But how do you fall in love? Is it really something that conveniently "just happens" to you? Or is it something that you have to make happen, see your opportunity and don't let it get away? Even though I'm only just seventeen, I have this scary conviction that if it was going to happen, it would have happened already. I mean, it's even happened to Sloane. Even though I'm the only one who knows that.

The phone rings. I smile and all the heavy thoughts disappear. Maybe Andrew has a new list of compliments that I can pretend to disapprove of. I snatch up my phone and glance at the screen. Oh.

"Hey, beautiful. I didn't wake you up, did I?" Thomas is using his bedroom voice. He's channeling George Clooney a little. Cheesy, but at least it isn't Jonah Hill. "I'm just sitting here, thinking of the dinner I wish I made for us and hoping I'll get a chance tomorrow night. Or do you have another family thing?"

"Nope. I'm all yours." God. Why did I put it that way? Calling Dr. Freud . . .

"Can you do me just one favor before I let you go?"

"Maybe."

"Tell me you actually meant what you just said."

"I certainly didn't," I say, glad he can't see my stupid smile.

"I figured. See you tomorrow."

CHAPTER FOURTEEN

SLOANE

I stare out at my tree with a smile. The wind tousles her spring leaves. The morning sun warms her thick bark. Crocuses and daffodils decorate the grass around her roots. She's so lovely. Maybe we all look better in the spring. Maybe all the birds and bees going about doing their thing puts something in the air and that's why James asked me to go on a date tonight. Maybe I need to not think so much about the why and just let myself be excited about it.

"I have a date," I tell her through my window.

There's a knock on my door and I wonder if whoever it is could've possibly heard me. My dad asks if he can come in. When I turned twelve, he started knocking before coming in even though I didn't shut my door until I was almost fifteen. It's not like I sleep in the nude or anything, but it's sweet that he respects my privacy.

He sits on the edge of my bed and whispers in a very serious tone, "I want to give you a heads-up before you come downstairs.

Your mom is going to ask you to go out to dinner tonight. I want you to say yes. And I want you to be grateful and excited to have the opportunity to make things right with your mother."

It's obvious this was his idea and he probably had to talk my mom into it, convincing her I wouldn't chop her hand off yet again if she reached out one more time. I am both touched to have this chance with my mom and scared to turn James down.

Of course it's tonight. My dad coaches Max's soccer team and always takes them out for pizza. It's my mom's only free night each week. But what if I never get another chance with James? If I don't go out with him tonight, will that give him enough pause to realize I'm not worth the trouble of pursuing? The truth is, though, if I turn my mom down, I won't like me enough to want to date me, and I've got to live with me.

In homeroom I tell James about my command performance with my mom. He's a little more understanding than I wish he'd be. In fact, he thinks it's great that I'm going to get to hang with my mom. He clearly wasn't as excited about the date as I was. But then he mentions that he misses his mom. He studies my face and asks, "Are you disappointed?"

"Very much so," I tell him honestly.

"Me too. Want to do something on Friday?"

Friday! Big-league, actual date night. Wednesday is just like a school night hangout, but Friday is unquestionably a date. I'm high as a kite until we spill out into the crowded hall after homeroom. The sea of faces brings me back to reality. There's very little you can get away with in Mystic without everyone knowing about it. A Friday date is not one of those things. Which creates a problem for me and Amanda.

Mom takes me to sushi at Go Fish! in the Olde Mystic Village. Mystic being the epicenter of culinary delights like the lobster roll (roll being a Wonder Bread hot dog bun), there is one sushi place in town. Bringing me here was obviously an olive branch offering since I once told her I liked sushi. Choosing this place shows she wants this to be the beginning of something good between us, and every cell in my brain wants to make this work.

I actually haven't eaten a ton of raw fish. But through Maggie, I've seen some of the best New York has to offer. I've also seen what fresh wasabi and ginger look like, which is nothing like the neon green paste and the fluorescent pink shavings of sugary ginger they plop in front of us.

"So," I begin, "I could use a little advice about James."

"Are you guys actually dating?"

"No. But he asked me on one." She smiles and I can see she's genuinely excited for me, which is nice since she's the only person I've told.

"And you want to go, and you're allowed to go. So what's the problem?"

"You know Amanda Porcella. Well, she's let everyone think that they're dating because they used to. But they broke up a long time ago."

"How does she let everyone think they're dating?" my mom asks as she munches on some edamame.

"She never actually lies about it, but she knows that everyone thinks they're together. And she just lets them think that. The thing is, I really like Amanda. I don't want to hurt her feelings and I don't want everyone to hate me. If I go out with him, it'll look like she got dumped and I'm a home wrecker because she's never going to embarrass herself by fessing up that she isn't even dating him in the first place. So what do I do?"

She thinks for a minute. I like that about her since I'm the type that starts running my mouth well ahead of my brain. The sushi chef (believe it or not, a Caucasian female) hands us a yellowtail scallion roll and some toro sushi. My mom is a ninja with her chopsticks. She's a woman of many hidden talents, my mother.

"I think you tell Amanda what's happened. Don't tell him first, even if he promises to keep his mouth shut, because he won't. Don't ask for Amanda's permission, just give her a heads-up. Tell her that she probably doesn't realize it, but some of the kids think she's dating James, and you wanted her not to be blindsided. That keeps her dignity and gives her a chance to be prepared. More importantly, if James hasn't told you the absolute truth, that's his problem. And deserves to be."

I'm stunned. I mean, I've known her all my life. Duh. And I know she's no dummy. But that was a lot of clear thinking in one well-organized burst. She makes it sound so easy.

"You're right. That's what I should do. But what if he was lying to me, and they really are dating?"

"Would you really want to date someone like that?"

On the one hand, I should be talking to this woman more often. On the other hand, I don't want to hear any bad news about Sparrow Boy.

Dinner turns out to be really nice. We never talk about the past or why things have been so tough for us. We just genuinely have fun together. I know it doesn't mean that things are miraculously okay or that I won't wake up tomorrow angry again. But I'm grateful to be with her like this again.

I'm so nervous getting ready for bed. Maybe it'd be easier on Amanda if I called her. That way she won't have to guard her reaction, and she can yell or swear at me or hang up if she wants. Of course, it is easier for me in exactly the same way. Her number is in my phone.

Unbelievably, she answers. I may throw up. Or have a complete panic attack. I start talking to keep myself from hanging up on her.

I tell her exactly the way Mom had suggested. And then there's silence. Great. It's probably a dropped call and I'll have to say the whole thing over again and it will sound all rehearsed.

But then she tells me in a very calm and friendly voice, which sounds a little tight and fake, that it's so nice of me to give her the benefit of the doubt, but she is fully aware that everyone thinks she and James are dating. She never announced they aren't because she's hoping they will be again. "We're very close," she says almost as a warning.

She thanks me for giving her the heads-up and asks if she and I are good.

"Totally. I'm good. Are you good?" I wish my mom could have scripted a better answer for me.

She says, "Sure," unconvincingly.

Nonetheless I hang up feeling proud of myself for being such an adult (for a change). Of course Amanda is bummed. I can't blame her. But it's also not my job to take care of her. Getting over this hurdle feels like any remote possibility I may have with James is at least on the up-and-up.

The next day, Amanda isn't in school. I feel like a criminal. She's at home feeling ashamed and afraid and didn't know how she would ever face anybody again. Anyway, that's how I would feel. Supposedly she just has the flu. I'll never know the truth of it.

At lunch, James finds me. He just walks right into my little hen circle and sits down with his turkey grinder. Lila drools. Kelly eats her lasagna as if she's parked in front of the TV.

"So I'm thinking for Friday night, maybe we drive down to Providence to hear Eric Clapton. We'll probably be the youngest people there by twenty years."

I nod in agreement, like I'm in these conversations all the time. Beautiful boys ask me to Stones concerts, sometimes Yo-Yo Ma, whatever. No big deal.

"But he is the greatest guitarist ever. I worship him. Sorry, no flamenco on the program."

"You just don't want me to have anybody to compare you to," I say.

"In any way," he says right back.

Kelly laughs out loud. I worry for a minute that my virginal status is that obvious, like I literally walk around with a V patch on my sweater. But then, who cares?! He is definitely flirting with me. It's a shame they don't build lunch yards so you can take a victory lap.

After school, Kelly and I go shopping for something a little more sophisticated than what's in my closet. I tell her we're definitely not looking for a dress; that'd be trying too hard. I wind up buying a dress. I will try as hard as I can.

The dress is lavender, which makes my eyes look really green. It is sweet and wispy and reminds me of spring. I show it to my mom when I tell her about the date. She does the mom thing about what time I'll be home but is clearly really happy for me.

Gordy stops by and stays for dinner. During dessert, Mom asks whether I want to borrow her gold bangles for tomorrow night. The ones she got in college when she traveled to India that I've drooled over since I was a little girl playing dress up. Yes, I want to borrow them. And I also cannot believe she brought this up at dinner. The old flash of anger flares again. But Gordy simply asks where I'm going. So I simply answer. And he simply looks, frankly, jealous.

"Who's the lucky guy?"

If I had Maggie's acting skill, I would know how to answer immediately and casually. I don't.

"Just James."

"James and Sloaney sitting in a tree. K-I-S-S-I-N-G!" Max sings obnoxiously. As if there's any other way to sing that. Gordy laughs and stuffs his napkin in Max's piehole.

Gordy and I walk to the Marble after dinner and I successfully avoid talking about my date with James. We then head next door to the Mystic Disc and look through all the albums. I linger over Eric Clapton's section to try to buff up for Friday. Bill loved the Mystic Disc. He not only had a record player but insisted on still buying CDs, even though almost everything could be purchased instantly as MP3s. Bill always used to chat up Dan, the owner and local music aficionado, and have him order rare releases from overseas. They put a picture of Bill up behind the register after the accident. I don't come in here without Gordy. On our walk home, the silence between us feels unusually awkward.

I wake up on Friday and decide to wear my cute jeans and a purple blouse that people say makes my eyes look like cat eyes. When I walk into homeroom, James has saved me a seat, but his face looks off somehow.

"I feel so bad about this, but I have to drive down to Kennedy really early tomorrow to pick up someone around seven. Is it okay if we just grab a bite tonight and we'll do a concert another time soon?"

He seems so sorry. Things happen to cancel plans. It's not a big deal, I tell myself. But it is very strange, a high school boy driving to "Kennedy," which I realize a beat too slow means the airport in New York.

"Who are you picking up?" It doesn't even feel like prying, but just a natural thing to ask. But the second I do, I can see in his eyes that something is off and I shouldn't have asked.

"Just somebody."

Whoa. That basically makes my heart throw up. Now I don't know what to do, but I won't be able to function if I'm left totally in the dark like this.

"Is it some kind of secret?" Clearly it is.

"Just a friend."

"Is he from California?" I feel like I'm sinking. He doesn't look angry; he looks like of course I'm asking these questions and he just doesn't know what to do. In an ordinary person, that wouldn't seem so odd. But I never thought that there would be anything that could make James feel uneasy or awkward. He was perfect. And now he isn't.

"Look, I am so sorry about this. It's just something I said I'd do, but I promise I'll make it up to you. I thought maybe tonight, we could drive out to the Ocean House for dinner."

The Ocean House is far and away the most awesome date anyone could offer in this area. He is really trying. That's part of what's scaring me. Why is he trying so hard?

In sixth period, he comes in late and has to sit far away from me. He keeps looking at me and smiling. And it dawns on me. He feels guilty. Who is he picking up? Is it the girl who owned Peaches? Is she flying into New York to say that they are destined to be together and to whisk him back to California or worse, move to Mystic and take a little job somewhere? I'm sick to my stomach. And every lame smile he throws my way is just another nail in my coffin.

That night, I stare into my closet. I don't want to wear the dress. I want to save it for a better time. Or for a guy who really likes me. So I have to decide right there, was my mom right? Am I going to compete, with Amanda or Cat Girl or any number of girls who want his attention? Can I turn this around? It will take more than a dress.

And of course, Lila texts me like eight times to say, *Have a NICE time in Providence. And after.* Great. Kelly texts me, *Send a picture of you in the dress with* Slowhand!

My mom knocks on my door to bring me her bracelets. I'm standing there in my dress with the tags still on. She comes over, zips me up, and pulls off the tags. I guess I'm wearing the dress tonight. She says I look amazing, and instead of hating her for her Pollyanna attitude, I feel comforted. Looking in the mirror, I suppose it's about the best I can look.

"We're just going to the Ocean House for dinner."

"Just? Your father and I go there for our anniversary."

"No. It's really nice. It's just weird why he changed plans. He said he's driving three and a half hours to pick 'someone' up at JFK tomorrow morning. And he was extremely dodgy when I asked who." Then I just stare at her. I feel my lip tremble.

"It could be another girl. Or not. And normally, a girl should play it cool. But if he was really dodgy, which I guess means sneaky and secretive . . ."

I nod like I'm four years old, yup.

"You should tell him that you're wondering if there's another girl in the picture, and given the circumstances, that's a question you have the right to ask."

"Mom, if I have to ask that, I'll just die."

"I know, honey. I would too. But on balance, I think it's better than the alternative of not eating, sleeping, or thinking about anything else until you actually know. And maybe you need to ask yourself, how much is a guy worth who could put you through something like that?"

It's a fair question. When he picks me up, he's real chatty with my parents. They are their usual warm and welcoming selves. He compliments my dress and looks very admiring, but it still doesn't feel completely natural.

On the way out to Watch Hill, he talks too much, and all about our mutual interests rather than his interest in me or us. Maybe I can just get him to slow the car enough so that I can hurl myself from it with minimal pain.

The Ocean House is a Victorian hotel that was recently restored to its original splendor, crisp yellow and white paint and wraparound porches. It is perched above white sand dunes and the blue Atlantic. The third floor used to be haunted by a woman whose husband murdered her on their wedding night.

We pull into the valet parking circle, which wouldn't be a big deal to Maggie, but I've never been in a car parked by a valet before. The guy opens my door and treats me like I'm a celebrity or something.

But for San Francisco Cat Girl, already boarding her plane out west, this would be my Cinderella moment, a dream come true, filled with a fluttering heart wondering whether he has booked a room for us tonight and how I could play this off with my parents if I decided to accept.

They don't even have a dinner reservation for us. He says he called one in, but they never called him back to confirm. They are "fully committed" in the dinning room but offer us two seats in the bar.

The bar is really nice but provides only a glimpse of the elegant dining room, which has magical views of the ocean. Through the French doors, we can see the diners enjoying their soft candlelight and romantic conversations. It's like looking through the looking glass into a night that could have been. So although I have no right to be disappointed, I really am.

They bring us dinner menus and as he's looking at his, I just take my heart in my hands and ask him.

"I have to ask you something."

He looks up with a nice smile. "Sure."

"You seemed kind of mysterious about who you're picking up tomorrow in New York."

He doesn't say anything. But he also doesn't look nervous. He just waits.

"So I guess I'm wondering if it is the girl from San Francisco whose cat you gave to your sister."

He laughs. The laugh seems pretty natural. But I can't tell what's funny.

"I promise you that's not who I'm picking up." And says no more.

"Not that there'd be anything wrong with that," I lie. "I would have just wanted to know." I'm such a chicken.

"I'm glad you asked. I'm kind of feeling like the rib eye. What do you think?"

Throughout dinner he is perfectly nice and I pretend I'm fine. I can't taste my food and can only think about what a coward I am for not busting him on the obvious truth that all he had to do was tell me who he was picking up. I wish he'd just lie and tell me it's a distant uncle. It'd be kinder. I don't know why he asked me out in the first place.

The drive home is virtually silent. He makes a couple of attempts at more impersonal conversation, and I just sit there trying not to completely humiliate myself by crying.

At my door, he points to a greasy blotch on the skirt of my dress, his finger hovers above the fabric, he doesn't touch me.

"Looks like you spilled something," he says, and I want to cry.

He tells me he had a great time, which is obviously completely insincere. Then he tells me I look really pretty tonight, which may be sincere but is certainly beside the point. He makes no attempt to kiss me or even touch me. I tell myself I should be relieved by this, but it's the most crushing moment of all.

It's not even nine. Of course my mom is waiting, reading her book. She takes one look at my face and just gives me a big hug. I ask if it's okay if we don't talk about anything, and she says absolutely. I show her the spot on my dress and she tells me to take it off and she'll be able to get it out if she does it right away.

Up in my room, I slip into my jeans. I call Gordy and ask him to meet me at Maxwell's boatyard in twenty minutes. He's at a party and immediately asks what happened, am I okay. Nothing and no, I tell him. He says he has a six-pack, and he will meet me on my front porch in ten minutes.

He pulls up in his truck. I jump in. And before he can say anything, I tell him . . .

"He's just not the guy I thought he was. That's all. It's no big deal."

"So if I rearrange his face, you'd be mad at me."

"I'd be humiliated forever and would have to leave town."

He smiles and drives off.

"I'm thinking," he says, "it would almost be worth it."

It isn't the Ocean House, but we have a full view of the sound, Ram Island and Fishers, a few boats drifting on their moorings, and the stars above. More to the point, I'm not sitting on the edge of the dock with my lifelong best friend. I'm sitting with a really attractive guy who wants no other girl in the world but me.

"So Sloane," he says leaning back on the planks to look up at the night sky.

"So Gordy," I say joining him.

"Want to go to prom? With me? Seeing as how everyone else

sucks, I figure we're each other's only chance for a non-brutal evening. At least I know you won't grope me on the dance floor."

His casual act isn't fooling anyone, except hopefully himself. It is sweet and innocent and awkward. And I mean it when I say . . .

"That's a great idea. We're going to have the best time."

CHAPTER FIFTEEN

MAGGIE

I walk Jade up to the Y for her swim class on Saturday morning. Nicole is at a photo shoot but promises she'll be finished in time to collect her. I will stay nearby awaiting the inevitable call from Jerome that she is delayed. Which is fine. For some reason I love the smell of chlorine in Jade's hair. But the photo shoot better be finished by dinner. I can't give Thomas the same excuse tonight. Jade gives me the hairy eyeball when I tell her she and Nicole are on their own for dinner.

"You will find this shocking, but I have a date," I inform her.

"You have a boyfriend?" she asks, incredulous that I may have kept such big news from her. "Is it Andrew?!"

"No. He's neither a boyfriend nor Andrew . . ." I take a breath to say it's Thomas, but she eagerly interrupts.

"So Andrew is available?"

"Actually, yes. He's very available. He and Carmen broke up."

"Saw that coming," she says, and I can't help but laugh. I'm sure she just hears Nicole and me say things like that, but I love that she incorporates it into her seven-year-old vernacular. "I should probably call him, just to make sure he's okay." And she starts skipping, her backpack bouncing up and down as she goes. Jade is clearly pleased Andrew is available.

He apparently isn't available to answer his phone, however. After dropping Jade, I walk toward SoHo. Andrew isn't picking up or replying to my incessant texting. He is either in an area with no coverage or his phone is off because it's going straight to voicemail. This is odd.

I meander down his street. There's the GEM, so maybe he's just asleep. I could look at the names on the buzzer lists of the buildings nearby and try to wake him up. But what if he's not alone?

I have time to kill in case I need to turn around and pick Jade up, so I pull out my Kindle and just decide that this would be a perfect spot to read *The Girl with the Dragon Tattoo* even though I've never been interested in it before. I feel the best place to do so is this one particular spot where I can see the GEM very clearly, sort of hidden by this van I'm leaning against. Yes, some might call this spying. But chances that I'm actually going to see him are so slim, I don't think it really constitutes full-on spying so much as waiting to pick up Jade in a place that is odd to be waiting.

And then, just as the full craziness of my being here is making me think I need to call Emma, Andrew walks out of a building two doors down from where I'm standing. He is with a very slender and pretty and intelligent-looking young woman. At eight thirty in the morning. Coming from his apartment. They actually walk right past me. I face the van and pretend to be engrossed in my Kindle, which is turned off. She is *extremely* pretty, and I catch a whiff of lavender as she passes. She says something to him that I can't understand, but her voice is soft and musical, and she rests her tiny hand on his arm as she says it. His dorky crooked smile is pleased or amused or something. They get in his GEM and simply drive away.

So I call him. Again. This time it rings. I can see him pull out his phone as he drives down the street. He glances at the screen, turns a corner, and I'm positive that he's screening my call. But then he answers.

"What's up?" which sounds abrupt, as in "please state your business and get the hell off my line."

"Feel like some breakfast?" I pitch.

"Already had mine." Now unless the blonde simply came to his place to share breakfast at, say, seven o'clock, there is only one other explanation.

"I've got the morning free," I say, "feel like hanging?"

"Wish I could. I'll check in with you later. Everything all right?"

"Totally!" I say a little too positively.

And he hangs up on me. What pops directly into my mind is whether he picked this skank up at Kennedy at seven in the morning—what James had told Sloane in the dream. My God. Maybe I am going crazy.

Of course, the real question is, why do I care? I resist the urge to manipulate Jade into actually calling Andrew when I pick her up from swimming. I ask myself "why do I care?" all day and into the evening, even while dressing for dinner with Thomas. Andrew never checks in with me later, and as far as I'm concerned, he can stick his future checking-ins where the sun will never find them.

First I put on matching bra and underwear. Not that anyone is going to see it, but if they do, they'll be impressed. I then go with a pair of my skinny jeans that make my butt look great, which is always a consideration because it needs just the right pocket and fit. For a top, I choose a Chloe peasant blouse I stole from the *Elle* closet. Thomas is the type of guy who might notice a designer piece. Shoes are the big debate: if I go for a python pump, they'll be classy and easy to kick off. Knee-high leather boots would look better, but they'll just be hard to take off. I mean, not that he'll be taking my boots or anything off, but he might be the kind of guy who likes you to be barefoot in his house. I go with the pumps because as Andrew (whoever he used to be) observed, I can handle the situation.

Thomas lives at 27 West 67th in a prewar building with a charming doorman who has to bring me up in the old cage elevator. This place is posh. Hard to square with Andrew's "flunky" handle, but I'm starting to learn that maybe certain statements from that source cannot be relied on. Not that he ever said specifically that he didn't dump Carmen for that scrawny blonde, who probably isn't nearly as intellectual as she looks (being an actress, and insecure, I believe against conventional wisdom that someone can actually look intelligent or intellectual). Anyway, what he had said was that he'd never been in love before and wouldn't settle for anything less. Which means there's a lie in there somewhere. Unless, of course, between Union Square Café and breakfast at his place, he met his potential soul mate, who really could use a little touch-up on her roots.

Thomas welcomes me into an apartment far more impressive

than even the building suggests. The brick ceilings are high and domed. The views are amazing; there is art everywhere. He catches me gawking and explains that the place belongs to his dad, who lives in Toronto, and even though it's far from his office, free rent is nice. I like that he's not trying to impress me and notice that he took some care to look his best. Which I also like. Certain other young men of my acquaintance have never done anything of the sort. Not that he should have.

He announces that he's making linguini with white Alba truffles. I know enough to know that those things are exactly a bazillion bucks a pound and are intoxicatingly yummy.

In the bathroom, I check for hair product (maybe the CIA needs me and my spying abilities). Unfortunately, I find plenty. Not that there's anything wrong with that. At least I don't find any blond dye; that could be a deal breaker. As if there's a deal to break. Which there definitely isn't. At this point.

He opens a bottle of his dad's fancy wine. It tastes really good and makes me feel warm and flush. He tells me I can drink up because there's a second bottle of the same wine, which he already opened. I feel a bit like that's a red flag, but I push the thought away.

He sets a cheese tray by the plushy couch, assuring me that while he prefers blue, these are "double cremes" that won't mask the taste of the wine. I'm sure Andrew wouldn't know what the hell he's talking about. I don't either, but I am here and he isn't. I kick off my pumps. I love cheese.

Thomas mentions casually that there will be three or four callbacks among the several (though unnumbered) women who are auditioning for Robin. He is "working on it." Well, he's certainly working on something.

On the bookshelf, there's an adorable picture of him with a five-year-old's version of the Hair. His mom is quite beautiful, duh, and seems very adoring. When I compliment her, he tells me that she passed away from breast cancer when he was nine. This brings tears to my eyes, and I tell him the story of my dad. He is only the second (and certainly nicest) boy that I have ever discussed my dad's death with. He really listens, and it's nice to share it with someone who understands. I don't know any other kids who have lost a parent. Not that Thomas is a kid, I suppose. My mom tried to get me to join a teen support group. I went once. Having a dead parent be the only thing I had in common with those kids just made me feel lonely.

Dinner begins with a salad that he overdressed (guys do that a lot). He made garlic bread, which is about the last thing anybody would want to eat if they are thinking of kissing someone. The table is set beautifully; there's a crystal vase with peonies, which happen to be my favorite flower. He is trying hard, as whatshisname once noted, and I like it. Especially tonight.

It's easy to make a case for Thomas. He's easy on the eyes, he's easy to be with, he promises an easy life. What's there even to debate? Well, how fast and how far to go with all this, of course, being barely seventeen and even more cautious realizing that I am basically (expensively) drunk.

Just as I reach this point in my rigged debate, a strong and confident hand reaches a plate down in front of me. The aroma of white truffles mixes with the alcohol in my system and the positive energy of my thoughts, so that when that masculine hand strokes the hair from my neck and begins massaging my shoulders, I realize something. Old Andrew is right about one thing. I do know how to handle this.

I wrap my fingers around his wrist, excited by how slender and delicate they look against his musculature. I only have to pull very slightly, and his mouth comes to mine, and I rise half out of my seat, twisting my body into a full, openmouthed, committed kiss that sends a definite (though slightly blurry) thrill through pretty much all of me.

He lifts me up, and I wrap my legs around his waist, pulling him closer. He rests me down on the table and starts to kiss my neck as his hands work the buttons of my peasant blouse. I weave my hands through his gorgeously thick hair. All of this feels good and exciting until, without really knowing why . . .

I push him away. Gently at first, and so he understandably feels it isn't a serious move but just me being playful. So I push him away harder and he stops. "I'm sorry," I tell him. And only then do I understand why.

"No, I'm so sorry, Maggie. Are you sure you're okay? I'm so sorry, I didn't mean to pressure you or make you feel uncomfortable or force myself on you . . ." He keeps a respectful distance between us and keeps apologizing, clearly worried that he pushed a young girl into the deep end.

"I'm the one who kissed you, Thomas," I remind him.

"And I took it further and faster than you were ready for. I want you to set the pace for us, Maggie. I have to keep reminding myself that you are much younger than you seem. I want you to take as much time as you need to figure out what you want. I'll be here. And whatever you decide, I promise it will have no relevance on your chances for Robin." Right.

I rebutton my shirt and pull my pumps back on as easily as I'd kicked them off. Thirty minutes later I ring the bell at Andrew's door. I don't really care if the little blond skank answers in a teddy or less. In fact, I don't really care about anything but seeing him right now.

The door opens. He's alone. So I don't even try to hide what I'm feeling. He looks sad and sympathetic and angry, and he gives me a big hug. I feel like a little girl. Which is what I am.

"What did he do to you?"

I tell him that Thomas was wonderful and didn't do anything wrong. I just picked the worst (but necessary) moment possible to remember Andrew's advice that it'd be wrong for me to settle for anything less than love.

At this point, he has one brotherly arm around my shoulders and invites me in. I freeze, and his surprise makes me ask to make sure he's alone. He doesn't understand why I'm asking.

"I told you Carmen and I broke up."

I don't have it in me to act my way out of this one.

"I saw you driving around with this very pretty blond girl."

He looks at me with his lopsided smile. "If I was driving someone around in my car, why would they necessarily be in my apartment at eleven o'clock tonight?"

Throwing all self-respect into the gutter, I say, "Because before she got into the GEM with you, she came out of your apartment at eight o'clock in the morning."

My mind floods with all the humiliating questions about how I could know something like that. But instead of asking them and instead of wearing a face that would hurt my feelings, he says . . .

"You're just having a really bad night. The person you're talking about is Cassie. She's my sister-in-law. She got into a horrible fight with my brother. And we're close, so she came over late and crashed. And then I spent half the day telling my idiot brother what an asshole he is and how lucky he is to be with someone who really loves him."

I stare in his eyes. "You should really charge for this stuff. Putting broken girls back together."

"You're not broken," Andrew tells me. If only he knew the half of it. Or the other half of me, as it were.

So we sit in his kitchen, and he makes me hot chocolate and we pitch mini-marshmallows into our mugs as we talk. He wants to know how I left things with Thomas, and I tell him that things aren't terrible. Thomas simply figures that being younger than I look, I got in over my head a little and need more time to figure out what I want. It would've been incredibly rude of me, not to mention courageous, to have told him that I already knew. So I didn't. I'm also worried once I tell him that, despite all his perfectness, I don't want to date him, my chances for Robin will go from slim to none. I'd like to believe he's genuine in his assurance that whether we date or not won't affect business. He's a good person. Andrew reminds me that ultimately it's not Thomas's decision who gets the role either way.

We talk for about an hour. He makes me bacon and eggs since I dashed out of Thomas's before dinner.

"You never asked why I was staking out your apartment when I saw Cassie and you this morning."

"And I'm not going to."

"Here's why. I had a dream last night. In this dream, I was sort of me, but my name was something else. I was just starting to date some guy in my high school, and he had to get up in the middle of the night to pick up some once-and-future girlfriend at the airport."

He stares at me. He's a terrific listener. So I tell him that this dream does not explain in any logical way why I was drawn to spy on him. But it is the reason.

"And I guess because the boy in my dream lied to me, it made me doubt how wonderful he was. And maybe I thought if you were lying about Carmen, it would mean that you weren't as terrific as I need you to be."

"Why do you need me to be terrific?"

"Because I need someone to be terrific. And you are, and you're very important to me."

"But this guy in your dream, that was like a boyfriend."

"Yeah. The dream is always different from my life. The same in some ways and modified and twisted and different."

"The dream."

I simply make one of the real threshold decisions of my life. "It's a dream I have every night. Every night since forever. It's never the same dream; it's the same alternate life."

I've said the words out loud. He is stunned by them. The second hand on the clock on the wall seems to move faster and the words tumble from my lips as I explain.

"Yes, alternate life. That's what it is. My name is Sloane, which is actually my real first name. I live in a little town called Mystic, Connecticut, where I have actually only been twice. I go to high school. I get to be blond and have actual breasts . . ."

He laughs in a very nice way, which helps me feel brave enough to continue.

"My father is alive there and very nice, though not my best friend like my dad was. I have no sister and two brothers. My mom there is the opposite of Nicole. We are close, but there's a huge anger thing in my heart toward her that I don't really understand. At least not there, I don't."

"But you understand it here?"

"I think I do. We can't read each other's minds."

"What do you mean 'we'?"

I take a deep breath. "This is the really hard part. This is the part where you learn how crazy I am and you'll have to decide if you're still going to be my friend."

"I already decided. And I already know you're crazy. And you can stop talking about this right now if you want."

"Here's what 'we' means. Every night, I dream about her life in Mystic. And when she falls asleep in Mystic, she dreams the whole day I live here in New York. And I think I'm real and she's my fantasy . . ."

"And she thinks the same?"

I'm too afraid to speak. The kitchen falls silent. I can hear the tick-tick of the clock on the wall.

"But you know the difference, right? I mean, you know you're real. If you weren't, I wouldn't be either, or Jade, or your dad, or everyone out there on the street right now. Right?"

I nod. And I quietly say, "That's what Sloane thinks too."

He smiles. "Only a storyteller like you could come up with something like this. Amazing."

I start to cry. He thinks it's a story. The truth of this is far more than insane. It separates me from everyone and everything. Anyone, who isn't my shrink, I tell this to will never really love me or be close to me.

Because of my tears, I can see in his face that he realizes this is actually true. And I am a freak. And this makes me cry harder, so that he comes over and hugs me tight to calm me down. But I know when he lets go, he and I will never be the same.

CHAPTER SIXTEEN

SLOANE

I wake up feeling utterly betrayed. Even if James never liked me the way I wish he'd liked me and I misread his actions and words as flirtatious, he must like me enough to want to be my friend. Why lie about this airport run? I guess he didn't lie so much as omit. Which leaves my mind to do horrible imagining. If it is an uncle or a guy friend, he'd just say it. It has to be some girl and he realized I have an enormous crush on him and he knew that telling me that would be devastating.

And I strangely feel betrayed by Maggie. We share the world's weirdest secret and she goes and blabs it to Andrew, what, to try to impress him or something? She obviously wants him to want her, even though she'd run like crazy if he did. Just like she ran like crazy from Thomas. Andrew has had plenty of opportunities and hasn't taken them. Showing up on his doorstep crying and spilling a sacred secret just seems desperate.

I would never tell anyone about us. Especially not a boy I wish liked me. I feel a tremendous ache to tell James everything else in my heart and soul and mind. Except Maggie.

I roll on my side to stare at my tree and see a star on my pillow. A fallen star. Looking up, I can tell it has fallen from the Field of Wildflowers, a constellation to the left of Delicioso, where all the great sky beings go to make wishes. I guess I should make a wish.

I suddenly feel inspired by Maggie's spying. I jump into jeans and a T-shirt, ones that fit pretty tight and great just in case he blows my cover. I take the time to coat my lashes with some mascara because he's an eyelash guy and all. Skip breakfast entirely, sneak out of the house undetected, and ride my bike down to James's house, throwing caution to the wind and leaving my life-sustaining helmet at home. A fatal head injury might be just the thing, particularly just outside his front yard, where he and his strumpet (Shakespeare for "slut") will drive by my mangled body in his stupid Targa, having to swerve wildly to avoid treating me as roadkill, only to jump from the car, run to my side, tears on his face as he desperately feels for my pulse, lifts me in his strong arms as if I were weightless, and turns to her and announces that I'm the one he really loves.

Sounds like a plan.

He isn't home. Nor does he come home during the nearly three hours that I sit behind that stupid tree, playing Fruit Ninja on my iPhone. Every time a car drives by, I lie flat on the ground so they can't see me from the road. Mystic is a small town. Not sure how I'd explain what I'm doing here.

Once I'd been at a keg party at Esker Point, basically just a bunch of kids from school sitting on the beach, drinking bad beer out of red plastic cups, your average rite of passage, and I responsibly walked home instead of getting a ride from Joe Stevens, who definitely had done at least one keg stand. The next morning our neighbor Mrs. Lamb came over to borrow some eggs and mentioned in front of my mom and dad that she'd seen me walking down by Beebee Cove. "Can't get away with anything in this town," she said, and winked. Luckily she made no reference to the fact that I most certainly had appeared inebriated.

Since my phone is running out of batteries and I'm losing my mind, I give up on my stakeout and hop on my trusty Schwinn. I take Marsh Road and bike through Noank, the little village right next to Mystic. I pass by the park and Carson's General Store, where I'd usually stop for an ice cream soda. Instead, I pedal as fast as I can and fly down the big hill toward the town dock. The water is sparkling out before me. If my brakes give out or if I was very adventurous, I could fly straight off the dock and into the mouth of the Mystic River. But I turn left at the last minute and coast onto Front Street. Right past Bill's house.

His family lives in the prettiest house. They moved to town when I was twelve. It is a green house, set back from the road with big gorgeous trees protecting it. The rolling lawn in front spills down to the water. As I coast by, I can see the corner window of Bill's room. The shades are open and I wonder what it looks like now, if they've turned it into a sewing room or an extra bedroom. Or if they left it just as it was.

I bike on, heading toward home. When I get downtown, I decide to head over the drawbridge and go visit Kelly. She works at Kitchen Little on Saturdays, which is the best breakfast spot in town. I get there just before she gets off at one. Neither of us has eaten all day, so she convinces the cook to make us Portuguese sweet muffins covered in hash and fried eggs. Of course, I can't eat a bite. Of course, she notices. We sit on the patio. Kelly takes the river view, leaving me staring out at traffic on Route 27.

She assumes I've come by to discuss last night's concert in Providence. I spend the next three minutes telling her what actually happened in one breath so I can get it over with. Although Lila is my friend from earliest childhood, she would've been a terrible choice for this moment because her idea of making me feel better would be to join me in a bitch fest against the pig who crushed my soul. I love Kelly because her insight into making me feel better is to walk me back from my completely uninformed and paranoid conclusion.

"Why in the world would he lead you on if he had a girlfriend? So that he could get some action until she showed up? He absolutely has Amanda available for that duty. More to the point, and I don't know him at all, but I feel like even if he may be a little bit in love with himself, he's basically a trustworthy guy. He doesn't seem like he'd hurt someone recklessly for no reason."

"You told me you didn't like him."

"I still don't. I think he's honorable, and he's certainly foxy, but like you originally said, I don't think he'll ever give his heart to anyone, and I'm sorry to say that includes you."

Her words have barely died away in the afternoon air when directly into my vision, braking to a stop at the light on Route 27, is an old red Targa. The woman in the seat beside him, touching his arm as she leans to speak in his ear, is not only stunning enough to put Amanda Porcella in the shade, exotic/intriguing enough to put

Angelina Jolie in the shade, she is clearly old enough to have her own apartment, big enough for a cat and a gorgeous boyfriend.

It doesn't feel real. And yet my shattered heart feels too sharp for it not to be real. I am completely ruined with grief and humiliated by my longing.

The light changes, and they simply drive away. It's true, you can't get away with anything in this town.

"You okay?" Kelly's back is to the road.

I take too many deep breaths.

"What is it? Come on, give."

"What if you're wrong? What if he has a girlfriend?"

Kelly looks at me strangely. "I don't understand the question. If he has a girlfriend, she wins, you lose, and the guy you lost is a lying d-bag."

"What if he's a lying d-bag who I can never get out of my heart?"

"That stuff is bullshit. You cry yourself to sleep. I give you tough love, Lila conspires to cut his jewels off, your mom tells you it's a teachable moment, you either have the good sense to run to Gordy or feel bad until freshman year at Columbia when twenty spectacular guys do amazing cartwheels to get your attention. Bitch, he ain't that cute."

The only thing she's wrong about is the last part.

Kelly and I hang out all afternoon so I won't be alone. We hike through Haley Farm all the way along the tracks to Bluff Point and sit up on the warm rocks looking out at the sound. She lets me think my thoughts without interruption. What comes clearly in focus is that I am even more obsessed with this boy. Does that mean I'm in love? What does it even mean to be in love? Is it the same thing as just being hypnotized, and mooning and irrational? I know that's not what I want love to be. I don't want to be in love with someone who is not in love with me back. It feels much better to be loved back.

It's bad enough not to get the thing I want. It's much worse to not know how to stop wanting it.

I lie to my folks and say that I'm grabbing a bite with the girls. Mom makes me feel extra bad by saying it's a great idea. But I don't really want to be with anyone, so I just wander all over alone. I wind up back in Noank at the park on the swing and just swing on that swing for what seems like hours, feeling more sorry for myself than Hedda Gabler or Ophelia or any other tragic heroine.

When I walk back up my street around ten, he's there. He. As in James. He is there alone sitting in his car in front of the house. He jumps out of the car, practically runs to me up the street, and stands there looking so awkward and unhappy that it makes me feel happy and vindicated. He feels guilty and came to confess and let me down face-to-face. And at least that means I'm important enough not to be kicked to the curb without a decent explanation.

I just stand there, saying nothing, determined not to show any weakness or desperation. He tells me that he knocked on our door two hours ago and my dad said I was out. So he waited because he has something important to tell me.

"Right here in the street?"

"I lied to you."

"Really? About what?"

"The person I picked up in New York is someone I used to be

201

with. I want to tell you everything about it, but only if you want to hear."

Unfortunately, my eyes completely flood with tears. I don't want to wipe them away or let them fall, so I just say, "Some other time." And walk quickly past him.

He grabs my arm before I can get by. "Please," he says, "please let me explain."

I guess I want to hear this so badly, I do the ridiculous and say, "Okay. Just make it quick." And brush the tears from my eyes as casually and absently as I can manage.

"There was no cat girl in San Francisco. That's why I laughed when you asked. I didn't want to tell you about who she really is, so I lied by omission. I should've explained it to you at the Ocean House. Her name is Caroline. She's two years older than I am; she's a sophomore at Northwestern. We met two summers ago in Paris when I was bumming around on my father's dime, just after Outward Bound."

"Meaning just after Amanda."

"That's right. I told you I met someone. She was taking a summer course at the Sorbonne, and we wound up living together in her little one-room place with Peaches."

"So why did she fly here to see you? And why was it such a secret?"

He looks down at the ground, as if getting up the nerve to tell me the truth. "I was pretty crazy about her. I thought I was in love, but I was definitely obsessed. When she dumped me, it hurt worse than anything I thought could ever hurt me. And for two years, I thought about her pretty much every day. Until . . ."

His voice becomes so quiet I can barely hear him.

"Until you."

I have no idea what he means, but my heart is racing as if somehow it could mean what I know it can't possibly mean.

"What's that supposed to mean?"

"It means, even though I didn't know you, and I still don't, this is the first time in two years that I wanted to be with someone other than Caroline. And I wasn't sure that would ever happen. So I kept my mouth shut for a while, to see if the feeling went away. And it just got stronger and stronger."

"So strong that you brought your ex-girlfriend out here to parade around town."

He just blinks.

"I saw you guys in the car on Route 27. She was wearing a striped sweater and big sunglasses. She's very pretty. Congratulations."

"Sloane, this is what happened and what you really saw. She called me out of the blue Thursday night. She said she'd been an idiot to break up with me; she was flying into New York on the red-eye just to see if we could make it work."

"And obviously, you told her you were crazy about this new girl and she was simply too late."

"I told her there was someone new. She asked if she could just come and talk to me. And I said yes. And I said it because I didn't know how I'd feel when I saw her. I mean, you're a normal person, you can't imagine what it's like to have been obsessed with someone, believing they are the key to your happiness, knowing that they will never want you, and all of a sudden hearing that they do."

Of course I know exactly what he means, and I know whatever the outcome of this story, I can never hate him for this.

"All the way to the airport, I was thinking about how I treated you last night."

"And how was that?"

"Like I had something else on my mind. Which I did. And I didn't know what was going to happen."

"So what happened? Where is she?"

"She got off the plane, there was one kiss, and I knew. I knew that I had been a stupid punk who had talked himself into some big tragic romance because a pretty girl had dumped him for the first time. And I knew that the girl who I really wanted to be with was probably hating me for being an asshole, and I couldn't believe that I'd blown it. And there I was with Caroline."

He waits for me to say something, but I don't.

"So. We had the awful, awkward day of my telling her that this wouldn't work and hoping that she was feeling the same."

"Did she?"

"Do you really care?"

"If you're saying that you want us to start over, then I don't care about anything else."

He looks so relieved and so happy. He actually didn't know how this would turn out. He doesn't know how much I want him to be mine.

Then he slides his arms around me and gives me a kiss so soft and so beautiful that I know I'll remember it forever.

He wants to go somewhere so we can talk. If only I was Maggie or Caroline and not a high school junior living at home, but since I'm already late for curfew and don't want to be grounded, I tear myself away. He walks me to my door. There is one more kiss, which is long and deep and completely thrilling. Then I'm inside, my house is still standing, the world is still spinning, and James Waters belongs to me.

It takes a while to fall asleep. I stare up at the constellations glowing above me. The Field of Wildflowers, missing my wish star. I have a boyfriend. He is going to call me, and be excited to see me, and hold my hand, and we'll make out, and every future in the world is possible.

Everything I thought about James this morning has been absolutely turned upside down. Except for one thing. Nothing on this earth or in heaven above will ever make me tell him that I am insane.

CHAPTER SEVENTEEN

MAGGIE

I wake up on Andrew's couch, snuggled in the down comforter that he took from his bed and placed over me while I slept. To a normal person, this wouldn't be a terrifying realization, but my stomach turns into a block of ice. What if he had woken me up in the middle of the night? What would have happened? I know the answer in a split second, and I know that Emma would be smirking triumphantly when she came to the same conclusion. If I were to be awakened in the middle of the night, Sloane's day would disappear, and there would no longer be the luxury of sort of pretending both lives exist. I would know that Sloane is simply a character I'm making up, like any stranger on the street.

Emma would say, of course I've always known this. And I have. But the big thing she misses is that the thrill of it is the ability to almost forget that I know it. To 90 percent believe that I can be two different people in two different places with two different lives. And as much as Emma denies it, I believe in my heart that anyone would do the same if they could.

Andrew's one-bedroom apartment is impeccably neat with thoughtful pieces of furniture he obviously put effort into finding. It's not your average nineteen-year-old's college dorm room with IKEA bookshelves and a ratty couch. He's clearly decorated the space on a budget, but rather than spending $129 on a flimsy Swedish bookcase you put together with an Allen key, he made one from rough planks of wood and glass blocks. Like all directors, he pays attention to detail: the books are organized by subject in a visually pleasing way.

He walks into the living room and sits on the couch, his body actually touching mine through the comforter.

"How did you sleep?" A loaded question.

"Sloane had the best day, if that's what you're asking."

"Details."

I take a breath. This is the Pandora's box I opened. Now he's going to be constantly interested in Sloane, and I will be defined by my craziness and he won't be interested in just me anymore.

"She is beyond ecstatic because the boy—"

"Wasn't cheating on her after all?"

"He was, sort of, but he dumped the other girl because he's in love with Sloane. Or at least really into her."

"So you're creating a situation where the guy who represents Thomas turns out to be a good guy after all so you can work it all through in a dream."

"First of all, one shrink is bad enough. Second, Thomas is absolutely nothing like James, and it doesn't work that way. I don't control Sloane's life. I just watch it. And the people who inhabit her world don't have anything to do with anyone in the real world. Or I should say, in my world."

He smiles. "No, you should say 'in the real world.' The only thing wrong with all of this is if you start to get confused."

I sigh. "That's the fun of it. To see how close I can come to believing she's real and not actually me at all. Otherwise, it's just like a story I'm writing."

"So what does your shrink say? Does he think that's a dangerous game?"

"*She* thinks it's dangerous. She thinks I could go truly crazy. Which I must be to be telling all this to you."

He strokes my arm, still through the comforter. "I'm honored you shared it with me. And I'm sorry if I'm prying. We can talk about this never, or always, or whenever you need to. I mean 24/7. Really."

He tells me that he doesn't want to know what I want for breakfast because what he is going to make me would be better. Andrew grew up on the Upper East Side. His parents divorced when he was eleven, and Andrew moved to Long Island with his mom while his brother, Todd, stayed with his dad. His mom is apparently an amazing cook, and Andrew always loved being in the kitchen with her. He proudly shows off a binder full of recipes they created together. Complete with photos of the dish and some shots of Andrew eating. His smile has always been like that.

He makes little pizzas with fresh buffalo mozzarella on top of English muffins topped with fried eggs. Then he sautés prosciutto with garlic and porcini mushrooms. I almost lose consciousness it is so delicious.

As we are eating, I get a text from Thomas. He hopes I'm okay and apologizes again for last night, as if he did something wrong, which he didn't. It is pretty sweet. I immediately get a second text (thereby separating business from business) apologizing for the late notice (forty-five minutes), but I need to get my scrawny butt down to a rehearsal stage because some actress they were flying in from LA missed her flight and Thomas has persuaded Macauley to give me a shot at a scene with Ryan O'Donnell, who has been cast as the male lead in *Innuendo*.

I just stare at the screen, having a total brain melt. But when I tell Andrew what's up, he swings into action. Pulls me out of the chair, throws me toward the bathroom, telling me Carmen left makeup in there. He irons my shirt. Seriously. He even pulls a full-size ironing board from the depths of his closet.

We jump into the GEM. "You realize, of course, I'm wearing my walk of shame clothes, and Thomas will see them. And it will be over between us."

"Okay. What exactly will be over between you? The not-having-a-relationship part? Or did he send you a text that made you fall in love?"

I have to smile. "Well, his text was pretty sweet."

"Concentrate. How well do you know this scene?"

"That's hard to answer. Since I have absolutely no idea what scene they want."

"Excellent," he says. "They will know this, and it will be easier for you to exceed their expectations."

He weaves through traffic at what seems like three hundred miles an hour (the GEM tops out at a maniacal thirty-five), defying all traffic rules, and occasionally gravity.

"Just one question," I say. "Is there anything I could say that you would interpret as bad news?"

"Absolutely not. Positive! Energy up! Confidence, confidence, confidence. You are going to absolutely blow this guy away; he's gonna can Blake Lively and you'll get the first lead."

He drops me off at the place, and I tell him there is no way I can do this without him. He is clearly delighted. As we sprint through the lobby, he is inspired. "We'll tell them I'm your dialect coach from a workshop at NYU!"

"Brilliant!" I exclaim.

Thomas isn't buying it. He looks at Andrew (who despite being very tall does not look older than his nineteen years) and my clothes from the night before and draws a logical conclusion. At first, I think this means he'll never speak to me again, after burying me with Macauley behind my back. But it eventually becomes evident that this has only fired up his competitive instincts; he's certain that he can mop the floor with this nobody. I leave them to compare whose bicep is bigger.

The PA hustles me into a makeshift wardrobe room and puts me into a nightgown, which is basically see-through. I feel a little weird about it, but I want this role so much that I try not to care. She insists I take off my bra and offers Nippies (which are every bit as repulsive as they sound). Then we argue over my underwear. The best she offers is a nude-colored thong, because if my butt isn't bare, they won't even do the scene. I steady myself and tell her to ask the director to come in so that I can discuss this with him. She gives me a look that means I'm not only risking her job, but that she will personally make it her life's work to ruin me.

"Fine," I say, "I'll go ask him myself."

The PA disappears. Macauley knocks on the door. When he comes in, he apologizes for Cheryl's behavior, tells me that of course I can wear my underpants, and asks if I'm comfortable without my bra. I lie and say that I am. I would not be truly comfortable with this even if I didn't personally know two of the guys watching the audition. More than the embarrassment that Thomas was fondling my bra strap last night, I'm so sorry that I invited Andrew to this rodeo.

Macauley then goes over the sides with me. It is a scene I know well, and it is pretty sexy. I have to hug the outrageously gorgeous Ryan from behind, nuzzle his ear, and sort of use my body to convince him to do what Robin wants him to do. He will then turn, kiss me, I will get incredibly turned on, he will tell me how beautiful I am, bury his hands in my hair, and that's it. Nothing terribly intrusive, except for the way I'm not dressed.

I tell Macauley that I understand why he chose this scene. The dialogue reveals the complexity of Robin's apparent desire being only a cover for her taking revenge on Blake Lively's character, but in a subtle enough way that the viewer will only realize this in retrospect.

Macauley nods like he appreciates I actually have a brain, but we are really all here to judge my ass. He is honest enough to say that the wardrobe choice is because he needs to see if we are physically right together on camera. Which means, can I play hot enough for the role. Which also means that I will have to really work it.

Quite an experience. Naked, in the arms of a godlike beautiful twenty-five-year-old man with a twelve-pack, while my once-and-possibly-future boyfriend watches alongside my platonic-friend-you-could-cut-the-sexual-tension-with-a-knife.

I have to get into Robin's sexuality, which is hard for me because I need to make it just manipulative enough to show a hint of hidden agenda while being totally hot on the surface. And, let's face it, I'm still fumbling through my own sexuality. Someone might ask if it's a turn-on to have Ryan's hands on my body. Sure. But at the same time, I don't have to think about where this is going or what is going to happen between us, so my mind is on my performance while my hormones are on autopilot.

Thomas thinks I'm wonderful, and very sexy. And tells me that was the biggest question to be answered in Macauley's mind. When we are alone back in wardrobe, Thomas asks if we are okay. I tell him, of course, and that all the apologies were on my end. He kisses me very sweetly and tells me we can take it as slow as I need to.

Then he gives me the grand inquisition about who is Andrew, how long has he been my dialect coach, what are his credentials, why have I never mentioned him, and why am I in last night's clothes.

I lie. Like a Persian rug.

Andrew is a friend of the family, who used me once for a student film, where he coached me on my Inuit accent. We became friends, and he needs me to see him through his breakup with a Latin bombshell. As to the clothes, I point out to Thomas that he gave me thirteen seconds notice, and I made the snap decision that last night's clothes were the best outfit to present myself to Macauley, all things considered. And by the way, what the hell is he implying? That I slept with Andrew last night?

He laughs and answers my lies with one of his own. That's the last thing on his mind.

This settled, he leaves my dressing room, Macauley enters, gives me an enthusiastic hug, and tells me I was nothing short of perfect. He thanks me for coming in and tells me that the role is now between me and the girl from LA, whom he still will have to read because he committed to her agent. I can't believe it. I feel giddy. And so grateful to Thomas for making this happen.

As Andrew and I are leaving, a male voice calls my name. I turn to see Ryan hurrying toward me in a shirt unbuttoned down to his pants. He looks too good to eat. An innocent smile lights his face as he takes both of my hands in his.

"Mags, you were magical. Where have you been? I mean did you feel it too?" He stares deep in my eyes.

"The gentleman asked you a question," says Andrew in a pleasant and neutral voice.

So gazing into Ryan's eyes with the required "I would do you right here on the floor" look, I say, "My God, I so did. All I've been wondering was whether you felt it too."

"How could you doubt it? I've been talking to Macauley and telling him that you can't waste chemistry like this. The show deserves it."

"Well." I smile. "Anything for the show."

"Mags. I want you. To work with me."

Andrew and I skip downstairs.

Doing a reasonable imitation of Ryan's voice, Andrew waggles his eyebrows: "Mags. I want you. To have sex with me. So that you'll think I'm getting Macauley to give you a role, but I'm also having sex with five other actresses, promising them the same thing."

"Hey. At least I'd get to have sex with him."

That stops him cold. It also reveals that he is utterly and over-whelmingly jealous. I love, love, love that.

He has schoolwork and a life to deal with. I promised Jade that she could pick a matinee, so of course she picks the debut feature of some chick from the Disney Channel who has yet to become a star, develop any discernible talent, or go to rehab. Although the film sucks and is completely cringe worthy, Jade loves it. To the point where she nearly loses my respect. She does bust me on humming along to one of the power ballads.

Afterward, she asks if we can have dinner with Andrew. I say, "Andrew who?"

"I made him cinnamon buns to thank him for my skates. I was only the fourth-worst skater at the party, so I fit right in."

So she texts him, he comes over and makes bucatini for us, and we have Pillsbury cinnamon buns for dessert. Nicole has a date with a bald guy in a turtleneck (don't even ask). Jade and Andrew have a dance-off with Wii Just Dance! He wins to a raucous rendition of Tina Turner's "Proud Mary." She asks if he'll put her to bed, and once she's asleep, I make tea and we plop on the couch.

He takes a *New Yorker* from the coffee table and flips pages so he can look casual when he asks, "You wouldn't really date that guy, would you?"

I laugh. "Depends on my alternatives. Which brings us to, what'd you think of Thomas?"

"Let's change the subject."

"Let's not."

"I think he's boring, I think there's a lot less there than meets the eye, and I think his manicure cost more than his hair goop, his eyebrows have been tweezed within an inch of their life. He's shallow and high maintenance. That was my first impression. The longer we spoke, the less I liked him."

"Then I guess we're back to Ryan. I mean I don't have other alternatives. At least not that I know of."

"Well, we don't want to disrespect Sloane's new boyfriend, do we? What's his name?"

"His name is James Waters."

"Who do you think James would prefer if he had the choice? Sloane or you?"

So I actually think about that. "Maybe me."

"Fascinating! I'm sorry, I know I promised not to bug you about this, but it is the single coolest thing I've ever heard of. Has James kissed you, I mean her, yet?"

"Yes."

"Yes which? You or her?"

"Her, of course. He hasn't met me, yet."

"So how are you and Sloane different, besides the blond and the boobs?"

"Um, would it be okay if that's enough about Sloane for tonight?"

"Sure. Sorry."

Then I make the mistake of offering, "Don't pout. You can ask one more question."

And straight back like a shot, "Who would I like better?"

I pause and pretend to be thinking it over, but really I'm digesting my annoyance at the question.

"I'll have to think about that," I say.

And I'm overwhelmed with a desire to have him leave. I can't say that, of course, and he stays for a few hours while we watch TiVo'd *Dancing with the Stars*, which he gets really into. I am totally shut down. Can barely engage in his game of creating wild-ass backstories for the professional dancers who work with the celebrities. The worst part is he doesn't even seem to notice.

During the third show, I pretend to fall asleep. He shakes me gently, and I open one sleepy eye; he says good night and lets himself out.

My eyes open. And stare into distance at the truth I now know. I am in love with Andrew. And have been from the first moment.

CHAPTER EIGHTEEN
SLOANE

I wake up and look out my window. There's my tree. She doesn't look different, but not a single molecule of my tree or my body or the world feels the same any longer. I've looked up *schizophrenia* online, and I think this is it. I know on the one hand that last night actually happened. Burned into my memory is every microsecond of his face, the fear in his eyes that I didn't want him, the sound of his voice so hopeful; it is absolutely true. And yet, it is of course completely impossible. I mean, I own a mirror. And that's just the outside of me. Obviously, he is making assumptions about the inside of me, matching some dream girl to the little glimpses that he's had. He doesn't know me yet. And I'm sure that when he does, he will be deeply disappointed. But for today, for this morning, James has chosen me. Unless of course he changed his mind overnight.

I turn on my phone. Maybe he's left a message like they do in those cheesy romantic comedies, where he says, "I'm halfway home and I miss you already."

There is a message. And it's much better. He's going to pick me up at eight thirty and take me away to places of his choosing until my curfew. He says he might be tired because he kissed a girl last night and it kept him awake for hours.

I text back: *Yes! Yes! Hell, yes!*

And there's a knock on my door. My dad comes in all smiling and happy. First, he thanks me for how much I took our little heart-to-heart to heart. I don't even know what he's talking about until I realize my mom must be really happy about me not ripping her head off anymore.

Then he offers to drive me to my SAT prep course for which I paid $200 (my vet salary for like four weeks), which starts in one hour and fifteen minutes and which (along with everything else in the world) I have totally forgotten.

Okay, time to lie. Course was postponed, nope. He might call and check. I promised Kelly that I'd take her to have both her legs amputated, nope, too much. To buy her prom dress? Nope, too little. There is only one option that seems realistic.

"Daddy there's something else I want to do today. There's a boy."

The smile on his face doesn't change, but I feel his body straighten.

"And I really like him. And he likes me. And I want to spend the day with him. And it won't hurt me on the SAT, I've studied a zillion hours already, so the whole thing is overkill."

He stares at me, obviously fighting the urge to give me a direct order.

"Of course, the money is your decision; you worked for it. Can you take the course another day?"

"No, but I really don't need it. Honest."

Not only is he absolutely not down with my decision, he can't even believe that this is consistent with his workaholic kid who would amputate both her own legs to get into Columbia.

"I'm sorry, honey, but I can't go along with this. Your boyfriend will understand, and if he doesn't, he's not the right guy for you anyway. You've worked so hard, and there's no way to know what is and isn't overkill. We always say leave no stone unturned and you'll have no regrets."

Of course James would understand. In fact, he'd probably give me the same advice. But that's not the point. I feel like I'm working on borrowed time with James since now that I have him, I might lose him, and there's no way I'm missing this day.

"I'm sorry, Dad. I'm choosing to spend the day with James. Only I know how completely prepared I am for this test."

He just stares at me, not knowing what to say in the face of absolute disobedience. Unsure of what to do with this version of me. I never say no or disappoint my father like this.

"Obviously, Daddy, this boy is really special to me."

"I think that's beside the point."

"Well, I think the point is that you need to trust me."

There is a real silence. "I don't appreciate your tone." And he walks out.

As I shower, I try to wash him from my thoughts. I don't want any dark clouds over my sunny day. Sadly, it just gets worse. He's right. Columbia used to be the most important thing in the world to me. And now it isn't. That's just the truth. At this point, I don't even know if I'll be *around* to go to Columbia.

As I get dressed I'm expecting the knock on the door. My mom comes in, sent by her husband, and basically agrees with him. They are trying to double-team me. I tell her what happened, that James dumped his old girlfriend so that he could be with me. It is the most exciting moment of my life so far, and there's no point in going to a practice test where I can't think about anything else but James.

She asks how long that's going to go on.

"Good question," I tell her. And I can see she's been here before. My mother was once a girl with an uncontrollable crush on a boy that consumed all her brainpower. Maybe that's why she was so strict about when I could start dating.

She gives me a hug and tells me she'll square things with Dad.

I'm too nervous to eat breakfast. At the last moment, I remember what Maggie said about matching your panties to your bra. I run upstairs and coordinate colors since I don't own an actual set. It doesn't necessarily make me feel anything in particular, except wondering if there's a chance that someone might see them.

I'm waiting on the porch steps when a red Targa sweeps up to the curb, just like in *Sixteen Candles*, and out jumps a guy who is hotter than Jake Ryan. I leap up because I don't want him to think I'm playing hard to get or anything. He pulls me into his arms and gives me a spectacular warm, lingering, shiver-all-over kiss, heedless of whoever's family or neighbors might be peeking out of a window.

He holds my face in his hands for a moment after, his forehead against mine, his thumb stroking my cheek, and gently presses his lashes to mine, fluttering a butterfly kiss. It feels so intimate and in a way excites me more than the big make-out kiss. I can feel his breath.

All he will say as we pull away from the curb is that we will be driving all the way to the Berkshire Mountains of Massachusetts. He offers to buy us breakfast at Kitchen Little, and I just lie and say I've eaten. He pulls into the drive-through line at Dunkin' Donuts, and I struggle to recall whether I know anyone who works here. Actually, The Weed works here, and I don't know his shift.

Sure enough, when we pull up to the window, The Weed turns to us with a huge wake-and-bake smile and hands James his extra-large coffee and full-dozen assorted. I look out the passenger window, hoping that The Weed won't recognize or care about the back of my head.

"Hey, Sloane, you sure you don't want anything? It's on me."

"Nope, thanks anyway."

Great. Now I will spend the entire day worrying whether this will zip straight through town or through the hollow chamber that lies between The Weed's ears.

Once on the highway, I dip into the dozen for a powdered jelly donut and ask if I can share his coffee. He starts asking about my entire life and personality all at once. Every detail, including is powdered my favorite donut and why? I can't fathom why anything about me is interesting to him. I tell him I actually prefer blueberry because of the gross purple dye they use; nothing else stains your mouth that particular color.

What was my favorite pet? I tell him that Schmulie, a runty black and white cat, was my first best friend in this world. I tell James everything. Schmulie licked my tears when I cried. And slept with me every night. When he was banished to my uncle's farm because of Tyler's allergies, I gave him special time on each visit and brought him special treats. And although I'm probably making this up, he seemed to love me and communicate with his big dark eyes. He died slowly and quietly, and I moved into my uncle's guest room that week and slept on the floor with him.

James seems very moved by this and doesn't speak for a while. I ask about Caroline's cat, and he says it was really hard getting the cat back to America, but by then it was all he had left of Caroline and he was determined not to lose Peaches.

"If you have another question about Caroline, you can ask that too," he offers.

"What if I have like fifteen thousand?"

"We may have to save a few for the ride back."

Caroline and James met in the Bois de Boulogne while they were running. Much to the horror of my enormous insecurities, she's French! Actually French. Two French parents. Her native language is French. The course she was taking at the Sorbonne was English. Holy shit. She is from Nice on the Riviera, and she once took him home to meet her folks, and they went on this nude beach (not with her parents) and sailed to Corsica (not nude, but with her parents). It is clear this French girl is very experienced. I badger him until he confirms my observation, but he refuses to elaborate. Which is to his credit. Though not to mine for asking five times.

"She's really pretty," I say, not letting it go.

"She is. But you are so much more attractive than anyone I've ever met."

I roll my eyes. He's just trying to make me feel better.

"Don't do that. You can't see how everyone sees you. You are beautiful, Sloane. But I'm not even talking about that. I mean attraction, like gravity. The connection I feel to you is overpowering. I don't think I could resist it if I tried."

I feel a familiar tingle when he says this. The thrill and the fear remind me of the sorcerer. I can't tell James that. And yet this perfect boy just gave me the greatest compliment I've ever received by confirming the spell I've been under since he rescued that sparrow. So I just reach out and take his hand.

Our fingers weave and dance around each other's for the rest of the drive. We never let go.

After two hours of driving, we pull into a fairgrounds. A big banner reads INTERNATIONAL PUPPET SHOW. Two twenty-foot dragon shadow puppets form an archway. We go through into a clearing surrounded by a dense forest. People are in costumes of different eras and cultures; some dressed as mythical creatures mingled. There are families, couples, a group of children gathered around a hand puppet stage. Chinese kites in the sky. There is a drum circle, strolling musicians playing flutes and pipes.

We settle down on a hill. James has packed a blanket and a picnic, and of course we still have five donuts. I can tell he is waiting for something. The drums stop; there is complete silence. And out of the trees comes a small army of towering puppets, maybe twenty feet tall. They are men on stilts, each portraying a different character, each with a gigantic moon-shaped face. Some are monsters, two are birds, there's a mermaid. Amazingly, the stilts don't make them awkward. Their movements are flowing and hypnotic like a tribe of giraffes. They act out a series of plays, the content of which is hard to precisely define but mesmerizing to watch.

So I lean my body into James's side, and he wraps me up in his long arm, and we watch like two people who have belonged to each other from the beginning of time. I have never been so completely content. It is a perfect moment.

On the drive back, the sunset gives way to a dusk of purple and deep blues. We drive in companionable silence for what seems like forever, and miraculously I don't worry that I should be saying something or that he's bored. I know everything is perfect between us.

"You know what I'm afraid of?"

It just pops out of my mouth. I am either possessed or insane or both.

"Silverfish? They're so slimy."

"Exactly."

He smiles. "Plus the other thing that you're reconsidering telling me about."

"Oh yeah, that. It's just this desperate fear that when you spend more time with me, you'll be bored out of your mind and wonder what you ever saw in me in the first place."

He glances from the road to my eyes so that I will know that he really means this. "You're endlessly fascinating just as you are."

"It's easier to be fascinated by someone you don't know."

"You don't have any deep dark secret, do you? No ax murders, meth labs, husbands in Utah, Kewpie doll collections?"

"Just one out of four. So we're good."

Actually, it's one out of five. The one being a secret he hasn't asked about, that I am clinically, irretrievably psychotic. But since there is absolutely no way he can ever find out, I will just put being out of my mind out of my mind.

I look over, and he is smiling so happily, looking so impossibly beautiful. And I relax again. Spending the day with me made him feel that way.

"Got a date for the prom?"

"Yep."

"One of your husbands from Utah?"

"Gordy, actually."

"I like him. So what's up with that?"

"He's like my brother; actually he's nothing like either of my brothers and I adore him. Neither of us was dating anyone, so we decided to go together."

I wonder if he will ask me to bail on Gordy and what I'll do if he does.

"Cool."

But it isn't. I'm terrified of Gordy learning about James. I'm living a secret life at the moment, and the roll-out of the truth is a delicate matter. Hopefully The Weed hasn't already taken it upon himself.

"Would it be okay," I begin hesitantly, "if we sort of kept us under wraps for a little while?"

"Does this mean I should retract the wedding announcement in the *New York Times*?"

He laughs. But just the words *wedding announcement* send an electric charge through every nerve ending in my body.

"No, let it run. No one in our class reads."

He really laughs. He actually thinks I'm funny. Maggie's funny, but I'm more grumpy and sarcastic than funny. Except to Gordy. And I guess Lila. Okay, the point is *he* thinks I'm funny.

"Sure. Can I ask why?"

"Sure, can you ask why what?"

"Why we're something secret."

"I don't want to make it weird for Amanda. I know you said she's fine, but I want to give her a heads-up and some time to deal with her image."

"Wow. Is this high school or Hollywood?"

"There's a difference?"

He laughs again. He's an easy audience.

"You are an exceptionally thoughtful person. It's not the reason I'm crazy about you, but it's actually more important."

Nothing bothers him. I can tell him anything. With the one exception, of course.

"When I was little, a sorcerer would float outside my window at night. I was terrified of him, but excited too. I knew that if I ever let my guard down, the sorcerer would be able to come through my window, into my bed, and take control of me. I kept him outside the window with these rituals I would do each night."

I looked over at his profile. My God, it's true.

"I never really knew what he looked like. Until the first moment I saw you."

He says nothing.

"You saved that sparrow in homeroom. And when you turned from the window, I thought I had never seen such a beautiful face on any creature before."

So not only have I just confessed that he is the embodiment of a lifelong fantasy but that he is also the most beautiful thing I've ever seen. His eyes were fixed on the road, so I could admit these things and at least feel unobserved and therefore protected. Of course, once saying them, I feel completely naked.

He says absolutely nothing. He doesn't even smile. And I know I ruined everything. I said too much, crazy too much. No boy could handle that without running for the hills.

And then, without explanation, he pulls to the side of the road and stops the car. It's twilight, and the leaves we park beneath are pastel colors. And my heart isn't beating anymore. He turns and looks at me.

"It was me," he says. "Outside your window, all your life. Hoping you'd let me in."

CHAPTER NINETEEN

MAGGIE

I'm sipping tea and picking at a bagel while attempting to read a horrible script my agent sent me. It's hard to focus on anything other than the fact I've fallen for my only true friend. As if on cue, my cell rings.

Andrew tells me that his next short film will be about kids talking back to a street performer, like a mime, or someone in gold lamé paint pretending to be a statue. I make the mistake of telling him that I used to do puppet shows for the Boys and Girls Club, and the kids would really get into shouting matches with my puppets. This confession is a mistake because he likes it. Next thing I know, he's found a cardboard puppet theater from the props department and four ridiculously mismatched hand puppets and announces that I won the coveted role of puppeteer.

We set up outside the Central Park Zoo next to the Good Humor guy. My ragtag puppets basically call out insults to little kids, not a single one of whom can resist stopping and shouting back.

For example, the Duck with a lazy eye on my right hand screams to this sniffly kid with his finger up his nose, "Hey booger brain, ever heard of a Kleenex?"

The kid stops, turns, and with his finger still second knuckle deep into his nostril yells, "You smell like a Kleenex!"

Five-year-olds come up with the best comebacks.

Once I have the kids' attention and that of their parent/nanny, the Milkmaid on my left hand tells the Duck some fanciful biography of the kid à la my normal shtick. The children scream and laugh and shout back rewrites of my stories, which are pretty clever, and the adults are so delighted they basically throw money. Several ask if I do birthday parties. The Duck answers that we only do bat mitzvahs and sweet sixteens because our material is so sophisticated.

Andrew shoots a ton of footage that will cut together into a masterpiece. At lunch, he fantasizes about taking it to festivals, licensing it to cable television. He's really lost it.

I've never seen him happier. And perhaps because I'm still feeling guilty for being a poophead last night or maybe because I now know I love him, I'm not even annoyed by his drumming and humming. He raves about my comedic timing and goes on and on about our future plans as a puppet troupe. There is even one stray reference to my shirt being really pretty.

Then just as his gigantic gross burger arrives, he casually asks where would be a good place for a first date. If a guy wanted to make a good impression without, you know, overdoing it and looking too whipped.

"Is this a hypothetical question? Or is there someone who's got you whipped?"

"The lady in question is a friend of Cassie's. I used to see her a lot at my brother's place."

I chew a fry, in the most casual way, while all the blood rushes to my head.

"So how come you never asked her out before?"

"Her boyfriend would've objected. She dumped him when she found out I'd broken up with Carmen, or at least the two events had quite the coincidental synchronicity."

My heart is actually breaking. Whether this anonymous rival is formidable or not, eventually one will be. I try to maintain the ridiculous smile I have plastered on my face while my insides turn to mush.

"So tell me all about her."

"Amy? I guess the basic attraction is attraction. She's model gorgeous. Maybe that's because she's a model. And she's real funny. And easy to hang with."

"What happened to only wanting to be with someone you love?"

"I've been thinking about that," he says, "and I don't know if I believe in love at first sight. And since we've been friends for a long time, maybe it'll be that thing you know where love comes out of friendship. So what do you think?"

"Take her to Little Owl."

To which the obviously appropriate response should be: "Let me take you there instead. In fact, let me take you everywhere for the rest of our lives."

"Perfect," he says. "Thanks."

Two hours later, I sit on Emma's couch and get up the courage to say, "I'm not sure I want to talk about it, but I'm in love with Andrew."

It's like hitting the world's biggest hornets' nest with a baseball bat. She doesn't know where to pry first. After asking eight questions at once, she settles on, "Tell me what you mean by 'being in love' with him."

"All my life I wondered, actually doubted, actually was pretty certain that I'd never be in love with anyone. And there was this moment last night, when absolutely nothing was going on between us, except me being a sour bitch, when the thought jumped into my mind that I'm in love with this guy. That I have been in love with him from the very first moment. That this is the thing I didn't know if I would recognize when it happened, and now I can't ignore it."

"Why would you want to ignore it?"

"Because I can't have him."

"Why not?"

I sit in silence for a moment. "Can we just end the session right here? I mean you'll get paid and everything."

She laughs.

"I'm actually not kidding, and if you laugh at my agony one more time, I'm not only walking out that door but I'm never coming back."

Another homerun to the hornets' nest. Which is great because now it becomes a whole bunch of questions about how do I feel about her and her process, and Nicole and her process, and Sloane's mother and her process, and I'm just looking at my watch hoping we never get back around to Andrew.

Which of course we do.

"Of course you can get Andrew. You're a lovely girl . . ."

Kill me now.

"You're very intelligent, you have an original sense of humor, though you rarely use it here . . ."

I interject, "And I can cook and have a darling personality. So what was I worried about?"

A silence follows that is meant to be meaningful. "I think this is the first time you've ever actually mocked me."

"I think you haven't been paying attention."

"Let's talk about why you're angry with me."

"Sure. I'm in love with my best friend, who really likes me a lot, so much that he's asking my advice on who to date and where to take them, and if you define your job as rubbing salt into people's wounds, expect them to be angry. It's called human behavior."

One thing is for sure, I will never tell her that Andrew knows about Sloane. I am not interested in hearing her tell me I'm certifiable for letting my crazy out of the bag. I'm already painfully aware it was a mistake since Andrew, or anyone for that matter, would prefer to be with a psychologically stable model.

For the remaining eleven minutes, I basically clam up. Which drives her crazy. And makes me feel I'm getting Nicole's money's worth. Which makes me wonder for the first time in a while why I do this at all. I used to think that it was this insurance policy against compete abnormality. At least I knew I was crazy and was seeing someone about it. So I was better off than Sloane. Then when

Emma raised the stakes from weirdo to psycho, I began feeling really in need of insurance. But I wonder whether this quack is up to providing it.

Her finest hours are always when I get sad about my dad. Mainly because she just shuts up and listens and lets me work it out for myself. But also because she really cares, and I can see that she is a genuinely nice person. Which is not the same as having the credentials to save you from schizophrenia.

I somehow waste three hours wandering around Central Park thinking about Andrew. It's pretty repetitive. Sort of like how I would imagine squirrels think about acorns in the winter. Rather than obsessing about productive things, like *Innuendo* and my career, or even the GED, my mind keeps coming back to Andrew. Even when I think about getting cast as Robin, I realize it will mean moving to Hollywood and never bumping into Andrew and Amy. Worse would be if I impulsively turn down the job because I can't move three thousand miles from him. Then I'd have to cry myself to sleep every night for the rest of my life because I wouldn't have Andrew or a career.

Of course, I'll always have Sloane. So at least I'm getting kissed in an alternate universe. I mean, of course, Sloane is.

All that obsessing and wandering gets me home less early than intended. It's Jade's night to cook (once a month) and it's usually best to have a disaster squad on hand, if not a full battalion of EMTs. So I walk into the apartment, hoping that it hasn't burned to the ground, only to find Nicole and Jade poring over VRBO (vacation rentals by owner). Jade is still wearing the swim goggles she dons while cutting onions. Sauce is on the stove and it smells good.

Jade announces that we are going to rent a beach house some-where this summer. Nicole tells me that she will make sure that the holiday fits within my production hiatus.

"My production what?"

"You can pretend all you want that you're not getting this show, but I know that you are."

"Just how do you know that?"

She looks in my eyes, and there is love in her voice as she says, "I just do."

"That's good enough for me," pipes in Jade, "and Boris."

I haven't felt the impulse to hug Nicole for a long time. When I reach out, she reaches back, and we hold each other, and I say in her ear, "I've got a chance, Mommy, I really do."

"You never call her Mommy; what's up with that?"

"She's getting older, dear," Nicole says. "Careful, it'll happen to you."

But all this time her eyes are locked to mine and I can see she is just proud of me. For a role I might never get? No. She's proud of me because she's proud of me.

As we are sitting down to our traditional bucatini diabolo deco-rated with Jade's famous broccoli trees, my cell rings. Looking at the screen, I excuse myself for a second. Shutting the bathroom door behind me, I offer, "You don't know what to wear to the Little Owl? I'd suggest a simple black dress."

Andrew laughs. It's an honest, spontaneous laugh, and it makes me a little sad because he doesn't know all the times I could make him laugh if he only chose me. And because I realize I'll do it any-way, so he doesn't have to choose me.

"Let's have dinner," he says. "You and me."

"She turned you down?" I'm kidding, of course.

"Yep."

"Oh, I see, you just called your one loser friend, who'll always be available as a last minute backup since she doesn't have a life."

"Basically."

I'm so happy. I'll get to see him tonight. "Can't leave for an hour."

"I'll try to be patient. Meet you at this place called the Little Owl. Where I overconfidently have a romantic corner table reserved."

"Super. I'll be the brunette in the little black dress."

"Me too."

I go back to the kitchen, and Nicole wonders why I look flushed and giddy. Jade says that Andrew must've called. Nicole says she's betting on Thomas. I tell them it was just a really entertaining tele-marketer and immediately begin shoveling down the pasta.

We spend dinner debating between Cape Cod and the Vineyard, like we can afford either, but Nicole is really excited about the three of us getting away together. And I like that. Very, very much. For the first time, I wonder if maybe everything is coming together.

I walk into the restaurant for my after-dinner dinner. The place is packed per usual, and I look around for a romantic table in the corner. There he is. There is a bottle of red wine on the table and two glasses have been poured.

He beams when he sees me.

"Excuse me, lady, I'm waiting for a brunette in a little black dress."

"She stood you up too. It's getting to be a trend."

He stands, kisses my cheek, and holds my chair. Like he'd do for his mother or his sister. But he does seem really happy to see me.

I pick up the wine bottle and look at the label, which is in French.

"We're celebrating you getting turned down?"

"I'm celebrating that they didn't card me when I walked in with the bottle. I got it in Paris with my dad last summer. It's going to really stand up to those gravy meatball sliders I have my eye on."

"Paris, huh? You've been holding out on me."

"Sure."

I hate that about him. He always says things that I both despise him for saying and wish I'd said myself.

My cell rings and I'm not sure why I even glance at the screen. It's Thomas. As I slip the phone back into my bag, Andrew smiles . . .

"Are you holding out on me?"

"Sure." Boy, that kind of immediate payback never happens in real life.

"I'm guessing it's Thomas because if it was Jade, you'd have answered."

"Oh, only two people call me?"

"Well, three, including me. Call him back. It might be about the role."

"I can't even believe you. What makes you think it's not some guy I'm dating that you've never heard of?"

"You didn't take the call. That's what makes me think it's not some guy you're dating that I've never heard of."

Rats. I hate that about him.

"Call him back, I mean it."

I want him to want me to never talk to a guy with hair like that for the rest of my life. Under his scrutiny, I call Thomas back.

"There you are," Thomas says in his George Clooney voice. "Feel like catching a late supper?"

"I've eaten, thanks anyway."

There's a brief silence and then no longer in his George Clooney voice, he says, "Yeah, I can hear the restaurant. Back at Jean-Georges, are you?"

"No, I'm at the Little Owl."

"With who?'

"Whom."

"I stand corrected, who is buying your dinner?" I don't like his tone, I don't like him anymore, and I don't care if he doesn't like the fact that it's . . .

"Just Andrew."

"Hey, thanks a lot." Andrew grins.

But at the other end of the phone, nobody is grinning. After a pause that makes me a little uncomfortable, "Okay," he says gravely, "I was going to do this face-to-face, but I think I need to let you know that Macauley is going with the other actress."

I am devastated. This must be what a head felt like in the French Revolution just after the guillotine blade fell. It is no longer connected to my body, but it can still manage to fix on one horrible thought.

"What happened?" Andrew is immediately alert, concerned, on my side.

"Wow," is all I can manage.

"Listen," Thomas offers in a softer voice, "Macauley really likes you and is already talking to Rosalie and me about putting you in his next feature. So I think you and I should maybe sit down and go over that and some other things I have up my sleeve."

Something in his voice just makes me feel I never want to see him again. Even if it means missing out on all the sparkly opportunities he dangles in front of me.

"Sounds good. Could you do me a favor and break it down with my agent first? She got all pissy about us running around behind her back."

Big silence. Confirming that he may have had more things up his sleeve than just his arm.

"Might be a problem," he says, "getting her in the middle of it. Let me call you tomorrow so you can get back to your date. And babe, I'm sorry about the role. You know how hard I tried."

I gather all my self-control. But have to at least go for: "Yeah, thanks. Thanks for everything."

"You didn't get it," Andrew says as if the loss is his own.

"No big surprise."

"Don't do that. You lost the Super Bowl. It was down to two actresses in the entire world. And you were one of those. And only seventeen, with no major credits, because you blew a huge director away. Here's to you." He lifts his glass in a toast.

I stare at him. And I know what I have to do. "Can we step outside for a second?"

He looks at me curiously. I stand up. So he does too. I'm already walking toward the door so he can't change his mind.

It's cold on the street, and I'm hugging myself with my back to the door and therefore to him. I hear . . .

"Are you okay?"

I turn around quickly, stand on my tiptoes, take his face in both my hands, and kiss him with everything I've got.

He kisses back right away. As if he's been waiting for this all his life.

Just like I have.

CHAPTER TWENTY

SLOANE

As I brush my teeth this morning, I can't get that kiss out of my mind. Not the one James and I shared when he dropped me off last night. We kissed for twenty glorious minutes in his car parked around the corner from my house, a spot I will probably refer to as heaven from now on. But it's the kiss outside of Little Owl that I keep thinking about.

On the one hand, I sort of know that I'm Maggie, and that I'm doing and feeling everything she does when I dream I'm her. And I know that means tasting her food, feeling her toothache, but I sort of push that to the back of my mind, and I think she does the same with me. And that's because neither of us wants to deal with the unreality of the dream. We're more comfortable feeling like we were watching someone else's life.

But that kiss was different. I can't pretend I didn't feel it. It was thrilling, and yet it was nothing like the feeling I have when James kisses me. And I guess that's the reason. James kisses *me*. But *Maggie kissed Andrew*. She's the kind of girl who takes the lead, who goes after what she wants, takes the risk of being rejected in a way so humiliating I know that I couldn't have recovered. I'm the "girl." I have to sit back and be all passive, and pray that my feminine softness will attract him. Maybe that's why I invented her. Because I want to be like that, I want to make my own life happen.

I go downstairs, and though I don't notice it at first, Jade is sitting at the breakfast table. I almost speak to her, as if I'm Maggie, as if we are in the West Village. All of this happens in half a second. A bolt of terrible fear rips through me; I shut my eyes tightly and pray that someone else will be there when my eyes open. I count to three. I open them. And she's not there—Max is.

It's a totally understandable thing. In fact, it's astonishing that it has never happened before. But it hasn't. Ever. And it scares the shit out of me. I go and hug Max, just to be sure he is real. He likes it, which is also a surprise.

"Maybe we should get out Mom's old telescope from the attic and look at Bill's stars," Max suggests.

"I love that idea," I tell him. Though the truth is I don't. I'm tired of being sad. I want to feel how I felt with James yesterday. I want to feel like that all the time.

On the bus ride to school, I listen to my iPod and stare out the window, remembering moments from yesterday that make me blush. I downloaded a flamenco album last night, and as the houses and woods on our route blur by, I imagine dancing to this music for James. In my mind, my body moves in graceful, rhythmic ways it never has before. I pull out my phone and text him that I'm excited to see him.

The instant I enter the school, it seems that every eye is on me. Either I forgot to put my pants on or James has spilled our beans. I turn off my iPod and hurry to my locker. There is whispering as I pass, and girls I barely know glare at me. All I can think about is finding Gordy. So of course I can't. He isn't at his locker or in his homeroom.

Lila ambushes me, pulling me into the girls' room.

"Tell me everything. Absolutely everything," she begs as she checks the stalls to make sure we're alone.

"Who did he tell?" I ask.

"The Weed? He sort of told everybody, but not on purpose. He walked into the Marble last night and mentioned to no one in particular that you guys had come by for donuts, but you wouldn't let Weed treat you. He just wondered what was up with that."

In other words, if I let him buy me a donut, I wouldn't be a pariah this morning. Something to remember.

"You slept with him. Don't deny it."

"Are you kidding? I barely know The Weed."

She grabs me by the ears. "I am your confidante in all matters juicy, and it really hurts my feelings that you wouldn't tell me. And everyone thinks that you and I have a problem because I didn't know."

"First, it's none of your business. Second, it's none of anyone's damn business. Third, of course I haven't slept with him; we're just starting to get to know each other. And most importantly, why does everybody hate me this morning? Is Amanda talking shit?"

"Everyone hates you because they're jealous. Even if they're not jealous because you scored James, and believe me most are, they'd just be jealous because you're in a relationship. It's high school, remember?"

"Does Gordy know?"

She stares at me silently, as if I asked an utterly random question.

"What's the difference?"

"Good point," I say. "I was just curious."

I skip homeroom. At first, I thought I'd just hang out in the bathroom, but people keep coming in and pretending they aren't staring at me. Kelly texts me asking if I'm okay.

I skip first period and go to conspire with Kelly, who works in the library during her free first period on Mondays. I help her shelve books so we can whisper and I can be out of the spotlight, hidden in the stacks.

"What has Amanda been saying?"

"Absolutely nothing. She's just going around with this noble, hurt look like she has too much class to actually call you out as a home wrecker. This way she doesn't have to lie, and everybody believes the rumors."

"Which are that I stole her boyfriend?"

"By sleeping with him."

There it is. And there's absolutely no way to do anything about it, ever. I try to shrug off the fact that I will be our high school's resident bitch and slut and cut to the chase . . .

"Have you seen Gordy?"

"He was there last night. And practically got in a fight defending you. He said James was a good guy, and the idea that everyone was sitting around talking about someone's sex life, let alone making you out to be a slut, was just about the lamest thing he'd ever heard."

I want to cry. And Kelly just says, "I know."

I rub the worn spine of a book on geodes. "I know you don't think James is worth it."

"I said I didn't think he would ever really give his heart for keeps. And I guess I'm still worried that's the case. But you're a big girl. I still believe the day will come when Gordy is for you and you are for Gordy. And I'm betting he'll still be there."

I decide to eat lunch inside with the nerd herd, the only crew that doesn't seem to be tapped into the rumor mill. And I cut sixth period and go to the darkroom. While I'm developing candids for the yearbook, I realize half my roll is of James. I know I'm avoiding him. I don't know how to have a boyfriend. I have no practice. I'm worried all this talk is going to put him off me. I'm just certain I don't want to be seen with him at school today, under the microscope of everyone staring at us and making up their own stories. I text him that I want to see him after dinner. And he writes back immediately, *K*.

I go out to the parking lot and take Gordy's hide-a-key from under the hood of his truck and wait for him in the cab. When school gets out, I think about ducking out of sight but don't want to alarm Gordy when he finds me stowed away. Just as I've convinced myself I'm being dramatic and ridiculous, an amazing number of female passersby stare at me with a variety of nasty looks.

A senior, who I've actually never spoken to, makes it her business to walk away from her jackal pack and knock on the window, which I foolishly roll down, permitting her to say . . .

"I hope you're proud of yourself."

I struggle to channel Maggie.

"Explain yourself," I demand calmly.

"You little bitch. I think you know what I mean."

"Not only that, I think I know what you are."

And I roll up the window. Which she spits on. I then recall that she was the girl who got two weeks' suspension in the fall for ripping Mily Burton's earrings out in the girl's locker room.

Why do they care? The truth is they don't. They don't care about Amanda or me or the morality of who is sleeping with who. They are just on autopilot. This is what you do in high school. Let's hope Columbia and the rest of life find bigger fish to fry.

Gordy shows up. He seems glad to see me. This makes me hope that things are going to be easy. His feelings aren't hurt. Maybe he's even happy for me.

"So what's new?" And he laughs.

"You're sharing your truck with Hester Prynne." And immediately fear that he won't place the reference. "She's—"

"The girl in *Scarlet Letter*, yeah. Eighth grade, I got an A, you got an A–."

"Well, now it's a scarlet A–."

He laughs again. "We could sit here and have everybody start saying you're cheating on your boyfriend with me. Or we could just get the hell out of here." He roars the truck's engine and pulls out.

On the drive to Maxwell's, I listen to Gordy rant about Amanda Porcella as if it's her duty to clear my good name.

"She was never dating him in the first place." He snorts.

"How do you know that?"

"Because you wouldn't be dating him if she had."

See, that's Gordy. I can do no wrong. Even though I completely betrayed him. I know deep in the pit of my stomach that I've betrayed him—the thing is, I just haven't quite figured out how. Is it because I didn't confide in him immediately? Why would that be a betrayal? I don't feel I betrayed Kelly. So why is this different? It's different because Gordy and I had that talk on my birthday about what would it be like if we ever dated. And I try never to think too much about whether Gordy really likes me in that way. But now I'm wondering. And I'm worried today will be the day I find out. And that would be the worst possible way.

The shipyard is quiet, just the yard guys working on the engine of a boat, getting it ready for the water. We walk down the dock and find some sunny planks and dangle our legs over the edge. The mooring field is still empty, a little lonely. But it gives us an open view of the sound and Ram Island and Watch Hill behind it. The light is crisp and clear, but I'm not in the mood to appreciate it.

"So tell me about it," he says, to my surprise. "How'd you guys get together?" He stares out at the island like we're talking about nothing in particular.

I don't know how to begin, so he fills in the silence: "He turned out to be the guy you'd thought he was after all, huh?"

"When I said that, it was because I thought he had a girlfriend, not Amanda, someone else. Turned out he didn't."

There's a long silence, but not an uncomfortable one. He clearly has something on his mind to ask, and I want to give him the space to do it.

"So is he kind of the first?"

A short laugh escapes me.

"First what?"

"You know, the first guy you ever really cared about. I mean, not like you and I care about each other, I mean, you know."

The corners of his eyes squint slightly; it could be glare from the water since he's looking straight out, not at me. He's asking if this is my first betrayal, or if there was a James before James. And the thing is—there was.

But I could never tell him. I have no choice but to flat-out lie.

"That's a good question. I guess I don't really know yet how I feel about James or where it's going. But I am excited. And I guess in a way that's new for me."

"Yeah, usually you're basically skeptical and underwhelmed by the human race. Except for me, of course." Then out of nowhere he says, "So you guys are gonna go to the prom, then."

"Hell, no. You and I are going to the prom, whether you like it or not."

He turns now and looks directly at me.

"No, we're not," is all he says. But his liquid eyes say so much more. They scream at me that I have hurt him, that he wants to be the first guy I ever really cared about, and that I have led him to this vulnerable place recklessly.

I can't bear it. I start to cry, which is weak and somehow makes me cry harder because I feel like by crying I'm trying to make it about me. But he doesn't comfort me. He doesn't ask why I'm crying. Because he seems to know. And he won't look away to make it any easier on me. Which I sort of respect, and it tells me that he has more backbone than I'd thought. Turns out I can do wrong in Gordy's eyes. And I have.

247

"This doesn't change anything about us," I say. "Past, present, or future."

I'm hoping for a smile, but it doesn't come.

"What's wrong?" I ask.

"Nothing's wrong. Just don't talk to me like that anymore. Okay?"

I have the choice of pretending I don't know what he means. And even though it makes me really cry, I just can't do that.

"Okay," I manage. And in that one word, I acknowledge that I have flirted with him all my life, unconsciously and intentionally, because I want to keep him as an option. And I pretended that there could be no consequences to that. And now I understand what a thoughtless, reckless, really despicable person I am. And he doesn't hug me to comfort me, or deny the truth of that in any way. Because we are no longer what we were and we aren't what we might have been.

All he says is, "I'll drive you home."

I don't cry on the way home. He doesn't say anything, but he doesn't look angry at all. Just strong and perversely very attractive. When we get to my house, he jumps out like always, and I let him open my door. He gives me a real strong hug and says, "We're okay." Which makes me almost cry again, but I contain myself. He just gets back into the truck and drives off.

I guess hating myself should make me cancel any plans with James tonight so that I don't do or say something I'll regret. But being me, it just makes me want to be with him immediately.

It's nearly dark. I apologize to my mom for skipping dinner and bike over to James's house. Because I'm in such a hurry, I go the direct route, which brings me by the cemetery where they buried Bill. At the service, I read from *The Little Prince*. "In one of the stars, I shall be living. In one of them, I shall be laughing." And Gordy in his handsome suit was a pallbearer with Tyler and Bill's cousins. We walked from the Noank Baptist Church, a full procession behind them to the Valley cemetery. We all put bright yellow daffodils on the casket. His dog, Mo, howled. And Gordy and I clung to each other.

There are few streetlights by the cemetery and it's a cloudy night, no moon, no stars. I bike faster and I realize that I haven't even called and have no idea if James is even home. He isn't. I sit on his doorstep and wait, which is progress from hiding behind a tree.

It's dark and really cold when he drives up. He is, of course, surprised to see me on his doorstep and worried that something is wrong.

"Something is really wrong. And it has nothing to do with you," I say, burying my face in his chest as he hugs me.

The place is empty. His dad is traveling for work, so he takes me into the kitchen and starts to make this homemade hot chocolate from a huge block of dark chocolate. I notice that the cupboards are pretty bare. I'm guessing he and his dad don't cook very much.

"What happened?" he asks since I'm just sitting at the table smooshing a marshmallow, unsure of where to start.

"I told Gordy about us." I wait for him to ask why that would upset me so. But he seems to know. He sits down with the hot chocolate and looks in my eyes.

"I wondered about that today. You don't really see who you are. You don't really know how any guy who got close to you would feel about you. It just wouldn't be possible for Gordy not to be hurt."

"I'm a despicable person."

"Because Gordy's hurt."

"Because I'm the one who hurt him." I turn the mug over in my hands. It's a souvenir from Muir Woods. It looks like his younger sister decorated his mug at Color Me Mine; it's purple swirls with a pink heart on the bottom.

"How? Did you lead him on? Did you make promises that you didn't keep?"

I don't know what to say. So I hold the mug to my lips but can't bring myself to take a sip.

"Of course you didn't."

"I did. I thought I could just be his best friend and at the same time sort of keep alive the possibility that maybe someday we could be even more than that."

"And that makes you despicable, huh?"

I nod. Tears flow from my eyes, but I'm not crying. It feels like something punctured the dam today and I'm leaking. I turn my gaze from him. The hardwood floor of their kitchen is immaculate. Not a crumb. A stray tear splashes by the leg of my chair.

"What you're not looking at is that Gordy felt exactly the same. Neither of you had found the person you really belonged to. And you were both wondering if maybe that meant someday you'd belong to each other."

He reaches out and strokes my hair. I hold the warm mug between both my hands and sit still, frozen in my chair, staring at the floor.

"And then you found me."

I sniffle and look up at his elegant hand curved around the purple cup. I can now smell the rich earthiness of the chocolate. "Oh and you're so great, huh?"

"It's not about me being great. We belong together."

My eyes dart to his and I study them briefly; the flecks of blue, brown, and green meld together into a solid granite color. "You say that. But you don't know me."

"But I do. There are a million little pieces that I don't know, and it may take the rest of our lives for me to learn them all. But I know that you're wonderful."

"Except you're wrong. You're really, really wrong. It's nothing to do with Gordy. I'm the last person in the world that someone like you should waste their time with." The mug suddenly feels hot and my hands are sweating. I put it down on the table and rest my hands under my thighs.

He grins. "Okay, just tell me why."

"Because I'm crazy." I say this softly, to the clock on the wall behind him.

"That's the most adorable part."

I look directly at him now. "No. Not adorable crazy. Actually, psychotically, clinically crazy. Secretly crazy. In a way no one could ever understand. No one could ever understand about me and Maggie."

Something in his face changes; he is alert. He immediately understands that there is something really wrong here. Something really wrong with me.

"Who's Maggie?"

I can't open my mouth. I can barely breathe.

"Sloane. Who's Maggie?"

"She's me."

CHAPTER TWENTY-ONE

MAGGIE

I'm a hot mess. My mouth is tacky and dry. My lips are raw and chapped. My hair looks like a hamster has gone loco in my locks. My cheeks appear as if they've been sandpapered, and last night's mascara is basically everywhere. Thank the good Lord I turned down Andrew's sweet begging for me to stay the night with him. If he could see me right now, he'd wonder whether his fancy French wine gave him beer goggles.

He raced back into the restaurant (after enough people on the street told us to get a room), grabbed the bottle, threw money on the table, ran back out, and we caught a cab for his place. I am not really experienced at making out (without a script). If someone told me to make out for four hours with (mostly) all my clothes on, I'd have no clue how to keep that interesting. Turns out, it wasn't interesting, it was spectacular. The secret is choosing the right guy.

By far the best night of my life.

This morning, I leave extra early to meet him for brunch. As I'm walking down Houston, I start to realize how pissed off I am at Sloane. After all that hand-wringing and whining about how she could never tell anyone about us, and least of all the amazing James, she just blurts it all out in the scariest, craziest way possible. The worst part is, she gave away so many private and secret things about my life. I would never do that to her.

The subject makes me walk faster and more aggressively, like a typical New Yorker. I weave through a crowd waiting for the walk signal at West Broadway and position myself in front. As I'm crossing the street, an attractive blonde coming toward me catches my eye. I have a feeling I know her from somewhere but know I really don't, so she must just be reminding me of someone I do know, and when we pass . . .

. . . she flashes this really warm smile and says, "Hey, Sloane," and walks right by.

Amanda Porcella.

I whip around. There is nobody there. There are hundreds of people there, but they are all real, they belong to the world. Not to my dream. I stand there in the middle of the crosswalk, terrified for a moment.

It must have been a real blonde, who thought she knew me, and I imagined the Sloane part. The light is about to change and I'm like a squirrel, turning back the way I came. I think she went south on West Broadway. I head down the block, almost pushing my way through to the curb, trying to beat the timing of the lights, but I can't get through the sea of people. Three blocks later I give up. I'm just tired. It's surprising that my mind doesn't play these tricks more often.

When I get to brunch, he's already at the table, and he looks really upset. More than upset, angry. What have I done? Or not done? It can't be that. When he sees me coming, he jumps up, kisses me, holds my chair. And when he sits back down, he says, "I've got to tell you something."

I take a sip of water, bracing myself. I blew it. I risked my friendship with him by crossing the line with that kiss, all those kisses last night, and now I'll have none of him. He's going to say this isn't working for him. Last night was a mistake. Every cornball line that every actor has ever said to every actress on-screen when dumping her rolls through my mind.

He must be able to see it happening because he reaches out and takes my hand, gently kisses each finger, and says, "I'm so happy I finally get to do this, and this, and this . . ."

And all is once again well in the world, until he tells me he spoke to Edward Duncan after class this morning. The Dunc, as Andrew calls him, is the professor who'd admired my Inuit accent and who is kind of a mentor and a friend to Andrew. He also happens to be good friends with Macauley Evans. Andrew asked the Dunc to find out why I lost the role.

"Macauley told Duncan that someone inside the situation, who knew you personally, confided that you have a serious drug problem and that your behavior is extremely erratic."

My whole life implodes before my eyes. All the work and sacrifice, the cattle call auditions, weathering every inch of me being picked apart and judged, all for nothing. I'll be known as uninsurable, unbankable, unworthy. It had to be Thomas. How could anyone be so vindictive and evil and hurtful?

"Duncan said you'd been Macauley's first choice."

"Then why wouldn't he come and talk to me about it?"

"Because people are cowards and take the easy way out. And I guess he would never assume that anyone would be a big enough asshole to lie about something like this. Particularly since Thomas, the prick, recommended you for the role in the first place."

"Thanks," I say. I jump up from the table and run out the door. I don't know if he's coming after me because I catch a cab so fast it doesn't matter.

On the way to Thomas's office, I realize that making a scene there will brand me as an unbalanced druggie. So I call on all of my training, pull out my cell phone (ignoring Andrew's third missed call), find my center (yep, we actually do that), and call Thomas. I make nice to his assistant, and when I get him on the phone, I'm bright and sunny. I tell him I miss him and that maybe now that I'm not going to be doing the show, we can pick things back up.

He buys it. He asks about Andrew. I say Andrew who? And he asks me to lunch.

I hang up and say a little prayer before I call to set the essential post-lunch appointment. It is carefully explained that I'm being squeezed in and there will only be a few minutes. That will be plenty. I turn off my phone after texting Andrew that I'm on a vigilante mission and will be in a much better mood by dinner. I need to focus.

I sort of hide halfway down the street until I see Thomas walk into Nobu. I take ten minutes to both gather my wits and make him wait. When I finally enter, I head straight toward his table. He jumps up with a smile. I smile back and say in my sweetest voice, "Sit the fuck down."

Having thus established the proper tone, I take a seat, lean forward keeping my smile in place and my voice low. "Rule number one of this conversation, you have no lines. Here's what's going to happen: your career, your professional life, is over. Thank you for your attention."

I stand up and walk out of the place. I can't help high-fiving a random businessman once I'm on the street.

After scarfing down two victory sandwiches at Pain Quotidien, I'm feeling that a beer or something stronger at some bar that will serve me might give me extra courage, but would also let my afternoon meeting smell something on my breath. Accordingly, my breath becomes laced with hot chocolate.

I walk into the lobby adorned with movie posters of all the films they've cast. The receptionist offers me a seat and a bottle of water. I take a seat as directed and pull out my Kindle. What will I do if Thomas shows up? I decide that if he gets in my face before I get into Rosalie's office, it will be the second-biggest mistake of his worthless life. The rat never shows and the receptionist misses out on the throw-down of the century.

Rosalie greets me warmly, probably figuring that this will simply be her chance to reassure a young actress that she has a bright future. Obviously, she has no idea that I know why I lost the role. She begins with all the expected positive and encouraging words, ending by telling me that it was extremely close between me and the other actress.

"I know it was close. I also know that Macauley had chosen me. I was only denied the role when your employee, Mr. Randazzo, defamed me to all of you by alleging that I had a substance abuse problem. Why no one came to me with this ridiculous story is a bit of a mystery. Why Mr. Randazzo told the lie is not." I sound a little bit like a lawyer on a procedural TV show, but too late to change tactics now.

Rosalie sits, listening with attention, revealing nothing on her face. For all I know, she's pressing some button beneath her desk to call security.

"Mr. Randazzo has been sexually pursuing me from the moment he met me, trying to dangle this role as an incentive to get me in bed. As you know, I'm underage. When he learned that I was rejecting him and dating someone else . . ."

"That nice guy who was with you at the audition. I thought so."

"So we have two choices. I turn this over to my attorney, and that's the end of it. Or you can do some belated due diligence. It's not possible for someone to have a serious drug problem with no trail of any kind. You can talk to my family, friends, physician, everyone in my life. Police. I'll happily take a drug test for you right now . . ."

"None of that is going to be necessary. You're a wonderful young actress, but you're not good enough to be faking this conversation. I will confront Thomas, and unless he can offer some kind of proof, he'll be fired immediately. I'm sorry to say, terribly sorry to say, that the role has been given to Rebecca McNally; her deal has been closed. I'll have to find some other way to make this up to you. I promise it will happen."

Then she looks at me in silence and says, "I'm sorry for my cowardice. It was easier for all of us to just take the other girl and let it go."

I don't smile. I simply say, "Apology accepted."

I stand up. We shake hands. I walk out.

When I hit the street, I try calling Andrew to explain and apologize. When he doesn't take my call, I try texting Andrew to explain and apologize, asking him to call me right away. Four ignored stalker calls later, I'm beginning to feel I'm in trouble.

I go by his apartment. Nope. I could wander the gaggle of buildings that comprise NYU's non-campus, but I wouldn't know where to look. I could go home to my apartment and wait, but the idea of being in my empty apartment, alone, makes me feel restless.

So I sit at Union Square Café and drink tea and worry. I stay there because it's the only place he knows I go to a lot. Maybe his phone broke again and he'll come find me here.

Jimmy puts the bread basket on the empty place setting and takes away the silverware. "I'm sorry, honey," he says, and touches my shoulder.

"No. I'm not alone. I mean, I'm alone right now. But that boy, he's my boyfriend," I try to explain. I think he's still my boyfriend.

At six o'clock, my phone rings. Finally. I give him my cheeriest, "Hi. I'm so sorry."

"You ought to be." But it isn't really Andrew's voice. It's a voice I can't place at all, apparently a wrong number.

For some reason, I say, "Excuse me?"

"I think you should know that I saw Mr. Wonderful with his arm around some French chick shopping for groceries at Puritan and Genesta. They couldn't keep their hands off each other."

And now I know the voice. It's Gordy.

"Sloane? Are you there? I mean, great choice. Just wanted to congratulate you."

"Gordy?"

"Who's Gordy?" Because the voice now belongs to Andrew. My brain freezes. What is happening? I can't deal with this, but I have to say something. Of course, I come up with the worst possible alternative.

"I thought you were someone else."

"Well, that was pretty clear, unless you'd forgotten my name."

I swallow hard. Close my eyes. "Please. Please don't be mad at me. It's been a tough day."

"I'm sorry about that. But who is Gordy?"

"Gordy's nobody. It was a bad connection, and I thought some guy said 'this is Gordy.' That's why I said 'excuse me.' "

He buys it. Or maybe not. I beg him to come meet me. There's a moment of silence. I'm sure I've lost him forever. Then . . .

"I don't think I want to see you tonight. Look, I'm really hurt. If we're together, that's the last time you shut me out. I'd never do that to you."

I try to agree and beg forgiveness, but he cuts me off: "Don't do that. Just sleep on it, think about it. Okay?"

"I promise."

"Just one more question," he says. "How did the Thomas thing turn out?"

"I lost the role. I cleared my name. I got the prick fired."

"Two out of three, not a bad day's work. I'll see you tomorrow. I love you."

And he hangs up. *He loves me.* No boy has ever said that to me before. It feels like a life raft I can cling to.

I walk around the city for hours. Tonight I'm not making up

stories about other people. Amanda this morning, Gordy on the phone. My stomach is in knots. This has never happened before. I have to keep Sloane's people in my dreams where they belong.

And as euphoric as I am to hear that Andrew loves me, I walk dark streets knowing that this is the very thing that will ultimately drive him away.

As I get undressed for bed, usually there is kind of a rising excitement that now I'll get to be Sloane for a while. Tonight it's a different feeling. I'm so scared to be in the real world, it'll be an escape to go to sleep, to run to Mystic, to the world of explaining myself to a fantasy boyfriend who can't really hurt me even if he leaves.

Just as I slide under the covers, there's a knock at my door. A little strange, only because both Nicole and Jade would open the door a nanosecond after knocking. But it doesn't really register, so I say, "Come in."

My door creaks open, slowly. Too slowly to be Nicole or Jade. Who is in my house? Who is coming into my room right now?

"Sweetheart? I know that every rule has its exceptions. And I know how much your time with James means to you . . ."

It's Sloane's mother. Walking into my room. Coming toward me, like she is going to touch me or something. I open my throat to scream, but nothing comes out. I pull the covers up so violently that my head bangs against the wall. But she keeps coming, like a ghost, a zombie . . .

"We have to talk about this, Sloane."

"Stop it!" I yell. "I'm not Sloane!"

I shut my eyes so tight they hurt. I plug my ears but can still hear . . .

"Your curfew is eleven o'clock, and that's perfectly generous for a girl who's just turned seventeen."

I can feel her body sitting down on the edge of my bed. And I actually say out loud, "Go away, go away, please, please, please . . ."

Her voice stops. I open my eyes. Of course there is nothing there.

But my door is open.

CHAPTER TWENTY-TWO

SLOANE

I'm awake, but afraid to open my eyes. So this is what a nightmare feels like. My heart beats in a way I can feel at the base of my throat. I'm sweating all over and my T-shirt is drenched like I have a fever. I force myself to open my eyes, and there is my tree and my room and the real world. It's raining outside.

I was right. The dam is leaking. I can't hold it all back anymore. My tears. My secret. The real world pouring in on Maggie. James punctured the dam. Maybe now that I have him I don't need her anymore. Maybe it's all for the best.

In the shower, I keep thinking about the relief I felt when I told him. I have been protecting and guarding this part of me because I believed it would be horrible for someone to know it. But the release of the pressure that had built up made every detail just gush out of me. And it felt good.

He didn't back away in horror as I'd expected. The more I

explained, the more he seemed to think it was the most fascinating thing he's ever heard. He kept saying that I must be brilliant and incredibly creative to be "doing something like this," as if it's something I can control.

The one question he asked over and over again was whether Maggie's world seems as real to me as my own. I told him that my world was the only real world to me, just as Maggie's was the only real world to her. So it's equal.

He noticed that sometimes I speak of Maggie as if we are separate people. I told him we couldn't be more different. I described her appearance. I told him all these stories and anecdotes about things that happen to Maggie and how she handles them. About Nicole and Jade, and acting, and Emma, even her flirtation with Thomas. I told him about everything. Except for Andrew.

I told him how Maggie makes up stories about people and how she sees the world so differently from me.

"So you get to be things as Maggie that you aren't willing to be in real life," he said.

"She's very exotic and free-spirited and imaginative and, well, glamorous, I guess. If you knew her, you'd probably prefer her to me," I told him.

"Actually, I'd prefer you."

"Why is that?"

"Because I prefer you to anyone."

I study my reflection in the mirror and expect to see an entirely different girl. A girl who James would prefer to anyone. A girl who doesn't have to keep secrets. But it's just me staring back.

When I walk into the kitchen for breakfast, my mom turns to

me with a serious look. I shudder as I remember seeing my mom in my dream.

"We have to talk," she says.

"We do?"

"Your curfew is eleven o'clock. And I think that's perfectly reasonable."

I try to remember if those are the exact words she said to Maggie last night. They aren't. They're similar, but that shouldn't be frightening. I did miss curfew, and there are only so many ways to say that.

"I'm really sorry. James and I were talking, just talking, and I know that's no excuse, and I'm going to be really careful that it doesn't happen again."

I gulp down my breakfast and hurry out to make the bus, grabbing an umbrella by the door. I skip down the porch steps zipping up my backpack, realizing I'm really late. But when I look up, I'm stopped cold.

The rain has stopped and there he is. Parked at the curb. Just beautiful and smiling at me, lit like in a movie, like a special ray of sunshine is streaming down just to illuminate those lips I get to kiss. All the snakes and demons in my mind are gone. Because the real world is my perfect boyfriend, deciding to surprise me with a ride to school. This is going to be my real life. Being taken care of by him. Belonging to him. I will cling to this, and never let it go, and everything will be all right.

I jump in the car and he kisses me. As if that is a small and normal and perfectly understandable thing to do.

He asks me if we can go somewhere tonight, promising in the same sentence not to break my curfew again. He has a gig playing with some guys at the Bank Street Café in New London. He can't wait for me to hear him play. He seems nervous and excited about the chance to impress me.

My boyfriend is a rock star driving a Porsche. Eat that, Maggie. I start to fantasize about the summer; maybe we can drive up to Cape Cod with the top down and I'll wear big sunglasses and a scarf in my hair, and we'll rent a shingled big house and roll around together in the surf. I'm already starting to plan my pitch to Mom; I mean, I'll be almost seventeen and a half—it is the twenty-first century.

"You know what we should do this summer? I was thinking maybe we could rent some place on the Cape?" I'll blow out my vet money.

He's silent and just keeps looking at the road.

"Unless you want to do something else," I say, backpedaling.

"It isn't that," he says. "I just have plans to go surfing in Costa Rica with these guys. I have been thinking about going to Peru and doing the Inca trail after that. I've been looking forward to it for a long time."

I am in shock. He's abandoning me and I look like an idiot for thinking otherwise.

"But," he adds, "I could come back like a week before school starts, and we could do something. Anything you want."

He throws me a bone. And I'm grateful. And even more embarrassed, my expectations in check. I've always wanted to do something different during the summer, something other than working at the vet, going to the beach or out on Gordy's boat on my days off, having dinner with my family every night on our back porch. I was getting ahead of myself by thinking James was my ticket out of town.

He reaches over and puts his hand on my thigh. As if that will make everything all right. And of course, it does. For the moment.

All morning long in class, it isn't so all right anymore. I mean, even if he isn't going to cancel on his buddies, he could invite me along. And certainly Peru, where it sounded like he was going alone anyway. Maybe he thinks my parents won't let me go, but that's no excuse for not asking. Maybe Kelly is right.

At lunch, we are all crammed into the cafeteria because the rain has left the grass muddy and messy. It is noisy and there's nowhere to hide. I still feel like an animal in the zoo the way people are staring at me. No one is gawking at James that way, of course. I watch him walk with his tray and sit down with Lee Parker and a bunch of guys from Double Negative, a surprisingly good local band that plays hot venues like the Elks club. No one is glaring at him or whispering when he walks by. They save it for me.

Kelly and Lila download me on the latest about my reputation as a backstabbing slutty man stealer. Not to worry, that rep is completely intact. Street cred to spare. Apparently, Amanda has put the word out that she and James broke up before I shamelessly seduced him. So technically, I'm not a complete felon. Just a hooker in the right place at the right time. You can imagine my relief.

Across the cafeteria, I catch a glimpse of Gordy eating with his boys. He gives me a tight, too-quick smile. I can tell we aren't so okay after all. All my instincts are to run over there and somehow make it all better. Obviously, I would only be making things incredibly worse. I have to give him the space to come around on his own. Something I am uniquely ill suited for.

In fact, so ill suited that I simply have to create an excuse to see just how bad things are. So I pull out my dad's old Nikon and go over to the guys, excusing myself for a second while I take pictures of them for the yearbook. Two of the three guys smile for the shot. Guess who doesn't? My heart is in my throat; I try one desperate, "Thanks, guys." Two guys say, "No problem." I have definitely made things worse.

After school I have to develop ten rolls of film for the yearbook. I've been ignoring the deadline, which of course is suddenly breathing down my neck. I find refuge in the darkroom. It almost feels like I'm underwater. Quiet, protected, in a world of my own that no one can intrude on.

Since I'm developing negatives and prints, I just kept the red light on outside the door so no one will come in. The egg timer goes off and I move some negatives to their last cold water rinse. I pull them out to hang and turn toward the dry wire.

There he is. Six inches away.

I scream and scream with everything in me. But Thomas just smiles this cruel, ugly smile.

"You little cock tease," he says. "You really thought you could mess with me."

I keep screaming and lurch backward against the metal counter; bottles of chemicals spill onto the floor. He starts toward me; I put my hands over my eyes and tell myself it's not real, he's not there, nothing can hurt you.

And he grabs my wrist.

He grabs it hard. Twists it, so it feels like my shoulder will dislocate. His face mocks my terror and relishes the moment, taking his time. My free hand finds a metal tray full of chemicals and I swing it at his face with all my strength, and just as the sharp edge slashes his cheek, he lets go of my wrist and I bolt out the door.

The light in the shop room is blindingly bright. Amanda is sitting on a desk, looking at her phone. I'm so shaken that it doesn't register that this is a place Amanda never comes. I'm relieved to see anyone.

"There's someone in there," I say, looking back through the open doors.

"No, there's not. I've been sitting out here waiting for that damn red light to go off for over an hour."

"You're wrong. There's somebody there."

She hops off the desk, brushes by me on her way into the darkroom. As she flips on the main lights, of course no one is there and I know that I can't explain my hallucination. She turns back with her hands on her hips.

"Can we talk?" It's more a demand than a question.

I don't know what to say. She walks right up to my face.

"Look," she says, in a voice so hard, so unlike a tone I've ever heard from her that I wonder if she is really there. Of course she is actually there; she's from my world. "I really don't appreciate you talking shit about me to James and making him come talk to me about clearing up your reputation."

My mind is spinning. I never did any such thing.

"I mean," she goes on, "everybody hates you anyway. Always so stuck up, so condescending; you think people don't notice? You think people are stupid? Everyone's just been waiting for you to pull something like this."

"Pull something like what?"

"Whether or not James and I were together, you knew how much I liked him. And you and I were friends."

"I called you. I told you."

"You think that makes it okay? You told me. You didn't ask me. You told me after you'd already gotten him to ask you out. So what was I supposed to say? You think everybody's got the wrong idea? Everybody has exactly the right idea. They see who you are."

"Whether you believe it or not, I had no idea he talked to you. What did he say?"

"He said that I was supposed to tell everyone that he and I were just friends when you got together. And he implied it was my fault everyone is mad at you. I've known James for years, and whatever it was you told him, it was the first time I've ever seen him angry with me. And that hurts, Sloane. More than you could ever know. Because when he's through with you, and believe me it won't be long, it's completely unfair of you to ruin things for me."

Without waiting for an answer, she pushes by me, grabs her bag from the desk, and is gone.

I sit down and start crying. My hands are shaking. I am losing my mind, and all of this high school drama with Amanda just makes me feel even more disoriented. Thomas isn't real, but he grabbed me, I felt it. What would've happened if I hadn't hit him? How far could he have gone? I have no Emma in my life. There is absolutely no one I can even tell this to.

I will just have to gut it out, pretend it isn't happening. Because, of course, it isn't. I'm fine. Really.

Later at home, I stand in front of the mirror, dressing for my big night out with James. I decide to wear a skirt so that if he puts his hand on my thigh again, he will feel my skin. I try on three different tops. As if my choosing the perfect one will make him love me. Love me enough to not leave me over the summer. Love me enough to not leave me if he finds out what is happening to me. No. No one could love me that much. Which is why no one can ever know.

When I come downstairs, James is already there, schmoozing my parents, who obviously are eating him up with a spoon. Even my dad, who is a tough audience. I don't know what it is, maybe the fact that he's going to be performing onstage, but he looks the best I've ever seen anyone look.

Driving to New London, he tells me I look beautiful. He just says it once, very simply, but it makes my heart pound.

I have to sneak in the back with him through the stage door because, well, I'm well underage and my fake ID sucks. Gordy scored it for me in Providence. My name is Shamika Jones. My explanation to bouncers or bartenders is that my mom speaks Swahili, and it means "beautiful soul." Maybe it does in some language.

He finds me a nice table and flirts with the waitress so that she won't card me. I order a rum and Coke. The band is in the middle of their first set, so we have time to talk. Even though it's a pretty ordinary bar, it's dark, our table has a little votive candle, and it feels really romantic. He wants to talk about Maggie, of course. But I anticipated this and know exactly what to do. Which is to talk about him. Never, ever fails.

"Okay, I can tell you don't want to talk about your dreams, or dream I should say; I just want you to know that whenever you do, I'm here."

I don't know what to start asking about him, so of course, I pick the very worst thing.

"Did your dad take you on a college tour? Mine did, but I was only looking at New York and Boston. And my heart is already set on Columbia."

"You have a very original way of asking about me."

I laugh. "Okay, enough about me; let's talk about you. So tell me, what do you think about me?"

"I think I'm really going to miss you when I'm in Oxford."

I never stopped to think that something like this could happen. He's a top student; he could go to Harvard or Yale or, God willing, slum it at Columbia with me. But he is going to abandon me for real. Not just a few weeks, but forever. There is no way he's going to Oxford and coming out the other end looking for me.

I keep my brightest smile shining. Maggie would be proud.

"Well, won't you miss me?" he asks with a playful smile.

"I don't know if I like you enough to miss you."

He plays with his napkin, folding the edges. "Lucky for me I was only kidding."

A wave of relief surges through me, and I try to maintain enough cool to hide it.

"I don't know where I want to go to school," he says, "or even what I want to study. Some days it's architecture, or engineering, languages . . ."

I'm kind of listening to what comes out of his mouth but more looking at it. There is something about the way he shapes his words that makes me want to lean across the table and kiss him.

So I lean across the table and kiss him. It is very sweet and playful.

He reaches over and takes my hand as we're kissing. I always kiss with my eyes closed. I'm not sure why. Maybe it's because in all the movies I've seen, the actresses look funny, almost cross-eyed, if they don't. But I want to see him, so I flutter one eye open, just a slit. His eyes are wide open; he is just staring at me. Like the length of my nose away. It seems funny, so I laugh. He isn't offended. He just looks like he'd like to do some more kissing. So we do.

When we stop, our drinks have magically appeared. It's nice of the waitress not to interrupt us. I'm beginning to feel, you know, all the world loves a lover, and everyone in the place and the entire universe thinks we're adorable. And I am not a crazy girl, just a lucky girl in love.

The band finishes their set. The lead guitarist leans to the mike, gives James this half-assed introduction, as if he is only there to fill in during their break (because it turns out that's the only reason he is there). And I applaud like crazy, even whistle as he makes his way to the stage. My enthusiasm encourages some copycat applause, which he finds highly amusing.

Once he's onstage, the lights come down. They hit him with a spotlight, and he begins to play some transcendently exquisite and complicated piece. While I really like listening to the flamenco album I purchased, it is now my favorite art form ever. I have absolutely no talent, except a small one in photography, and animals like me if you can call that a talent. How long has he been doing this? How often does he practice? How cool is he to never have bragged about this? Almost the best part is that this is the kind of guitar-playing he's chosen, not the I-want-to-rock-out-and-get-girls garage band type.

His playing is so physical, as if he were part of the instrument.

His arm muscles are flexed, but he's cradling the guitar so lovingly. I am aware of the strength in his fingers as they move along the neck of the guitar and the unexpected, rhythmic slaps against the wood. And his face. The concentration, the almost devotion to strumming each phrase. None of the people in this place deserve to be hearing this. They are talking and slurping their American drafts. People are so inconsiderate.

Just as I'm wondering what I can do about it, someone puts a hand on my shoulder. I turn, irritated by the intrusion.

"I've been calling you for hours. You have to come with me right now."

For a second, I don't even recognize this crazy woman who clearly has me confused with someone else. I raise my finger to my lips to quiet her and suddenly realize.

It is Nicole.

"Jade is in the hospital. They think it was an aneurysm. She's been in surgery. We have to get back."

She stares at me, incredulous that I'm not reacting as she'd expect.

"Did you hear what I just said?" she asks angrily.

I nod dumbly. She shoots me a dirty look and takes off through the crowd toward the door, assuming I'll follow. I can't move, I can't think. Suddenly, a hand is on my shoulder again, and I scream so loud half the place whips around.

"Are you okay?"

It's James. He'd finished, everyone had applauded or not, and he is already at the table. How long was I hypnotized? There he is, smile, damn it. Keep it together.

"Yeah! You were so amazing!" I try to shout as loudly as I screamed.

He smiles back and leans to my ear. "I liked knowing you were watching." He kisses my ear, which only one boy has ever done before. It is my spot. It makes me melt in a way that is so exciting I kind of squirm.

In the car ride home I try not to obsess on the hallucination. But I'm lost in my thoughts.

"I bet I know why you're so quiet," he says.

"Oh, I bet you don't."

"I could tell you were bummed that I'd made plans for the summer. So am I. So I'm thinking, how would you like to wander around Spain for a while? We could start in the south. Marbella has incredible beaches." As he is talking, he reaches over and starts rubbing the back of my neck, as if he is playing it like his guitar. "We'll skip the bullfights in Toledo, and hang out in Madrid, and finish in Barcelona. Because that's the best."

He's clearly expecting me to be thrilled out of my mind. Unfortunately, I am. Apart from how difficult it would be to talk my parents into something like this, there's the small matter that I will most likely be committed to a mental hospital long before.

"What? I'll talk to your parents. I know I can sell it."

This perfect, unattainable life is so near and will never really be mine. I guess there are tears standing in my eyes.

"What's wrong?"

"Nothing's wrong," I say, blinking the tears away. "Everything is more perfect than I ever dreamed it could be."

CHAPTER TWENTY-THREE

MAGGIE

My eyes snap open. I fight the urge to jump out of bed and race down to Jade's room. Obviously, that was just a dream, Jade is okay, and if I start chasing down every nightmare, I'll have completely lost control. So I climb out of bed, and as slowly as I'm able to make myself walk, I go down the hall and peek in on my angelically sleeping baby sister.

She may be the most precious thing I stand to lose.

I can't resist climbing into bed with her, spooning her little body, listening to that soft puppy breath she makes when she sleeps. Jade would literally keep snoring if a marching band stormed down the hall. She doesn't stir as I kiss her head and sneak back out of her room. I wonder what she's dreaming about.

I call Emma and leave a message asking if she can squeeze me in today for an extra session because I'm having an emergency.

I start to call Andrew and stop myself, panicked that if something happens while I'm with him, something like what happened to Sloane at the bar, I could never hide it from Andrew. If he knew that I am finally unraveling, it would be over between us. Eventually, if not immediately. Of course that's the inevitable. I'm only trying to buy a little bit of time.

He doesn't pick up. He's preparing for finals and has probably locked himself in the stacks or an editing bay. I wish him good luck and tell him to call me as soon as he needs a break.

I run cold water in the bathroom sink, splash my face, and when I look up into the mirror . . .

Sloane is staring back at me. I scream. The bathroom reflected in the mirror is hers and not mine. I shut my eyes and take a deep breath. My hands grip the sink for support, and rather than smooth porcelain, I can feel the grooves of small tiles. I spin around, open my eyes, and . . .

Gasp. I am standing in her bathroom. The towels are blue, outside the window is her tree, her shampoo is on the tub ledge. I feel dizzy and reach back to brace myself on the sink. I stare at the drain. Just focus on the drain. I close my eyes and lift my head back to face the mirror.

I'm myself again. The bathroom is mine once more. My toothbrush is on the sink. I stand there gripping the sink with both hands, listening to my heart pounding. I'm afraid to take my eyes from the mirror. Afraid to lose myself in it again.

Jade drags herself sleepily through the door, sits on the toilet, and pees.

"What are you doing?"

"What does it look like?" I manage.

"Um. Either you're acting or you're trying to hypnotize yourself."

"God, I wish I could do that." I laugh weakly. "Can you show me how?"

"Sure," she says. She wipes, flushes, and shoves me out of the way so she can wash her hands. Then she motions for me to get down to her level. She opens her eyes absurdly wide.

"Look deep into my eyes." So I do. "You are getting sleepy. Very sleepy. When I clap, you will cluck like a chicken." And she claps. I moo like a cow.

"Close enough," she says proudly. "Now when I snap my fingers, you will make me silver dollar pancakes. Swimming in maple syrup."

Try as she might, however, the Great Jadini cannot snap her fingers. But I make her pancakes anyway.

Even though it's Nicole's day to drop her, I walk Jade to school because I can't bear to let her go, not knowing when I might break down completely and never see her again. She asks when Andrew is going to make her dinner again. I say I'll ask him tonight. She rolls her eyes at me.

"I would hope that you and he are close enough that you'd know he's studying for finals. And you should respect that. Schoolwork comes first, but when it's over, he can make me spaghetti and butter sauce."

"He and I are close enough that I kiss him."

Her eyes get huge and she does this little jazz hand motion. After a moment's reflection, she looks at me suspiciously. "Does he kiss back?"

I nod, yep.

"On the lips?"

"And on my neck and my ear."

"Gross. Like a wet willy?"

"Exactly."

We walk on in silence.

"Are you jealous?" I ask.

"Of course. I liked him first."

"Are you mad at me?"

"No. I have three boyfriends at school and Rico in swim class and sort of Ben in arts and crafts. Not to mention the whole Josh Hinkle thing. And you really needed one."

"Thanks," I say. "I owe you one."

I'm distracted as we walk. A bit paranoid, checking out every face that passes, each storefront, the shopkeeper sweeping his stoop, the dog raising its leg on the tulips to make sure everything is in its place and from the real world.

Emma cancels another patient to meet my emergency. When I walk in, she does this super-calm thing that seems so artificial I regret ever calling her.

So I sit on her sofa, holding the box of Kleenex, and tell her all the horrible stuff without holding back. She keeps nodding support-ively, as if to reassure me that this isn't freaking her out and that we can absolutely handle it. When I've talked myself dry, she asks . . .

"Are you ready to let Sloane go?"

"I don't know if I can. I don't know how to."

"But do you want to?"

"I don't know."

"Talk about that."

So I think about whether I want to finally say goodbye to Sloane.

The real answer is absolutely not. At the very least, she's my best friend. Only she knows who I really am and everything there is to know about me. I don't know where I'd be without her.

"I guess I'm afraid of losing her."

"How much would you give up to keep her?"

"A lot."

"Would you give up Andrew?"

The truth is yes, I would. Because Sloane isn't actually my best friend. She is me. It'd be giving up myself.

"Yes."

"Would you give up Jade?"

I stare at the floor.

"Because, Maggie, that's where you're heading. You're afraid that people you love will leave you. But you're leaving them. And you're picking up speed."

"How would it work, anyway? I just wouldn't ever go to sleep or something?"

My cell phone rings. I reach for it to turn it off.

"That's all right. If you left it on, you left it on because you needed to. Is it Andrew?"

I look at the screen. It isn't Andrew.

Of course I can't find a cab, so I run across the park and up Madison. I walk the last block to Sant Ambroeus so I can gather my breath. As I enter the restaurant, I see my reflection. My cheeks are flushed, my skin is glowing from my unexpected jog. I look healthy and alive and totally not crazy.

Macauley is sitting at a choice table. Wearing the most welcoming smile, he jumps to his feet and waves me over. I can't believe this is happening. I am going to be Robin.

He holds my shoulders, kisses both cheeks, and tells me how excited he is.

"What happened?" I ask. "Did she get sick or take another role?"

"Nope. I just came to my senses and realized that you were Robin and I would be the luckiest of men if you forgave me."

I glance beyond his shoulder—and my heart jolts in my chest. The girls at the next table, incongruously drinking martinis, are Sloane's best friends Kelly and Lila. They're dressed as young Upper East Siders, but there is no mistaking who they are.

"Well. Don't keep me in suspense." He smiles, clearly not in suspense at all. "If you wait any longer to say yes, I'm going to have to start increasing your salary."

"That will hardly be necessary. This is basically the happiest moment of my life, and I promise you that you'll never regret it."

And over his shoulder, Lila stands to make her way to the bathroom while Kelly calls the server over for a refill.

"Everything all right?" Macauley asks, craning to see what has my attention.

"I thought I saw someone I know."

"We're going to shoot the pilot in July, when Blake wraps her feature. Gives you plenty of time to get settled in LA. Do you think your mom will come with you?"

My mind is beyond spinning. Everything about this moment feels surreal. I hang on to the edge of the table. "She couldn't; her work is here."

"No problem, you'll just go through the emancipation process. It's simple and quick."

Easier, I guess, than emancipating myself from Sloane.

"Can you do me a favor?" Macauley asks. "I'm reading an actress for Zoey, and I'd like to do the scene she does with you and Ryan, where you catch them together. And it'd be nice to see the two of you in frame. Are you free after lunch?"

As we leave the restaurant, I glance back. Lila and Kelly are still at the table. They're sharing a pile of pasta. Kelly looks up while delicately sucking a strand of linguine and stares right at me. And winks.

In the cab down to the rehearsal hall, Macauley rolls calls. I stare out the window, grounding myself with the New York streetscape. And I realize that if this actually happens, I'll be moving to Los Angeles. But I wonder what it would be like to move away from Andrew and Jade and Nicole and the city and everything I've known all my life, outside of Mystic, Connecticut. Maybe my insanity has the one silver lining that I won't be put to the decision of separating from everything I love.

At the rehearsal hall I'm introduced to Layne Seebran. I've seen her work on a soap and remember she was good despite the ridiculous story line. I think she played a girl who moves to town with the horrible secret that she received a brain transplant from a famous villainous character who died a mysterious death. No one ever dies for long in soap opera land. She is pretty and well trained. Without the training, she'd be a weather girl or a beauty contestant.

She's nervous, eagerly trying to make friends with me and with Ryan as if we might actually be able to help her land the role. I'm sympathetic because I've been there more times than I'd like to remember.

Ryan greets me with a gropey hug and a kiss on the mouth. He talks about how happy he is that we'll be moving to LA, almost as if we are moving there together. He tells me all about how well he knows the city and that he'll show me the ropes.

During wardrobe and makeup, Layne pops a Xanax. She confides that she self-medicates a lot. She seems very insecure about her look for this particular character, over-instructing the makeup artist as to how best to line her eyes. I wonder what meds they'll be dishing out in those tiny Dixie cups after my breakdown. Which leads to the major question of whether Nicole will be able to keep me at home or whether I'll be institutionalized. That question, as if those were the only two possible alternative futures, just slips into my head like the most natural thing in the world. This is going to happen to me, is already happening to me.

The scene requires Layne to show up at Ryan's apartment and boldly seduce him, almost immediately following her entrance. I will be Ryan's girlfriend at this point and will interrupt them. Not much for me to do except slap the shit out of Layne, spit on Ryan, and slam the door. This might be the last time I ever get to act in a scene. Foolishly that makes me feel like crying.

Macauley stays really close to me. Tells me how fantastic I look and generally seems intent on bonding with me, trying to ingratiate himself in case I secretly hate him for treating me like a drug addict.

As the scene begins, Macauley watches the action in the monitor, and I space out a little since my entrance won't come for a while. At one point, he beckons to me to look in the monitor, and when I do . . .

I see James with his back against the wall, Caroline's body pressed up against his. She is kissing his neck, whispering in his ear. Then he reaches down and hikes her up, her legs circling around him. He carries her to the bed and excitedly starts to undress her.

I feel really detached. I wonder who I'll see if I look up from the monitor. I take a deep breath, then look up. It's still James and Caroline, seemingly writhing together in a passion they can't control. I know this isn't really happening in Sloane's world, though I feel a little sorry for her that she must be seeing it in her dream. Then all of a sudden, I start to feel something different. I'm angry. I'm hurt. James is betraying me, he lied, he broke his promise, and worst of all, he doesn't really love me. But I still love him.

It's my cue. I enter the scene, watch James and Caroline, and all the sadness and bitterness and loss just wells up within me and I sink to my knees and I start to sob. The crying takes me over, and I'm oblivious to the fact that the lovers have now become Ryan and Layne, that Macauley called cut and is now crouching in front of me, taking hold of my shoulders.

"Wow," he says softly, "what an interesting choice. Let's hang on to that and do another one on script, huh? Will that be okay?"

I dry my eyes, somehow smile as if I was acting, and say, "Sure." I can tell he isn't crazy about me going all Meryl Streep on him with my own improv take.

"Sorry about that; it just happened in the moment." Lame. He is nodding and smiling like, let's just not let that moment reoccur.

He has us pick up the scene with the couple on the bed. They are still Ryan and Layne. When my entrance comes, I whirl the girl around as I'm supposed to and stage-slap her appropriately, but when I turn to Ryan, I'm overwhelmed with anger. Instead of following script, I just lose it. I hit him with a closed fist and, ignoring his shock, just start swinging at him and hitting him with everything I have.

The next thing I know, Macauley is pulling me off Ryan. The look in everyone's eyes is completely appropriate. They just saw a crazy person doing something crazy. There is no way to cover this, no way to explain. All I can do is apologize to Ryan.

Macauley calls it a day and asks me to wait in the little room he's using as an office. I apologize to everyone again and head to my execution. I sit on a folding chair waiting to be fired so that I can leave here and go screw up the rest of my life one piece at a time.

Macauley comes in and shuts the door. He asks what I'm on. I tell him it isn't drugs.

"It was an emotional episode. I'm sorry. I can't explain. But I swear from my heart, it will never happen again," I promise him.

Macauley studies me. Deciding what to say. I just sit there vulnerable in front of him and let him judge for himself.

"I'll sleep on it, Maggie," he finally says. "I'm sorry for whatever trouble you're going through. But I can't risk the project by moving forward with you in this state. Let's talk tomorrow and see how we're both feeling."

In the cab, I desperately try to understand what I've done. Where was that rage coming from? Is it just the anger I feel in losing my mind, my life, my family, my love, my future? Or is it something even scarier? Was I Sloane in that moment, hitting my boyfriend who I thought had betrayed me, humiliated me, and robbed me of my dream of forever belonging to him?

I go home and hide on the roof of our building, watching the sun's path, watching it sink below the horizon, watching twilight become dusk become dark. The lights dance on the river and a soft breeze blows through the trees along our street. I feel safer here because I can't encounter anyone who could become someone from the other world.

I was wrong.

It's probably a little past midnight when he comes and silently sits down next to me. I don't recognize him, but I'm not afraid; his obvious intent is to be kind and reassure me.

"How are you doing?"

His name is Bill. He's Sloane's friend who died in a car crash on our birthday. I've seen him before, of course, in the dream. But I turn and look at his face as if for the first time. He smiles this beautiful sideways smile.

"I know it's hard for you to believe right now. But it's going to be all right."

"That's easy for you to say. You're dead."

He laughs. "There's worse things."

So we sit and look at each other for the longest time. And I finally feel comfortable and calm and peaceful. He points up at the sky above my head. The stars. There are never stars in Manhattan, but we can see them all.

"Which ones are mine?" he asks.

"We can't see them from here," I say, mesmerized by the vision of the twinkling heavens above this twinkling city.

Finally, I ask, "How is this all going to end?"

"The way it should."

CHAPTER TWENTY-FOUR

SLOANE

I've never dreamt of Bill. As far back as I can remember, I have never dreamt of anyone from the real world, have never put anyone like that into Maggie's world, until these last two days.

Seeing Bill's face and hearing his voice breaks my heart. I miss him so much. It almost seems as if I caught his scent through Maggie. It's just like him to be so reassuring and calm and to want us to not be afraid. Bill was never afraid of the future or anything.

God, I miss him. Gordy has been my friend since we were little, but no one has ever meant to me anything close to what Bill did. I think after he died, I sort of leaned extra hard on Gordy, and maybe that's where I started to give him the wrong impression.

There isn't a day that goes by that I don't think about Bill and little moments together. Even now, even with loving James, I still think of Bill all the time. I wonder if I could ever share that much of myself again, with James or anyone.

Max knocks our secret knock on my bedroom door. I tap the reply on the wall, letting him know it's safe to come in. As soon as I see his face, I'm overwhelmed with guilt. He pulled out my mom's old telescope last night and set it up in the backyard. And I avoided him because I didn't want to look for Bill in the stars before my date with James.

He's carrying a piece of tracing paper that he's drawn on with markers. It looks as if he's made his own star chart. He sits down on my floor and stares at it. I sit down next to him and tell him I'm sorry. He shrugs.

"I couldn't find him anyway. I don't think Mom's telescope works anymore."

I pick up his star chart and lie down on my back, holding it up against my constellations, overlapping some of the points with the stickers on my ceiling. He lies down next to me, his head touching mine.

"You were just looking at the wrong sky," I tell him. I don't want Max to hurt or miss Bill as much as I do.

Max gets very quiet. I start to speak, but he shushes me and reaches out, holding my arm. After a moment he giggles softly.

"I think I can hear him laughing," he says.

And the pieces of my broken heart shatter. Tears streak my face. Max turns his head and kisses one from my cheek. He then gets up and leaves me on the floor.

"You can keep the chart in case you lose him," he tells me.

I dress for school and as I head downstairs, I feel a stab of panic wondering who will be at the breakfast table. Maybe somehow it will be Bill. Maybe when I truly go crazy, I'll get to see him all the time.

It's my dad, waiting for me with a blueberry donut and a big smile. He asks if I'm willing to miss school today. I tell him he can twist my arm. He has a meeting in Manhattan and offers to take me along, give me a chance to wander the Columbia campus, grab a yummy meal with him. I guess I haven't been doing a great job of hiding the fact that these have been two of the worst days of my life, spiraling toward far worse than that. I'm no longer convincing everyone I'm fine. He wants to cheer me up and clearly thinks his company can do it, which is pretty sweet.

On the train, he seems awkward for a few minutes.

"So. Jim seems like a really nice guy."

"He also seems like a James. And yes, he's very nice."

A silence follows that is kind of funny.

"Good," he says. And that is the end of our James discussion.

He seems to feel more comfortable having displayed his support for my choice. He leans back, tries to read the paper for a few minutes, and dozes off. I gave him the window, even though it was always my spot when I was little. He'd said thank you, but he probably doesn't care about the seat, just likes me taking care of him.

There's less to look at on the aisle because everyone's heads block your view. I'm staring at this piece of gunk ground into the Amtrak blue carpet in the aisle when a familiar pair of purple Converse high-tops with neon pink laces comes into my eye line. The scribbles and designs in Sharpie across the toe are signed by their artist owner, Jade.

"Can I have some money, please?"

I look up into her bright hazel eyes. The amazing thing is that

I'm no longer frightened. Am I adjusting to insanity? Or am I Maggie's dream, getting ready to disappear?

"Maggie, you promised! I know it's only ten, but I really, really need a Strawberry Shortcake Good Humor bar. I'm ravished. Or am I ravishing?"

"You're actually both," I say, marking my first official conversation with a hallucination.

"Two dollars, please. I'll bring you change." Jade likes to stay on message at times like these.

"Will you give me a bite?"

"I'll give you half. You're my sister."

"I only wish," I say. And am sad to see that she doesn't register this. I open my purse and find a five-dollar bill. When I look up to hand it over, the aisle is empty. And I'm sorry. Maybe if I'd had a little sister to love so much, I wouldn't have gone crazy. No. I've had Max to love so much and I still went crazy.

When I turn around, my dad is just staring at me.

"Have a nice nap?"

"Who were you talking to?" he asks, looking at the five dollars in my hand.

"My imaginary friend," I say with the brightest smile I can find.

"Do you have to pay her five dollars to be your friend?"

"I was just heading to the food car. Want anything?"

He stares at me. "Sweetie, are you okay?"

"Totally." And I jump out of my seat as fast I can.

When I come back with my Strawberry Shortcake Good Humor bar, he asks if I've been sleeping well lately. By which he means am I still having that dream I told him about, the one that has apparently disturbed me so much. Of course I tell him I've been sleeping well. And just to put it all to bed, so to speak, I tell him I feel so much better since that recurring nightmare went away.

Just before we pull into Penn Station, I get a text from James asking if I'm sick, why aren't I at school. I totally spaced on letting him know I wouldn't be there. As I furiously text my apology, I wonder how this could happen. Of course, if I'm only Maggie's fantasy, that would explain it. How could any girl forget the love of her life for even a minute, let alone all morning? Maggie never forgets Andrew.

My dad drops me off at Columbia's Low Plaza and gives me a cheerful kiss. Clearly, he's still nervous about my phantom chat with Jade because he says that his cell will be on all the time, and if I need anything at all, I should call him right away. I figure that reassuring him will only create more concern, so I say thanks, you're the best, and act all excited about my day at Columbia. He looks in my eyes just a half second too long—dads are really transparent creatures—and then heads back downtown for his meeting.

I stand staring at Butler Library across the immaculate quadrangle. It's beautiful and represents everything exciting about getting out of your small town high school and starting life for real.

Then I realize. I've never visited Columbia before. Of course, I know that, but I've never stopped to wonder why. After all, I've been in Manhattan before. I've been on a college tour with my dad before. Wouldn't it make sense that this would be the first place I'd come? And yet I didn't. What suddenly makes sense, terrifying sense, is the vision of this as a blank space in Maggie's fantasy. That's right. I've seen it before, in my dream. Maggie went there with Benjamin. He taught English here, creative writing. He worked in the building two blocks from where I'm standing. Maggie never wanted to go to college. She gave that to me, at her father's college, and never bothered (as if she controlled the dream enough to bother) to fill in the blank of having me visit.

I've heard the phrase "my blood ran cold" in books and movies. This is what it feels like. It's your body that's cold, and really frightened in a way that you don't know how to fix. I literally can't move. I don't notice any sound, though life is going on around me. I'm staring at the air in front of me but can't focus my eyes on anything. I'm not real. I'm not.

There must be a thousand explanations and a thousand examples of how Maggie could be having the same experience that I'm having. I try to slow my breathing, which makes me feel light-headed. A strangely familiar voice says, "Hi."

I turn directly into a charming and friendly smile that I've seen many times. In my dreams.

"Are you okay?" Andrew asks.

I swallow hard. I'm aware of a conscious effort to keep from blacking out. I take my best shot. "Do I know you?"

"Nope. I'm just a random citizen who thought you looked a little ill or something. I didn't mean to intrude or bother you."

He doesn't know me. Obviously, since I'm not real, he can't know me. Then a ray of hope. Andrew is showing up in Maggie's dream, just like Bill showed up in mine. But of course, this hope is dashed. Andrew is alive and real. Bill is only a memory.

"I'm sorry to push this, but you're not looking any better. Do you want to sit down on that bench over there?"

I should send him away. But I can't.

"Sure."

He takes my elbow, gently, so different from Thomas's terrifying attack. He leads me to the bench and sits beside me.

"Can I get you some water? Or maybe you need some food in your stomach?"

"I'll be fine in a second." I look at him and smile. I want to talk to him, even if I don't know why. "I like your bracelet." He's wearing an awkwardly tied multicolor friendship bracelet.

"Thanks. My girlfriend's sister made it for me."

"Her younger sister, I hope."

He laughs in a really easy and appealing way. It reminds me of someone else's laugh.

"Oh yeah," he says. "My girlfriend's older than seven."

"Good to know. Do you guys go to Columbia?"

"I go to NYU and she's an actress."

"She must be a handful."

"You'd think so. She'd probably say that. But I think when you really want to be with someone, all that stuff goes away."

"She's lucky to have a guy who feels that way."

"We're both lucky we found each other. I mean, I don't know what I'd do with the rest of my life if I ever lost her. Crazy, huh?"

I stare in his eyes. And remember the smile his smile now reminds me of.

"There's worse things than crazy," I say. And wonder if that could be true.

I tell him I'm feeling better. He points me toward the visitors' center and heads off with a little wave. I watch him go and suddenly wonder what he's doing here. His life is downtown. Why would Maggie put him uptown to meet me? For the same reason I put my mom in her bedroom. We wouldn't. We just can't control this thing anymore. If we ever did.

I don't go to the visitor's center. Instead, I walk into the library. Gaze at the elegant high ceilings, imagine hiding out in the stacks fifteen hours at a time, cramming for finals, the life I've longed to have. Know that I never will. In fact, there probably isn't even a me in the first place. Being here is unbearable. I catch a cab and head downtown.

I know where I'm going. I come down Hudson, get out at Horatio, and head west. I soak in the neighborhood. I've seen it a million times but never really looked at it. Probably because I always thought it wasn't real, like a fake street in a movie.

All of a sudden I'm there. Staring up at where she lives. Where I live? With my sister, Jade? I summon all my courage and go to the call box. I scroll for Jameson, but just as I get to the *D*s . . .

"Lose your key?"

I turn to see a lean, handsome man in his mid-forties. I feel as if I've known him all my life. And that feeling is like a knife in my gut. Maggie's father, Benjamin, is dead, as dead as Bill. Yet here he is, thinking that I'm his daughter who has lost her key.

"I can't believe I did that. I'm a bonehead."

He sits down on the stoop, and I sit alongside him. There are tears in my eyes. How much Maggie, or I, really loved this guy. And this might be the last moment either of us will ever speak to him. I lean my head on his shoulder, and he strokes my hair.

"Tell me a story," I ask.

"You first."

I take a deep breath. "There once was a girl who was very, very unhappy. But she didn't know it. She invented an imaginary world and told herself it was her special, fun place to go visit."

"But it was her place to hide," he says.

"Hey, who's telling this story?"

"We are," he says. Which suddenly makes me feel warm and comforted. Someone else once said those words to me. And they made me feel less alone.

"She visits her special place every night. It's a secret from everyone. And she looks forward to it. Even though it isn't always easy there."

"And then one day . . ." he prompts.

I look over at him questioningly.

"Every story has a point. Every story has a reason and a journey. Every story has an end."

"That's where this one is different. Because the girl doesn't want it to end. Won't let it end."

He looks at me with a wisdom that reminds me of the way Bill looked at Maggie last night.

"Oh, it will end all right. The storyteller just needs to find a nice soft place for her to land."

I start to cry. "Can she find it?"

He studies me. Almost as if he can read the answer to that question in my eyes.

"She will," he says. "Even if it's not the one she's planning on."

I'm not sure how to take that. But his face looks so kind, I know he meant it well. He doesn't comment on the fact that I'm crying.

Maybe being a ghost, he doesn't notice. But then he reaches over and dries my face with his fingertips.

"I have to go now," he says. "I wish I didn't."

He stands, leaning down to kiss the top of my head. I feel this glow and sadness as if he is my own father, which in this moment I wish he were. He walks off down the street and I watch with this unbearable regret that I will never see him again even though he is someone I never really knew.

I wander around for hours. My dad calls, asking if I'm ready to meet up. We talk about getting an early dinner before our train. I tell him to meet me at Union Square Café.

I stand in the park, across the street from the place Maggie goes to be alone in a crowd. To watch the strangers she makes up stories about. If I sit there tonight, will she be somewhere in the room, maybe in a parallel universe, watching me and creating me? Maybe she's in there right now.

I cross the street, and just before I can enter . . .

"There you are."

I know the voice even before I turn around. Emma is looking at me in a very different way from the way everyone else from Maggie's world has looked at me. She knows who I am. She knows I'm Sloane.

"Do you know who I am?" she asks.

I'm struck dumb. This really isn't possible.

"Sloane, can you hear me?"

I nod slowly, like a three-year-old.

"Go away, Sloane. Let her be. Leave her alone so she can have a life."

She glares at me, actually angry, blaming me for everything.

"Why doesn't she let me go so I can have a life?"

"You know why. Maggie can't go away. Any more than her sister, or her mother, or I can."

"Oh, but I can, huh?"

"You can if you want to. You can just let go, and fade away, and be happy that she can live without you now."

"Because of Andrew?"

"Because of the possibility of Andrew. She can't really be with anyone until you're gone. I know you love her. Please, please let it happen."

"So I'm supposed to, what, kill myself?"

"Stop it!" That isn't Emma. I close my eyes. But I know he won't go away.

"Sloane, what are you doing? What are you saying?"

I open my eyes and stare at my dad for the longest moment.

"I don't know," I say. "I'm just confused, I guess. Just. Really confused."

I've never seen tears in my dad's eyes before. His arms slide around me. He holds me tight.

"It's going to be okay," he whispers. "We'll figure it out."

CHAPTER TWENTY-FIVE

MAGGIE

My eyes spring open. I'm completely disoriented. My head whirls to my left to see the clock, but it's not there. Who took it? I turn back, and it's on the right. But I don't keep my clock there. Suddenly, I focus on the time; my God, I'm late for school.

I throw back the comforter, my feet hit the floor, and then I remember. This is Saturday. There's no school today. I can calm down. I can slow my breathing. Everything's fine.

Then I realize. I'm not Sloane. I don't go to school. Ever.

I sit on the edge of my bed and try to swallow back the panic. This is worse. Things are getting worse. I can't let them.

I have to get up the courage to go to the bathroom because what if it's Sloane in the mirror? What if it's her bathroom? What if I can never find my way back? But I can't sit here all day. I have to take the chance.

I walk to the bathroom so slowly. I open the door a crack. It's still my bathroom. I enter and look bravely into the mirror. It's me.

On the wall are all these framed family photos: my first carousel ride, Jade and I building a sand castle, my mom and dad skiing. My school play. I was a cucumber. I was so cute.

And suddenly, I feel blind, utter panic. What school was that? I don't remember. I don't remember anything about any schools. Suddenly, I don't remember anything before I was like twelve or thirteen. I mean, nothing. No Christmas, no best friend, no stomachaches where Mom kept me home and made me pudding. I called her Mom, not Nicole. Like Sloane calls her mom.

I can remember Sloane's mom making her egg drop soup and rubbing her back when she was getting over the chicken pox. I can remember everything about Sloane's childhood. Why can't I remember mine? There's only one reason.

I've been waiting in Emma's stupid, fussy, little waiting room for forty minutes. My heart pounds so hard, I know I'm going to throw up. I keep trying to remember. Back to age twelve, I know everything. My God, it's actually true. But how can it be? How can a person not be real? It would mean that nothing and no one in my world is real. Even Emma. So of course, she'll defend this world with everything she's got.

She opens the door, gives me that phony, sweet smile. As I enter, she tries to give me a hug, and I just can't let her today. I flinch at her touch, and I know this offends her. And I don't care. Not today.

I tell her everything. I am Sloane's creation, nothing exists before I was twelve, that must be when Sloane's dream started.

Emma remains calm. I hate her so much in this moment.

"Calm down. It's only a panic attack. And luckily, it's one I can solve in a heartbeat. I know everything about your childhood because you've told me everything during our three years together. You went to Calhoun on the Upper West Side because you lived near Columbia, where your father worked. Your favorite teacher was Ms. Wallace in fourth grade. You made a clay turtle and fired it in the school's kiln. The glaze was maroon, I think you said. Can you remember the turtle?"

"Shelly." Suddenly, I remember everything. I wanted a pet like Eloise's turtle, Skipperdee. So I made my own. My best friend was Ashley Goldberg; we swam in a fountain somewhere and got into heaps of trouble. Central Park. It was the one with the boats.

For one blessed moment, I am so relieved and overjoyed.

And then I realize Sloane is making me remember. This is her dream. She would be scared that I am figuring things out. The game would be over. So I say all of this into Emma's complacent smile.

"You have to stop this, Maggie. You act as if you have no control over the situation. And the truth is since neither I nor any of the doctors that I have consulted with have ever seen anything like this before, none of us really know how far you can push it. But we all agree on one thing. You have to take responsibility for yourself. You have to try to hold on to reality."

"But I am, don't you see? How ridiculous for me to ever think that the girl who doesn't go to school, who lives in Manhattan, who's an actress moving to Los Angeles with a plum role waiting for her, that this person could be real and the small town high school girl squabbling with her girlfriends and flirting with the cutest guy in class would be the fantasy. There's no way you can defend that."

"If I try," she says, "will you listen? Will you give me a chance to save your life?" And in that moment, I feel she cares, even loves me, and I say yes. I will listen.

"You've got the wrong end of the stick, Maggie. The starting point is which of you has the creativity, the imagination, the individuality to create something like this. An entire world, populated with well-defined and realistic people. It's an achievement of will, of need. You are the one who makes up stories. You see strangers everywhere, and you invent entire lives for them. You are so devoted to maintaining a second life for yourself that you refuse to see the obvious. This invention is what you do, even in your waking life."

"Sloane doesn't have to do this in her waking life; she does it every night in her dream. And the only way she can keep from knowing that I'm the fantasy is to give me exactly the kind of behavior you're talking about. See, we can play traits in either direction; none of that proves anything."

I watch her gather her thoughts. My panic is rising again. She has no answers. What am I going to do?

"Here's why you've created Sloane. You have lost your father, the most important person in the world to you, the one person you could trust with your problems. Your relationship with your mother is so disconnected that she's basically a girlfriend and not even a terribly close one. You adore your sister, but she needs you and you feel the weight of that responsibility. You have no truly close friends except for Andrew, who wasn't around when you started this."

Andrew. He's not real either. Sloane just made him up.

"You haven't made up Sloane to exchange your life for hers. What you're doing is adding her life to yours. You get to have your career, your sister, your freedom, everything you love, and you get to have a close-knit family, girlfriends, all the comforts of a so-called normal life. It's like having a weekend house. Who wants to live in the city every minute? You'd go crazy."

"It's your fault!" I'm suddenly screaming. "I mean everything's Sloane's fault, of course, you're not even real. But she put you here to keep me in line, to keep telling me, convincing me that I'm a flesh and blood person who's just crazy. If you weren't here, I'd have been out of this long ago."

"Good. This is progress. You're down to blaming me . . ."

"Fuck you! Shut up! Just shut your mouth!" I jump up, but she opens her mouth to say something. "No!" I scream at the very top of my lungs, and grab the nearest thing, a table lamp, and just throw it as hard as I can against the wall. She shouts my name, like a schoolteacher who feels this is the time to be firm, but she's way too late.

I'm out the door, pounding down the stairs, and out onto the street, straight into two-way traffic. The cars aren't real. I'm not real. It won't hurt. They honk and swerve and pretend to be real. Even the people shout all the predictable pretend-to-be-real things. They can't fool me anymore. I get across the street, and see, I'm fine. Nothing's touched me. Nothing here can. Sadly, nothing anywhere can.

I start running. I don't know where I'm going. But of course it can't possibly matter. It's my last chance to feel my lungs bursting for air and my legs burning with the effort. I turn toward the river and there's a line of traffic at a dead stop.

The bridge must be up. I slow down. I'm hungry. Maybe I'll

grab a muffin at the Green Marble. I'm not that far from home; maybe Mom will make me some waffles. I don't want to see her right now. That's right, it's Saturday, she's picking up Max from soccer anyway. I turn down the alley at the Army Navy Store, but somehow there's the Hudson. I'm in New York. I stand still and blink. I look down at my body. It's Maggie's body. So of course I'm in New York.

I walk slowly, just trying to keep it together. I can't really be Sloane, even though I am. This is my last chance to be anything at all. It's so sunny out. Maybe Jade is walking Boris. I hate Boris. I had a bunny growing up, but Tyler was allergic, and I had to give him to Uncle Fred to keep on his farm. No, the bunny's mine and the uncle is Sloane's. Bunny, mine. Uncle, Sloane's. That's easy. I won't forget again.

If I don't turn a corner, I can stay out of Mystic, and I can stay Maggie. This is lucky because Riverside Park runs down the whole island. I can just go from one end to the other, and when it gets dark, I can sleep under a bench; it's not that cold. Of course I shouldn't sleep at all. So Sloane can't take me away. As long as I'm awake, she's screwed. Which is exactly what she deserves.

I stare out at the water. Across the sound, Fishers Island, where Gordy and I will build our dream house. Of course, that's crazy. Gordy is only my friend. I'll build my dream house with James. Maybe in Spain; he loves Spain. It goes with his guitar. There are pheasants on Fishers. I like their feathers. I wish my ears were pierced.

Oh, that's right, they are. If I'm Maggie. So I touch my lobe. And I smile. I am Maggie. The Circle Line boat goes by full of German tourists, taking pictures of Manhattan's skyline and all the

German tourists on the shore, who are taking pictures back at them. Germans are the new Japanese. They're everywhere, but of course, since they're not real, they're nowhere.

I sit down on a bench and comfort myself with this reality. Nothing can hurt me. Nothing I say or do matters. I realize that I'm safe.

He puts his hand on my thigh. I like that. I turn to see who he is. It's the love of my life. James kisses my neck, right in the perfect spot. I melt into him and he engulfs me. I'm warm and tingly. I look at him. He's so beautiful. He's actually perfect. In every way. I lean in to taste his mouth. He teases me, nibbling my lower lip. And then he kisses me full. Pulls my thigh up to rest on top of his lap so he's between my legs.

He rests my head back on the bench seat. And I open my eyes, wanting to see just his face and sky above him.

He's Tyler.

I kick and hit him, and he tries to block my fists. He stands up, bewildered.

"What are you doing?!" I scream. And everyone in the park looks at me.

"Whoa, I'm sorry. I thought you were into it."

"I'm your sister!"

"No, you're not. Why are you saying that?"

But before I can ask him what he meant, he isn't there anymore. No one is there with me, and no one was there at all. Only the people staring. Of course, they aren't real either. So it hardly matters. I pluck a piece of my hair. It's black. So I'm Maggie, who is not his sister. So there.

I start walking home. I'll risk turning corners. I just need to be alone. If an imaginary person can be alone. I want Bill to walk with me. To take me home. Bill has such long legs, it takes two of my steps to meet one of his. I'm running through all of my favorite jokes because I want to make Bill laugh when he gets here. My most favorite joke, at least of the ones Sloane hasn't told him, is the parrot joke. Parrots live forever. They're mean. They bite, even if you own them for a hundred years. Even Sloane doesn't like parrots all that much.

I turn onto my street. Someone's waiting on the steps. Maybe it's Bill. Wasn't he supposed to walk me home? Hold my hand?

It isn't Bill. It's my dad. He's got that stern face that used to scare me so much. How can he be angry at me? Maybe he's embarrassed that I'm crazy. Blaming himself that this all started in the first place. When, of course, it was Mom's rule. She started it all. I don't hate her. She thought it was best.

I sit on the stoop beside him. He's tying his running shoes to go for his jog before work. Oh, wait, it's Saturday.

"Sloane, your mother and I had a talk about, you know, your confusion in New York."

We are in New York, but I feel it would be rude to point that out.

"We're going to take you to a very good doctor. Gordy's parents recommended him . . ."

"You told them?! Don't you know they'll tell Gordy, and everyone will know!"

"Of course they won't. They understand and they're worried for you. And if Gordy did ever hear something, he would never ever spread anything like that. He loves you."

I know he does. It just gets sadder and sadder.

"We're all going to talk to the doctor together. Then they'll give you some medication and you'll feel better, and they'll shave your head and lie you down on the table and strap your arms and legs tight so you won't hurt yourself when the electricity starts."

He smiles and I know he loves me.

"Thanks, Daddy. I'm so happy we get to go together. But let's not bring Max; he might not understand."

"Who's Max?" Benjamin asks. It's Benjamin now. He looks fine, not dead at all.

"He's no one, just someone real I made up."

Benjamin understands. Dads always do. At least my dad.

"I can't stay long," he says.

"Because you're dead." I want him to know I understand.

"I miss you," he says. And there are tears in his eyes. It's good to know that you can cry when you're dead.

"When Sloane makes me go away, will I be dead?"

"No, it's different."

"Will I get to be with you?"

"Of course," and he kisses my head.

Maybe that's the soft landing.

He isn't there anymore, and I go up to the apartment.

I have to pee. It's good that the toilet is in the darkroom because I realize that my deadline for yearbook is Monday. This is Saturday, I think. I take the next print and begin to swish it in the stop bath so that it won't overdevelop. It's taking longer than it should. It's my favorite picture of Bill. But I can always reshoot it when I'm dead.

I go to hang the print on the line, but there are no pins. I start opening all the drawers, rummaging. Where are they? This is crazy. Who would do this? Take all the pins and not replace them? It must've been Thomas. It's just like him.

I rip the drawers free and turn them upside down. Stuff clatters everywhere, but no pins yet. I throw open the medicine cabinet . . .

"What are you doing?"

I see Jade's face in the mirror. I whirl around. "Shut the door! You'll ruin all the film!"

She's shocked somehow. Confused. Poor kid.

"What film?"

I hold up the print. "It's my best picture of Bill. For the tribute page. I can't let you spoil it."

"Maggie, it's just a washcloth. You're scaring me." Her little voice is so soft. I have to calm her down.

"Don't worry. Maggie will be here soon. And you and she can walk Bella. No, it's Boris. It's a boy. Bella is the one with the broken leg that Dr. French rescued. She doesn't look anything like Boris. I'm sorry."

"Maggie?"

"She's coming, honey. I'm her friend Sloane. Just let me finish this, and we'll call her." I kneel down to find those damn pins. I'll have to make do with this little girl's barrette. I hang the picture of Bill on the line. I've never noticed before, but James is in the crowd in the background. He's staring straight at me.

The little girl is gone. I walk through her apartment, which I've always liked. Even though I wouldn't give up my yard and my tree for anything. I open the front door.

"Maggie?"

I turn back. My sister, Jade, is standing there. She looks desperately upset about something. I go to her, but the closer I get, the more I can see how terrified she is. So I drop to my knees and hold out my arms. She hesitates only a heartbeat and comes into my hug, clutching me tighter than I can ever remember. Her hair smells like strawberries.

"Are you okay, sweetie?"

"Are you?" she asks with those wide eyes.

The question catches me off guard. Why wouldn't I be?

"Totally. But I could use one more hug."

I get the hug. But it comes with a question. "Who's Sloane?"

I blink. What a strange, strange thing to ask. "I don't know," I say. "Is it a friend of yours?"

I can feel her tense in my arms. She's getting scared again.

"You said your name was Sloane. In the bathroom."

I laugh. "You know, for an actress, you'd think I'd learn better diction. That is my real first name, you know. But I can't imagine why I used it."

"Maybe you were, like, rehearsing something."

I can't remember anything like that, but it seems to calm her down. So I nod as if suddenly remembering. I laugh again. "You know, I think I'd forget my head if it wasn't screwed on sometimes."

"That was the scariest thing I ever saw you rehearse. Is it for a scary movie?"

"The scariest. I have to go find Andrew; will you be okay alone until Nicole gets home?"

"Boris is here. He's our watchdog, you know. Will you tell Andrew that he owes me a spaghetti and butter sauce?"

The street is very dirty. They haven't picked up the garbage and it's hot out. That never happens in our little town; we've had the same garbageman since I was in kindergarten. Arthur. There was something about the way he would wave at me that made me uncomfortable.

This is obviously a part of town I don't know. Which confuses me because I thought I lived here. Unless of course I'm Maggie, in which case I know this street quite well. It's taking me to that place with the salad I like. And all the weird people who eat there and try to hide their lives from me.

The restaurant is packed because it's raining now. Umbrellas are such odd ways of staying dry. You'd think with all the technology and everything, I mean spaceships and iPhones, somebody would have invented something a little more elegant and effective. Though I wish I had one because I'm very wet.

I have a friend in this restaurant who brings me my salad; I'm hoping he will get me dry. He sees me. I wave cheerfully since I've forgotten his name. He has a life partner who's an architect and quite successful. When Andrew and I build our dream house, we'll hire him. Bill used to paint houses in the summer. White houses are the worst. They burn your eyes. I wonder what happens to your eyeballs when you die. Sloane carries a little card with her that gives her eyeballs away to someone who needs them. She's a good person. Better than me.

It's a license, that card. From Connecticut. I can't drive. I take the subway. Or the GEM. Now that Andrew is my life partner. It's sad to have a life partner and no life. I wonder if this is how Sloane feels about Bill.

My friend the architect's friend finds me a table. I kiss his cheek as a tip. It's cheaper than money. I stare around at all the people pretending not to hate me. They don't fool me. Nobody fools me. That one over there is really a criminal. If I watch her long enough, I will be able to discern her felony. I doubt that it's violent, but contemptible nonetheless. My salad comes. It's cold. I wish it was soup.

That woman in the blue top is a kind of hooker. A special kind. Like in Russia, where all the pretty girls make their living by being pretty. Sort of like actresses. She's from Iowa. Where I've never been, although I could certainly play a girl from Iowa. Play it in my sleep. No. I laugh out loud. I play a girl from Connecticut in my sleep.

The man she's with. The man who is paying her to be pretty. I can't even believe this. I'm sorry, he cannot be allowed to get away with this. Someone has to do something. I stand and go to their table. They look up quizzically. As if they don't know exactly why I'm there.

"I saw, you know. I saw you slip the gun into your pocket. That's illegal and wrong; this isn't that kind of a restaurant."

They stare at me with predictably dumb expressions. Unfortunately for them, they are not professional actors, and I can see right through them.

"You have to leave," I say, "you have to leave right now."

The man squeezes the woman's hand across the table. She won't look at me. "Listen, I don't know what you're on, but if you don't leave us alone, I'll have them throw you out of here."

"I know who you are. I know why you've been following me. You work with Thomas. And I know what you did to Bill."

"Waiter?!" the hooker says nervously. But the killer holds up his hand. He wants to see how much I know.

"Bill, huh? What did I do to old Bill?"

"You killed him. You left that puppy in the road. Her name was Bella. And he had to swerve, and his car swung into that tree. And he was killed. In less than a second. His neck snapped and his head smashed on the steering wheel and there was blood all over the windshield and the leather and his blue-striped sweater. Bones popped out of his skin. And his eyes were just staring open like a fish on ice. Don't look at me like that. You know that's how you planned it."

He smiles.

"Just take your gun and your skanky hooker and get out of here. These are nice people."

He stands. He's very big. And he smells like bad cologne, which is customarily used by his type.

"Fun time is over, sweetie. Now get the hell out of this place before I call the cops."

I stand my ground.

"Go on. Go."

And he shoves me. It doesn't hurt, but hard enough to make me step back into another table. Glasses and a bottle of wine crash on the floor. I look around and the world is watching. They don't have to pretend anymore. They can hate me and I can hate them.

The architect's life partner comes and grabs my arm. He's against me too. I'm surprised and hurt. He starts to pull me toward the door.

"Get your hands off of me!"

But he doesn't. Now he's pulling me across the floor. I swing my arms and kick, but he drags me anyway. Everyone shouts.

"I need my umbrella!" I scream. But no one cares. It's raining outside.

One of them pushes through everyone, running toward me. I'm frightened. I cover my face so he can't hit me.

"I'm sorry," he says. "I'll take care of her."

It's him. It's someone I know. It isn't James, though. James is beautiful and perfect. And James would be angry. This is the other one. The one who loves me.

Andrew wraps his jacket around me. And hugs me tight as he takes me to the door. I'm grounded in my body by his touch. It's raining harder now. He holds his jacket over my head and we go to his tiny, ridiculous car. He settles me in the passenger seat and buckles my seat belt for me as if I am Jade. He ignores the rain pounding down on him and leans close and tells me everything is going to be all right.

If he only knew.

Come to think, he probably does.

As we drive to his place, I'm not listening to his soft words. I'm wondering if he can read my mind. Since all of us are Sloane's creation, then all of our minds are hers, and even if they can't read my mind, they're all following her orders, trying to make me stay. So that she can kiss Andrew instead of James. That's not as crazy as it sounds. She dreams of Andrew because he's the one she really wants to kiss, which she can only do through me.

We climb the steps to his apartment. I realize how cold I've been because now I'm shaking so hard I can't control it. He turns on his shower, steamy hot. He takes off all of my clothes. They are sticking to me from the rainwater. He puts me in the shower and I sit down on the tile. He sticks his hand through the curtain to hold mine. He's never seen me naked before. I'm very naked. I think I'm crying because there's salty water on my face.

When I'm warm and dry, I climb into his big bed, under his down comforter. I'm not naked now. He gave me a sweatshirt and sweatpants from his high school track team. They're blue. He was a quarter miler.

He leaves the room to make me hot chocolate. I'm fine. I'm Maggie, no doubt about it. Andrew is really here and I love him. When he comes back in, I'll tell him. I just have to be careful not to fall asleep and lose myself, because I know I won't be coming back.

"Here, drink this," he says. He sits next to me in the bed, on top of the covers. I don't want the hot chocolate. But I feel bad because he made it.

"The dream came to town, huh?"

I nod. His comforter feels like a warm cloud around me.

"You have to let go of it. You know that, don't you?"

"Don't leave me." Now I'm crying for sure.

"You're the one leaving me," he says. "And I can't stand that. So just for my sake. Please." His hand is so gentle and big as it holds mine.

I look in his eyes. I tell him the truth.

"It's too late."

CHAPTER TWENTY-SIX

SLOANE

My eyes open. I'm completely disoriented. My head whirls to my right to see the clock. But it's not there. Who took it? I turn back, and it's on the left. But I don't keep my clock there. Suddenly, I realize why. I'm in Andrew's bed, of course. Where is he? And more importantly, what happened last night?

Did we have sex? We were talking. He gave me hot chocolate. He was being really sweet to me. Maybe I just fell asleep. I look around. This isn't his room, I don't think. Was there a tree outside his window? Maybe.

But that's not his tree. That's Sloane's tree.

"Andrew?" I call out. There's no answer.

So I sit on the edge of the bed and try to collect my thoughts. That's Sloane's tree, so maybe I'm dreaming now. I'm dreaming I'm Sloane. Shit, she's late for school. No, it's Saturday. Thank God. I'm not sure I could go through some surreal day pretending that all those kids are real and everything in their world is real and trying to pay attention in some classroom.

But Monday will come. That's okay. I won't have until Monday. I'll be gone. Emma knows. She knows that only Maggie could invent something like this, only Maggie is brilliant enough and weird enough and lonely enough. Especially lonely.

So it's okay. I still wonder why I'm here today. And then I realize. Maggie wants me to say goodbye to everyone in her dream. I can't really do that, can I? It would freak everybody out. But they're not real. But it would freak Maggie out and she'd wake up and then I'd never get to say goodbye.

Not saying goodbye wouldn't be all right with me. Whoever I am, there's enough of me to love everyone in my life and to feel sad about losing them. I'm not sad to be losing me. I'm sad to be losing them.

I feel very calm, not like how confused and panicked I was last night when I was Maggie. Thank God for Andrew. He'll keep me safe once I stop dreaming. Everything will get better then.

In the mirror I notice how red and puffy my eyes are. But that can't be from last night. Maggie's eyes are ice blue. And asleep. My eyes are puffy because Sloane was crying last night. And they're green, like hers. And she digs her fingernails into her palms when she's upset and my hands are cut. Maggie never does that. We made my dad so scared. And I'm sure he told Mom after he put me to bed. So Sloane will have to deal with their worry. No problem. I'll just lie. I'll think of something. I'm fine.

I come downstairs, and Dad is making pancakes for Max. I've seen this a million times when Mom is at the church doing the altar flowers for Sunday. And now it hits me like a train running through my chest at full speed. I'll never see this again. I'll never see them again. Tears fill my eyes. I can't let them see that. I turn away and wipe them quickly. I hear Dad say, "Morning, honey, I'll be right back."

I'm alone with Max. He looks over and says something I don't even hear. I remember the first time I saw him at the hospital. He was the most precious thing I've ever seen. I love him so much. I just walk over and grab his ears and give him this kiss on his syrupy mouth while he's still talking. He squirms from the cooties and asks what do I think I'm doing.

What I think I'm doing is kissing him goodbye, but what I say is, "Just messing around. Can I have a pancake?"

"No."

I'm going to miss this kid. But then again, will Maggie really miss any of this? Any of them? Or will my missing disappear too?

"You can have two," Max offers. He flops them on the empty plate at my seat. The same chair where I've eaten seventeen years' worth of breakfasts. Suddenly, I wish I could take it with me. As if there was a me and a somewhere.

My dad appears with his too-bright smile. Here we go. He asks to "show me something" in the yard. I play along. As soon as we get outside, he asks me how I'm feeling and how I slept last night.

"So much better, Daddy. Thank you. I'm sorry I scared you yesterday. I scared me too. I don't know what the heck was going on. But I feel fine now."

"Your mom and I want you to talk to someone about this. Her name is Dr. Barrows, and she's really nice, and she wants to see you Monday morning; is that okay?"

I listen with my serious and good-daughter face.

"I'm so glad that you found someone for me to talk to. Only, please can I see her after school? I have finals coming up, and I just can't afford to miss the prep. Especially in calculus. Would that be okay?"

He actually has to think for a moment before agreeing. He's so scared but of course realizes that if he's not going to commit me to Bellevue or something, I would have to live a normal life during therapy. Assuming there would have been a life to live.

He seems relieved that I'm acting so responsibly and taking things so well. I just want to hug him. So I do. He squeezes me so tight. And rubs his head against mine like we are bears. I love that. It's my last time to love that. Unless Maggie will let me remember. Unless Maggie will remember.

I make sure that Mom is coming back for lunch so that I have my chance to see her one last time. Which makes me wonder if I'm safe all day until I fall asleep one last time. Or if Maggie can just wake up in the middle somehow. I can't take the chance. I have to make every minute count.

I tell my dad that I'm going to drop by Kelly's and then go see Gordy and that I'll have my cell with me if he needs me for something. Right. Like making sure I haven't jumped off a bridge or something. He seems pretty okay with it.

"Remember the first time we took a whole Saturday and went to Napatree so you could teach me to take pictures? And we spent so much time at the fort, when we came around the point, the tide had come in and you had to carry me through the freezing water?"

"I sure do. Let's do that again. Maybe next week?"

"I'd love to." I mean that.

I text Kelly to meet me at the Green Marble. She wonders what's up since I know she has to be at work by ten. As I wait for her, I feel jealous that Kelly will get to go to college and grow up, have babies and a career. Then I laugh out loud. Kelly is as unreal as I am. She won't get to do anything. At least she'll never have to take her physics final. She hates physics. She is looking forward to prom.

Kelly shows up with one of her sly smiles.

"So did you sleep with him?" she asks.

"Stop beating around the bush. If you want to know something, just come right out and ask."

"Okay. Did you sleep with him?"

"Not yet." And this is the moment I realize that I'm going to. It has to be today. I have to make it happen. And it is the most important thing of all to me.

Kelly babbles on about things I need to know for my first time. Like, wear a condom. Duh. Don't put pressure on it to be a dream come true (I love that phrase in this situation) because it will probably be awkward. Trust that it will get better. Just think about how much you care about him.

As she talks and we giggle, I almost forget that this isn't real. It's all so normal. I guess that's why Maggie invented it.

When we say goodbye, I don't feel as sad as I thought I would. Maybe I'm getting used to this. Maybe it'll all be easy.

I decide to cut through Haley Farm to get to Gordy's. I take the long path, the one that winds past the foundation of the old farmhouse and up into the shade of the trees. It is so green and dense this way. I follow the Indian stone wall. But hit briars. Am I on a deer path? I haven't been in this part of Central Park before. Which is odd. Because I've been everywhere in the park. I think Sheep Meadow is right through there.

But it isn't. I'm lost. Lost in the middle of Manhattan. I listen for traffic, but there's nothing. How is that possible? I hear a stick break and leaves shuffle. Something is coming. I turn in every direction but don't know which way to go. I can't tell where the sound came from. Or who is following me. But he's dangerous. Because when I stop walking, he stops walking.

I pull out my cell phone. I'll call Andrew and he'll find me. But there's no reception, which is crazy because I always have service in the park.

I hear the man again. I think I can hear his breathing. And I start to run. But the faster I run, the closer he gets. My heart is pounding. I'm gulping for air. I see a main path up ahead, but I trip hard over a rock. My knee hurts so badly, and when I look up . . .

He's right there. I don't know him at first.

"Hi there, sweetie. I wasn't sure I'd see you again." He's the guy from Union Square Café. The one with the hooker. The big guy. And he has the most awful smile. A smile that is thinking of terrible things. He reaches down with both meaty hands and I kick as hard as I can between his legs. He screams and falls to his knees.

And I'm running. Even if my knee is broken, I'm running on it. He is swearing and screaming horrible things he's going to do to me. I can't even bear to hear them. But I'm dodging through trees, looking for Fifth Avenue somewhere. It has to be somewhere.

Suddenly, I see the cow tunnel. It's where the farmer used to bring his cows safely under the train tracks. I've taken this train. Dad and I took it yesterday to New York and back. We must have passed over this tunnel.

Instead of going through the tunnel, I climb up onto the tracks. And I sit down. And wait. I have an idea. When the train comes, it will go right through me. Because neither of us is real. I don't know why I want that. Maybe it will make me feel safe.

I feel the buzzing in the tracks. And it makes my heart jump in a good way. Almost like being alive. I stand up for the last time. Then I think, why would that be? I see the train now, but I'm still wondering why I think this will be the end if it's going to go through me.

Then I realize. When that happens, Maggie won't be able to pretend anymore. She'll know she's real. Game over. And no more goodbyes. No more last times. And no first time. No first time with him.

And now the train is blaring its horn and coming so impossibly fast. Here it comes.

But I can't let it hit me. I step off the tracks and remember to run so the rush of air doesn't suck me under the wheels. I feel the blast of air and I slip and roll on the grass. I guess I don't want Maggie to wake up yet. Miles to go before I sleep. Maggie thinks that poem, all of Frost really, is obvious and dumb. I think it's obvious and smart.

I'm something of a mess when I get to Gordy's. He seems really glad to see me, which makes me happy and sad. It's nice that our last time together won't be awkward, like when Sloane took that picture at lunch. When I took that picture at lunch.

He isn't expecting me. I never knock at his house, just let myself in. He's out back, reading *The Three Musketeers*. I sit in the chair next to him and he reaches over and pulls a twig from my hair. I close my eyes and let the sun warm my lids.

"Are you okay?" he asks. I can feel him looking at me. I smile convincingly.

"Just really tired," I tell him. Which is true.

"Want to take Tiller for a walk?" Gordy asks. I feel Tiller's wet nose lift my hand up, encouraging me to scratch behind his ears. I open my eyes.

Tiller is old. He's a black Lab. His chin is gray now. I worry about his arthritis.

"Sure," I say. And Gordy smiles that same smile he's had since he was three years old. I love that smile.

As we walk along Mumford's Cove, he asks what's up. I tell him I've really missed him. I tell him it's really important that we're okay. He reaches one long arm and sort of hugs me as we walk. Which is the best answer.

"I had a dream about Bill last night." He says that, not me. Even though Sloane did too.

"What happened?" I ask.

"You guys were hanging out and you wouldn't tell me where you were going."

"That doesn't sound very friendly," I say.

"Well," he says, "you guys always had your own thing. I think the dream means I was missing both of you. As if you were gone too, the way he is."

I am gone, of course. Just not the way Bill is.

Actually, I'm not gone at all. It's Sloane that's gone. And as he talks and smiles and looks so relieved that the awkwardness is gone and they can go back to being best friends, I start to wonder. I understand why I created Sloane. And James. And girlfriends and, of course, a family. But why Gordy? This guy who she mistreats and lies to. I've just made him her dog to kick.

Maybe I should have her tell him about Bill. No. It would kill him.

We come to the flood wall, and after lifting Tiller over the wall, Gordy takes my hand to help me climb up. Just like he's done since we were five years old. His hand feels warm and innocent. I start to cry. He sees. And bless his heart, he doesn't ask what's wrong. He circles his arms around me and kisses the top of my head. And we just rock back and forth a little.

Who does Maggie think she is? To talk like that about him. What does she know about anything? He is so decent and she is so screwed up. Just because she's real and I'm the dream doesn't give her the right to do that. I hate her. I really hate her.

We get back to Gordy's and he heads for the house, but I hold back on the walkway.

"I've got to go," I tell him. He's halfway through the door, almost gone.

"Let me drive you," he says, standing there in the doorway.

"I feel like walking." I shrug. He skips down the stairs and holds his hand up. I interlace my fingers in his and pull him into a hug, nuzzle my face into his chest, and pull away.

"Bye, Gordy," I say, looking right at him, hoping to sear this image into my brain, to tuck it into some pocket so it can stow away to wherever I'm going. His handsome face, his kind smile, his sparkling eyes, the years and the memories between us. I want to take them with me.

"Thanks for coming by," he says. I start down the road. "See you on the other side," he calls coincidentally as he heads back into the house.

I walk home on Groton Long Point Road. As I pass Esker Point, I see my mom's friend Hillary rowing her dingy out by Mouse Island. It looks like she's collecting mussels. At Marsh Road, I turn right.

Somehow, I'm lost. It's as if I've never seen this part of Tribeca. If I turn left, it should bring me back to the West Village, I think. It seems dangerous here. Dark alleys, tough-looking kids sitting on a stoop. One calls out as I walk by. Don't look at him. Nicole says never make eye contact. I walk faster.

Oh. Up there, I see Macauley enter some local bar. That's probably why I'm here, meeting him about the show. I start to run, but it takes strangely long to cover the distance. But I guess dreams are like that. I could probably fly if I put my mind to it. Concentrate. You don't want Macauley to think you're on something. This may be your last chance.

I enter the dark bar. Macauley's at the bar. I sit down on the stool next to him. I smile my prettiest smile. It's not flirting, exactly, but it's the way actresses establish rapport with directors.

"What are you drinking?" I ask. He looks at me with great surprise.

"You can't be in here. You're underage."

"Oh, no one's carded me in the city in two years."

He stares for an odd beat. "Sloane, are you okay?"

I want to say neither. I am not Sloane and I am not okay. But what I say is, "Sure."

"Um, does Michael know that you're in a bar on Saturday afternoon? Because I feel I really ought to call him. I don't want to get you in trouble with your folks. Maybe you should just go home, huh? You sure you're okay?"

It's a test. An audition of some sort. He wants me to play Sloane, which of course is my favorite role. "Totally," I say, "I just came in here to use the bathroom and saw you. And just wanted to say hi."

I head toward the restrooms. That wasn't Macauley at all. It may have been the guy with the hooker. Sometimes they can make themselves look different. Actresses know that. I find an exit to the alley and slip out the door.

I jog down to what should be West Broadway, I think. I head uptown. A car pulls over. A woman leans to open the passenger door.

"There you are," she says. "I've been trying to track you down."

I know her. She's the one who came into my bedroom that night to talk about my curfew. I don't have a curfew. She's the one who plays Sloane's mom. Is Sloane's mom. She's actually very nice, even though Sloane has hated her for a year. Not hated her, blamed her.

But I like her. So I get in the car.

"Gordy said you were walking home, so I thought I'd give you a lift. It looks like it's going to rain soon. I picked up a meatball grinder for you at the Mystic Market. Are you hungry?"

If I try to eat anything, I'll throw up. But it's so sweet of my mom to do that, I nod eagerly and gratefully. She smiles and holds my hand. She's much better at hiding her terror than my dad is. Maggie could take acting tips from my mom.

We get home and she's unpacking our lunch. I go to the book-shelf and pull down the white album—as in wedding, not the Beatles. It's very old and yellowing a bit. It's very precious. I open the cover carefully and she comes to look over my shoulder. Together, we turn the pages of her wedding pictures. We've been doing this together since I was three. But it's been over a year since the last time, which is why she seems so happy we're doing it again.

"Tell me," I say, "what it's going to be like when we have my wedding."

I probably haven't said it just that way since I was little, and now there are big tears in her eyes.

She runs her fingers gently across my scalp and starts to play with my hair. "We'll put your hair up to show off your face and your sweet earlobes. You can wear Grandma's diamond clip-ons."

"You're going too fast. Start at the beginning."

"Okay. It will take us, oh, at least a couple months to pick out everything together. The places for the rehearsal dinner and the reception. The menus, the music, the flowers, the cake. All that good stuff."

"The invitations. Don't forget the invitations."

"And most of all, your dress. That's where the real work is. We'll probably go to New York."

"Just for ideas. It's pretty expensive there."

"Well, the idea is you're only doing this once, so we won't worry quite so much about that."

She hugs me and kisses me. I'm so glad I thought to do this before Maggie takes me away.

We have lunch together, and I make myself laugh and eat the whole sandwich. And everything is perfect. Like it used to be.

"You know," I say, "someday I may be far away. But I'll always remember everything about you. Because you're just the best mom."

She gets a little teary again. "You won't ever be that far away. There are airplanes, you know. And that Skype thing."

"Sure," I lie. And even though I know she can't be real, I know she's real to me. And I know in this moment that I don't want Maggie to take her away from me. I don't know how, but I'll fight for her. I'm not ready to give her up. Not ever.

And then. I suddenly know. I know why all this is happening. And I know how to stop it. I know how to stop Maggie. How to stop her from taking me away.

I stand in the shower. I need to be with him. *Sleep* with him. I want to be with him more than anything I've ever wanted. I wonder about it all the time. What it will feel like. I won't be confused or sad about it being the only time. I'll make it perfect; I know I will. It will make up for a lifetime of times.

But more important, it will make it okay when I tell him good-bye. It will make him understand that I don't blame him or hate him, even though it's all his fault. Even though he's made everything happen. He didn't know. It isn't anyone's fault.

Biking to his house at dusk, I see no cars and I can ride down the hill with my arms stretched out like wings. No hands. Maggie can't do this down Park Avenue. I've spent my whole life loving this town. The coolness of the shady woods, the sound of the crickets, the painted sky reflected in the stillness of the cove. It all whizzes by. And I am so grateful in this moment to Maggie for choosing it. After a year of sadness, I'm starting to remember why I love my life.

All afternoon I spent saying goodbye to everything in my so-called life, big and small. The noisy furnace in the basement. The big gross spider outside my bathroom window. My stoic tree. Stoic because she never talks, but she is so brave.

All the animals at the vet watched me cry, some with real concern. Others, mostly cats, were just curious. I held them all, which takes some doing with an Irish wolfhound. I had a real conversation with my favorite patient, a blind tabby named Willow. I told her there is a place where we would meet again. And I promised we would. And I kissed her.

It is just dark as I reach James's. Stars are starting to appear in the purple sky. He comes down the steps and grabs me up in a big hug and kiss. He hasn't seen me for two days, and he's missed me. I force myself to realize that he doesn't know anything is wrong. Just like Gordy and Kelly and Max. I'm fine.

I don't know when Andrew will wake Maggie up. So I have to hurry.

Once inside, he heads for the kitchen, thinking I'll follow. I don't have time for cooking and eating and all that.

"You know, I just realized. I've never seen your room." I head up the stairs. He follows.

"Hey," he calls out, "this is easier than I thought." He is joking, of course. I'm not.

His room is painted dark, midnight blue. There are books

everywhere, piles and stacks on the floor. There is a photo of him surfing somewhere. No doubt about it, he looks like a god in that shot. Lots of other pictures in frames on shelves and his desk of friends, far-off places, his mom and sister. Then I notice a small shot of me, which looks like it was taken from a phone and printed by a normal laser printer on regular paper. It's taped above his dresser. I'm standing at the microphone on the football field, speaking at Bill's memorial. The boy who sleeps in this room, with all these books I haven't read, all this music I'll never listen to, the beautiful guitar I'll never hear again, this boy wanted my picture in this room before we were ever together. Does it mean that he always hoped we would be?

He has a big bed, a queen or maybe even a king. Big, pillowy dark blue comforter, every bit as nice as Andrew's. My stomach jumps knowing that I'll be under that comforter soon. I'm excited and scared. Still, I know what I want and what I need to do.

He picks up his guitar and starts strumming. He hikes himself up on the corner of his desk so that the chair is free for me. But I lie down on his bed instead. The comforter billows around me like water. It's going to happen.

"Come here," I tell him. He puts down his guitar and smiles at me. It's a smile I've never seen before and it sends shivers down the front of me.

He walks over slowly and slides down the length of the bed, the length of my body. He never touches me, but I feel his body heat as he moves closer. His beautiful face hits the pillow next to mine and he turns to me and we just look at each other.

He opens his mouth to say something, but I lean in when his

lips part, and I kiss him. I don't want to have to tell him what I want. I want him to feel it. We kiss deeper. I take his hand and put it on my bare stomach, under my shirt. But he just rubs my side, my hip. I guide it farther up. And I feel hesitation in his kiss. So I kneel and pull my shirt over my head. But then I see the look on his face. Something is wrong. There's no time for anything to be wrong.

I bury one hand in his hair, kiss him hard. My other hand reaches down to his belt buckle. As I start to fumble with it, I feel his hand on top of mine, stopping me.

"What's wrong?" I ask, frightened. Maybe I am being clumsy or something.

"Nothing's wrong," he says softly. "We've got all night." He brushes my hair behind my ear. "We've got forever if we want it."

I'm so embarrassed. He thinks I'm nervous and just doing this to please him. I have to slow down. I make myself smile. I kiss him on the nose.

"Be right back," I say.

I head to the bathroom down the hall to collect myself. I open the door and it's dark. I shut the door as I feel along the wall for the switch.

The light goes on. Someone's cleaned up Sloane's mess. I wonder if they found those stupid pins she was looking for. I look and see all of Jade's bath things in my tub. And I smile. We haven't taken a bath together in more than a year. Maybe she's too big a girl now. Makeup is next.

I look into the mirror. And she's there. Just staring back at me. All the rage, and pity, and sadness just explodes inside me.

"What the hell do you think you're doing here?!" I demand.

But Sloane just grins that snotty, condescending little smirk. Like she knows something you don't. Like her silence is filled with meaningful thoughts that are just so above your intelligence level.

"You're the idiot, you know," I hiss. "Just tell me one time, try to defend yourself, what you're doing."

No answer. Her smile is gone. She's waiting to hear what she needs to hear.

"You didn't learn your lesson? You're going to kill this one too?"

"Sloane, what's wrong, what are you doing?" His voice cuts through everything.

I whip around.

"You!"

But he doesn't understand. He just stands there looking stupid with no regret, no sorrow. Not even an apology for what he's done.

"All of this. All of this! It's all because of you! You're the one breaking us up!"

"Calm down. We're not breaking up. I love you."

He is so stupid.

"I'm not talking about you and me; no one can break up two people who aren't even real. You know what I'm talking about. I told you."

"You told me what, Sloane?"

"Stop calling me that!!"

He registers something. "Should I call you Maggie?"

"Don't say her name. You have no right to say her name! It's all your fault. You're doing this."

"Doing what?"

"Killing me. You're killing me. You're the reason she's doing it. You're the reason she's taking me away. Everything was fine before you came. Everything was fine before she wanted you. Before she wanted to kiss you."

"What's wrong with me, Sloane? What's wrong with wanting to kiss me?"

"Because you can *never* be him. You can never, ever and she won't let you. She'll take me away before she'll let you."

He is talking now. Saying stupid boy things about everything will be okay and how he'll take care of me and he's sorry he didn't know. I can barely see him through my fury and tears.

He comes toward me, reaching out his hands, and I knock them away as hard as I can. He tries to grab me and I hit him and hit him and he can't stop me. He gets arms around me and I claw at him and scrape his shin with my boot and spit at him. And scream and scream and scream.

He lets go. I back out the door.

"You need to go away." It is my last warning.

"Not going to happen," he says. "You can't get rid of me."

I screw my face up so tight that he can see the ugliness of how much I hate him. My finger stabs at him.

"Never see me again. Never call. Never see me. Never. Never."

I turn and run. I fly down the stairs, out his door, onto my bike. And am gone from him. Forever.

I'm lying in Sloane's bed. Of course I am. I am Sloane. Whatever being Sloane means. It's very late. I know that once I sleep, I will never wake. I stare at my stars. I try to focus on each one, to make them anchors to keep me here.

Please. Please, I beg again and again. Please don't make me disappear. Don't take me away from my mom and my tree and my world. He's gone. Maggie, I promise. I'll never see him again. Everything will be perfect. I'll be good. I'll never let anyone be him again.

You did it, anyway. You made him up in your dream. You made up both of them. And you made me do what I did. You have to take responsibility for your dream. It isn't fair to take me away.

There's a tapping at the window. I used to imagine that sound was the sorcerer. Trying to get into my room. Trying to get into my bed. Trying to control me. That was before I realized that the wind could make branches of my tree scrape the window. I would lie, a little girl, with my eyes closed and see if there was a pattern to the tapping. As long as it was random, I knew it was the tree. Because if it was him, he would tap four times and then stop. And then two more.

So now I listen with my eyes closed. And I count. One. Two. Three. Four. Silence. My breath catches in my throat. An accident, of course. A coincidence. And then, one. Two. I gasp.

I whirl toward the window.

The sorcerer is there. He will come into my room. Into my bed. He will control me. And I will be so happy.

I don't have to get up and open the window. He sees my happiness and knows he's allowed in. Welcomed in.

He crosses the room. He sits on my bed. He smiles the most beautiful smile.

"Happy birthday, beautiful," he tells me.

There are tears on my face. I barely manage to say, "It isn't my birthday anymore."

"I'm sorry I'm late. How does it feel to be sixteen?"

I smile back. I'm so happy he's here. I don't know what to do.

"I've almost forgotten," I say. "I'm seventeen now."

He lies down beside me and gently turns me so that his body curls close to mine like a spoon. All the fear, all the madness, even doubt, all vaporize. I am with Bill. I am in heaven. We are together in the sea of stars above us. He entwines his fingers through mine.

He whispers, "Your mom won't be angry. She only said you couldn't date until your birthday. So everyone can know now. Everyone can know that you belong to me and I belong to you. Forever."

He kisses the back of my neck. My body glows. My heart is so full. I know we will lie like this forever. And that's all I want. It's the thought that's never been more than a heartbeat away for this past year. Since he died.

How comforting to learn what death really is. It's forever. And that's a good thing. As long as you're together. That's the answer. To the desperate problem I couldn't solve. How to live without him. Now I know. Love is stronger than death. Stronger than anything. I'll never be without him again.

I can fall asleep now. I can fall asleep in his arms.

Maggie won't take me away. At least, not from him.

My eyes close.

"I love you," I say.

CHAPTER TWENTY-SEVEN

MAGGIE

My eyes open. I'm lying on my side, spooned into Andrew's protective embrace. He's cuddled into me. Even in his sleep he loves me.

So very carefully, an inch at a time, I ease my way free from his arms. I slide from the bed, turning back for a moment to watch him in peaceful sleep. I love him so much.

When I'm dressed, I leave a note. I'll see him later. I write *I love you*. I haven't said it out loud before. I will tonight.

I step onto the street. The sky is the clearest blue. The clouds are the purest white, billowing in the gentlest breeze that has cleaned everything imperfect from the air. The sun illuminates the city's angles with precision and clarity that I've never seen before. It is wonderful. As is my life.

I run through the city, seeing everything, everyone. Just as it, as they, truly are. Perfect. Needing no story from my mind to be safe for me.

I run up my steps, hoping to catch my mom and my sister. They've already left, but that's no problem. I'll track them down.

In the meantime, I wander our apartment. Looking at everything. Touching everything. A blind person who has suddenly been granted the grace of sight. I want to cry with joy. And relief. I'm awake now, for the first time. I'm awake.

I go to my mom's closet. I pull down the old Olivetti case gathering dust behind shoe boxes. I open the case and run my fingers over the keys of my dad's ancient typewriter. It had been my grandpa's, and my dad used it for all the stories he wrote in college. He would threaten to make me use this when I went to college too, saying it built character to write in a careful way because mistakes took time to correct.

I'd like to have character. Maybe this would help.

I decide to write a love letter to my sister that she mustn't open until her wedding day. A little fanciful, yes, but I'm in that mood, and I've got all day. I hope the typewriter still works. And it does, although the little holes in the *e*'s are kind of filled in.

Dear Jade,

What a beautiful bride you are today. What a perfect choice you've made of the man to spend your life with. Whatever the weather, the sun is shining on you today. Whether or not there are birds, they are singing to you right now. The world loves you, as you deserve. And of course, so do I.

As I write this, you are only seven. It is my deepest wish to be there at your side today. But because none of us know where life will take us, it is important to me that certain things be said:

Don't change. Everything you need to be is already there inside you. I see it every day. You are curious and brave and honest and so very alive. So very real. You are the light in every room you enter. You grow every day, every minute, and you always will. It's your nature and your gift. Share that with the man you love and your own babies. Who will be so lucky that you are their mommy.

As you're putting on your gown and pulling up your hair, I will be with you. Wherever I am. I will be with you.

I seal it in an envelope and put it in my desk drawer. After all, the kid is only seven. She'd tear it open in a New York minute.

I catch a cab up to *Elle*. Haven't been there in a while. Jerome is glad to see me. Everyone's glad to see me today. I just charge into Mom's cubicle as she's sorting through a million photos. I announce that I'm treating her to lunch. I'm completely ready not to take no for an answer when she says, "Great."

I take her to the Palm Court at the Plaza because she used to take me there for tea so I could hope to spot Eloise and Skipperdee. I think I gave up on Santa Claus and the Easter Bunny way before I let go of Skipperdee.

"Wow," she says as the maitre d' seats us. "How big is that pilot fee again?"

I laugh and tell her she'll have to call my agent for that. I'm an artist and don't involve myself in such matters.

We eat big sloppy burgers and have the best time. She asks when I'm moving to Los Angeles, and I realize we've never actually discussed the specifics of that. She looks quite sad beneath her smile, and I guess I never realized how much she'd miss me.

She tells me that she's taking all three weeks of her vacation, plus eight days of accumulated sick leave, and instead of Martha's Vineyard, we're all going to drive out to California together to get me settled. I remind her that if the show is canceled, I'll be coming back to New York with my tail between my legs. She says that's never going to happen. She knows in her heart what I'm destined to be. And that this is the start of all that. I lean over and kiss her.

Then she chokes up a little. She wishes Benjamin were here to see this. I do too. I tell her that I've been dreaming of him and that what I know in my heart is that he sees all of this. She nods, trying to pretend she believes this and trying not to cry.

I think of how much Andrew means to me. It makes me think in a new way what it must be like for her to think of my dad. We never know what our parents really have together. It's funny, but we don't think of them as real people in that way. I reach over and wrap my fingers around her hand. I debate whether to say that he loved her very much. I decide against it. She knows. She doesn't need me to tell her.

Our cab drops her at the office. Just before she opens the door, she looks in my eyes.

"Thank you," she says. "For everything you mean to Jade. It means everything to me to have you as my partner in raising her."

"Don't mention it," I say, trying to keep it light. But I guess my voice betrays me because she gives me this quick, fierce hug before she jumps out.

As the cab rolls on toward Jade's school, it strikes me as strange that my mom has said this. She never has before, not quite this way. As if she's saying goodbye. I wonder if it's because she's feeling the weight of me moving to Hollywood, of our impending separation. And just now, I'm feeling it too.

I sit on the curb in front of Jade's Montessori. I've seen this place a million times, but it looks new today as everything does. The kids run out to waiting cars and moms and nannies. They seem particularly adorable today, filled with the promise of after-school snacks and playdates. Bless their hearts.

Tiny hands reach from behind me to cover my eyes. She never says "guess who" during these tests of my intelligence because she fears I'll recognize her voice. Among the hundreds of people with whom I play this game on a regular basis. I start with the Princess of Wales, as she and I have decided to call Kate Middleton, even though she is a commoner to some. I am wrong. I move along to Lady Gaga. I get a giggle, but I'm wrong again. I think harder. I try Sean Connery since Jade has decided he will always be the only real James Bond. A deep voice with a horrible Scottish accent says, "Getting warmer." I smile.

"Jade Jameson, of course."

"Our board of judges," says the Scottish accent, which has become even horribler, "requires a complete answer."

"Jade Grace Jameson." Which is of course correct. I've always loved the fact that Grace is also Sloane's mom's name.

We walk home holding hands. We pick up Boris, who for some reason looks absolutely semi-acceptable today. We head to the Hudson River Greenery, stopping at the bodega for Japanese donuts, a special treat. They're made of chewy mochi, filled with sweet red beans, and smothered in powdered sugar.

It is one of the best afternoons of my life. I just lie in the grass and let New York's greatest undiscovered comedienne keep me in stitches. Hours pass. Let them. I could stay here forever.

The sun sets. We walk home, arms around each other. Not Boris, of course.

I cook her dinner because Mom won't be home until eight. I try to re-create the exquisite spaghetti and butter sauce. She tries not to show her disdain, but she refers to them as buttery noodles. As I watch her eat, we are planning big fun in Los Angeles. Disneyland gets mentioned a lot. Maybe too much.

Then to my shock, she tells me that she's going to move to Los Angeles and live with me. She already asked; there's a Montessori school there. She wants my help in breaking the news to Mom because it turns out there isn't an *Elle* there.

This is a tough one. I start with a smile. I tell her that one of us needs to stay in New York and take care of Mom. Mom may be a grown-up, but she needs taking care of too. We're young—we have our whole lives to live together some other time.

She thinks this over. Holds up one hand.

"Pinky swear," she says.

So we each kiss our pinkies and lock them together in a solemn promise that one day we will live together again.

Then I look in her eyes. "You know, the way things work out, we won't always be in the same place."

"Because you'll be a famous actress, actressing all over the world, and I'll be a famous zookeeper."

"Right. But here's the thing I need you to really hear. Are you really, really listening right now?"

I've never said anything quite like that before, and she responds by scrunching up her face to show how hard she's listening.

"Wherever I am, I'm with you. Across whatever distance there is. I send you my love."

She drinks that in. She really was listening.

"Me too," she says. And leans across her spaghetti and kisses my face.

I slip on my jacket. My stomach does this flip as I head for the door. I don't want to leave her tonight. I keep going. At the door, I turn back and she's there. There's the strangest look in her eyes. Lost and lonely. She reaches out her arms and I grab her up into mine.

"What's wrong?" I ask.

"I'm practicing," she says. "For when you're far away and I have to pretend we're together."

"When that happens," I tell her, "if that happens, we both have to work very hard at understanding something. We're not pretending we're together. We're realizing that we actually are together in the ways that count the most."

She stares in my eyes. Nods once, decisively.

"Okay," she says. "I'll practice that."

I told Andrew to meet me outside of City Hall at the corner of Center and Chambers. It's such a beautiful night. You never see stars like this in the city. Maybe I never looked hard enough. But I can clearly make out Orion and Rooibus and El Delicioso. I feel energy and excitement and love. Definitely love.

There he is. So happy to see me. I run to him, to hold him, to kiss him.

"Thank you for taking care of me last night. It was all I needed. I've had the best day."

I take his hand and lead him onto the Brooklyn Bridge. I tell him we're going to Grimaldi's for pizza. And then to the Ice Cream Factory for dessert. My treat.

Crossing the bridge at night is the most romantic thing to do. The views up and down the river of the city, of Brooklyn, make you feel so small. The lights dance on the water so far below until you can't tell whether they're city lights or stars. We walk in silence so comfortable, like two people who have forever. Which we do.

It's warm and cozy in the restaurant. We don't know anyone, and yet it feels like family. We share a carafe of their best Chianti, which is not too good. We share pizza with extra cheese, extra pepperoni, extra onion. Because he likes the pepperoni and I like onion. Of course we could've ordered two pizzas, but it's more fun to share.

We eat the slices messily, with one hand because we don't want to let go of each other. He suggests a second carafe. I laugh and ask if he's trying to get me drunk. I smile and say this shows a lack of confidence on his part. He insists he's just developed a taste for really shitty wine.

The ice cream is perfect. I have a waffle cone filled with butter pecan. His is vanilla, which he says is proof that he's no longer trying to impress me. I tell him it's working.

We walk back across the bridge so slowly. At the midpoint, I stop us. And lean on the rail and stare out at the world. He nestles up beside me and I grab his hand. Too tight. But I can't help it.

"I have to tell you a story," I say. "But I have to kiss you first."

And I do. His eyes are wondering. I'm not a good actress in this moment.

"There was a girl who fell in love with her best friend. And he fell in love with her. It was the deepest kind of love there could be. The kind that most people never find. But they were only fifteen years old. And the girl's mother, who knew nothing of this secret love, had forbidden her daughter to date before her sixteenth birthday."

The night and Andrew are very still right now. Both are waiting.

"So the girl and the boy kept their love secret from everyone and satisfied themselves with stolen kisses. For her sixteenth birthday, all she wanted was for them to be together. That became the promise they made to each other."

I look at him for the first time.

"Are you okay?" I ask.

He nods once.

I look back at the water.

"The night of her sixteenth birthday, she lay in her bed and waited for him to tap on her window. She would let him in so they could make love for the first time and then tell the world they belonged to each other. But as Bill was driving to her, something happened that we will never know, and his car crashed headlong into a tree. In her grief, she had to keep their secret. He had been only her best friend. Instead of the boy she was destined to belong to forever."

"She's Sloane," he says.

"And you're Bill."

And when I turn to him, he is.

We look at each other with all the love we feel. We kiss a kiss that will last forever.

"Do you know why I'm here?" he asks.

I don't.

"Because you think it was all your fault. Because I was coming to be with you. As if it was your love for me that killed me. But it was your love for me that made my life mean something. Did my love do that for you?"

"You know that it did."

"Then let me go."

And so I do. And he is gone.

I walk home alone through this city that I love so much.

I enter my darkened bathroom. I flick on the light.

She's in the mirror. I'm in the mirror.

We don't need any words.

I want her to smile first. So I can go.

And when she does, I smile back.

And I'm gone.

CHAPTER TWENTY-EIGHT

SLOANE MARGARET JAMESON

I open my eyes. I'm still smiling.

Acknowledgments

The authors would like to acknowledge Marty Bowen for the idea and the opportunity. Isaac Klausner for his countless contributions and kindness. Jenn Joel for being a patient advocate and advisor. Jocelyn Davies for her enthusiasm and thoughtful guidance throughout this process. GB, Mema, and Nessa for their encouragement and sweet support. The staff at the Montage for tolerating us. And of course Mystic, Connecticut, the most idyllic little town a girl could dream to call home.

For another chilling read,
check out *Zoe Letting Go*
by Nora Price:

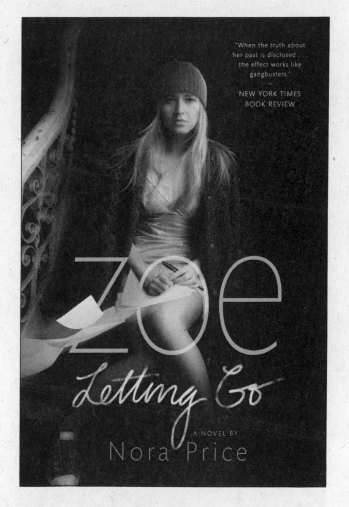

"When the truth about her past is disclosed . . .
the effect works like gangbusters."

—*New York Times Book Review*

These four best friends share memories too, but in *Five Summers* by Una LaMarche, they are the secret memories of camp:

UNA LaMARCHE

FIVE SUMMERS

"Vivid, warm, familiar and bittersweet, *Five Summers* is a welcome escape, full of moments that linger beyond the final pages."
—Jodi Lynn Anderson, *New York Times* bestselling author of *Peaches*